SIX
OF
CROWS

Praise for *Six of Crows*

'This has all the right elements to keep readers enthralled: a cunning leader with a plan for every occasion, nigh-impossible odds, an entertaining combative team of skilled misfits, a twisty plot, and a nerve-wracking cliffhanger.'
Publishers Weekly, starred review

'Cracking page-turner with a multiethnic band of misfits with differing sexual orientations who satisfyingly, believably jell into a family.' *Kirkus Reviews, starred review*

'Bardugo outdoes herself with this book, creating the gorgeously built backdrop of Ketterdam and populating it with a sophisticated cast of rogues and criminals. *Six of Crows* is a twisty and elegantly crafted masterpiece that thrilled me from beginning to end.' *Holly Black*

Praise for *The Grisha Trilogy*

'A New York Times bestseller, it's like *The Hunger Games* meets *Potter* meets *Twilight* meets *Lord Of The Rings* meets *Game Of Thrones*; basically epic magical fantasy but completely for grown-ups.' *Stylist*

'Unlike anything I've ever read.'
Veronica Roth, author of the Divergent trilogy

'A heady blend of fantasy, romance and adventure.'
Rick Riordan, author of the Percy Jackson series

SIX
OF
CROWS

LEIGH BARDUGO

Indigo

First published in Great Britain in 2015
by Indigo
An imprint of Hachette Children's Group
Part of Hodder and Stoughton Ltd
Carmelite House
50 Victoria Embankment
London EC4Y 0DZ
An Hachette UK company

1 3 5 7 9 10 8 6 4 2

Text © Leigh Bardugo 2015

Map © Keith Thompson 2015
Ice Court illustration © Keith Thompson 2015

A catalogue record for this book is
available from the British Library.

ISBN 978 1 78062 227 9

Typeset by Input Data Services Ltd, Bridgwater, Somerset

Printed and bound by CPI Group (UK) Ltd, Croydon, CR0 4YY

www.orionchildrensbooks.com

To Kayte – secret weapon, unexpected friend

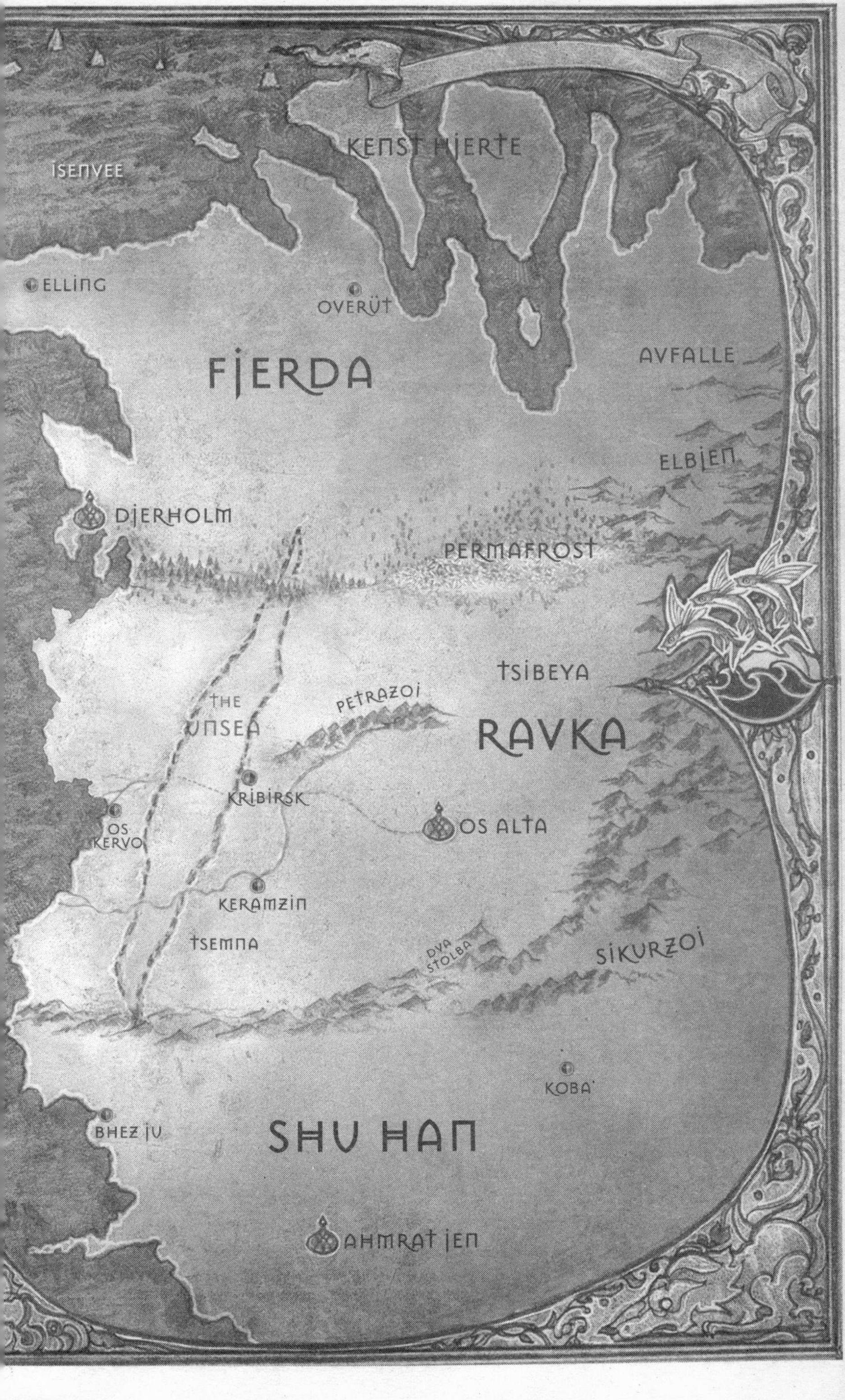
ISENVEE
KENST HJERTE
ELLING
OVERÜT
FJERDA
AVFALLE
ELBJEN
DJERHOLM
PERMAFROST
TSIBEYA
THE UNSEA
PETRAZOI
RAVKA
KRIBIRSK
OS KERVO
OS ALTA
KERAMZIN
TSEMNA
DVA STOLBA
SIKURZOI
KOBA
BHEZ JU
SHU HAN
AHMRAT JEN

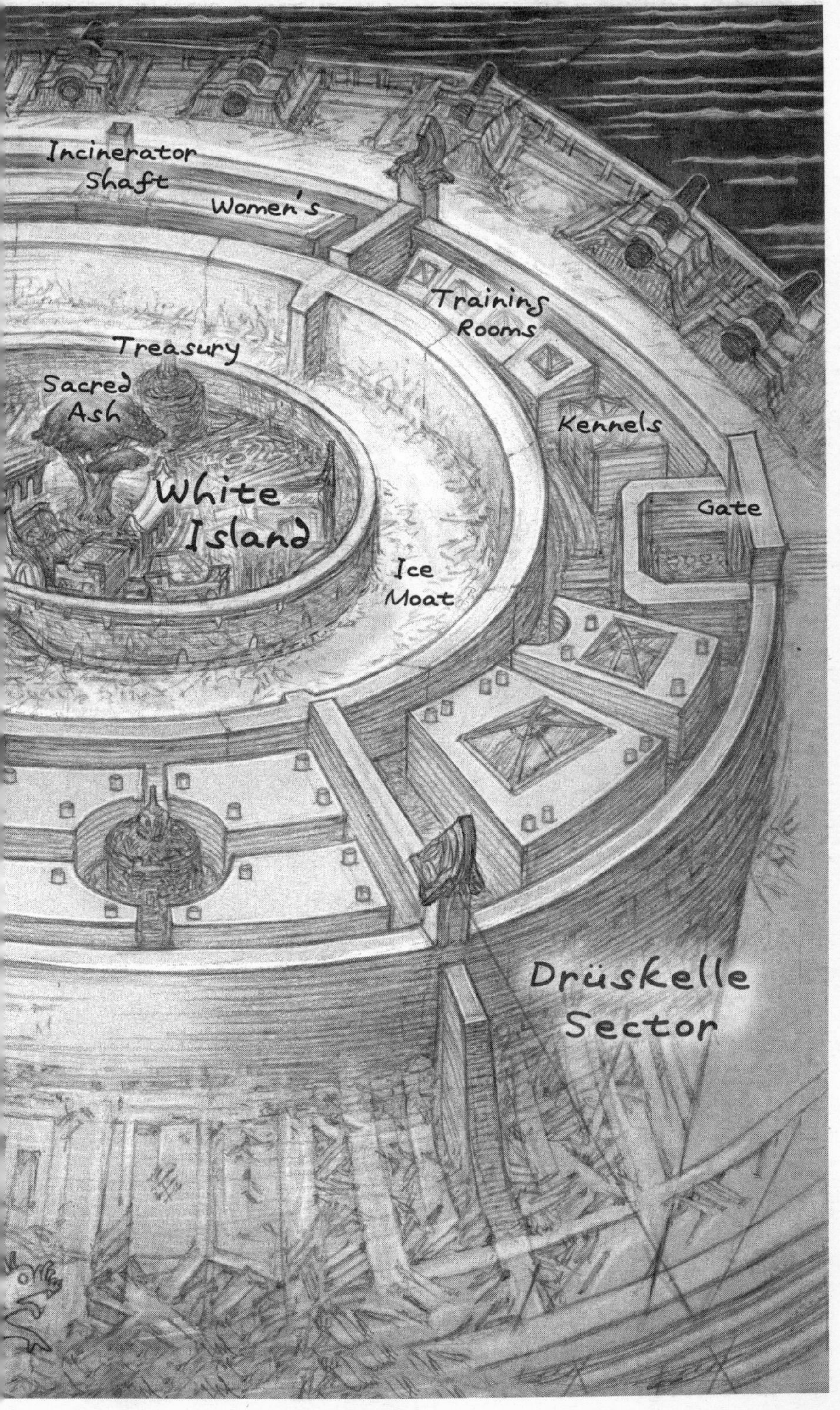

Incinerator
Shaft

Women's

Training
Rooms

Treasury

Sacred
Ash

Kennels

White
Island

Gate

Ice
Moat

Drüskelle
Sector

THE GRISHA

SOLDIERS OF THE SECOND ARMY
MASTERS OF THE SMALL SCIENCE

CORPORALKI
(The Order of the Living and the Dead)

Heartrenders
Healers

ETHEREALKI
(The Order of Summoners)

Squallers
Inferni
Tidemakers

MATERIALKI
(The Order of Fabrikators)

Durasts
Alkemi

PART 1

SHADOW BUSINESS

1

JOOST

Joost had two problems: the moon and his moustache.

He was supposed to be making his rounds at the Hoede house, but for the last fifteen minutes, he'd been hovering around the south-east wall of the gardens, trying to think of something clever and romantic to say to Anya.

If only Anya's eyes were blue like the sea or green like an emerald. Instead, her eyes were brown – lovely, dreamy . . . melted chocolate brown? Rabbit fur brown?

"Just tell her she's got skin like moonlight," his friend Pieter had said. "Girls love that."

A perfect solution, but the Ketterdam weather was not cooperating. There'd been no breeze off the harbour that day, and a grey milk fog had wreathed the city's canals and crooked alleys in damp. Even here among the mansions of the Geldstraat, the air hung thick with the smell of fish and bilge water, and smoke from the refineries on the city's outer islands had smeared the night sky in a briny haze. The full moon looked less like a jewel than a yellowy blister in need of lancing.

Maybe he could compliment Anya's laugh? Except he'd never heard her laugh. He wasn't very good with jokes.

Joost glanced at his reflection in one of the glass panels set into the double doors that led from the house to the side garden. His mother was right. Even in his new uniform, he still looked like a baby. Gently, he brushed his finger along his upper lip. If only his moustache would come in. It definitely felt thicker than yesterday.

He'd been a guard in the *stadwatch* less than six weeks, and it wasn't nearly as exciting as he'd hoped. He thought he'd be running down thieves in the Barrel or patrolling the harbours, getting first look at cargo coming in on the docks. But ever since the assassination of that ambassador at the town hall, the Merchant Council had been grumbling about security, so where was he? Stuck walking in circles at some lucky mercher's house. Not just any mercher, though. Councilman Hoede was about as high placed in Ketterdam government as a man could be. The kind of man who could make a career.

Joost adjusted the set of his coat and rifle, then patted the weighted baton at his hip. Maybe Hoede would take a liking to him. *Sharp eyed and quick with the cudgel*, Hoede would say. *That fellow deserves a promotion.*

"Sergeant Joost Van Poel," he whispered, savouring the sound of the words. "*Captain* Joost Van Poel."

"Stop gawking at yourself."

Joost whirled, cheeks going hot as Henk and Rutger strode into the side garden. They were both older, bigger, and broader of shoulder than Joost, and they were house guards, private servants of Councilman Hoede. That meant they wore his pale green livery, carried fancy rifles from Novyi Zem, and never let Joost forget he was a lowly grunt from the city watch.

"Petting that bit of fuzz isn't going to make it grow any faster," Rutger said with a loud laugh.

Joost tried to summon some dignity. "I need to finish my rounds."

Rutger elbowed Henk. "That means he's going to go stick his head in the Grisha workshop to get a look at his girl."

"*Oh, Anya, won't you use your Grisha magic to make my moustache grow?*" Henk mocked.

Joost turned on his heel, cheeks burning, and strode down the eastern side of the house. They'd been teasing him ever since he'd arrived. If it hadn't been for Anya, he probably would have pleaded with his captain for a reassignment. He and Anya only ever exchanged a few words on his rounds, but she was always the best part of his night.

And he had to admit, he liked Hoede's house, too, the few peeks he'd managed through the windows. Hoede had one of the grandest mansions on the Geldstraat – floors set with gleaming squares of black and white stone, shining dark wood walls lit by blown-glass chandeliers that floated like jellyfish near the coffered ceilings. Sometimes Joost liked to pretend that it was his house, that he was a rich mercher just out for a stroll through his fine garden.

Before he rounded the corner, Joost took a deep breath. *Anya, your eyes are brown like . . . tree bark?* He'd think of something. He was better off being spontaneous anyway.

He was surprised to see the glass-panelled doors to the Grisha workshop open. More than the hand-painted blue tiles in the kitchen or the mantels laden with potted tulips, this workshop was a testimony to Hoede's wealth. Grisha indentures didn't come cheap, and Hoede had three of them.

But Yuri wasn't seated at the long worktable, and Anya was nowhere to be seen. Only Retvenko was there, sprawled out on a chair in dark blue robes, eyes shut, a book open on his chest.

Joost hovered in the doorway, then cleared his throat.

"These doors should be shut and locked at night."

"House is like furnace," Retvenko drawled without opening his eyes, his Ravkan accent thick and rolling. "Tell Hoede I stop sweating, I close doors."

Retvenko was a Squaller, older than the other Grisha indentures, his hair shot through with silver. There were rumours he'd fought for the losing side in Ravka's civil war and had fled to Kerch after the fighting.

"I'd be happy to present your complaints to Councilman Hoede," Joost lied. The house was always overheated, as if Hoede were under obligation to burn coal, but Joost wasn't going to be the one to mention it. "Until then—"

"You bring news of Yuri?" Retvenko interrupted, finally opening his heavily hooded eyes.

Joost glanced uneasily at the bowls of red grapes and heaps of burgundy velvet on the worktable. Yuri had been working on bleeding colour from the fruit into curtains for Mistress Hoede, but he'd fallen badly ill a few days ago, and Joost hadn't seen him since. Dust had begun to gather on the velvet, and the grapes were going bad.

"I haven't heard anything."

"Of course you hear nothing. Too busy strutting around in stupid purple uniform."

What was wrong with his uniform? And why did Retvenko even have to be here? He was Hoede's personal Squaller and often travelled with the merchant's most precious cargos, guaranteeing favourable winds to bring the ships safely and quickly to harbour. Why couldn't he be away at sea now?

"I think Yuri may be quarantined."

"So helpful," Retvenko said with a sneer. "You can stop craning neck like hopeful goose," he added. "Anya is gone."

Joost felt his face heat again. "Where is she?" he asked, trying to sound authoritative. "She should be in after dark."

"One hour ago, Hoede takes her. Same as night he came for Yuri."

"What do you mean, 'he came for Yuri'? Yuri fell ill."

"Hoede comes for Yuri, Yuri comes back sick. Two days later, Yuri vanishes for good. Now Anya."

For good?

"Maybe there was an emergency. If someone needed to be healed—"

"First Yuri, now Anya. I will be next, and no one will notice except poor little Officer Joost. Go now."

"If Councilman Hoede—"

Retvenko raised an arm and a gust of air slammed Joost backwards. Joost scrambled to keep his footing, grabbing for the doorframe.

"I said *now*." Retvenko etched a circle in the air, and the door slammed shut. Joost let go just in time to avoid having his fingers smashed, and toppled into the side garden.

He got to his feet as quickly as he could, wiping muck from his uniform, shame squirming in his belly. One of the glass panes in the door had cracked from the force. Through it, he saw the Squaller smirking.

"That's counting against your indenture," Joost said, pointing to the ruined pane. He hated how small and petty his voice sounded.

Retvenko waved his hand, and the doors trembled on their hinges. Without meaning to, Joost took a step back.

"Go and make your rounds, little watchdog," Retvenko called.

"That went well," snickered Rutger, leaning against the garden wall.

How long had he been standing there? "Don't you have something better to do than follow me around?" Joost asked.

"All guards are to report to the boathouse. Even you. Or are you too busy making friends?"

"I was asking him to shut the door."

Rutger shook his head. "You don't ask. You tell. They're servants. Not honoured guests."

Joost fell into step beside him, insides still churning with humiliation. The worst part was that Rutger was right. Retvenko had no business talking to him that way. But what was Joost supposed to do? Even if he'd had the courage to get into a fight with a Squaller, it would be like brawling with an expensive vase. The Grisha weren't just servants; they were Hoede's treasured possessions.

What had Retvenko meant about Yuri and Anya being taken anyway? Had he been covering for Anya? Grisha indentures were kept to the house for good reason. To walk the streets without protection was to risk getting plucked up by a slaver and never seen again. *Maybe she's meeting someone*, Joost speculated miserably.

His thoughts were interrupted by the blaze of light and activity down by the boathouse that faced the canal. Across the water he could see other fine mercher houses, tall and slender, the tidy gables of their rooftops making a dark silhouette against the night sky, their gardens and boathouses lit by glowing lanterns.

A few weeks before, Joost had been told that Hoede's boathouse would be undergoing improvements and to strike it from his rounds. But when he and Rutger entered, he saw no paint or scaffolding. The *gondels* and oars had been pushed up against the walls. The other house guards were there in their sea-green livery, and Joost recognised two *stadwatch* guards in purple. But most of the interior was taken up by a huge box – a kind of freestanding cell that looked as if it was made from reinforced steel, its seams thick with rivets, a huge window embedded in one of its walls. The glass had a wavy bent, and through it, Joost could see a girl seated at a table, clutching her red silks tight around her. Behind her, a *stadwatch* guard stood at attention.

Anya, Joost realised with a start. Her brown eyes were wide and frightened, her skin pale. The little boy sitting across from her looked doubly terrified. His hair was sleep-tousled and his legs dangled from the chair, kicking nervously at the air.

"Why all the guards?" asked Joost. There had to be more than ten of them crowded into the boathouse. Councilman Hoede was there, too, along with another merchant Joost didn't know, both of them dressed in mercher black. Joost stood up straighter when he saw they were talking to the captain of the *stadwatch*. He hoped he'd got all the garden mud off his uniform. "What is this?"

Rutger shrugged. "Who cares? It's a break in the routine."

Joost looked back through the glass. Anya was staring out at him, her gaze unfocused. The day he'd arrived at Hoede house, she'd healed a bruise on his cheek. It had been nothing, the yellow-green remnants of a crack he'd taken to the face during a training exercise, but apparently Hoede had caught sight of it and didn't like his guards looking like thugs. Joost had been sent to the Grisha workshop, and Anya had sat him down in a bright square of late winter sunlight. Her cool fingers had passed over his skin, and though the itch had been terrible, bare seconds later it was as if the bruise had never been.

When Joost thanked her, Anya had smiled and Joost was lost. He knew his cause was hopeless. Even if she'd had any interest in him, he could never afford to buy her indenture from Hoede, and she would never marry unless Hoede decreed it. But it hadn't stopped him from dropping by to say hello or to bring her little gifts. She'd liked the map of Kerch best, a whimsical drawing of their island nation, surrounded by mermaids swimming in the True Sea and ships blown along by winds depicted as fat-cheeked men. It was a cheap souvenir, the kind tourists bought along East Stave, but it had seemed to please her.

Now he risked raising a hand in greeting. Anya showed no reaction.

"She can't see you, moron," laughed Rutger. "The glass is mirrored on the other side."

Joost's cheeks pinked. "How was I to know that?"

"Open your eyes and pay attention for once."

First Yuri, now Anya. "Why do they need a Grisha Healer? Is that boy injured?"

"He looks fine to me."

The captain and Hoede seemed to reach some kind of agreement.

Through the glass, Joost saw Hoede enter the cell and give the boy an encouraging pat. There must have been vents in the cell because he heard Hoede say, "Be a brave lad, and there's a few *kruge* in it for you." Then he grabbed Anya's chin with a liver-spotted hand. She tensed, and Joost's gut tightened. Hoede gave Anya's head a little shake. "Do as you're told, and this will soon be over, *ja*?"

She gave a small, tight smile. "Of course, Onkle."

Hoede whispered a few words to the guard behind Anya, then stepped out. The door shut with a loud clang, and Hoede slid a heavy lock into place.

Hoede and the other merchant took positions almost directly in front of Joost and Rutger.

The merchant Joost didn't know said, "You're sure this is wise? This girl is a Corporalnik. After what happened to your Fabrikator—"

"If it was Retvenko, I'd be worried. But Anya has a sweet disposition. She's a Healer. Not prone to aggression."

"And you've lowered the dose?"

"Yes, but we're agreed that if we have the same results as the Fabrikator, the Council will compensate me? I can't be asked to bear that expense."

When the merchant nodded, Hoede signalled to the captain. "Proceed."

The same results as the Fabrikator. Retvenko claimed Yuri had vanished. Was that what he'd meant?

"Sergeant," said the captain, "are you ready?"

The guard inside the cell replied, "Yes, sir." He drew a knife.

Joost swallowed hard.

"First test," said the captain.

The guard bent forwards and told the boy to roll up his sleeve. The boy obeyed and stuck out his arm, popping the thumb of his other hand into his mouth. *Too old for that*, thought Joost. But the boy must be very scared. Joost had slept with a sock bear until he was nearly fourteen, a fact his older brothers had mocked mercilessly.

"This will sting just a bit," said the guard.

The boy kept his thumb in his mouth and nodded, eyes round.

"This really isn't necessary—" said Anya.

"Quiet, please," said Hoede.

The guard gave the boy a pat then slashed a bright red cut across his forearm. The boy started crying immediately.

Anya tried to rise from her chair, but the guard placed a stern hand on her shoulder.

"It's alright, sergeant," said Hoede. "Let her heal him."

Anya leaned forwards, taking the boy's hand gently. "Shhhh," she said softly. "Let me help."

"Will it hurt?" the boy gulped.

She smiled. "Not at all. Just a little itch. Try to hold still for me?"

Joost found himself leaning closer. He'd never actually *seen* Anya heal someone.

Anya removed a handkerchief from her sleeve and wiped away the excess blood. Then her fingers brushed carefully over the boy's wound. Joost watched in astonishment as the skin slowly seemed to re-form and knit together.

A few minutes later, the boy grinned and held out his arm. It looked a bit red, but was otherwise smooth and unmarked. "Was that magic?"

Anya tapped him on the nose. "Of a sort. The same magic your own body works when given time and a bit of bandage."

The boy looked almost disappointed.

"Good, good," Hoede said impatiently. "Now the *parem*."

Joost frowned. He'd never heard that word.

The captain signalled to his sergeant. "Second sequence."

"Put out your arm," the sergeant said to the boy once again.

The boy shook his head. "I don't like that part."

"Do it."

The boy's lower lip quivered, but he put out his arm. The guard cut him once more. Then he placed a small wax paper envelope on the table in front of Anya.

"Swallow the contents of the packet," Hoede instructed Anya.

"What is it?" she asked, voice trembling.

"That isn't your concern."

"*What is it?*" she repeated.

"It's not going to kill you. We're going to ask you to perform some simple tasks to judge the drug's effects. The sergeant is there to make sure you do only what you're told and no more, understood?"

Her jaw set, but she nodded.

"No one will harm you," said Hoede. "But remember, if you hurt the sergeant, you have no way out of that cell. The doors are locked from the outside."

"What is that stuff?" whispered Joost.

"Don't know," said Rutger.

"What do you know?" he muttered.

"Enough to keep my trap shut."

Joost scowled.

With shaking hands, Anya lifted the little wax envelope and opened the flap.

"Go on," said Hoede.

She tipped her head back and swallowed the powder. For

a moment she sat, waiting, lips pressed together.

"Is it just *jurda*?" she asked hopefully. Joost found himself hoping, too. *Jurda* was nothing to fear, a stimulant everyone in the *stadwatch* chewed to stay awake on late watches.

"What does it taste like?" Hoede asked.

"Like *jurda* but sweeter, it—"

Anya inhaled sharply. Her hands seized the table, her pupils dilating enough that her eyes looked nearly black. "Ohhh," she said, sighing. It was nearly a purr.

The guard tightened his grip on her shoulder.

"How do you feel?"

She stared at the mirror and smiled. Her tongue peeked through her white teeth, stained like rust. Joost felt suddenly cold.

"Just as it was with the Fabrikator," murmured the merchant.

"Heal the boy," Hoede commanded.

She waved her hand through the air, the gesture almost dismissive, and the cut on the boy's arm sealed instantly. The blood lifted briefly from his skin in droplets of red then vanished. His skin looked perfectly smooth, all trace of blood or redness gone. The boy beamed. "That was definitely magic."

"It *feels* like magic," Anya said with that same eerie smile.

"She didn't touch him," marvelled the captain.

"Anya," said Hoede. "Listen closely. We're going to tell the guard to perform the next test now."

"Mmm," hummed Anya.

"Sergeant," said Hoede. "Cut off the boy's thumb."

The boy howled and started to cry again. He shoved his hands beneath his legs to protect them.

I should stop this, Joost thought. *I should find a way to protect her, both of them.* But what then? He was a nobody, new to the *stadwatch*, new to this house. *Besides,* he discovered in a burst of shame, *I want to keep my job.*

Anya merely smiled and tilted her head back so she was looking at the sergeant. "Shoot the glass."

"What did she say?" asked the merchant.

"Sergeant!" the captain barked out.

"Shoot the glass," Anya repeated. The sergeant's face went slack. He cocked his head to one side as if listening to a distant melody, then unslung his rifle and aimed at the observation window.

"Get down!" someone yelled.

Joost threw himself to the ground, covering his head as the rapid hammer of gunfire filled his ears and bits of glass rained down on his hands and back. His thoughts were a panicked clamour. His mind tried to deny it, but he knew what he'd just seen. Anya had commanded the sergeant to shoot the glass. She'd *made* him do it. But that couldn't be. Grisha Corporalki specialised in the human body. They could stop your heart, slow your breathing, snap your bones. They couldn't get inside your head.

For a moment there was silence. Then Joost was on his feet with everyone else, reaching for his rifle. Hoede and the captain shouted at the same time.

"Subdue her!"

"Shoot her!"

"Do you know how much money she's worth?" Hoede retorted. "Someone restrain her! Do not shoot!"

Anya raised her hands, red sleeves spread wide. "Wait," she said.

Joost's panic vanished. He knew he'd been frightened, but his fear was a distant thing. He was filled with expectation. He wasn't sure what was coming, or when, only that it would arrive and that it was essential he be ready to meet it. It might be bad or good. He didn't really care. His heart was free of worry and desire. He longed for nothing, wanted for nothing, his mind silent, his breath steady. He only needed to *wait*.

He saw Anya rise and pick up the little boy. He heard her crooning tenderly to him, some Ravkan lullaby.

"Open the door and come in, Hoede," she said. Joost heard the words, understood them, forgot them.

Hoede walked to the door and slid the bolt free. He entered the steel cell.

"Do as you're told, and this will soon be over, *ja?*" Anya murmured with a smile. Her eyes were black and bottomless pools. Her skin was alight, glowing, incandescent. A thought flickered through Joost's mind – *beautiful as the moon.*

Anya shifted the boy's weight in her arms. "Don't look," she murmured against his hair. "Now," she said to Hoede. "Pick up the knife."

2

INEJ

Kaz Brekker didn't need a reason. Those were the words whispered on the streets of Ketterdam, in the taverns and coffeehouses, in the dark and bleeding alleys of the pleasure district known as the Barrel. The boy they called Dirtyhands didn't need a reason any more than he needed permission – to break a leg, sever an alliance, or change a man's fortunes with the turn of a card.

Of course they were wrong, Inej considered as she crossed the bridge over the black waters of the Beurscanal to the deserted main square that fronted the Exchange. Every act of violence was deliberate, and every favour came with enough strings attached to stage a puppet show. Kaz *always* had his reasons. Inej could just never be sure they were good ones. Especially tonight.

Inej checked her knives, silently reciting their names as she always did when she thought there might be trouble. It was a practical habit, but a comfort, too. The blades were her companions. She liked knowing they were ready for whatever the night might bring.

She saw Kaz and the others gathered near the great stone

arch that marked the eastern entrance to the Exchange. Three words had been carved into the rock above them: *Enjent, Voorhent, Almhent*. Industry, Integrity, Prosperity.

She kept close to the shuttered shop fronts that lined the square, avoiding the pockets of flickering gaslight cast by the streetlamps. As she moved, she inventoried the crew Kaz had brought with him: Dirix, Rotty, Muzzen and Keeg, Anika and Pim, and his chosen seconds for tonight's parley, Jesper and Big Bolliger. They jostled and bumped each other, laughing, stamping their feet against the cold snap that had surprised the city this week, the last gasp of winter before spring began in earnest. They were all bruisers and brawlers, culled from the younger members of the Dregs, the people Kaz trusted most. Inej noted the glint of knives tucked into their belts, lead pipes, weighted chains, axe handles studded with rusty nails, and here and there, the oily gleam of a gun barrel. She slipped silently into their ranks, scanning the shadows near the Exchange for signs of Black Tip spies.

"Three ships!" Jesper was saying. "The Shu sent them. They were just sitting in First Harbour, cannons out, red flags flying, stuffed to the sails with gold."

Big Bolliger gave a low whistle. "Would have liked to see that."

"Would have liked to *steal* that," replied Jesper. "Half the Merchant Council was down there flapping and squawking, trying to figure out what to do."

"Don't they want the Shu paying their debts?" Big Bolliger asked.

Kaz shook his head, dark hair glinting in the lamplight. He was a collection of hard lines and tailored edges – sharp jaw, lean build, wool coat snug across his shoulders. "Yes and no," he said in his rocksalt rasp. "It's always good to have a country in debt to you. Makes for friendlier negotiations."

"Maybe the Shu are done being friendly," said Jesper.

"They didn't have to send all that treasure at once. You think they stuck that trade ambassador?"

Kaz's eyes found Inej unerringly in the crowd. Ketterdam had been buzzing about the assassination of the ambassador for weeks. It had nearly destroyed Kerch-Zemeni relations and sent the Merchant Council into an uproar. The Zemeni blamed the Kerch. The Kerch suspected the Shu. Kaz didn't care who was responsible; the murder fascinated him because he couldn't figure out how it had been accomplished. In one of the busiest corridors of the Stadhall, in full view of more than a dozen government officials, the Zemeni trade ambassador had stepped into a washroom. No one else had entered or left, but when his aide knocked on the door a few minutes later, there had been no answer. When they'd broken down the door, they'd found the ambassador facedown on the white tiles, a knife in his back, the taps still running.

Kaz had sent Inej to investigate the premises after hours. The washroom had no other entrance, no windows or vents, and even Inej hadn't mastered the art of squeezing herself through the plumbing. Yet the Zemeni ambassador was dead. Kaz hated a puzzle he couldn't solve, and he and Inej had concocted a hundred theories to account for the murder – none of which satisfied. But they had more pressing problems tonight.

She saw him signal to Jesper and Big Bolliger to divest themselves of weapons. Street law dictated that for a parley of this kind each lieutenant be seconded by two of his foot soldiers and that they all be unarmed. *Parley.* The word felt like a deception – strangely prim, an antique. No matter what street law decreed, this night smelled like violence.

"Go on, give those guns over," Dirix said to Jesper.

With a great sigh, Jesper removed the gunbelts at his hips. She had to admit he looked less himself without them. The Zemeni sharpshooter was long-limbed, brown-skinned, constantly in motion. He pressed his lips to the pearl handles of his prized revolvers, bestowing each with a mournful kiss.

"Take good care of my babies," Jesper said as he handed them over to Dirix. "If I see a single scratch or nick on those, I'll spell *forgive me* on your chest in bullet holes."

"You wouldn't waste the ammo."

"And he'd be dead halfway through *forgive*," Big Bolliger said as he dropped a hatchet, a switchblade, and his preferred weapon – a thick chain weighted with a heavy padlock – into Rotty's expectant hands.

Jesper rolled his eyes. "It's about sending a message. What's the point of a dead guy with *forg* written on his chest?"

"Compromise," Kaz said. "*I'm sorry* does the trick and uses fewer bullets."

Dirix laughed, but Inej noted that he cradled Jesper's revolvers very gently.

"What about that?" Jesper asked, gesturing to Kaz's walking stick.

Kaz's laugh was low and humourless. "Who'd deny a poor cripple his cane?"

"If the cripple is you, then any man with sense."

"Then it's a good thing we're meeting Geels." Kaz drew a watch from his vest pocket. "It's almost midnight."

Inej turned her gaze to the Exchange. It was little more than a large rectangular courtyard surrounded by warehouses and shipping offices. But during the day, it was the heart of Ketterdam, bustling with wealthy merchers buying and selling shares in the trade voyages that passed through the city's ports. Now it was nearly twelve bells, and the Exchange was deserted but for the guards who patrolled the perimeter and the rooftop. They'd been bribed to look the other way during tonight's parley.

The Exchange was one of the few remaining parts of the

city that hadn't been divvied up and claimed in the ceaseless skirmishes between Ketterdam's rival gangs. It was supposed to be neutral territory. But it didn't *feel* neutral to Inej. It felt like the hush of the woods before the snare yanks tight and the rabbit starts to scream. It felt like a trap.

"This is a mistake," she said. Big Bolliger started; he hadn't known she was standing there. Inej heard the name the Dregs preferred for her whispered among their ranks – *the Wraith*. "Geels is up to something."

"Of course he is," said Kaz. His voice had the rough, abraded texture of stone against stone. Inej always wondered if he'd sounded that way as a little boy. If he'd ever been a little boy.

"Then why come here tonight?"

"Because this is the way Per Haskell wants it."

Old man, old ways, Inej thought but didn't say, and she suspected the other Dregs were thinking the same thing.

"He's going to get us all killed," she said.

Jesper stretched his long arms overhead and grinned, his teeth white against his dark skin. He had yet to give up his rifle, and the silhouette of it across his back made him resemble a gawky, long-limbed bird. "Statistically, he'll probably only get *some* of us killed."

"It's not something to joke about," she replied. The look Kaz cast her was amused. She knew how she sounded – stern, fussy, like an old crone making dire pronouncements from her porch. She didn't like it, but she also knew she was right. Besides, old women must know something, or they wouldn't live to gather wrinkles and yell from their front steps.

"Jesper isn't making a joke, Inej," said Kaz. "He's figuring the odds."

Big Bolliger cracked his huge knuckles. "Well, I've got lager and a skillet of eggs waiting for me at the Kooperom, so I can't be the one to die tonight."

"Care to place a wager?" Jesper asked.

"I'm not going to bet on my own death."

Kaz flipped his hat onto his head and ran his gloved fingers along the brim in a quick salute. "Why not, Bolliger? We do it every day."

He was right. Inej's debt to Per Haskell meant she gambled her life every time she took on a new job or assignment, every time she left her room at the Slat. Tonight was no different.

Kaz struck his walking stick against the cobblestones as the bells from the Church of Barter began to chime. The group fell silent. The time for talk was done. "Geels isn't smart, but he's just bright enough to be trouble," said Kaz. "No matter what you hear, you don't join the fray unless I give the command. Stay sharp." Then he gave Inej a brief nod. "And stay hidden."

"No mourners," Jesper said as he tossed his rifle to Rotty.

"No funerals," the rest of the Dregs murmured in reply. Among them, it passed for 'good luck'.

Before Inej could melt into the shadows, Kaz tapped her arm with his crow's head cane. "Keep a watch on the rooftop guards. Geels may have them in his pocket."

"Then—" Inej began, but Kaz was already gone.

Inej threw up her hands in frustration. She had a hundred questions, but as usual, Kaz was keeping a stranglehold on the answers.

She jogged towards the canal-facing wall of the Exchange. Only the lieutenants and their seconds were allowed to enter during the parley. But just in case the Black Tips got any ideas, the other Dregs would be waiting right outside the eastern arch with weapons at the ready. She knew Geels would have his crew of heavily armed Black Tips gathered at the western entrance.

Inej would find her own way in. The rules of fair play among the gangs were from Per Haskell's time. Besides, she was the Wraith – the only law that applied to her was gravity, and some days she defied that, too.

The lower level of the Exchange was dedicated to windowless warehouses, so Inej located a drainpipe to shin up. Something made her hesitate before she wrapped her hand around it. She drew a bonelight from her pocket and gave it a shake, casting a pale green glow over the pipe. It was slick with oil. She followed the wall, seeking another option, and found a stone cornice bearing a statue of Kerch's three flying fishes within reach. She stood on her toes and tentatively felt along the top of the cornice. It had been covered in ground glass. *I am expected*, she thought with grim pleasure.

She'd joined up with the Dregs less than two years ago, just days after her fifteenth birthday. It had been a matter of survival, but it gratified her to know that, in such a short time, she'd become someone to take precautions against. Though, if the Black Tips thought tricks like this would keep the Wraith from her goal, they were sadly mistaken.

She drew two climbing spikes from the pockets of her quilted vest and wedged first one then the other between the bricks of the wall as she hoisted herself higher, her questing feet finding the smallest holds and ridges in the stone. As a child learning the highwire, she'd gone barefoot. But the streets of Ketterdam were too cold and wet for that. After a few bad spills, she'd paid a Grisha Fabrikator working in secret out of a gin shop on the Wijnstraat to make her a pair of leather slippers with nubbly rubber soles. They were perfectly fitted to her feet and gripped any surface with surety.

On the second story of the Exchange, she hoisted herself onto a window ledge just wide enough to perch on.

Kaz had done his best to teach her, but she didn't quite have his way with breaking and entering, and it took her a few tries to finesse the lock. Finally she heard a satisfying *click*, and the window swung open on a deserted office, its walls covered in maps marked with trade routes, and chalkboards listing share prices and the names of ships. She ducked inside, refastened the latch, and picked her way past the empty desks with their neat stacks of orders and tallies.

She crossed to a slender set of doors and stepped onto a balcony that overlooked the central courtyard of the Exchange. Each of the shipping offices had one. From here, callers announced new voyages and arrivals of inventory, or hung the black flag that indicated that a ship had been lost at sea with all its cargo. The floor of the Exchange would erupt into a flurry of trades, runners would spread the word throughout the city, and the price of goods, futures, and shares in outgoing voyages would rise or fall. But tonight all was silence.

A wind came in off the harbour, bringing the smell of the sea, ruffling the stray hairs that had escaped the braided coil at the nape of Inej's neck. Down in the square, she saw the sway of lamplight and heard the thump of Kaz's cane on the stones as he and his seconds made their way across the square. On the opposite side, she glimpsed another set of lanterns heading towards them. The Black Tips had arrived.

Inej raised her hood. She pulled herself onto the railing and leaped soundlessly to the neighbouring balcony, then the next, tracking Kaz and the others around the square, staying as close as she could. His dark coat rippled in the salt breeze, his limp more pronounced tonight, as it always was when the weather turned cold. She could hear Jesper keeping up a lively stream of conversation, and Big Bolliger's low, rumbling chuckle.

As she drew nearer to the other side of the square, Inej saw that Geels had chosen to bring Elzinger and Oomen – exactly as she had predicted. Inej knew the strengths and weaknesses of every member of the Black Tips, not to mention Harley's Pointers, the Liddies, the Razorgulls, the Dime Lions, and every other gang working the streets of Ketterdam. It was her job to know that Geels trusted Elzinger because they'd come up through the ranks of the Black Tips together, and because Elzinger was built like a stack of boulders – nearly seven feet tall, dense with muscle, his wide, mashed-in face jammed low on a neck thick as a pylon.

She was suddenly glad Big Bolliger was with Kaz. That Kaz had chosen Jesper to be one of his seconds was no surprise. Twitchy as Jesper was, with or without his revolvers, he was at his best in a fight, and she knew he'd do anything for Kaz. She'd been less sure when Kaz had insisted on Big Bolliger as well. Big Bol was a bouncer at the Crow Club, perfectly suited to tossing out drunks and wasters, but too heavy on his feet to be much use when it came to a real tussle. Still, at least he was tall enough to look Elzinger in the eye.

Inej didn't want to think too much on Geels' other second. Oomen made her nervous. He wasn't as physically intimidating as Elzinger. In fact, Oomen was made like a scarecrow – not scrawny, but as if beneath his clothes, his body had been put together at wrong angles. Word was he'd once crushed a man's skull with his bare hands, wiped his palms clean on his shirtfront, and kept right on drinking.

Inej tried to quiet the unease roiling through her, and listened as Geels and Kaz made small talk in the square while their seconds patted each of them down to make sure no one was carrying.

"Naughty," Jesper said as he removed a tiny knife from Elzinger's sleeve and tossed it across the square.

"Clear," declared Big Bolliger as he finished patting down Geels and moved on to Oomen.

Kaz and Geels discussed the weather, the suspicion that the Kooperom was serving watered-down drinks now that the rent had been raised – dancing around the real reason they'd come here tonight. In theory, they would chat, make their apologies, agree to respect the boundaries of Fifth Harbour, then all head out to find a drink together – at least that's what Per Haskell had insisted.

But what does Per Haskell know? Inej thought as she looked for the guards patrolling the roof above, trying to pick out their shapes in the dark. Haskell ran the Dregs, but these days, he preferred to sit in the warmth of his room, drinking lukewarm lager, building model ships, and telling long stories of his exploits to anyone who would listen. He seemed to think territory wars could be settled as they once had been: with a short scuffle and a friendly handshake. But every one of Inej's senses told her that was not how this was going to play out. Her father would have said the shadows were about their own business tonight. Something bad was going to happen here.

Kaz stood with both gloved hands resting on the carved crow's head of his cane. He looked totally at ease, his narrow face obscured by the brim of his hat. Most gang members in the Barrel loved flash: gaudy waistcoats, watch fobs studded with false gems, trousers in every print and pattern imaginable. Kaz was the exception – the picture of restraint, his dark vests and trousers simply cut and tailored along severe lines. At first, she'd thought it was a matter of taste, but she'd come to understand that it was a joke he played on the upstanding merchers. He enjoyed looking like one of them.

"I'm a business man," he'd told her. "No more, no less."

"You're a thief, Kaz."

"Isn't that what I just said?"

Now he looked like some kind of priest come to preach to a group of circus performers. A *young* priest, she thought with another pang of unease. Kaz had called Geels old and washed up, but he certainly didn't seem that way tonight.

The Black Tips' lieutenant might have wrinkles creasing the corners of his eyes and burgeoning jowls beneath his sideburns, but he looked confident, experienced. Next to him Kaz looked . . . well, seventeen.

"Let's be fair, *ja*? All we want is a bit more scrub," Geels said, tapping the mirrored buttons of his lime-green waistcoat. "It's not fair for you to cull every spend-happy tourist stepping off a pleasure boat at Fifth Harbour."

"Fifth Harbour is ours, Geels," Kaz replied. "The Dregs get first crack at the pigeons who come looking for a little fun."

Geels shook his head. "You're a young one, Brekker," he said with an indulgent laugh. "Maybe you don't understand how these things work. The harbours belong to the city, and we have as much right to them as anyone. We've all got a living to make."

Technically, that was true. But Fifth Harbour had been useless and all but abandoned by the city when Kaz had taken it over. He'd had it dredged, and then built out the docks and the quay, and he'd had to mortgage the Crow Club to do it. Per Haskell had railed at him and called him a fool for the expense, but eventually he'd relented. According to Kaz, the old man's exact words had been, "Take all that rope and hang yourself." But the endeavour had paid for itself in less than a year. Now Fifth Harbour offered berths to mercher ships, as well as boats from all over the world carrying tourists and soldiers eager to see the sights and sample the pleasures of Ketterdam. The Dregs got first try at all of them, steering them – and their wallets – into brothels, taverns, and gambling dens owned by the gang. Fifth Harbour had made the old man very rich, and cemented the Dregs as real players in the Barrel in a way that not even the success of the Crow Club had. But with profit came unwanted attention. Geels and the Black Tips had been making trouble for the Dregs all year, encroaching on Fifth Harbour, picking off pigeons that weren't rightfully theirs.

"Fifth Harbour is ours," Kaz repeated. "It isn't up for negotiation. You're cutting into our traffic from the docks, and you intercepted a shipment of *jurda* that should have docked two nights ago."

"Don't know what you're talking about."

"I know it comes easy, Geels, but try not to play dumb with me."

Geels took a step forwards. Jesper and Big Bolliger tensed.

"Quit flexing, boy," Geels said. "We all know the old man doesn't have the stomach for a real brawl."

Kaz's laugh was dry as the rustle of dead leaves. "But *I'm* the one at your table, Geels, and I'm not here for a taste. You want a war, I'll make sure you eat your fill."

"And what if you're not around, Brekker? Everyone knows you're the spine of Haskell's operation – snap it and the Dregs collapse."

Jesper snorted. "Stomach, spine. What's next, spleen?"

"Shut it," Oomen snarled. The rules of parley dictated that only the lieutenants could speak once negotiations had begun. Jesper mouthed "sorry" and elaborately pantomimed locking his lips shut.

"I'm fairly sure you're threatening me, Geels," Kaz said. "But I want to be certain before I decide what to do about it."

"Sure of yourself, aren't you, Brekker?"

"Myself and nothing else."

Geels burst out laughing and elbowed Oomen. "Listen to this cocky little piece of crap. Brekker, you don't own these streets. Kids like you are fleas. A new crop of you turns up every few years to annoy your betters until a big dog decides to scratch. And let me tell you, I'm about tired of the itch." He crossed his arms, pleasure rolling off him in smug waves. "What if I told you there are two guards with city-issue rifles pointed at you and your boys right now?"

Inej's stomach dropped. Was that what Kaz had meant when he said Geels might have the guards in his pocket?

Kaz glanced up at the roof. "Hiring city guards to do your killing? I'd say that's an expensive proposition for a gang like the Black Tips. I'm not sure I believe your coffers could support it."

Inej climbed onto the railing and launched herself from the safety of the balcony, heading for the roof. If they survived the night, she was going to kill Kaz.

There were always two guards from the *stadwatch* posted on the roof of the Exchange. A few *kruge* from the Dregs and the Black Tips had ensured they wouldn't interfere with the parley, a common enough transaction. But Geels was implying something very different. Had he really managed to bribe city guards to play sniper for him? If so, the Dregs' odds of surviving this night had just dwindled to a knife's point.

Like most of the buildings in Ketterdam, the Exchange had a sharply gabled roof to keep off heavy rain, so the guards patrolled the rooftop via a narrow walkway that overlooked the courtyard. Inej ignored it. It was easier going but would leave her too exposed. Instead she scaled halfway up the slick roof tiles and started crawling, her body tilted at a precarious angle, moving like a spider as she kept one eye on the guards' walkway and one ear on the conversation below. Maybe Geels was bluffing. Or maybe two guards were hunched over the railing right now with Kaz or Jesper or Big Bolliger in their sights.

"Took some doing," Geels admitted. "We're a small operation right now, and city guards don't come cheap. But it'll be worth it for the prize."

"That being me?"

"That being you."

"I'm flattered."

"The Dregs won't last a week without you."

"I'd give them a month on sheer momentum."

The thought rattled noisily around in Inej's head. *If Kaz was gone, would I stay? Or would I skip out on my debt? Take my chances with Per Haskell's enforcers?* If she didn't move faster, she might well find out.

"Smug little slum rat." Geels laughed. "I can't wait to wipe that look off your face."

"So do it," Kaz said. Inej risked a look down. His voice had changed, all humour gone.

"Should I have them put a bullet in your good leg, Brekker?"

Where are the guards? Inej thought, picking up her pace. She raced across the steep pitch of the gable. The Exchange stretched nearly the length of a city block. There was too much territory to cover.

"Stop *talking*, Geels. Tell them to shoot."

"Kaz—" said Jesper nervously.

"Go on. Find your balls and give the order."

What game was Kaz playing? Had he expected this? Had he just assumed Inej would find her way to the guards in time?

She glanced down again. Geels radiated anticipation. He took a deep breath, puffing out his chest. Inej's steps faltered, and she had to fight not to go sliding straight off the edge of the roof. *He's going to do it. I'm going to watch Kaz die.*

"Fire!" Geels shouted.

A gunshot split the air. Big Bolliger let loose a cry and crumpled to the ground.

"Damn it!" shouted Jesper, dropping to one knee beside Bolliger and pressing his hand to the bullet wound as the big man moaned. "You worthless podge!" he yelled at Geels. "You just violated neutral territory."

"Nothing to say you didn't shoot first," Geels replied. "And who's going to know? None of you are walking out of here."

Geels' voice sounded too high. He was trying to maintain his composure, but Inej could hear panic pulsing against his words, the startled wingbeat of a frightened bird. Why? Moments before he'd been all bluster.

That was when Inej saw Kaz still hadn't moved. "You don't look well, Geels."

"I'm just fine," he said. But he wasn't. He looked pale and shaky. His eyes were darting right and left as if searching the shadowed walkway of the roof.

"Are you?" Kaz asked conversationally. "Things aren't going quite as planned, are they?"

"Kaz," Jesper said. "Bolliger's bleeding bad—"

"Good," Kaz said ignoring him.

"Kaz, he needs a medik!"

Kaz spared the wounded man the barest glance. "What he needs to do is stop his bellyaching and be glad I didn't have Holst take him down with a headshot."

Even from above, Inej saw Geels flinch.

"That's the guard's name, isn't it?" Kaz asked. "Willem Holst and Bert Van Daal – the two city guards on duty tonight. The ones you emptied the Black Tips' coffers to bribe?"

Geels said nothing.

"Willem Holst," Kaz said loudly, his voice floating up to the roof, "likes to gamble almost as much as Jesper does, so your money held a lot of appeal. But Holst has much bigger problems – let's call them urges. I won't go into detail. A secret's not like coin. It doesn't keep its value in the spending. You'll just have to trust me when I say this one would turn even your stomach. Isn't that right, Holst?"

The response was another gunshot. It struck the cobblestones near Geels' feet. Geels released a shocked bleat and sprang back.

This time Inej had a better chance to track the origin of the gunfire. The shot had come from somewhere near the west side of the building. If Holst was there, that meant the other guard – Bert Van Daal – would be on the east side. Had Kaz managed to neutralise him, too? Or was he counting on her? She sped over the gables.

"Just shoot him, Holst!" Geels bellowed, desperation sawing at his voice. "Shoot him in the head!"

Kaz snorted in disgust. "Do you really think that secret would die with me? Go on, Holst," he called. "Put a bullet in my skull. There will be messengers sprinting to your wife and your watch captain's door before I hit the ground."

No shot came.

"How?" Geels said bitterly. "How did you even know who would be on duty tonight? I had to pay through the gills to get that roster. You couldn't have outbid me."

"Let's say my currency carries more sway."

"Money is money."

"I trade in information, Geels, the things men do when they think no one is looking. Shame holds more value than coin ever can."

He was grandstanding, Inej saw that, buying her time as she leaped over the slate shingles.

"Are you worrying about the second guard? Good old Bert Van Daal?" Kaz asked. "Maybe he's up there right now, wondering what he should do. Shoot me? Shoot Holst? Or maybe I got to him, too, and he's getting ready to blow a hole in your chest, Geels." He leaned in as if he and Geels were sharing a great secret. "Why not give Van Daal the order and find out?"

Geels opened and closed his mouth like a carp, then bellowed, "Van Daal!"

Just as Van Daal parted his lips to answer, Inej slipped up behind him and placed a blade to his throat. She'd barely had time to pick out his shadow and slide down the rooftiles. Saints, Kaz liked to cut it close.

"Shhhh," she whispered in Van Daal's ear. She gave him a tiny jab in the side so that he could feel the point of her second dagger pressed against his kidney.

"Please," he moaned. "I—"

"I like it when men beg," she said. "But this isn't the time for it."

Below, she could see Geels' chest rising and falling with panicked breaths. "Van Daal!" he shouted again. There was rage on his face when he turned back to Kaz. "Always one step ahead, aren't you?"

"Geels, when it comes to you, I'd say I have a running start."

But Geels just smiled – a tiny smile, tight and satisfied. *A victor's smile*, Inej realised with fresh fear.

"The race isn't over yet." Geels reached into his jacket and pulled out a heavy black pistol.

"Finally," Kaz said. "The big reveal. Now Jesper can stop keening over Bolliger like a wet-eyed woman."

Jesper stared at the gun with stunned, furious eyes. "Bolliger searched him. He . . . Oh, Big Bol, you idiot," he groaned.

Inej couldn't believe what she was seeing. The guard in her arms released a tiny squeak. In her anger and surprise, she'd accidentally tightened her grip. "Relax," she said, easing her hold. But, all Saints, she wanted to put a knife through something. Big Bolliger had been the one to pat down Geels. There was no way he could have missed the pistol. He'd betrayed them.

Was that why Kaz had insisted on bringing Big Bolliger here tonight – so he'd have public confirmation that Bolliger had gone over to the Black Tips? It was certainly why he'd let Holst put a bullet in Bolliger's gut. But so what? Now everyone knew Big Bol was a traitor. Kaz still had a gun pointed at his chest.

Geels smirked. "Kaz Brekker, the great escape artist. How

are you going to wriggle your way out of this one?"

"Going out the same way I came in." Kaz ignored the pistol, turning his attention to the big man lying on the ground. "Do you know what your problem is, Bolliger?" He jabbed at the wound in Big Bol's stomach with the tip of his cane. "That wasn't a rhetorical question. Do you know what your biggest problem is?"

Bolliger mewled. "Noooo . . ."

"Give me a guess," Kaz hissed.

Big Bol said nothing, just released another trembling whimper.

"All right, I'll tell you. You're lazy. I know it. Everyone knows it. So I had to ask myself why my laziest bouncer was getting up early twice a week to walk two extra miles to Cilla's Fry for breakfast, especially when the eggs are so much better at the Kooperom. Big Bol becomes an early riser, the Black Tips start throwing their weight around Fifth Harbour and then intercept our biggest shipment of *jurda*. It wasn't a tough connection to make." He sighed and said to Geels, "This is what happens when stupid people start making big plans, *ja?*"

"Doesn't matter much now, does it?" replied Geels. "This gets ugly, I'm shooting from close range. Maybe your guards get me or my guys, but no way you're going to dodge this bullet."

Kaz stepped into the barrel of the gun so that it was pressed directly against his chest. "No way at all, Geels."

"You think I won't do it?"

"Oh, I think you'd do it gladly, with a song in your black heart. But you won't. Not tonight."

Geels' finger twitched on the trigger.

"Kaz," Jesper said. "This whole 'shoot me' thing is starting to concern me."

Oomen didn't bother to object to Jesper mouthing off this time. One man was down. Neutral territory had been violated. The sharp tang of gunpowder already hung in the air – and along with it a question, unspoken in the quiet, as if the Reaper himself awaited the answer: How much blood will be shed tonight?

In the distance a siren wailed.

"Nineteen Burstraat," Kaz said.

Geels had been shifting slightly from foot to foot; now he went very still.

"That's your girl's address, isn't it, Geels?"

Geels swallowed. "Don't have a girl."

"Oh yes, you do," crooned Kaz. "She's pretty, too. Well, pretty enough for a fink like you. Seems sweet. You love her, don't you?" Even from the rooftop, Inej could see the sheen of sweat on Geels' waxen face. "Of course you do. No one that fine should ever have looked twice at Barrel scum like you, but she's different. She finds you charming. Sure sign of madness if you ask me, but love is strange that way. Does she like to rest her pretty head on your shoulder? Listen to you talk about your day?"

Geels looked at Kaz as if he was finally seeing him for the first time. The boy he'd been talking to had been cocky, reckless, easily amused, but not frightening – not really. Now the monster was here, dead-eyed and unafraid. Kaz Brekker was gone, and Dirtyhands had come to see the rough work done.

"She lives at Nineteen Burstraat," Kaz said in his gravelly rasp. "Three floors up, geraniums in the windowboxes. There are two Dregs waiting outside her door right now, and if I don't walk out of here whole and feeling righteous, they will set that place alight from floor to rooftop. It will go up in seconds, burning from both ends with poor Elise trapped in the middle. Her blonde hair will catch first. Like the wick of a candle."

"You're bluffing," said Geels, but his pistol hand was trembling.

Kaz lifted his head and inhaled deeply. "Getting late now. You heard the siren. I smell the harbour on the wind, sea and salt, and maybe – is that smoke I smell, too?" There was pleasure in his voice.

Oh, Saints, Kaz, Inej thought miserably. *What have you done now?*

Again, Geels' finger twitched on the trigger, and Inej tensed.

"I know, Geels. I know," Kaz said sympathetically. "All that planning and scheming and bribing for nothing. That's what you're thinking right now. How bad it will feel to walk home knowing what you've lost. How angry your boss is going to be when you show up empty-handed and that much poorer for it. How satisfying it would be to put a bullet in my heart. You can do it. Pull the trigger. We can all go down together. They can take our bodies out to the Reaper's Barge for burning, like all paupers go. Or you can take the blow to your pride, go back to Burstraat, lay your head in your girl's lap, fall asleep still breathing, and dream of revenge. It's up to you, Geels. Do we get to go home tonight?"

Geels searched Kaz's gaze, and whatever he saw there made his shoulders sag. Inej was surprised to feel a pang of pity for him. He'd walked into this place buoyed on bravado, a survivor, a champion of the Barrel. He'd leave as another victim of Kaz Brekker.

"You'll get what's coming to you some day, Brekker."

"I will," said Kaz, "if there's any justice in the world. And we all know how likely that is."

Geels let his arm drop. The pistol hung uselessly by his side.

Kaz stepped back, brushing the front of his shirt where the gun barrel had rested. "Go and tell your general to keep the Black Tips out of Fifth Harbour and that we expect him to make amends for the shipment of *jurda* we lost, plus five per cent for drawing steel on neutral ground and five per cent more for being such a spectacular bunch of asses."

Then Kaz's cane swung in a sudden sharp arc. Geels screamed as his wrist bones shattered. The gun clattered to the paving stones.

"I stood down!" cried Geels, cradling his hand. "I stood down!"

"You draw on me again, I'll break both your wrists, and you'll have to hire someone to help you take a piss." Kaz tipped the brim of his hat up with the head of his cane. "Or maybe you can get the lovely Elise to do it for you."

Kaz crouched down beside Bolliger. The big man whimpered. "Look at me, Bolliger. Assuming you don't bleed to death tonight, you have until sunset tomorrow to get out of Ketterdam. I hear you're anywhere near the city limits, and they'll find you stuffed in a keg at Cilla's Fry." Then he looked at Geels. "You help Bolliger, or I find out he's running with the Black Tips, don't think I won't come after you."

"Please, Kaz," moaned Bolliger.

"You had a home, and you put a wrecking ball through the front door, Bolliger. Don't look for sympathy from me." He rose and checked his pocket watch. "I didn't expect this to go on so long. I'd best be on my way or poor Elise will be getting a trifle warm."

Geels shook his head. "There's something wrong with you, Brekker. I don't know what you are, but you're not made right."

Kaz cocked his head to one side. "You're from the suburbs, aren't you, Geels? Came to the city to try your luck?" He smoothed his lapel with one gloved hand. "Well, I'm the kind of bastard they only manufacture in the Barrel."

Despite the loaded gun at the Black Tips' feet, Kaz turned his back on them and limped across the cobblestones towards the eastern arch. Jesper squatted down next to

Bolliger and gave him a gentle pat on the cheek. "Idiot," he said sadly, and followed Kaz out of the Exchange.

From the roof, Inej continued to watch as Oomen picked up and holstered Geels' gun and the Black Tips said a few quiet words to each other.

"Don't leave," Big Bolliger begged. "Don't leave me." He tried to cling to the cuff of Geels' trousers.

Geels shook him off. They left him curled on his side, leaking blood onto the cobblestones.

Inej plucked Van Daal's rifle from his hands before she released him. "Go home," she told the guard.

He cast a single terrified glance over his shoulder and sprinted off down the walkway. Far below, Big Bol had started trying to drag himself across the floor of the Exchange. He might be stupid enough to cross Kaz Brekker, but he'd survived this long in the Barrel, and that took will. He might make it.

Help him, a voice inside her said. Until a few moments ago, he'd been her brother in arms. It seemed wrong to leave him alone. She could go to him, offer to put him out of his misery quickly, hold his hand as he passed. She could fetch a medik to save him.

Instead, she spoke a quick prayer in the language of her Saints and began the steep climb down the outer wall. Inej pitied the boy who might die alone with no one to comfort him in his last hours or who might live and spend his life as an exile. But the night's work wasn't yet over, and the Wraith didn't have time for traitors.

3

KAZ

Cheers greeted Kaz as he emerged from the eastern arch, Jesper trailing behind him and, if Kaz was any judge, already working himself into a sulk.

Dirix, Rotty, and the others charged at them, whooping and shouting, Jesper's revolvers held aloft. The crew had got the barest glimpse of the proceedings with Geels, but they'd heard most of it. Now they were chanting, "The Burstraat is on fire! The Dregs don't have no water!"

"I can't believe he just turned tail!" jeered Rotty. "He had a loaded pistol in his hand!"

"Tell us what you had on the guard," Dirix begged.

"Can't be the usual stuff."

"I heard about a guy in Sloken who liked to roll around in apple syrup and then get two—"

"I'm not talking," said Kaz. "Holst could prove useful in the future."

The mood was jittery, and their laughter had the frantic serration that came with near disaster. Some of them had expected a fight and were still itching for one. But Kaz knew there was more to it, and he hadn't missed the fact that no one had mentioned Big Bolliger's name. They'd been badly shaken by his betrayal – both the revelation and the way Kaz had delivered punishment. Beneath all that jostling and whooping, there was fear. *Good*. Kaz relied on the fact that the Dregs were all murderers, thieves, and liars. He just had to make sure they didn't make a habit of lying to *him*.

Kaz dispatched two of them to keep an eye on Big Bol and to make sure that if he made it to his feet, he left the city. The rest could return to the Slat and the Crow Club to drink off their worry, make some trouble, and spread word of the night's events. They'd tell what they'd seen, embroider the rest, and with every retelling, Dirtyhands would get crazier and more ruthless. But Kaz had business to attend to, and his first stop would be Fifth Harbour.

Jesper stepped into his path. "You should have let me know about Big Bolliger," he said in a furious whisper.

"Don't tell me my business, Jes."

"You think I'm dirty, too?"

"If I thought you were dirty, you'd be holding your guts in on the floor of the Exchange like Big Bol, so stop running your mouth."

Jesper shook his head and rested his hands on the revolvers he'd reclaimed from Dirix. Whenever he got cranky, he liked to lay hands on a gun, like a child seeking the comfort of a favoured doll.

It would have been easy enough to make peace. Kaz could have told Jesper that he knew he wasn't dirty, reminded him that he'd trusted him enough to make him his only real second in a fight that could have gone badly wrong tonight. Instead, he said, "Go on, Jesper. There's a line of credit waiting for you at the Crow Club. Play till morning or your luck runs out, whichever comes first."

Jesper scowled, but he couldn't keep the hungry gleam from his eye. "Another bribe?"

"I'm a creature of habit."

"Lucky for you, I am, too." He hesitated long enough to say, "You don't want us with you? Geels' boys are gonna be riled after that."

"Let them come," Kaz said, and turned down Nemstraat without another word. If you couldn't walk by yourself through Ketterdam after dark, then you might as well just hang a sign that read 'soft' around your neck and lie down for a beating.

He could feel the Dregs' eyes on his back as he headed over the bridge. He didn't need to hear their whispers to know what they would say. They wanted to drink with him, hear him explain how he'd known Big Bolliger had gone over to the Black Tips, listen to him describe the look in Geels' eyes when he'd dropped his pistol. But they'd never get it from Kaz, and if they didn't like it, they could find another crew to run with.

No matter what they thought of him, they'd walk a little taller tonight. It was why they stayed, why they gave their best approximation of loyalty for him. When he'd officially become a member of the Dregs, he'd been twelve and the gang had been a laughing stock, street kids and washed-up cadgers running shell games and penny-poor cons out of a run-down house in the worst part of the Barrel. But he hadn't needed a great gang, just one he could make great – one that needed him.

Now they had their own territory, their own gambling hall, and that run-down house had become the Slat, a dry, warm place to get a hot meal or hole up when you were wounded. Now the Dregs were feared. Kaz had given them that. He didn't owe them small talk on top of it.

Besides, Jesper would smoothe it all over. A few drinks in and a few hands up and the sharpshooter's good nature would return. He held a grudge about as well as he held his liquor, and he had a gift for making Kaz's victories sound like they belonged to everyone.

As Kaz headed down one of the little canals that would take him past Fifth Harbour, he realised he felt – Saints, he almost felt hopeful. Maybe he should see a medik. The Black Tips had been nipping at his heels for weeks, and now he'd forced them to play their hand. His leg wasn't too bad either, despite the winter chill. The ache was always there, but tonight it was just a dull throb. Still, a part of him wondered if the parlay was some sort of test Per Haskell had set for him. Haskell was perfectly capable of convincing himself that he was the genius making the Dregs prosper, especially if one of his cronies was whispering in his ear. That idea didn't sit easy, but Kaz could worry about Per Haskell tomorrow. For now, he'd make sure everything was running on schedule at the harbour and then head home to the Slat for some much-needed sleep.

He knew Inej was shadowing him. She'd been with him all the way from the Exchange. He didn't call out to her. She would make herself visible when she was good and ready. Usually he liked the quiet; in fact, he would have happily sewn most people's lips shut. But when she wanted to, Inej had a way of making you feel her silence. It tugged at your edges.

Kaz managed to endure it all the way past the iron railings of Zentzbridge, the grating covered in little bits of rope tied in elaborate knots, sailors' prayers for safe return from sea. Superstitious rot. Finally he gave in and said, "Spit it out already, Wraith."

Her voice came from the dark. "You didn't send anyone to Burstraat."

"Why would I?"

"If Geels doesn't get there in time—"

"No one's setting fires at Nineteen Burstraat."

"I heard the siren . . ."

"A happy accident. I take inspiration where I find it."

"You *were* bluffing, then. She was never in danger."

Kaz shrugged, unwilling to give her an answer. Inej was always trying to wring little bits of decency from him. "When everyone knows you're a monster, you needn't waste time doing every monstrous thing."

"Why did you even agree to the meet if you knew it was a set-up?" She was somewhere to the right of him, moving without a sound. He'd heard other members of the gang say she moved like a cat, but he suspected cats would sit attentively at her feet to learn her methods.

"I'd call the night a success," he said. "Wouldn't you?"

"You were nearly killed. So was Jesper."

"Geels emptied the Black Tips' coffers paying useless bribes. We've outed a traitor, re-established our claim on Fifth Harbour, and I don't have a scratch on me. It was a good night."

"How long have you known about Big Bolliger?"

"Weeks. We're going to be short-staffed. That reminds me, let Rojakke go."

"Why? There's no one like him at the tables."

"Lots of sobs know their way around a deck of cards. Rojakke is a little too quick. He's skimming."

"He's a good dealer, and he has a family to provide for. You could give him a warning, take a finger."

"Then he wouldn't be a good dealer any more, would he?"

When a dealer was caught skimming money from a gambling hall, the floor boss would cut off one of his pinkie fingers. It was one of those ridiculous punishments that had somehow become codified in the gangs. It threw off the skimmer's balance, forced him to relearn his shuffle, and showed any future employer that he had to be watched. But it also made him clumsy at the tables. It meant he was focusing on simple things like the mechanics of the deal instead of watching the players.

Kaz couldn't see Inej's face in the dark, but he sensed her disapproval.

"Greed is your god, Kaz."

He almost laughed at that. "No, Inej. Greed bows to me. It is my servant and my lever."

"And what god do you serve, then?"

"Whichever will grant me good fortune."

"I don't think gods work that way."

"I don't think I care."

She blew out an exasperated breath. Despite everything she'd been through, Inej still believed her Suli Saints were watching over her. Kaz knew it, and for some reason he loved to rile her. He wished he could read her expression now. There was always something so satisfying about the little furrow between her black brows.

"How did you know I would get to Van Daal in time?" she asked.

"Because you always do."

"You should have given me more warning."

"I thought your Saints would appreciate the challenge."

For a while she said nothing, then from somewhere behind him he heard her. "Men mock the gods until they need them, Kaz."

He didn't see her go, only sensed her absence.

Kaz gave an irritated shake of his head. To say he trusted Inej would be stretching the point, but he could admit to himself that he'd come to rely on her. It had been a gut decision to pay off her indenture with the Menagerie, and it had cost the Dregs sorely. Per Haskell had needed convincing, but Inej was one of the best investments Kaz had ever made. That she was so very good at remaining unseen made her an excellent thief of secrets, the best in the Barrel. But the fact that she could simply erase herself bothered him. She didn't even have a scent. *All* people carried scents, and those scents told stories – the hint of carbolic on a woman's fingers or woodsmoke in her hair, the wet wool of a man's suit, or the tinge of gunpowder lingering in his shirt cuffs. But not Inej. She'd somehow mastered invisibility. She was a valuable asset. So why couldn't she just do her job and spare him her moods?

Suddenly, Kaz knew he wasn't alone. He paused, listening. He'd cut through a tight alley split by a murky canal. There were no streetlamps here and little foot traffic, nothing but the bright moon and the small boats bumping against their moorings. He'd dropped his guard, let his mind give in to distraction.

A man's dark shape appeared at the head of the alley.

"What business?" Kaz asked.

The shape lunged at him. Kaz swung his cane in a low arc. It should have made direct contact with his attacker's legs, but instead it sailed through empty space. Kaz stumbled, thrown off balance by the force of his swing.

Then, somehow, the man was standing right in front of him. A fist connected with Kaz's jaw. Kaz shook off the stars that rocketed through his head. He spun back around and swung again. But no one was there. The weighted head of Kaz's walking stick whooshed through nothing and cracked against the wall.

Kaz felt the cane torn from his hands by someone on his right. Was there more than one of them?

And then a man stepped *through* the wall. Kaz's mind stuttered and reeled, trying to explain what he was seeing as a cluster of mist became a cloak, boots, the pale flash of a face.

Ghosts, Kaz thought. A boy's fear, but it came with absolute surety. Jordie had come for his vengeance at last. *It's time to pay your debts, Kaz. You never get something for nothing.*

The thought passed through Kaz's mind in a humiliating, gibbering wave of panic, then the phantom was upon him, and he felt the sharp jab of a needle in his neck. *A ghost with a syringe?*

Fool, he thought. And then he was in the dark.

Kaz woke to the sharp scent of ammonia. His head jerked back as he returned fully to consciousness.

The old man in front of him wore the robes of a university medik. He had a bottle of wuftsalts in his hand that he was waving beneath Kaz's nose. The stink was nearly unbearable.

"Get away from me," Kaz rasped.

The medik eyed him dispassionately, returning the wuftsalts to their leather pouch. Kaz flexed his fingers, but that was all he could do. He'd been shackled to a chair with his arms behind his back. Whatever they'd injected him with had left him groggy.

The medik moved aside, and Kaz blinked twice, trying to clear his vision and make sense of the absurd luxury of his surroundings. He'd expected to wake in the den of the Black Tips or some other rival gang. But this wasn't cheap Barrel flash. A squat decked out like this took real money – mahogany panels dense with carvings of frothing waves and flying fish, shelves lined with books, leaded windows, and he was fairly sure that was a real DeKappel. One of those demure oil portraits of a lady with a book open in her lap and a lamb lying at her feet. The man observing him from behind a broad desk had the prosperous look of a mercher. But if this was his house, why were there armed members of the *stadwatch* guarding the door?

Damn it, Kaz thought, *am I under arrest?* If so, this merch was in for a surprise. Thanks to Inej, he had information on every judge, bailiff, and high councilman in Kerch. He'd be out of his cell before sunrise. Except he wasn't in a cell, he was chained to a chair, so what the hell was going on?

The man was in his forties with a gaunt but handsome face and a hairline making a determined retreat from his forehead. When Kaz met his gaze, the man cleared his throat and pressed his fingers together.

"Mister Brekker, I hope you're not feeling too poorly."

"Get this old canker away from me. I feel fine."

The merch gave a nod to the medik. "You may go. Please send me your bill. And I would, of course, appreciate your discretion in this matter."

The medik secured his bag and exited the room. As he did, the mercher rose and picked up a sheaf of papers from his desk. He wore the perfectly cut frock coat and vest of all Kerch merchants – dark, refined, deliberately staid. But the pocket watch and tie pin told Kaz all he needed to know: Heavy links of laurel leaves made up the watch's gold fob, and the pin was a massive, perfect ruby.

I'm going to pry that fat jewel from its setting and jab the pin right through your mercher neck for chaining me to a chair, Kaz thought. But all he said was, "Van Eck."

The man nodded. No bow, of course. Merchants didn't bow to scum from the Barrel. "You know me, then?"

Kaz knew the symbols and jewels of all the Kerch merchant houses. Van Eck's crest was the red laurel. It didn't take a professor to make the connection.

"I know you," he said. "You're one of those merch crusaders always trying to clean up the Barrel."

Van Eck gave another small nod. "I try to find men honest work."

Kaz laughed. "What's the difference between wagering at the Crow Club and speculating on the floor of the Exchange?"

"One is theft and the other is commerce."

"When a man loses his money, he may have trouble telling them apart."

"The Barrel is a den of filth, vice, violence—"

"How many of the ships you send sailing out of the Ketterdam harbours never return?"

"That doesn't—"

"One out of five, Van Eck. One out of every five vessels you send seeking coffee and *jurda* and bolts of silk sinks to the bottom of the sea, crashes on the rocks, falls prey to pirates. One out of five crews dead, their bodies lost to foreign waters, food for deep sea fishes. Let's not speak of violence."

"I won't argue ethics with a stripling from the Barrel."

Kaz didn't really expect him to. He was just stalling for time as he tested the tightness of the cuffs around his wrists. He let his fingers feel along the length of chain as far as they were able, still puzzling over where Van Eck had brought him. Though Kaz had never met the man himself, he'd had cause to learn the layout of Van Eck's house inside and out. Wherever they were, it wasn't the mercher's mansion.

"Since you didn't bring me here to philosophise, what business?" It was the question spoken at the opening of any meeting. A greeting from a peer, not a plea from a prisoner.

"I have a proposition for you. Rather, the Council does."

Kaz hid his surprise. "Does the Merchant Council begin all negotiations with a beating?"

"Consider it a warning. And a demonstration."

Kaz remembered the shape from the alley, the way it had appeared and disappeared like a ghost. *Jordie.*

He gave himself an internal shake. *Not Jordie, you podge. Focus.* They'd nabbed him because he'd been flush off a victory and distracted. This was his punishment, and it wasn't a mistake he'd make again. *That doesn't explain the phantom.* For now, he pushed the thought aside.

"What possible use would the Merchant Council have for me?"

Van Eck thumbed through the papers in his hand. "You were first arrested at ten," he said, scanning the page.

"Everyone remembers his first time."

"Twice again that year, twice at eleven. You were picked up when the *stadwatch* rousted a gambling hall when you were fourteen, but you haven't served any time since."

It was true. No one had managed a pinch on Kaz in three years. "I cleaned up," Kaz said. "Found honest work, live a life of industry and prayer."

"Don't blaspheme," Van Eck said mildly, but his eyes flashed briefly with anger.

A man of faith, Kaz noted, as his mind sorted through everything he knew about Van Eck – prosperous, pious, a widower recently remarried to a bride not much older than Kaz himself. And, of course, there was the mystery of Van Eck's son.

Van Eck continued paging through the file. "You run book on prize fights, horses, and your own games of chance. You've been floor boss at the Crow Club for more than two years. You're the youngest to ever run a betting shop, and you've doubled its profits in that time. You're a blackmailer—"

"I broker information."

"A con artist—"

"I create opportunity."

"A bawd and a murderer—"

"I don't run whores, and I kill for a cause."

"And what cause is that?"

"Same as yours, merch. Profit."

"How do you get your information, Mister Brekker?"

"You might say I'm a lockpick."

"You must be a very gifted one."

"I am indeed." Kaz leaned back slightly. "You see, every man is a safe, a vault of secrets and longings. Now, there are those who take the brute's way, but I prefer a gentler approach – the right pressure applied at the right moment, in the right place. It's a delicate thing."

"Do you always speak in metaphors, Mister Brekker?"

Kaz smiled. "It's not a metaphor."

He was out of his chair before his chains hit the ground. He leaped the desk, snatching a letter opener from its surface in one hand, and catching hold of the front of Van Eck's shirt with the other. The fine fabric bunched as he pressed the blade to Van Eck's throat. Kaz was dizzy, and his limbs felt creaky from being trapped in the chair, but everything seemed sunnier with a weapon in his hand.

Van Eck's guards were facing him, all with guns and swords drawn. He could feel the merch's heart pounding beneath the wool of his suit.

"I don't think I need to waste breath on threats," Kaz said. "Tell me how to get to the door or I'm taking you through the window with me."

"I think I can change your mind."

Kaz gave him a little jostle. "I don't care who you are or how big that ruby is. You don't take me from my own streets. And you don't try to make a deal with me while I'm in chains."

"Mikka," Van Eck called.

And then it happened again. A boy walked through the library wall. He was pale as a corpse and wore an embroidered blue Grisha Tidemaker's coat with a red-and-gold ribbon at the lapel indicating his association with Van Eck's house. But not even Grisha could just stroll through a wall.

Drugged, Kaz thought, trying not to panic. *I've been drugged.* Or it was some kind of illusion, the kind they performed in the theatres off East Stave – a girl cut in half, doves from a teapot.

"What the hell is this?" he growled.

"Let me go and I'll explain."

"You can explain right where you are."

Van Eck huffed a short, shaky breath. "What you're seeing are the effects of *jurda parem*."

"*Jurda* is just a stimulant." The little dried blossoms were grown in Novyi Zem and sold in shops all over Ketterdam. In his early days in the Dregs, Kaz had chewed them to stay alert during stakeouts. It had stained his teeth orange for days after. "It's harmless," he said.

"*Jurda parem* is something completely different, and it is most definitely not harmless."

"So you did drug me."

"Not *you*, Mister Brekker. Mikka."

Kaz took in the sickly pallor of the Grisha's face. He had dark hollows beneath his eyes, and the fragile, trembling build of someone who had missed several meals and didn't seem to care.

"*Jurda parem* is a cousin to ordinary *jurda*," Van Eck continued. "It comes from the same plant. We're not sure of the process by which the drug is made, but a sample of it was sent to the Kerch Merchant Council by a scientist named Bo Yul-Bayur."

"Shu?"

"Yes. He wished to defect, so he sent us a sample to convince us of his claims regarding the drug's extraordinary effects. Please, Mister Brekker, this is a most uncomfortable position. If you'd like, I will give you a pistol, and we can sit and discuss this in more civilised fashion."

"A pistol and my cane."

Van Eck gestured to one of his guards, who exited the room and returned a moment later with Kaz's walking stick – Kaz was just glad he used the damn door.

"Pistol first," Kaz said. "Slowly." The guard unholstered his weapon and handed it to Kaz by the grip. Kaz grabbed and cocked it in one quick movement, then released Van Eck, tossed the letter opener on to the desk, and snatched his cane from the guard's hand. The pistol was more useful, but the cane brought Kaz a relief he didn't care to quantify.

Van Eck took a few steps backwards, putting distance between himself and Kaz's loaded gun. He didn't seem eager to sit. Neither was Kaz, so he kept close to the window, ready to bolt if need be.

Van Eck took a deep breath and tried to set his suit to rights. "That cane is quite a piece of hardware, Mister Brekker. Is it Fabrikator made?"

It was, in fact, the work of a Grisha Fabrikator, lead-lined and perfectly weighted for breaking bones. "None of your business. Get talking, Van Eck."

The mercher cleared his throat. "When Bo Yul-Bayur sent us the sample of *jurda parem*, we fed it to three Grisha, one from each Order."

"Happy volunteers?"

"Indentures," Van Eck conceded. "The first two were a Fabrikator and a Healer indentured to Councilman Hoede. Mikka is a Tidemaker. He's mine. You've seen what he can do using the drug."

Hoede. Why did that name ring a bell?

"I don't know what I've seen," Kaz said as he glanced at Mikka. The boy's gaze was focused intently on Van Eck as if awaiting his next command. Or maybe another fix.

"An ordinary Tidemaker can control currents, summon water or moisture from the air or a nearby source. They manage the tides in our harbour. But under the influence of *jurda parem*, a Tidemaker can alter his own state from solid to liquid to gas and back again, and do the same with other objects. Even a wall."

Kaz was tempted to deny it, but he couldn't explain what he'd just seen any other way. "How?"

"It's hard to say. You're aware of the amplifiers some Grisha wear?"

"I've seen them," Kaz said. Animal bones, teeth, scales. "I hear they're hard to come by."

"Very. But they only increase a Grisha's power. *Jurda parem* alters a Grisha's perception."

"So?"

"Grisha manipulate matter at its most fundamental levels. They call it the Small Science. Under the influence of *parem*, those manipulations become faster and far more precise. In theory, *jurda parem* is just a stimulant like its ordinary cousin. But it seems to sharpen and hone a Grisha's senses. They can make connections with extraordinary speed. Things become possible that simply shouldn't be."

"What does it do to sorry sobs like you and me?"

Van Eck seemed to bristle slightly at being lumped in with Kaz, but he said, "It's lethal. An ordinary mind cannot tolerate *parem* in even the lowest doses."

"You said you gave it to three Grisha. What can the others do?"

"Here," Van Eck said, reaching for a drawer in his desk.

Kaz lifted his pistol. "Easy."

With exaggerated slowness, Van Eck slid his hand into the desk drawer and pulled out a lump of gold. "This started as lead."

"Like hell it did."

Van Eck shrugged. "I can only tell you what I saw. The Fabrikator took a piece of lead in his hands, and moments later we had this."

"How do you even know it's real?" asked Kaz.

"It has the same melting point as gold, the same weight and malleability. If it's not identical to gold in every way, the difference has eluded us. Have it tested if you like."

Kaz tucked his cane under his arm and took the heavy lump from Van Eck's hand. He slipped it into his pocket. Whether it was real or just a convincing imitation, a chunk of yellow that big could buy plenty on the streets of the Barrel.

"You could have got that anywhere," Kaz pointed out.

"I would bring Hoede's Fabrikator here to show you himself, but he isn't well."

Kaz's gaze flicked to Mikka's sickly face and damp brow. The drug clearly came with a price.

"Let's say this is all true and not cheap, coin-trick magic. What does it have to do with me?"

"Perhaps you heard of the Shu paying off the entirety of their debt to Kerch with a sudden influx of gold? The assassination of the trade ambassador from Novyi Zem? The theft of documents from a military base in Ravka?"

So that was the secret behind the murder of the ambassador in the washroom. And the gold in those three Shu ships must have been Fabrikator made. Kaz hadn't heard anything about Ravkan documents, but he nodded anyway.

"We believe all these occurrences are the work of Grisha under the control of the Shu government and under the influence of *jurda parem*." Van Eck scrubbed a hand over his jaw. "Mister Brekker, I want you to think for a moment about what I'm telling you. Men who can walk through walls – no vault or fortress will ever be safe again. People who can make gold from lead, or anything else for that matter, who can alter the very material of the world – financial markets would be thrown into chaos. The world economy would collapse."

"Very exciting. What is it you want from me, Van Eck? You want me to steal a shipment? The formula?"

"No, I want you to steal the man."

"Kidnap Bo Yul-Bayur?"

"Save him. A month ago we received a message from Yul-Bayur begging for asylum. He was concerned about his government's plans for *jurda parem*, and we agreed to help him defect. We set up a rendezvous, but there was a skirmish at the drop point."

"With the Shu?"

"No, with Fjerdans."

Kaz frowned. The Fjerdans must have spies deep in Shu Han or Kerch if they had learned about the drug and Bo Yul-Bayur's plans so quickly. "So send some of your agents after him."

"The diplomatic situation is somewhat delicate. It is essential that our government not be tied to Yul-Bayur in any way."

"You have to know he's probably dead. The Fjerdans hate Grisha. There's no way they'd let knowledge of this drug get out."

"Our sources say he is very much alive and that he is awaiting trial." Van Eck cleared his throat. "At the Ice Court."

Kaz stared at Van Eck for a long minute, then burst out laughing. "Well, it's been a pleasure being knocked unconscious and taken captive by you, Van Eck. You can be sure your hospitality will be repaid when the time is right. Now have one of your lackeys show me to the door."

"We're prepared to offer you five million *kruge*."

Kaz pocketed the pistol. He wasn't afraid for his life now, just irritated that this fink had wasted his time. "This may come as a surprise to you, Van Eck, but we canal rats value our lives just as much as you do yours."

"Ten million."

"There's no point to a fortune I won't be alive to spend. Where's my hat – did your Tidemaker leave it behind in the alley?"

"Twenty."

Kaz paused. He had the eerie sense that the carved fish on the walls had halted mid-leap to listen. "Twenty million *kruge*?"

Van Eck nodded. He didn't look happy.

"I'd need to convince a team to walk into a suicide mission. That won't come cheap." That wasn't entirely true.

Despite what he'd said to Van Eck, there were plenty of people in the Barrel who didn't have much to live for.

"Twenty million *kruge* is hardly cheap," Van Eck snapped.

"The Ice Court has never been breached."

"That's why we need you, Mister Brekker. It's possible Bo Yul-Bayur is already dead or that he's given up all his secrets to the Fjerdans, but we think we have at least a little time to act before the secret of *jurda parem* is put into play."

"If the Shu have the formula—"

"Yul-Bayur claimed he'd managed to mislead his superiors and keep the specifics of the formula secret. We think they're operating from whatever limited supply Yul-Bayur left behind."

Greed bows to me. Maybe Kaz had been a bit too cocky on that front. Now greed was doing Van Eck's bidding. The lever was at work, overcoming Kaz's resistance, moving him into place.

Twenty million *kruge.* What kind of job would this be? Kaz didn't know anything about espionage or government squabbles, but why should stealing Bo Yul-Bayur from the Ice Court be any different from liberating valuables from a mercher's safe? *The most well-protected safe in the world*, he reminded himself. He'd need a very specialised team, a desperate team that wouldn't balk at the real possibility that they'd never come back from this job. And he wouldn't be able to just pull from the Dregs. He didn't have the talent he'd need in their ranks. That meant he'd have to watch his back more than usual.

But if they managed it, even after Per Haskell got his cut, Kaz's share of the scrub would be enough to change everything, to finally put into motion the dream he'd had since he'd first crawled out of a cold harbour with revenge burning a hole in his heart. His debt to Jordie would be paid at last.

There would be other benefits, too. The Kerch Council

would owe him, to say nothing of what this particular heist would do for his reputation. To infiltrate the impenetrable Ice Court and snatch a prize from the bastion of Fjerdan nobility and military might? With a job like this under his belt and that kind of scrub at his fingertips, he wouldn't need Per Haskell any more. He could start his own operation.

But something was off. "Why me? Why the Dregs? There are more experienced crews out there."

Mikka started to cough, and Kaz saw blood on his sleeve.

"Sit," Van Eck instructed gently, helping Mikka into a chair and offering the Grisha his handkerchief. He signalled to a guard. "Some water."

"Well?" prodded Kaz.

"How old are you, Mister Brekker?"

"Seventeen."

"You haven't been arrested since you were fourteen, and since I know you are not an honest man any more than you were an honest boy, I can only assume you have the quality I most need in a criminal: *You don't get caught.*" Van Eck smiled slightly then. "There's also the matter of my DeKappel."

"I'm sure I don't know what you mean."

"Six months ago, a DeKappel oil worth nearly one hundred thousand *kruge* disappeared from my home."

"Quite a loss."

"It was, especially since I had been assured that my gallery was impenetrable and that the locks on its doors were foolproof."

"I do seem to remember reading about that."

"Yes," admitted Van Eck with a small sigh. "Pride is a perilous thing. I was eager to show off my acquisition and the lengths I'd gone to in order to protect it. And yet, despite all my safeguards, despite dogs and alarms and the most loyal staff in all of Ketterdam, my painting is gone."

"My condolences."

"It has yet to surface anywhere on the world market."

"Maybe your thief already had a buyer lined up."

"A possibility, of course. But I'm inclined to believe that the thief took it for a different reason."

"What would that be?"

"Just to prove that he could."

"Seems like a stupid risk to me."

"Well, who can guess at the motives of thieves?"

"Not me, certainly."

"From what I know of the Ice Court, whoever stole my DeKappel is exactly who I need for this job."

"Then you'd be better off hiring him. Or her."

"Indeed. But I'll have to settle for you."

Van Eck held Kaz's gaze as if he hoped to find a confession written between his eyes. At last, Van Eck asked, "We have a deal then?"

"Not so fast. What about the Healer?"

Van Eck looked baffled. "Who?"

"You said you gave the drug to a Grisha from each Order. Mikka's a Tidemaker – he's your Etherealnik. The Fabrikator who mocked up that gold was a Materialnik. So what happened to the Corporalnik? The Healer?"

Van Eck winced slightly, but simply said, "Will you accompany me, Mister Brekker?"

Warily, keeping one eye on Mikka and the guards, Kaz followed Van Eck out of the library and down the hall. The house dripped mercher wealth – walls panelled in dark wood, floors tiled in clean black and white, all in good taste, all perfectly restrained and impeccably crafted. But it had the feel of a graveyard. The rooms were deserted, the curtains drawn, the furniture covered in white sheets so that each shadowy chamber they passed looked like some kind of forgotten seascape cluttered with icebergs.

Hoede. Now the name clicked into place. There'd been some kind of incident at Hoede's mansion on the Geldstraat last week. The whole place had been cordoned off and crawling with *stadwatch*. Kaz had heard rumours of a firepox outbreak, but even Inej hadn't been able to learn more.

"This is Councilman Hoede's house," Kaz said, skin crawling. He wanted no part of a plague, but the merch and his guards didn't seem remotely concerned. "I thought this place was under quarantine."

"What happened here is no danger to us. And if you do your job, Mister Brekker, it never will be."

Van Eck led him through a door and into a manicured garden, thick with the new nectar scent of early crocuses. The smell hit Kaz like a blow to the jaw. Memories of Jordie were already too fresh in his mind, and for a moment, Kaz wasn't walking through the canal-side garden of a rich merch, he was knee-deep in spring grasses, hot sun beating down on his cheeks, his brother's voice calling him home.

Kaz gave himself a shake. *I need a mug of the darkest, bitterest coffee I can find*, he thought. *Or maybe a real punch to the jaw.*

Van Eck was leading him to a boathouse that faced the canal. The light filtering out between its shuttered windows cast patterns on the garden path. A single city guard stood at attention beside the door as Van Eck slid a key from his pocket and into the heavy lock. Kaz put his sleeve up to his mouth as the stink from the closed-up room reached him – urine, excrement. So much for spring crocuses.

The room was lit by two glass lanterns on the wall. A group of guards stood facing a large iron box, shattered glass littering the floor at their feet. Some wore the purple uniform of the *stadwatch*, others the sea green livery of the Hoede house. Through what Kaz now understood had been an observation window, he saw another city guard standing in front of an empty table and two overturned chairs. Like the others, the guard stood with his arms loose at his sides, face blank, eyes forwards, gazing at nothing. Van Eck turned up the light on one of the lanterns, and Kaz saw a body in a purple uniform slumped on the floor, eyes closed.

Van Eck sighed and crouched down to turn the body over. "We've lost another," he said.

The boy was young, the bare scraps of a moustache on his upper lip.

Van Eck gave orders to the guard who had let them in, and with help from one of Van Eck's retinue they lifted the corpse and took it from the room. The other guards didn't react, just continued to stare ahead.

Kaz recognised one of them – Henrik Dahlman, the captain of the *stadwatch*.

"Dahlman?" he queried, but the man made no response. Kaz waved a hand in front of the captain's face, then gave him a hard flick on the ear. Nothing but a slow, disinterested blink. Kaz raised his pistol and aimed it directly at the captain's forehead. He cocked the hammer. The captain didn't flinch, didn't react. His pupils didn't contract.

"He's as good as dead," said Van Eck. "Shoot. Blow his brains out. He won't protest and the others won't react."

Kaz lowered his weapon, a chill settling deep into his bones. "What is this? What happened to them?"

"The Grisha was a Corporalnik serving her indenture with Councilman Hoede's household. He thought because she was a Healer and not a Heartrender, he was making the safe choice to test the *parem*."

Seemed smart enough. Kaz had seen Heartrenders at work. They could rupture your cells, burst your heart in your chest, steal the breath from your lungs, or lower your pulse so that you dropped into a coma, all while never laying a finger on you. If even part of what Van Eck said was true, the idea of one of them dosed with *jurda parem* was a daunting proposition. So the merchers had tried the drug on a Healer instead. But apparently things hadn't gone according to plan.

"You gave her the drug, and she killed her master?"

"Not exactly," Van Eck said, clearing his throat. "They had her in that observation cell. Within seconds of consuming the *parem*, she took control of the guard inside the chamber—"

"How?"

"We don't know exactly. But whatever method she used, it allowed her to subdue these guards as well."

"That's not possible."

"Isn't it? The brain is just one more organ, a cluster of cells and impulses. Why shouldn't a Grisha under the influence of *jurda parem* be able to manipulate those impulses?"

Kaz's disbelief must have shown.

"Look at these people," Van Eck insisted. "She told them to wait. And that's exactly what they've done – that's *all* they've done since."

Kaz studied the silent group more closely. Their eyes weren't blank or dead, their bodies weren't quite at rest. They were *expectant*. He suppressed a shiver. He'd seen peculiar things, extraordinary things, but nothing like what he'd witnessed tonight.

"What happened to Hoede?"

"She commanded him to open the door, and when he did, she ordered him to cut the thumb from his hand. We only know how it all happened because a kitchen boy was present. The Grisha girl left him untouched, but he claims Hoede carved away his own thumb, smiling all the while."

Kaz didn't like the idea of some Grisha moving things around in his head. But he wouldn't be surprised if Hoede deserved whatever he'd got. During Ravka's civil war, a lot of Grisha had fled the fighting and paid their way to Kerch by becoming indentures without realising that they'd essentially sold themselves into slavery.

"The merch is dead?"

"Councilman Hoede lost a great deal of blood, but he's

in the same state as these men. He's been removed to the country with his family and the staff from his house."

"Did the Grisha Healer go back to Ravka?" Kaz asked.

Van Eck gestured Kaz out of the eerie boathouse and locked the door behind them.

"She may have attempted it," he said as they retraced their steps through the garden and along the side of the house. "We know she secured a small craft, and we suspect she was headed to Ravka, but we found her body washed up two days ago near Third Harbour. We think she drowned trying to get back into the city."

"Why would she come back here?"

"For more *jurda parem*."

Kaz thought of Mikka's glittering eyes and waxy skin. "It's that addictive?"

"It seems to take only one dose. Once the drug has run its course, it leaves the Grisha's body weakened and the craving is intense. It's quite debilitating."

Quite debilitating seemed like a bit of an understatement. The Council of Tides controlled entry to the Ketterdam harbours. If the drugged Healer had tried to return at night in a small boat, she wouldn't have had much of a chance against the current. Kaz thought of Mikka's gaunt face, the way his clothes hung from his body. The drug had done that to him. He'd been high on *jurda parem* and already greedy for the next dose. He'd also looked ready to keel over. How long could a Grisha go on that way?

It was an interesting question, but not relevant to the matter at hand. They'd arrived at the front gate. It was time to settle up.

"Thirty million *kruge*," Kaz said.

"We said twenty!" sputtered Van Eck.

"*You* said twenty. It's clear you're desperate." Kaz glanced back in the direction of the boathouse, where a room full of men simply waited to die. "And now I see why."

"The Council will have my head."

"They'll sing your praises once you have Bo Yul-Bayur safely hidden away wherever you intend to keep him."

"Novyi Zem."

Kaz shrugged. "You can put him in a coffeepot for all I care."

Van Eck's gaze locked on his. "You've seen what this drug can do. I assure you it is just the beginning. If *jurda parem* is unleashed on the world, war is inevitable. Our trade lines will be destroyed, and our markets will collapse. Kerch will not survive it. Our hopes rest with you, Mister Brekker. If you fail, all the world will suffer for it."

"Oh, it's worse than that, Van Eck. If I fail, I don't get paid."

The look of disgust on the merch's face was something that deserved its own DeKappel oil to commemorate it.

"Don't look so disappointed. Just think how miserable you would have been to discover this canal rat had a patriotic streak. You might actually have had to uncurl that lip and treat me with something closer to respect."

"Thank you for sparing me that discomfort," Van Eck said disdainfully. He opened the door, then paused. "I do wonder what a boy of your intelligence might have amounted to under different circumstances."

Ask Jordie, Kaz thought with a bitter pang. But he simply shrugged. "I'd just be stealing from a better class of sucker. Thirty million *kruge*."

Van Eck nodded. "Thirty. The deal is the deal."

"The deal is the deal," Kaz said. They shook.

As Van Eck's neatly manicured hand clasped Kaz's leather-clad fingers, the merch narrowed his eyes.

"Why do you wear the gloves, Mister Brekker?"

Kaz raised a brow. "I'm sure you've heard the stories."

"Each more grotesque than the last."

Kaz had heard them, too. Brekker's hands were stained

with blood. Brekker's hands were covered in scars. Brekker had claws and not fingers because he was part demon. Brekker's touch burned like brimstone – a single brush of his bare skin caused your flesh to wither and die.

"Pick one," Kaz said as he vanished into the night, thoughts already turning to thirty million *kruge* and the crew he'd need to help him get it. "They're all true enough."

4

INEJ

Inej knew the moment Kaz entered the Slat. His presence reverberated through the cramped rooms and crooked hallways as every thug, thief, dealer, conman, and steerer came a little more awake. Per Haskell's favoured lieutenant was home.

The Slat wasn't much, just another house in the worst part of the Barrel, three storeys stacked tight on top of each other, crowned with an attic and a gabled roof. Most of the buildings in this part of the city had been built without foundations, many on swampy land where the canals were haphazardly dug. They leaned against each other like tipsy friends gathered at a bar, tilting at drowsy angles. Inej had visited plenty of them on errands for the Dregs, and they weren't much better on the inside – cold and damp, plaster sliding from the walls, gaps in the windows wide enough to let in the rain and snow. Kaz had spent his own money to have the Slat's drafts shorn up and its walls insulated. It was ugly, crooked, and crowded, but the Slat was gloriously dry.

Inej's room was on the third floor, a skinny slice of space barely big enough for a cot and a trunk, but with a window that looked out over the peaked roofs and jumbled chimneys of the Barrel. When the wind came through and cleared away the haze of coal smoke that hung over the city, she could even make out a blue pocket of harbour.

Though dawn was just a few hours away, the Slat was wide awake. The only time the house was ever really quiet was in the slow hours of the afternoon, and tonight everyone was buzzing with the news of the showdown at the Exchange, Big Bolliger's fate, and now poor Rojakke's dismissal.

Inej had gone straight from her conversation with Kaz to seek out the card dealer at the Crow Club. He'd been at the tables dealing Three Man Bramble for Jesper and a couple of Ravkan tourists. When he'd finished the hand, Inej had suggested they speak in one of the private gaming parlours to spare him the embarrassment of being fired in front of his friends, but Rojakke wasn't having it.

"It's not fair," he'd bellowed when she'd told him Kaz's orders. "I ain't no cheat!"

"Take it up with Kaz," Inej had replied quietly.

"And keep your voice down," Jesper added, glancing at the tourists and sailors seated at the neighbouring tables. Fights were common in the Barrel, but not on the floor of the Crow Club. If you had a gripe, you settled it outside, where you didn't risk interrupting the hallowed practice of separating pigeons from their money.

"Where's Brekker?" growled Rojakke.

"I don't know."

"You always know everything about everything," Rojakke sneered, leaning in, the stink of lager and onions on his breath. "Isn't that what Dirtyhands pays you for?"

"I don't know where he is or when he's getting back. But I *do* know you won't want to be here when he does."

"Give me my cheque. I'm owed for my last shift."

"Brekker doesn't owe you anything."

"He can't even face me? Sends a little girl to give me the

boot? Maybe I'll just shake a few coins out of you." He'd reached to grab her by the collar of her shirt, but she'd dodged him easily. He fumbled for her again.

Out of the corner of her eye, Inej saw Jesper rise from his seat, but she waved him off and slipped her fingers into the brass knuckles she kept in her right hip pocket. She gave Rojakke a swift crack across the left cheek.

His hand flew up to his face. "Hey," he said. "I didn't hurt you none. It was just words."

People were watching now, so she hit him again. Regardless of the Crow Club rules, this took precedence. When Kaz had brought her to the Slat, he'd warned her that he wouldn't be able to watch out for her, that she'd have to fend for herself, and she had. It would have been easy enough to turn away when they called her names or sidled up to ask for a cuddle, but do that and soon it was a hand up your blouse or a try at you against a wall. So she'd let no insult or innuendo slide. She'd always struck first and struck hard. Sometimes she even cut them up a bit. It was fatiguing, but nothing was sacred to the Kerch except trade, so she'd gone out of her way to make the risk much higher than the reward when it came to disrespecting her.

Rojakke touched his fingers to the ugly bruise forming on his cheek, looking surprised and a bit betrayed. "I thought we was friendly," he protested.

The sad part was that they were. Inej *liked* Rojakke. But right now, he was just a frightened man looking to feel bigger than someone.

"Rojakke," she'd said. "I've seen you work a deck of cards. You can get a job in almost any den. Go home and be grateful Kaz doesn't take what you owe him out of your hide, hmmm?"

He'd gone, a bit wobbly on his feet, still clutching his cheek like a stunned toddler, and Jesper had sauntered over.

"He's right, you know. Kaz shouldn't send you to do his dirty work."

"It's all dirty work."

"But we do it just the same," he said with a sigh.

"You look exhausted. Will you sleep at all tonight?"

Jesper just winked. "Not while the cards are hot. Stay and play a bit. Kaz will stake you."

"Really, Jesper?" she'd said, pulling up her hood. "If I want to watch men dig holes to fall into, I'll find myself a cemetery."

"Come on, Inej," he'd called after her as she passed through the big double doors onto the street. "You're good luck!"

Saints, she'd thought, *if he believes that, he really must be desperate.* She'd left her luck behind in a Suli camp on the shores of West Ravka. She doubted she'd see either again.

Now Inej left her tiny chamber in the Slat and headed downstairs by way of the banisters. There was no reason to cloak her movements here, but silence was a habit, and the stairs tended to squeak like mating mice. When she reached the second floor landing and saw the crowd milling below, she hung back.

Kaz had been gone longer than anyone had expected, and as soon as he'd entered the shadowy foyer, he'd been waylaid by people looking to congratulate him on his routing of Geels and asking for news of the Black Tips.

"Rumour has it Geels is already putting together a mob to move on us," said Anika.

"Let him!" rumbled Dirix. "I've got an axe handle with his name on it."

"Geels won't act for a while," said Kaz as he moved down the hall. "He doesn't have the numbers to face us in the streets, and his coffers are too empty to hire on more hands. Shouldn't you be on your way to the Crow Club?"

The raised eyebrow was enough to send Anika

scurrying away, Dirix on her heels. Others came to offer congratulations or make threats against the Black Tips. No one went so far as to pat Kaz on the back, though – that was a good way to lose a hand.

Inej knew Kaz would stop to speak to Per Haskell, so instead of descending the final flight of stairs, she moved down the hallway. There was a closet here, full of odds and ends, old chairs with broken backs, paint-spattered canvas sheeting. Inej moved aside a bucket full of cleaning supplies that she'd placed there precisely because she knew no one in the Slat would ever touch it. The grate beneath it offered a perfect view of Per Haskell's office. She felt slightly guilty for eavesdropping on Kaz, but he was the one who had turned her into a spy. You couldn't train a falcon, then expect it not to hunt.

Through the grate she heard Kaz's knock on Per Haskell's door and the sound of his greeting.

"Back and still breathing?" the old man inquired. She could just see him seated in his favourite chair, fiddling with a model ship he'd been building for the better part of a year, a pint of lager within arm's reach, as always.

"We won't have a problem with Fifth Harbour again."

Haskell grunted and returned to his model ship. "Close the door."

Inej heard it shut, muffling the sounds from the hallway. She could see the top of Kaz's head. His dark hair was damp. It must have started raining.

"You should have asked permission from me to deal with Bolliger," said Haskell.

"If I had talked to you first, word might have got out—"

"You think I'd let that happen?"

Kaz's shoulders lifted. "This place is like anything in Ketterdam. It leaks." Inej could have sworn he looked directly at the vent when he said it.

"I don't like it, boy. Big Bolliger was *my* soldier, not yours."

"Of course," Kaz said, but they both knew it was a lie. Haskell's Dregs were old guard, conmen and crooks from another time. Bolliger had been one of Kaz's crew – new blood, young and unafraid. Maybe too unafraid.

"You're smart, Brekker, but you need to learn patience."

"Yes, sir."

The old man barked a laugh. "*Yes, sir. No, sir*," he mocked. "I know you're up to something when you start getting polite. Just what have you got brewing?"

"A job," Kaz said. "I may need to be gone for a spell."

"Big money?"

"Very."

"Big risk?"

"That, too. But you'll get your twenty per cent."

"You don't make any major moves without my say-so, understood?" Kaz must have nodded because Per Haskell leaned back in his chair and took a sip of lager. "Are we to be very rich?"

"Rich as Saints in crowns of gold."

The old man snorted. "Long as I don't have to live like one."

"I'll talk to Pim," Kaz said. "He can pick up the slack while I'm gone." Inej frowned. Just where was Kaz going? He hadn't mentioned any big job to her. *And why Pim?* The thought shamed her a bit. She could almost hear her father's voice: *So eager to be Queen of the Thieves, Inej?* It was one thing to do her job and do it well. It was quite another to want to succeed at it. She didn't want a permanent place with the Dregs. She wanted to pay off her debts and be free of Ketterdam forever, so why should she care if Kaz chose Pim to run the gang in his absence? *Because I'm smarter than Pim. Because Kaz trusts me more.* But maybe he didn't trust the crew to follow a girl like her, only two years out of the brothels, not even seventeen years old. She wore her sleeves long and the sheath of her knife mostly hid the scar on the inside of her left forearm where the Menagerie tattoo had once been, but they all knew it was there.

Kaz exited Haskell's room, and Inej left her perch to wait for him as he limped his way up the stairs.

"Rojakke?" he asked as he passed her and started up the second flight.

"Gone," she said, falling in behind him.

"He put up much of a fight?"

"Nothing I couldn't handle."

"Not what I asked."

"He was angry. He may come back around looking for trouble."

"Never a shortage of that to hand out," Kaz said as they reached the top floor. The attic rooms had been converted into his office and bedroom. She knew all those flights of stairs were brutal on his bad leg, but he seemed to like having the whole floor to himself.

He entered the office and without looking back at her said, "Shut the door."

The room was mostly taken up by a makeshift desk – an old warehouse door atop stacked fruit crates – piled high with papers. Some of the floor bosses had started using adding machines, clanking things crowded with stiff brass buttons and spools of paper, but Kaz did the Crow Club tallies in his head. He kept books, but only for the sake of the old man and so that he had something to point to when he called someone out for cheating or when he was looking for new investors.

That was one of the big changes Kaz had brought to the gang. He'd given ordinary shopkeepers and legitimate businessmen the chance to buy shares in the Crow Club. At first they'd been skeptical, sure it was some kind of swindle, but he'd brought them in with tiny stakes and managed to gather enough capital to purchase the dilapidated old building, spruce it up, and get it running. It had paid back big for those early investors. Or so the story went. Inej could never be sure which stories about Kaz were true and which were rumours he'd planted to serve his own ends. For all she knew, he'd conned some poor honest trader out of his life savings to make the Crow Club thrive.

"I've got a job for you," Kaz said as he flipped through the previous day's figures. Each sheet would go into his memory with barely a glance. "What would you say to four million *kruge*?"

"Money like that is more curse than gift."

"My little Suli idealist. All you need is a full belly and an open road?" he said, the mockery clear in his voice.

"And an easy heart, Kaz." That was the difficult part.

Now he laughed outright as he walked through the door to his tiny bedroom. "No hopes of that. I'd rather have the cash. Do you want the money or not?"

"You're not in the business of giving gifts. What's the job?"

"An impossible job, near certain death, terrible odds, but should we scrape it . . ." He paused, fingers on the buttons of his waistcoat, his look distant, almost dreamy. It was rare that she heard such excitement in his raspy voice.

"Should we scrape it?" she prompted.

He grinned at her, his smile sudden and jarring as a thunderclap, his eyes the near-black of bitter coffee. "We'll be kings and queens, Inej. Kings and queens."

"Hmm," she said noncommittally, pretending to examine one of her knives, determined to ignore that grin. Kaz was not a giddy boy smiling and making future plans with her. He was a dangerous player who was always working an angle. *Always*, she reminded herself firmly. Inej kept her eyes averted, shuffling a stack of papers into a pile on the desk as Kaz stripped out of his vest and shirt. She wasn't sure if she was flattered or insulted that he didn't seem to give a second thought to her presence.

"How long will we be gone?" she asked, darting a glance at him through the open doorway. He was corded muscle, scars, but only two tattoos – the Dregs' crow and cup on his forearm and above it, a black *R* on his bicep. She'd never asked him what it meant.

It was his hands that drew her attention as he shucked off his leather gloves and dipped a cloth in the wash basin. He only ever removed them in these chambers, and as far as she knew, only in front of her. Whatever affliction he might be hiding, she could see no sign of it, only slender lockpick's fingers, and a shiny rope of scar tissue from some long ago street fight.

"A few weeks, maybe a month," he said as he ran the wet cloth under his arms and the hard planes of his chest, water trickling down his torso.

For Saints' sake, Inej thought as her cheeks heated. She'd lost most of her modesty during her time with the Menagerie, but really, there were limits. What would Kaz say if she suddenly stripped down and started washing herself in front of him? *He'd probably tell me not to drip on the desk*, she thought with a scowl.

"A month?" she said. "Are you sure you should be leaving with the Black Tips so riled up?"

"This is the right gamble. Speaking of which, round up Jesper and Muzzen. I want them here by dawn. And I'll need Wylan waiting at the Crow Club tomorrow night."

"Wylan? If this is for a big job—"

"Just do it."

Inej crossed her arms. One minute he made her blush and the next he made her want to commit murder. "Are you going to explain any of this?"

"When we all meet." He shrugged on a fresh shirt, then hesitated as he fastened the collar. "This isn't an assignment, Inej. It's a job for you to take or leave as you see fit."

An alarm bell rang inside her. She endangered herself

every day on the streets of the Barrel. She'd murdered for the Dregs, stolen, brought down bad men and good, and Kaz had never hinted that any of the assignments were less than a command to be obeyed. This was the price she'd agreed to when Per Haskell had purchased her contract and liberated her from the Menagerie. So what was different about this job?

Kaz finished with his buttons, pulled on a charcoal waistcoat, and tossed her something. It flashed in the air, and she caught it with one hand. When she opened her fist, she saw a massive ruby tie pin circled by golden laurel leaves.

"Fence it," Kaz said.

"Whose is it?"

"Ours now."

"Whose was it?"

Kaz stayed quiet. He picked up his coat, using a brush to clean the dried mud from it. "Someone who should have thought better before he had me jumped."

"*Jumped?*"

"You heard me."

"Someone got the drop on you?"

He looked at her and nodded once. Unease snaked through her and twisted into an anxious, rustling coil. No one got the better of Kaz. He was the toughest, scariest thing walking the alleys of the Barrel. She relied on it. So did he.

"It won't happen again," he promised.

Kaz pulled on a clean pair of gloves, snapped up his walking stick, and headed out the door. "I'll be back in a few hours. Move the DeKappel we lifted from Van Eck's house to the vault. I think it's rolled up under my bed. Oh, and put in an order for a new hat."

"*Please.*"

Kaz heaved a sigh as he braced himself for three painful

flights of stairs. He looked over his shoulder and said, "Please, my darling Inej, treasure of my heart, won't you do me the honour of acquiring me a new hat?"

Inej cast a meaningful glance at his cane. "Have a long trip down," she said, then leaped onto the banister, sliding from one flight to the next, slick as butter in a pan.

5

KAZ

Kaz followed East Stave towards the harbour, through the beginnings of the Barrel's gambling district. The Barrel was bracketed by two major canals, East Stave and West Stave, each catering to a particular clientele, and separated by a tangle of narrow streets and minor waterways. The buildings of the Barrel were different from anywhere else in Ketterdam, bigger, wider, painted in every garish colour, clamouring for attention from passersby – the Treasure Chest, the Golden Bend, Weddell's Riverboat. The best of the betting halls were located further north, in the prime real estate of the Lid, the section of the canal closest to the harbours, favourably situated to attract tourists and sailors coming into port.

But not the Crow Club, Kaz mused as he looked up at the black-and-crimson façade. It had taken a lot to lure tourists and risk-hungry merchers this far south for entertainment. Now the hour was coming up on four bells, and the crowds were still thick outside the club. Kaz watched the tide of people flowing past the portico's black columns, beneath the watchful eye of the oxidised silver crow that spread its wings above the entrance. *Bless the pigeons*, he thought. *Bless all you kind and generous folk ready to empty your wallets into the Dregs' coffers and call it a good time.*

He could see barkers out front shouting to potential customers, offering free drinks, hot pots of coffee, and the fairest deal in all of Ketterdam. He acknowledged them with a nod and pressed further north.

Only one other gambling den on the Stave mattered to him: the Emerald Palace, Pekka Rollins' pride and joy. The building was an ugly green, decked out in artificial trees laden with fake gold and silver coins. The whole place had been done up as some kind of tribute to Rollins' Kaelish heritage and his gang, the Dime Lions. Even the girls working the chip counters and tables wore glittering green sheaths of silk and had their hair tinted a dark, unnatural red to mimic the look of girls from the Wandering Isle. As Kaz passed the Emerald, he looked up at the false gold coins, letting the anger come at him. He needed it tonight as a reminder of what he'd lost, of what he stood to gain. He needed it to prepare him for this reckless endeavour.

"Brick by brick," he muttered to himself. They were the only words that kept his rage in check, that prevented him from striding through the Emerald's garish gold-and-green doors, demanding a private audience with Rollins, and slitting his throat. *Brick by brick.* It was the promise that let him sleep at night, that drove him every day, that kept Jordie's ghost at bay. Because a quick death was too good for Pekka Rollins.

Kaz watched the flow of customers in and out of the Emerald's doors and caught a glimpse of his own steerers, men and women he hired to seduce Pekka's customers south with the prospect of better deals, bigger wins, prettier girls.

"Where are you coming from, looking so flush?" one said to the other, talking far more loudly than necessary.

"Just got back from the Crow Club. Took one hundred *kruge* off the house in just two hours."

"You don't say!"

"I do! Just came up the Stave to get a beer and meet a friend. Why don't you join us, and we'll all go together?"

"The Crow Club! Who would have thought it?"

"Come on, I'll buy you a drink. I'll buy everyone a drink!"

And they walked off together laughing, leaving all the patrons around them to wonder if maybe they ought to head just a few bridges down the canal and see if the odds weren't kinder there – Kaz's servant, greed, luring them south like a piper with flute in hand.

He made sure to cycle steerers in and out, changing the faces so Pekka's barkers and bouncers never got wise, and customer by customer, he leeched away the Emerald's business. It was one of the infinite tiny ways he'd found to make himself strong at Pekka's expense – intercepting his shipments of *jurda*, charging him fees for access to Fifth Harbour, undercutting his rents to keep his properties free of tenants, and slowly, slowly tugging at the threads that made up his life.

Despite the lies he'd spread and the claims he'd made to Geels tonight, Kaz wasn't a bastard. He wasn't even from Ketterdam. He'd been nine and Jordie thirteen when they'd first arrived in the city, a cheque from the sale of their father's farm sewn safely into the inner pocket of Jordie's old coat. Kaz could see himself as he was then, walking the Stave with dazzled eyes, hand tucked into Jordie's so he wouldn't be swept away by the crowd. He hated the boys they'd been, two stupid pigeons waiting to be plucked. But those boys were long gone, and only Pekka Rollins was left to punish.

One day Rollins would come to Kaz on his knees, begging for help. If Kaz managed this job for Van Eck, that day would come much sooner than he ever could have hoped. *Brick by brick, I will destroy you.*

But if Kaz had any hope of getting into the Ice Court, he needed the right crew, and the next hour's business would bring him a step closer to securing two very vital pieces of the puzzle.

He turned onto a walkway bordering one of the smaller canals. The tourists and merchers liked to keep to well-lit thoroughfares, so the foot traffic here was sparser, and he made better time. Soon, the lights and music of West Stave came into view, the canal choked with men and women of every class and country seeking diversion.

Music floated out of parlours where the doors had been flung open, and men and women lounged on couches in little more than scraps of silk and gaudy baubles. Acrobats dangled from cords over the canal, lithe bodies garbed in nothing but glitter, while street performers played their fiddles, hoping to garner a coin or two from passersby. Hawkers shouted at the sleek private *gondels* of rich merchers in the canal and the larger browboats that brought tourists and sailors inland from the Lid.

A lot of tourists never entered the brothels of West Stave. They just came to watch the crowd, which was a sight in itself. Many people chose to visit this part of the Barrel in disguise – in veils or masks or capes with nothing but the glint of their eyes visible. They bought their costumes in one of the speciality shops off the main canals, and sometimes disappeared from their companions for a day or a week, or however long their funds held out. They dressed as Mister Crimson or the Lost Bride, or wore the grotesque, goggle-eyed mask of the Madman – all characters from the Komedie Brute. And then there were the Jackals, a group of rowdy men and boys who cavorted through the Barrel in the red lacquered masks of Suli 'fortune-tellers'.

Kaz remembered when Inej had first seen the jackal masks in a shop window. She hadn't been able to contain her contempt. "Real Suli fortune-tellers are rare. They're holy men and women. These masks that are handed around like party favours are sacred symbols."

"I've seen Suli tellers ply their trade in caravans and pleasure ships, Inej. They didn't seem so very holy."

"They are pretenders. Making themselves clowns for you and your ilk."

"My ilk?" Kaz had laughed.

She'd waved her hand in disgust. "*Shevrati*," she'd said. "Know-nothings. They're laughing at you behind those masks."

"Not at me, Inej. I'd never lay down good coin to be told my future by anyone – fraud or holy man."

"Fate has plans for us all, Kaz."

"Was it fate that took you from your family and stuck you in a pleasure house in Ketterdam? Or was it just very bad luck?"

"I'm not sure yet," she'd said coldly.

In moments like that, he thought she might hate him.

Kaz wove his way through the crowd, a shadow in a riot of colour. Each of the major pleasure houses had a speciality, some more obvious than others. He passed the Blue Iris, the Bandycat, bearded men glowering from the windows of the Forge, the Obscura, the Willow Switch, the dewy-eyed blondes at the House of Snow, and of course the Menagerie, also known as the House of Exotics, where Inej had been forced to don fake Suli silks. He spotted Tante Heleen in her peacock feathers and famous diamond choker holding court in the gilded parlour. She ran the Menagerie, procured the girls, made sure they behaved. When she saw Kaz, her lips thinned to a sour line, and she lifted her glass, the gesture more threat than toast. He ignored her and pressed on.

The House of the White Rose was one of the more luxurious establishments on West Stave. It had its own dock, and its gleaming white stone façade looked less like a pleasure house than a mercher mansion. Its window boxes were always bursting with climbing white roses, and their scent clung dense and sweet over this portion of the canal.

The parlour was even stickier with perfume. Huge alabaster vases overflowed with more white roses, and men and women – some masked or veiled, some with faces bare – waited on ivory couches, sipping near-colourless wine and nibbling little vanilla cakes soaked in almond liqueur.

The boy at the desk was dressed in a creamy velvet suit, a white rose in his buttonhole. He had white hair and eyes the colour of boiled eggs. Barring the eyes, he looked like an albino, but Kaz happened to know that he'd been tailored to match the decor of the House by a certain Grisha on the payroll.

"Mister Brekker," the boy said, "Nina is with a client."

Kaz nodded and slipped down a hallway behind a potted rose tree, resisting the urge to bury his nose in his collar. Onkle Felix, the bawd who ran the White Rose, liked to say that his house girls were as sweet as his blossoms. But the joke was on the clients. That particular breed of white rose, the only one hardy enough to survive the wet weather of Ketterdam, had no natural scent. All the flowers were perfumed by hand.

Kaz trailed his fingers along the panels behind the potted tree and pressed his thumb into a notch in the wall. It slid open, and he climbed a corkscrew staircase that was only used by staff.

Nina's room was on the third floor. The door to the bedroom beside it was open and the room unoccupied, so Kaz slipped in, moved aside a still life, and pressed his face to the wall. The peepholes were a feature of all the brothels. They were a way to keep employees safe and honest, and they offered a thrill to anyone who enjoyed watching others take their pleasure. Kaz had seen enough slum dwellers seeking satisfaction in dark corners and alleys that the allure was lost on him. Besides, he knew that anyone looking through this particular peephole and hoping for excitement would be sorely disappointed.

A little bald man was seated fully clothed at a round table draped in ivory baize, his hands neatly folded beside an untouched silver coffee tray. Nina Zenik stood behind him, swathed in the red silk *kefta* that advertised her status as a Grisha Heartrender, one palm pressed to his forehead, the other to the back of his neck. She was tall and built like the figurehead of a ship carved by a generous hand. They were silent, as if they'd been frozen there at the table. There wasn't even a bed in the room, just a narrow settee where Nina curled up every night.

When Kaz had asked Nina why, she'd simply said, "I don't want anyone getting ideas."

"A man doesn't need a bed to get ideas, Nina."

Nina fluttered her lashes. "What would you know about it, Kaz? Take those gloves off, and we'll see what ideas come to mind."

Kaz had kept his cool eyes on her until she'd dropped her gaze. He wasn't interested in flirting with Nina Zenik, and he happened to know she wasn't remotely interested in him. Nina just liked to flirt with everything. He'd once seen her make eyes at a pair of shoes she fancied in a shop window.

Nina and the bald man sat, unspeaking, as the minutes ticked by, and when the hour on the clock chimed, he rose and kissed her hand.

"Go," she said in solemn tones. "Be at peace."

The bald man kissed her hand again, tears in his eyes. "Thank you."

As soon as the client was down the hall, Kaz stepped out of the bedroom and knocked on Nina's door.

She opened it cautiously, keeping the chain latched. "Oh," she said when she saw Kaz. "You."

She didn't look particularly happy to see him. No surprise. Kaz Brekker at your door was rarely a good thing.

She unhooked the chain and let him show himself in as she shucked off the red *kefta*, revealing a slip of satin so thin it barely counted as cloth.

"Saints, I hate this thing," she said, kicking the *kefta* away and pulling a threadbare dressing gown from a drawer.

"What's wrong with it?" Kaz asked.

"It isn't made right. And it itches." The *kefta* was of Kerch manufacture, not Ravkan – a costume, not a uniform. Kaz knew Nina never wore it on the streets; it was simply too risky for Grisha. Her membership in the Dregs meant anyone acting against her would risk retribution from the gang, but payback wouldn't matter much to Nina if she was on a slaver ship bound for who knew where.

Nina threw herself into a chair at the table and wriggled her feet out of her jewelled slippers, digging her toes into the plush white carpet. "Ahhh," she said contentedly. "So much better." She shoved one of the cakes from the coffee service into her mouth and mumbled, "What do you want, Kaz?"

"You have crumbs on your cleavage."

"Don't care," she said, taking another bite of cake. "So hungry."

Kaz shook his head, amused and impressed at how quickly Nina dropped the wise Grisha priestess act. She'd missed her true calling on the stage. "Was that Van Aakster, the merch?" Kaz asked.

"Yes."

"His wife died a month ago, and his business has been a wreck since. Now that he's visiting you, can we expect a turnaround?"

Nina didn't need a bed because she specialised in emotions. She dealt in joy, calm, confidence. Most Grisha Corporalki focused on the body – to kill or to cure – but Nina had needed a job that would keep her in Ketterdam and out of trouble. So instead of risking her life and making major money as a mercenary, she slowed heartbeats, eased breathing, relaxed muscles. She had a lucrative side business as a Tailor, seeing to the wrinkles and jowls of the wealthy Kerch, but her chief source of income came from altering moods. People came to her lonely, grieving, sad for no reason, and left buoyed, their anxieties eased. The effect didn't last long, but sometimes just the illusion of happiness was enough to make her clients feel like they could face another day. Nina claimed it had something to do with glands, but Kaz didn't care about the specifics as long as she showed up when he needed her and she paid Per Haskell his percentage on time.

"I expect you'll see a change," Nina said. She finished off the last cake, licking her fingers with relish, then set the tray outside the door and rang for a maid. "Van Aakster started coming at the end of last week and has been here every day since."

"Excellent." Kaz made a mental note to buy up some of the low stock in Van Aakster's company. Even if the man's mood shift was the result of Nina's handiwork, business would pick up. He hesitated then said, "You make him feel better, ease his woe and all that . . . but could you compel him to do something? Maybe make him forget his wife?"

"Alter the pathways in his mind? Don't be absurd."

"The brain is just another organ," Kaz said, quoting Van Eck.

"Yes, but it's an incredibly complex one. Controlling or altering another person's thoughts . . . well, it's not like lowering a pulse rate or releasing a chemical to improve someone's mood. There are too many variables. No Grisha is capable of it."

Yet, Kaz amended. "So you treat the symptom, not the cause."

She shrugged. "He's avoiding the grief, not treating it. If I'm his solution, he'll never really get over her death."

"Will you send him on his way then? Advise him to find a new wife and stop darkening your door?"

She ran a brush through her light brown hair and glanced at him in the mirror. "Does Per Haskell have plans to forgive my debt?"

"None at all."

"Well then Van Aakster must be allowed to grieve in his own way. I have another client scheduled in a half hour, Kaz. What business?"

"Your client will wait. What do you know about *jurda parem*?"

Nina shrugged. "There are rumours, but they sound like nonsense to me." With the exception of the Council of Tides, the few Grisha working in Ketterdam all knew each other and exchanged information readily. Most were on the run from something, eager to avoid drawing the attention of slavers or interest from the Ravkan government.

"They aren't just rumours."

"Squallers flying? Tidemakers turning to mist?"

"Fabrikators making gold from lead." He reached into his pocket and tossed the lump of yellow to her. "It's real."

"Fabrikators make textiles. They fuss around with metals and fabrics. They can't turn one thing into another." She held the lump up to the light. "You could have got this anywhere," she said, just as he had argued to Van Eck a few hours earlier.

Without being invited, Kaz sat down on the plush settee and stretched out his bad leg. "*Jurda parem* is real, Nina, and if you're still the good little Grisha soldier I think you are, you'll want to hear what it does to people like you."

She turned the lump of gold over in her hands, then wrapped her dressing gown more tightly around her and curled up at the end of the settee. Again, Kaz marvelled at the transformation. In these rooms, she played the part her clients wanted to see – the powerful Grisha, serene in her knowledge. But sitting there with her brow furrowed and her feet tucked under her, she looked like what she truly was: a girl of seventeen, raised in the sheltered luxury of the Little Palace, far from home and barely getting by every day.

"Tell me," she said.

Kaz talked. He held back on the specifics of Van Eck's proposal, but he told her about Bo Yul-Bayur, *jurda parem*, and the addictive properties of the drug, placing particular emphasis on the recent theft of Ravkan military documents.

"If this is all true, then Bo Yul-Bayur needs to be eliminated."

"That is not the job, Nina."

"This isn't about money, Kaz."

It was always about money. But Kaz knew a different kind of pressure was required. Nina loved her country and loved her people. She still believed in the future of Ravka and in the Second Army, the Grisha military elite that had nearly disintegrated during the civil war. Nina's friends back in Ravka believed she was dead, a victim of Fjerdan witchhunters, and for now, she wanted it to stay that way. But Kaz knew she hoped to return one day.

"Nina, we're going to retrieve Bo Yul-Bayur, and I need a Corporalnik to do it. I want you on my crew."

"Wherever he's hiding out, once you find him, letting him live would be the most outrageous kind of irresponsibility. My answer is no."

"He isn't hiding out. The Fjerdans have him at the Ice Court."

Nina paused. "Then he's as good as dead."

"The Merchant Council doesn't think so. They wouldn't be going to this trouble or offering up this kind of reward if they thought he'd been neutralised. Van Eck was worried. I could see it."

"The mercher you spoke to?"

"Yes. He claims their intelligence is good. If it's not, well, I'll take the hit. But if Bo Yul-Bayur is alive, *someone* is going to try to break him out of the Ice Court. Why shouldn't it be us?"

"The Ice Court," Nina repeated, and Kaz knew she'd begun to put the pieces together. "You don't just need a Corporalnik, do you?"

"No. I need someone who knows the Court inside and out."

She leaped to her feet and began pacing, hands on hips, dressing gown flapping. "You're a little skiv, you know that? How many times have I come to you, begging you to help Matthias? And now that you want something . . ."

"Per Haskell isn't running a charity."

"Don't put this on the old man," she snapped. "If you'd wanted to help me, you know you could have."

"And why would I do that?"

She whirled on him. "Because . . . because . . ."

"When have I ever done something for nothing, Nina?"

She opened her mouth, closed it again.

"Do you know how many favours I would have had to call in? How many bribes I'd have had to pay out to get Matthias Helvar out of prison? The price was too high."

"And now?" she managed, her eyes still blazing anger.

"Now, Helvar's freedom is worth something."

"It—"

He held up a hand to cut her off. "Worth something *to me*."

Nina pressed her fingers to her temples. "Even if you could get to him, Matthias would never agree to help you."

"It's just a question of leverage, Nina."

"You don't know him."

"Don't I? He's a person like any other, driven by greed

and pride and pain. You should understand that better than anyone."

"Helvar is driven by honour and only honour. You can't bribe or bully that."

"That may have been true once, Nina, but it's been a very long year. Helvar is much changed."

"You've seen him?" Her green eyes were wide, eager. *There*, thought Kaz, *the Barrel hasn't beaten the hope out of you yet.*

"I have."

Nina took a deep, shuddering breath. "He wants his revenge, Kaz."

"That's what he wants, not what he needs," said Kaz. "Leverage is all about knowing the difference."

6
NINA

The sick feeling in Nina's stomach had nothing to do with the rocking of the rowboat. She tried to breathe deeply, to focus on the lights of the Ketterdam harbour disappearing behind them and the steady splash of the oars in the water. Beside her, Kaz adjusted his mask and cloak, while Muzzen rowed with relentless and aggressive speed, driving them closer to Terrenjel, one of Kerch's tiny outlying islands, closer to Hellgate and Matthias.

Fog lay low over the water, damp and curling. It carried the smell of tar and machinery from the shipyards on Imperjum, and something else – the sweet stink of burning bodies from the Reaper's Barge, where Ketterdam disposed of the dead who couldn't afford to be buried in the cemeteries outside the city. *Disgusting*, Nina thought, drawing her cloak tighter around her. Why anyone would want to live in a city like this was beyond her.

Muzzen hummed happily as he rowed. Nina knew him only in passing – a bouncer and an enforcer, like the ill-fated Big Bolliger. She avoided the Slat and the Crow Club as much as possible. Kaz had branded her a snob for it, but she didn't much care what Kaz Brekker had to say about her tastes. She glanced back at Muzzen's huge shoulders. She wondered if Kaz had just brought him along to row or because he expected trouble tonight.

Of course there will be trouble. They were breaking into a prison. It wasn't going to be a party. *So why are we dressed for one?*

She'd met Kaz and Muzzen at Fifth Harbour at midnight, and when she'd boarded the little rowboat, Kaz had handed her a blue silk cape and a matching veil – the trappings of the Lost Bride, one of the costumes pleasure seekers liked to don when they sampled the excesses of the Barrel. He'd had on a big orange cape with a Madman's mask perched atop his head; Muzzen had worn the same. All they needed was a stage, and they could perform one of those dark, savage little scenes from the Komedie Brute that the Kerch seemed to find so hilarious.

Now Kaz gave her a nudge. "Lower your veil." He pulled down his own mask; the long nose and bulging eyes looked doubly monstrous in the fog.

She was about to give in and ask why the costumes were necessary when she realised that they weren't alone. Through the shifting mists, she caught sight of other boats moving through the water, carrying the shapes of other Madmen, other Brides, a Mister Crimson, a Scarab Queen. What business did these people have at Hellgate?

Kaz had refused to tell her the specifics of his plan, and when she'd insisted, he'd simply said, "Get in the boat." That was Kaz all over. He knew he didn't have to tell her anything because the lure of Matthias' freedom had already overridden every bit of her good sense. She'd been trying to talk Kaz into breaking Matthias out of jail for the better part of a year. Now he could offer Matthias more than freedom, but the price would be far higher than she had expected.

Only a few lights were visible as they approached the rocky shoal of Terrenjel. The rest was darkness and crashing waves.

"Couldn't you just bribe the warden?" she muttered to Kaz.

"I don't need him knowing he has something I want."

When the boat's hull scraped sand, two men rushed forward to haul them further onto land. The other boats she'd seen were making ground in the same cove, being pulled ashore by more grunting and cursing men. Their features were vague through the gauze of her veil, but Nina glimpsed the tattoos on their forearms: a feral cat curled into a crown – the symbol of the Dime Lions.

"Money," one of them said as they clambered out of the boat.

Kaz handed over a stack of *kruge* and once it was counted, the Dime Lion waved them on.

They followed a row of torches up an uneven path to the leeward side of the prison. Nina tilted her head back to gaze at the high black towers of the fortress known as Hellgate, a dark fist of stone thrusting up from the sea. She'd seen it from afar before, when she'd paid a fisherman to take her out to the island. But when she'd asked him to bring her closer, he'd refused. "Sharks get mean there," he'd claimed. "Bellies full of convict blood." Nina shuddered at the memory.

A door had been propped open, and another member of the Dime Lions led Nina and the others inside. They entered a dark, surprisingly clean kitchen, its walls lined with huge vats that looked better suited to laundry than cooking. The room smelled strange, like vinegar and sage. *Like a mercher's kitchen*, Nina thought. The Kerch believed that work was akin to prayer. Maybe the merchant wives came here to scrub the floors and walls and windows, to honour Ghezen, the god of industry and commerce, with soap and water and the chafing of their hands. Nina resisted the urge to gag. They could scrub all they liked. Beneath that wholesome scent was the indelible stench of mildew, urine, and unwashed bodies. It might take an actual miracle to dislodge it.

They passed through a dank entry hall, and she thought they would head up into the cells, but instead they passed through another door and onto a high stone walkway that connected the main prison to what looked like another tower.

"Where are we going?" Nina whispered. Kaz didn't answer. The wind picked up, lifting her veil and lashing her cheeks with salt spray.

As they entered the second tower, a figure emerged from the shadows, and Nina barely stifled a scream.

"Inej," she said on a wavering breath. The Suli girl wore the horns and high-necked tunic of the Grey Imp, but Nina recognised her anyway. No one else moved liked that, as if the world were smoke and she was just passing through it.

"How did you even get here?" Nina whispered to her.

"I came earlier on a supply barge."

Nina ground her teeth. "Do people just come and go from Hellgate for fun?"

"Once a week they do," said Inej, her little imp horns bobbing along with her head.

"What do you mean once a—"

"Keep quiet," Kaz growled.

"Don't shush me, Brekker," Nina whispered furiously. "If it's this easy to get into Hellgate—"

"The problem isn't getting in, it's getting out. Now shut up and stay alert."

Nina swallowed her anger. She had to trust Kaz to run the game. He'd made sure she didn't have any other choice.

They entered a tight passageway. This tower felt different from the first, older, its rough-hewn stone walls blackened by smoking torches. Their Dime Lion guide pushed open a heavy iron door and gestured for them to follow him down a steep staircase. Here the smell of bodies and refuse was worse, trapped by the sweating moisture of salt water.

They spiralled lower, into the bowels of the rock. Nina clung to the wall. There was no banister, and though she could not see the bottom, she doubted the fall would be kind. They didn't go far, but by the time they reached their destination, she was trembling, her muscles wound taut, less from exertion than the knowledge that Matthias was somewhere in this terrible place. *He is here. He is under this roof.*

"Where are we?" she whispered as they ducked through cramped stone tunnels, passing dark caves fitted with iron bars.

"This is the old prison," Kaz said. "When they built the new tower, they left this one standing."

She heard moaning from inside one of the cells.

"They still keep prisoners here?"

"Only the worst of them."

She peered between the bars of an empty cell. There were shackles on the wall, dark with rust and what might have been blood.

Through the walls, a sound reached Nina's ears, a steady pounding. She thought it was the ocean at first, but then she realised it was chanting. They emerged into a curving tunnel. To her right were more old cells, but light poured into the tunnel from staggered archways on the left, and through them she glimpsed a roaring, rowdy crowd.

The Dime Lion led them around the tunnel to the third archway, where a prison guard dressed in a blue-and-grey uniform was posted, rifle slung across his back. "Four more for you," the Dime Lion shouted over the crowd. Then he turned to Kaz. "If you need to leave, the guard will call for an escort. No one goes wandering off without a guide, understood?"

"Of course, of course, wouldn't dream of it," Kaz said from behind his ridiculous mask.

"Enjoy," the Dime Lion said with an ugly grin. The prison guard waved them through.

Nina stepped under the arch and felt as if she'd fallen into some strange nightmare. They were on a jutting stone ledge, looking down into a shallow, crudely made amphitheatre. The tower had been gutted to create an arena. Only the black walls of the old prison remained, the roof long since fallen in or destroyed so that the night sky was visible high above, dense with clouds and free of stars. It was like standing in the hollowed-out trunk of a massive tree, something long dead and howling with echoes.

Around her, masked and veiled men and women crowded onto the terraced ledges, stamping their feet as the action proceeded below. The walls surrounding the fighting pit blazed with torchlight and the sand of the arena floor was red and damp where it had soaked up blood.

In front of the dark mouth of a cave, a scrawny, bearded man in shackles stood next to a big wooden wheel marked with what looked like drawings of little animals. He'd clearly once been strong, but now his skin hung in loose folds and his muscles sagged. A younger man stood beside him in a mangy cape made from a lion's skin, his face framed by the big cat's mouth. A garish gold crown had been secured between the lion's ears, and its eyes had been replaced with bright silver dimes.

"Spin the wheel!" the young man commanded.

The prisoner lifted his shackled hands and gave the wheel a hard spin. A red needle ticked along the edges as it spun, making a cheerful clattering noise, then slowly the wheel came to a stop. Nina couldn't quite make out the symbol, but the crowd bellowed, and the man's shoulders drooped as a guard came forward to unlock his chains.

The prisoner cast them aside into the sand, and a second later Nina heard it – a roar that carried even over the excited baying of the crowd. The man in the lion cape and the prison guard stepped hurriedly onto a rope ladder and were lifted out of the pit to the safety of a ledge as the prisoner seized a flimsy-looking knife from a bloody bunch of weapons lying in the sand. He backed as far away from the mouth of the tunnel as he could get.

Nina had never seen a creature like the one that crawled into view from the tunnel. It was some kind of reptile, its thick body covered in grey-green scales, its head wide and flat, its yellow eyes slitted. It moved slowly, sinuously, its low-slung body sliding lazily over the ground. There was a white crust around the broad crescent of its mouth, and when it opened its jaws to roar again, something wet, white, and foaming dripped from its pointed teeth.

"What is that thing?" Nina asked.

"*Rinca moten*," said Inej. "A desert lizard. The poison from its mouth is lethal."

"It seems pretty slow on its feet."

"Yes. It seems that way."

The prisoner lunged forward with his knife. The big lizard moved so quickly Nina could barely track it. One moment the prisoner was bearing down on it; the next, the lizard was on the other side of the arena. Bare seconds later, it had slammed into the prisoner, pinning him to the ground as he screamed, its poison dripping over his face, leaving smoky trails wherever it touched his skin.

The creature dropped its weight on the prisoner with a sickening crunch and set about slowly mauling his shoulder as he lay there shrieking.

The crowd was booing.

Nina averted her eyes, unable to watch. "What is this?"

"Welcome to the Hellshow," said Kaz. "Pekka Rollins got

the idea a few years back and pitched it to the right Council member."

"The Merchant Council knows?"

"Of course they know, Nina. There's money to be made here."

Nina dug her fingernails into her palms. That condescending tone made Kaz so slappable.

She knew Pekka Rollins' name well. He was the reigning king of the Barrel, the owner of not one but two gambling palaces – one luxurious, the other catering to sailors with less to line their pockets – and several of the higher-end brothels. When Nina had arrived in Ketterdam a year ago, she'd been friendless, penniless, and far from home. She'd spent the first week in the Kerch law courts, dealing with the charges against Matthias. But once her testimony was complete, she'd been unceremoniously dumped at First Harbour with just enough money to book passage back to Ravka. Desperate as she'd been to return to her country, she'd known she couldn't leave Matthias to languish in Hellgate.

She had no idea what to do, but it seemed rumours of a new Grisha Corporalnik in Ketterdam had already circulated through the city. Pekka Rollins' men had been waiting for her at the harbour with the promise of safety and a place to stay. They'd taken her to the Emerald Palace, where Pekka himself had leaned heavily on Nina to join the Dime Lions and had offered to set her up in business at the Sweet Shop. She'd been close to saying yes, desperate for cash and terrified of the slavers who patrolled the streets. But that night, Inej had crawled through her window on the top floor of the Emerald Palace with a proposal from Kaz Brekker in hand.

Nina never could figure out how Inej had managed to scale six rain-slick storeys of stone in the middle of the night, but the Dregs' terms were far more favourable than those offered by Pekka and the Dime Lions. It was a contract that she might actually pay off in a year or two if she was smart with her money. And Kaz had sent the right person to argue his case – a Suli girl just a few months younger than Nina who had grown up in Ravka and who had spent a very ugly year indentured at the Menagerie.

"What can you tell me about Per Haskell?" Nina had asked that night.

"Not much," Inej had admitted. "He's no better or worse than most of the bosses in the Barrel."

"And Kaz Brekker?"

"A liar, a thief, and utterly without conscience. But he'll keep to any deal you strike with him."

Nina had heard the conviction in her voice. "He freed you from the Menagerie?"

"There is no freedom in the Barrel, only good terms. Tante Heleen's girls never earn out of their contracts. She makes sure they don't. She—" Inej had broken off then, and Nina had sensed the vibrant anger coursing through her. "Kaz convinced Per Haskell to pay off my indenture. I would have died at the Menagerie."

"You may still die in the Dregs."

Inej's dark eyes had glinted. "I may. But I'll die on my feet with a knife in my hand."

The next morning, Inej had helped Nina sneak out of the Emerald Palace. They'd met with Kaz Brekker, and despite his cold ways and those strange leather gloves, she'd agreed to join the Dregs and work out of the White Rose. Less than two days later, a girl died at the Sweet Shop, strangled in her bed by a customer dressed as Mister Crimson who was never found.

Nina had trusted Inej, and she hadn't been sorry for it, though right now she just felt furious with everyone. She watched a group of Dime Lions prod the desert lizard with long spears. Apparently, the monster was sated after its meal; it allowed itself to be herded back to the tunnel, its thick body moving side to side in a lazy, sinuous roll.

The crowd continued to boo as guards entered the arena to remove the prisoner's remains, tendrils of smoke still curling from his ruined flesh.

"Why are they complaining?" Nina asked angrily. "Isn't this what they came here for?"

"They wanted a fight," said Kaz. "They were expecting him to last longer."

"This is disgusting."

Kaz shrugged. "Only disgusting thing about it is that I didn't think of it first."

"These men aren't slaves, Kaz. They're prisoners."

"They're murderers and rapists."

"And thieves and con artists. *Your* people."

"Nina, sweet, they aren't forced to fight. They line up for the chance. They earn better food, private cells, liquor, *jurda*, conjugals with girls from West Stave."

Muzzen cracked his knuckles. "Sounds better than we got it at the Slat."

Nina looked at the people screaming and shouting, the barkers walking the aisles taking bets. The prisoners of Hellgate might line up to fight, but Pekka Rollins made the real money.

"Helvar doesn't . . . Helvar doesn't fight in the arena, does he?"

"We aren't here for the ambience," Kaz said.

Beyond slappable. "Are you aware that I could waggle my fingers and make you wet your trousers?"

"Easy, Heartrender. I like these trousers. And if you start messing with my vital organs, Matthias Helvar will never see sunshine again."

Nina blew out a breath and settled for glowering at no one.

"Nina—" Inej murmured.

"Don't you start on me."

"It will all work out. Let Kaz do what he does best."

"He's horrible."

"But effective. Being angry at Kaz for being ruthless is like being angry at a stove for being hot. You know what he is."

Nina crossed her arms. "I'm mad at you, too."

"Me? Why?"

"I don't know yet. I just am."

Inej gave Nina's hand a brief squeeze, and after a moment, Nina squeezed back. She sat through the next fight in a daze, and the next. She told herself she was ready for this – to see him again, to see him here in this brutal place. After all, she was a Grisha and a soldier of the Second Army. She'd seen worse.

But when Matthias emerged from the mouth of the cave below, she knew she'd been wrong. Nina recognised him instantly. Every night of the past year, she had fallen asleep thinking of Matthias' face. There was no mistaking the gilded brows, the sharp cut of his cheekbones. But Kaz hadn't lied: Matthias was much changed. The boy who looked back at the crowd with fury in his eyes was a stranger.

Nina remembered the first time she'd seen Matthias in a moonlit Kaelish wood. His beauty had seemed unfair to her. In another life, she might have believed he was coming to rescue her, a shining saviour with golden hair and eyes the pale blue of northern glaciers. But she'd known the truth of him by the language he spoke, and by the disgust on his face every time his eyes lighted on her. Matthias Helvar was a *drüskelle*, one of the Fjerdan witchhunters tasked with hunting down Grisha to face trial and execution, though to her he'd always resembled a warrior Saint, illuminated in gold.

Now he looked like what he truly was: a killer. His bare torso seemed hewn from steel, and though she knew it wasn't possible, he seemed bigger, as if the very structure of his body had changed. His skin had been gilded honey; now it was fish-belly white beneath the grime. And his hair – he'd had such beautiful hair, thick and golden, worn long in the way of Fjerdan soldiers. Now, like the other prisoners, his head had been shaved, probably to prevent lice. Whichever guard had done it had made a mess of the job. Even from this distance, she could see the cuts and nicks on his scalp, and little strips of blond stubble in the places the razor had missed. And yet, he was beautiful still.

He glared at the crowd and gave the wheel a hard spin that nearly knocked it off its base.

Tick tick tick tick. Snakes. Tiger. Bear. Boar. The wheel ticked merrily along, then slowed and finally stopped.

"No," Nina said when she saw where the needle was pointing.

"It could be worse," said Muzzen. "Could have landed on the desert lizard again."

She grabbed Kaz's arm through his cloak and felt his muscles tense. "You have to stop this."

"Let go of me, Nina." His gravel-rough voice was low, but she sensed real menace in it.

She dropped her hand, "Please, you don't understand. He—"

"If he survives, I'll take Matthias Helvar out of this place tonight, but this part is up to him."

Nina gave a frustrated shake of her head. "You don't get it."

The guard unbolted Matthias' shackles, and as soon as the chains dropped into the sand, he leaped onto the ladder with the announcer to be lifted to safety. The crowd screamed and stamped. But Matthias stood silent, unmoving, even when the gate opened, even when the wolves charged out of the tunnel – three of them snarling and snapping, tumbling over one another to get to him.

At the last second, Matthias dropped into a crouch, knocking the first wolf into the dirt, then rolling right to pick up the bloodied knife the previous combatant had left in the sand. He sprang to his feet, blade held out before him, but Nina could sense his reluctance. His head was cocked to one side, and the look in his blue eyes was pleading, as if he was trying to engage the two wolves circling him in some silent negotiation. Whatever the plea might have been, it went unheard. The wolf on the right lunged. Matthias crouched low and spun, lodging his knife in the wolf's belly. It gave a miserable yelp, and Matthias seemed to shudder at the sound. It cost him precious seconds. The third wolf was on him, knocking him to the sand. Its teeth sank into his shoulder. He rolled, taking the wolf with him. The wolf's jaws snapped, and Matthias caught them. He wrenched them apart, the muscles of his arms flexing, his face grim. Nina squeezed her eyes shut. There was a sickening *crack*. The crowd roared.

Matthias kneeled over the wolf. Its jaw was broken, and it lay on the ground twitching in pain. He reached for a rock and slammed it hard into the poor animal's skull. It went still and Matthias' shoulders slumped. The people howled, stomping their feet. Only Nina knew what this was costing him, that he'd been a *drüskelle*. Wolves were sacred to his kind, bred for battle like their enormous horses. They were friends and companions, fighting side by side with their *drüskelle* masters.

The first wolf had recovered and was circling. *Move, Matthias*, she thought desperately. He got to his feet, but his movements were slow, weary. His heart wasn't in this fight. His opponents were grey wolves, rangy and wild, but cousins to the white wolves of the Fjerdan north. Matthias had no knife, only the bloody rock in his hand, and the remaining wolf prowled the arena between him and the pile of weapons. The wolf lowered its head and bared its teeth.

Matthias dove left. The wolf lunged, sinking its teeth into his side. He grunted, and hit the ground hard. For a moment, Nina thought he might simply give in and let the wolf take his life. Then he reached out, hand scrabbling through the sand, searching for something. His fingers closed over the shackles that had bound his wrists.

He seized them, looped the chain across the wolf's throat, and pulled, the veins in his neck cording from the strain. His bloody face was pressed against the wolf's ruff, his eyes tightly shut, his lips moving. What was he saying? A *drüskelle* prayer? A farewell?

The wolf's hind legs scrabbled at the sand. Its eyes rolled, frightened whites showing bright against its matted fur. A high whine rose from its chest. And then it was over. The creature's body stilled. Both fighters lay unmoving in the sand. Matthias kept his eyes closed, his face still buried in the creature's fur.

The crowd thundered its approval. The ladder was lowered, and the announcer sprang down, hauling Matthias to his feet and grabbing his wrist to raise his hand in victory. The announcer gave him a little nudge, and Matthias lifted his head. Nina caught her breath.

Tears streaked the dirt on Matthias' face. The rage was gone, and it was like some flame had gone out with it. His north sea eyes were colder than she'd ever seen them, empty of feeling, stripped of anything human at all. This was what Hellgate had done to him. And it was her fault.

The guards took hold of Matthias again, pulling the shackles from the wolf's throat and clapping them back on his wrists. As he was led away, the crowd chanted its disapproval, clamouring "More! More!"

"Where are they taking him?" Nina asked, voice trembling.

"To a cell to sleep off the fight," Kaz said.

"Who will see to his injuries?"

"They have mediks. We'll wait to make sure he's alone."

I could heal him, she thought. But a darker voice rose in her, rich with mocking. *Not even you can be that foolish, Nina. No Healer can cure that boy. You made sure of it.*

She thought she would leap from her skin as the minutes burned away. The others watched the next fight – Muzzen avidly, flexing his fingers and speculating on the outcome, Inej silent and still as a statue, Kaz inscrutable as always, scheming away behind that hideous mask. Nina slowed her own breathing, forced her pulse lower, trying to calm herself, but she could do nothing to mute the riot in her head.

Finally, Kaz gave her a nudge. "Ready, Nina? The guard first."

She cast a glance at the prison guard standing by the archway.

"How down?" It was a Barrel turn of phrase. *How badly do you want him hurt?*

"Shut eye." *Knock him out, but don't actually hurt him.*

They followed Kaz to the arch through which they'd entered. The rest of the crowd took little notice, eyes focused on the fighting below.

"Need your escort?" the guard asked as they approached.

"I had a question," said Kaz. Beneath her cape, Nina lifted her hands, sensing the flow of blood in the guard's veins, the tissue of his lungs. "About your mother and whether the rumours are true."

Nina felt the guard's pulse leap and sighed. "Never can make it easy, can you, Kaz?"

The guard stepped forward, lifting his gun. "What did you say? I—" His eyelids drooped. "You don't—" Nina dropped his pulse, and he toppled forward.

Muzzen grabbed him before he could fall as Inej swept

him into the cloak Kaz had been wearing just moments before. Nina was only mildly surprised to see that Kaz was wearing a prison guard's uniform beneath it.

"Couldn't you have just asked him the time or something?" Nina said. "And where did you get that uniform?"

Inej slid the Madman's mask down over the guard's face, and Muzzen threw his arm around him, holding him up as if the guard had been drinking too much. They deposited him on one of the benches pressed against the back wall.

Kaz tugged on the sleeves of his uniform. "Nina, people love to give up authority to men in nice clothes. I have uniforms for the *stadwatch*, the harbour police, and the livery of every merch mansion on the Geldstraat. Let's go."

They slipped down the passageway.

Instead of turning back the way they'd come, they moved counter-clockwise around the old tower, the wall of the arena vibrating with voices and stomping feet to their left. The guards posted at each archway paid them little more than a glance, though a few nodded at Kaz, who kept a brisk pace, his face buried in his collar.

Nina was so deep in thought that she nearly missed it when Kaz held up a hand for them to slow. They'd rounded a bend between two archways and were in the cover of deep shadow. Ahead of them, a medik was emerging from a cell accompanied by guards, one carrying a lantern. "He'll sleep through the night," the medik said. "Make sure he drinks something in the morning and check his pupils. I had to give him a powerful sleeping draft."

As the men moved off in the opposite direction, Kaz gestured his group forward. The door in the rock was solid iron, broken only by a narrow slot through which to pass the prisoner's meals. Kaz bent to the lock.

Nina eyed the crude iron door. "This place is barbaric."

"Most of the better fighters sleep in the old tower," Kaz replied. "Keeps them away from the rest of the population."

Nina glanced left and right to where bright light spilled from the arena entryways. There were guards standing in those doorways, distracted maybe, but all one needed to do was turn his head. If they were caught here, would the guards bother giving them over to the *stadwatch* for trial or would they simply force them into the ring to be eaten by a tiger? *Maybe something less dignified*, she thought bleakly. *A swarm of angry voles.*

It took Kaz a few quick heartbeats to pick the lock. The door creaked open and they slipped inside.

The cell was pitch-black. A brief moment passed, and the cold green glow of a bonelight flickered to life beside her. Inej held the little glass sphere aloft. The substance inside was made from the dried and crushed bodies of luminous deep-sea fishes. They were common among crooks in the Barrel who didn't want to get caught in a dark alley, but couldn't be bothered to lug around lanterns.

At least it's clean, Nina thought, as her eyes adjusted to the gloom. *Barren and icy cold, but not filthy.* She saw a pallet of horse blankets and two buckets placed against the wall, one with a bloody cloth peeking over the rim.

This was what the men of Hellgate competed for: a private cell, a blanket, clean water, a bucket for waste.

Matthias slept with his back to the wall. Even in the dim illumination of the bonelight, she could see his face was starting to swell. Some kind of ointment had been smeared over his wounds – calendula. She recognised the smell.

Nina moved towards him, but Kaz stopped her with a hand on her arm. "Let Inej assess the damage."

"I can—" Nina began.

"I need you to work on Muzzen."

Inej tossed Kaz the crow-headed cane she must have been hiding beneath her Grey Imp costume, and kneeled over Matthias' body with the bonelight. Muzzen stepped forward. He removed his cloak and shirt and the Madman's mask. His head was shaved, and he wore prison-issue trousers.

Nina looked at Matthias then back to Muzzen, grasping what Kaz had in mind. The two boys were about the same height and the same build, but that was where the similarities ended.

"You can't possibly mean for Muzzen to take Matthias' place."

"He isn't here for his sparkling conversation," Kaz replied. "You'll need to reproduce Helvar's injuries. Inej, what's the inventory?"

"Bruised knuckles, chipped tooth, two broken ribs," Inej said. "Third and fourth on the left."

"His left or your left?" Kaz asked.

"His left."

"This isn't going to work," Nina said in frustration. "I can match the damage to Helvar's body, but I'm not a good enough Tailor to make Muzzen look like him."

"Just trust me, Nina."

"I wouldn't trust you to tie my shoes without stealing the laces, Kaz." She peered at Muzzen's face. "Even if I swell him up, he'll never pass."

"Tonight, Matthias Helvar – or rather, our dear Muzzen – is going to appear to contract firepox, the lupine strain, carried by wolves and dogs alike. Tomorrow morning, when his guards discover him so covered in pustules that he is *unrecognisable*, he will be quarantined for a month to see if he survives the fever and to outwait the contagion. Meanwhile Matthias will be with us. Get it?"

"You want me to make Muzzen look like he has firepox?"

"Yes, and do it quickly, Nina, because in about ten minutes, things are going to get very hectic around here."

Nina stared at him. What was Kaz planning? "No matter what I do to him, it won't last a month. I can't give him a permanent fever."

"My contact in the infirmary will make sure he stays sick enough. We just need to get him through diagnosis. Now get to work."

Nina looked Muzzen up and down. "This is going to hurt just as much as if you'd been in the fight yourself," she warned.

He scrunched up his face, bracing for the pain. "I can take it."

She rolled her eyes, then lifted her hands, concentrating. With a sharp slice of her right hand over her left, she snapped Muzzen's ribs.

He let out a grunt and doubled over.

"That's a good boy," said Kaz. "Taking it like a champion. Knuckles next, then face."

Nina spread bruises and cuts over Muzzen's knuckles and arms, matching the wounds to Inej's descriptions.

"I've never seen firepox up close," Nina said. She was only familiar with illustrations from books they'd used in their anatomy training at the Little Palace.

"Count yourself lucky," Kaz said grimly. "Hurry it up."

She worked from memory, swelling and cracking the skin on Muzzen's face and chest, raising blisters until the swelling and pustules were so bad that he was truly unrecognisable. The big man moaned.

"Why would you agree to do this?" Nina murmured.

The swollen flesh of Muzzen's face quivered, and Nina thought he might be trying to smile. "Money was good," he said thickly.

She sighed. Why else did anyone do anything in the Barrel? "Good enough to get locked up in Hellgate?"

Kaz tapped his cane on the cell floor. "Stop making trouble, Nina. If Helvar cooperates, he and Muzzen will both have their freedom just as soon as the job is done."

"And if he doesn't?"

"Then Helvar gets locked back in his cell, and Muzzen

still gets paid. And I'll take him to breakfast at the Kooperom."

"Can I have waffles?" Muzzen mumbled.

"We'll all have waffles. And whisky. If this job doesn't come off, no one's going to want to be around me sober. Finished, Nina?"

Nina nodded, and Inej took her place to bandage Muzzen to look like Matthias.

"All right," said Kaz. "Get Helvar on his feet."

Nina crouched beside Matthias as Kaz stood over her with the bonelight. Even in sleep, Matthias' features were troubled, his pale brows furrowed. She let her hands travel over the bruised line of his jaw, resisting the urge to linger there.

"Not the face, Nina. I need him mobile, not pretty. Heal him fast and only enough to get him walking for now. I don't want him spry enough to vex us."

Nina lowered the blanket and went to work. *Just another body*, she told herself. She was always getting late-night calls from Kaz to heal wounded members of the Dregs who he didn't want to bring around to any legitimate medik – girls with stabbing punctures, boys with broken legs or bullets lodged inside them, victims of a scuffle with the *stadwatch* or another gang. *Pretend it's Muzzen*, she told herself. *Or Big Bolliger or some other fool. You don't know this boy.* And it was true. The boy she knew might have been the scaffold, but something new had been built upon it.

She touched his shoulder gently. "Helvar," she said. He didn't stir. "Matthias."

A lump rose in her throat, and she felt the ache of tears threatening. She pressed a kiss to his temple. She knew that Kaz and the others were watching and that she was making an idiot of herself, but after so long he was finally here, in front of her, and so very broken. "Matthias," she repeated.

"Nina?" His voice was raw but as lovely as she remembered.

"Oh, Saints, Matthias," she whispered. "Please wake up."

His eyes opened, groggily, palest blue. "Nina," he said softly. His knuckles brushed her cheek; his rough hand cupped her face tentatively, disbelievingly. "Nina?"

Her eyes filled with tears. "Shhhh, Matthias. We're here to get you out."

Before she could blink he had hold of her shoulders and had pinned her to the ground.

"Nina," he growled.

Then his hands closed over her throat.

PART 2

SERVANT AND LEVER

7
MATTHIAS

Matthias was dreaming again. Dreaming of her.

In all his dreams he hunted her, sometimes through the new green meadows of spring, but usually through the ice fields, dodging boulders and crevasses with unerring steps. Always he chased, and always he caught her. In the good dreams, he slammed her to the ground and throttled her, watching the life drain from her eyes, heart full of vengeance – *finally, finally*. In the bad dreams, he kissed her.

In these dreams, she didn't fight him. She laughed as if the chase was nothing but a game, as if she'd known he would catch her, as if she'd wanted him to and there was no place she'd rather be than beneath him. She was welcoming and perfect in his arms. He kissed her, buried his face in the sweet hollow of her neck. Her curls brushed his cheeks, and he felt that if he could just hold her a little longer, every wound, every hurt, every bad thing would melt away.

"Matthias," she would whisper, his name so soft on her lips. These were the worst dreams, and when he woke, he hated himself almost as much as he hated her. To know that he could betray himself, betray his country again even in sleep, to know that – after everything she'd done – some sick part of him still hungered after her . . . it was too much.

Tonight was a bad dream, very bad. She was wearing blue silk, clothes far more luxurious than anything he'd ever seen her in; some kind of gauzy veil was caught up in her hair, the lamplight glinting off of it like caught rain. *Djel*, she smelled good. The mossy damp was still there, but perfume, too. Nina loved luxury and this was expensive – roses and something else, something his pauper's nose didn't recognise. She pressed her soft lips to his temple, and he could swear she was crying.

"Matthias."

"Nina," he managed.

"Oh, Saints, Matthias," she whispered. "Please wake up."

And then he was awake, and he knew he'd gone mad because she was here, in his cell, kneeling beside him, her hand resting gently on his chest. "Matthias, please."

The sound of her voice, pleading with him. He'd dreamed of this. Sometimes she pleaded for mercy. Sometimes there were other things she begged for.

He reached up and touched her face. She had the softest skin. He'd laughed at her for it once. No real soldier had skin like that, he'd told her – pampered, coddled. He'd mocked the lushness of her body, ashamed of his own response to her. He cupped the warm curve of her cheek, felt the soft brush of her hair. So lovely. So real. It wasn't fair.

Then he registered the bloody wrappings on his hands. Pain rushed at him as he came fully awake – cracked ribs, aching knuckles. He'd chipped a tooth. He wasn't sure when, but he'd cut his tongue against it at some point. His mouth still held the coppery taste of blood. *The wolves.* They'd made him murder wolves.

He was awake.

"Nina?"

There were tears in her beautiful green eyes. Rage

coursed through him. She had no right to tears, no right to pity.

"Shhhh, Matthias. We're here to get you out."

What game was this? What new cruelty? He'd just learned to survive in this monstrous place, and now she'd come to heap some fresh torture on him.

He launched himself forward, flipping her to the ground, hands fastened tight around her throat, straddling her so that his knees pinned her arms to the ground. He knew damn well that Nina with her hands free was a deadly thing.

"Nina," he gritted out. She clawed at his hands. "Witch," he hissed, leaning over her. He saw her eyes widen, her face getting redder. "Beg me," he said. "Beg me for your life."

He heard a click, and a gravelly voice said, "Hands off her, Helvar."

Someone behind him had pressed a gun to his neck. Matthias didn't spare him a glance. "Go ahead and shoot me," he said. He dug his fingertips deeper into Nina's neck – nothing would deprive him of this. Nothing.

Traitor, witch, abomination. All those words came to him, but others crowded in, too: *beautiful, charmed one. Röed fetla,* he'd called her, little red bird, for the colour of her Grisha Order. The colour she loved. He squeezed harder, silencing that weak-willed strain inside him.

"If you've actually lost your mind, this is going to be a lot tougher than I thought," said that raspy voice.

He heard a whoosh like something moving through the air, then a wrenching pain shot through his left shoulder. It felt like he'd been punched by a tiny fist, but his entire arm went numb. He grunted as he fell forward, one hand still clamped around Nina's throat. He would have fallen directly onto her, but he was yanked backwards by the collar of his shirt.

A boy wearing a guard's uniform stood before him, dark eyes glittering, a pistol in one hand, a walking stick in the other. Its handle was carved to look like a crow's head, with a cruelly pointed beak.

"Get hold of yourself, Helvar. We're here to break you out. I can do to your leg what I did to your arm, and we can drag you out of here, or you can leave like a man, on two feet."

"No one gets out of Hellgate," Matthias said.

"Tonight they do."

Matthias sat forward, trying to get his bearings, clutching his dead arm. "You can't just walk me out of here. The guards will recognise me," he snarled. "I'm not losing fighting privileges to be carted off Djel knows where with you."

"You'll be masked."

"If the guards check—"

"They're going to be too busy to check," said the strange, pale boy. And then the screaming started.

Matthias' head jerked up. He heard the thunder of footsteps from the arena, cresting like a wave as people burst into the passageway outside his cell. He heard the shouts of guards, and then the roaring of a great cat, the trumpet of an elephant.

"You opened the cages." Nina's voice was shaky with disbelief, though who knew what might be real or performance with her. He refused to look in her direction. If he did, he'd lose all sense of reality. He was barely hanging on as it was.

"Jesper was supposed to wait until three bells," said the pale boy.

"It is three bells, Kaz," replied a small girl in the corner with dark hair and deep bronze Suli skin. A figure covered in welts and bandages was leaning against her.

"Since when is Jesper punctual?" the boy complained with a glance at his watch. "On your feet, Helvar."

He offered him a gloved hand. Matthias stared at it. *This is a dream. The strangest dream I've ever had, but definitely a dream.* Or maybe killing the wolves had finally driven him truly mad. He'd murdered family tonight. No whispered prayers for their wild souls would make it right.

He looked up at the pale demon with his black-gloved hands. Kaz, she'd called him. Would he lead Matthias out of this nightmare or just drag him into another kind of hell? *Choose, Helvar.*

Matthias clasped the boy's hand. If this was real and not illusion, he'd escape whatever trap these creatures had set for him. He heard Nina release a long breath – was she relieved? Exasperated? He shook his head. He would deal with her later. The little bronze girl swept a cloak around Matthias' shoulders and propped an ugly, beak-nosed mask on his head.

The passageway outside the cell was chaos. Costumed men and women surged past, screaming and pushing each other, trying to get away from the arena. Guards had their guns out, and he could hear shots being fired. He felt dizzy, and his side ached badly. His left arm was still useless.

Kaz signalled towards the far right archway, indicating that they should move against the flow of the crowd and into the arena. Matthias didn't care. He could plunge through the mob instead, force his way up that staircase and onto a boat. *And then what?* It didn't matter. There was no time for planning.

He stepped into the throng and was instantly hauled back.

"Boys like you weren't meant to get ideas, Helvar," said Kaz. "That staircase leads to a bottleneck. You think the guards won't check under that mask before they let you through?"

Matthias scowled and followed the others through the crowd, Kaz's hand at his back.

If the passage had been chaos, then the arena was a special kind of madness. Matthias glimpsed hyenas leaping and bounding over the ledges. One was feeding over a body in a crimson cape. An elephant charged the wall of the stadium, sending up a cloud of dust and bellowing its frustration. He saw a white bear and one of the great jungle cats from the Southern Colonies crouching in the eaves, its teeth bared. He knew there were snakes in the cages as well. He could only hope that this Jesper character hadn't been foolish enough to set them free, too.

They plunged across the sands where Matthias had fought for privileges for the last six months, but as they headed towards the tunnel, the desert lizard came pounding towards them, its mouth dripping foaming white poison, its fat tail lashing the ground. Before Matthias could think to move, the bronze girl had vaulted over its back and dispatched the creature with two bright daggers wedged beneath the armour of its scales. The lizard groaned and collapsed on its side. Matthias felt a pang of sadness. It was a grotesque creature, and he'd never seen a fighter survive its attack, but it was also a living thing. *You've never seen a fighter survive until now*, he corrected himself. *The bronze girl's daggers merit watching.*

He'd assumed they'd cross the arena and head back up into the stands to avoid the crowds clogging the passageway, possibly just storm the stairs and hope to make it through the guards who must be waiting at the top. Instead, Kaz led them down the tunnel past the cages. The cages were old cells that had been turned over to whatever beasts the masters of the Hellshow had got their hands on that week – old circus animals, even diseased livestock in a pinch, creatures culled from forest and countryside. As they raced past the open doors, he glimpsed a pair of yellow eyes glaring at him from the shadows, and then he was moving on. He cursed his deadened arm and lack of weapon. He was virtually defenceless. *Where is this Kaz leading us?* They wended past a wild boar feeding on a guard and a spotted cat that hissed and spit at them but did not draw near.

And then, through the musk of animals and the stink of their waste, he smelled the clean tang of salt water. He heard the rush of waves. He slipped and discovered the stones beneath his feet were damp. He was deeper in the tunnel than he'd ever been permitted to go. It must lead to the sea. Whatever Nina and her people intended, they really were taking him out of the bowels of Hellgate.

In the green light from the orbs carried by Kaz and the bronze girl, he spotted a tiny boat moored up ahead. It looked like a guard was seated in it, but he raised a hand and waved them forward.

"You were early, Jesper," Kaz said as he nudged Matthias towards the boat.

"I was on time."

"For you, that's early. Next time you plan to impress me give me some warning."

"The animals are out, and I found you a boat. This is when a thank you would be in order."

"Thank you, Jesper," said Nina.

"You're very welcome, gorgeous. See, Kaz? That's how the civilised folk do."

Matthias was only half listening. The fingers of his left hand had started to tingle as sensation returned. He couldn't fight all of them, not in this state and not when they were armed. But Kaz and the boy in the boat, Jesper, looked to be the only ones with guns. *Unhook the rope, disable Jesper.* He'd have a gun and possession of the boat. *And Nina can stop your heart before you've taken hold of the oars*, he reminded himself. *So shoot her first. Put a bullet in her heart. Stay long enough to watch her fall and then be done with this place.* He could do it. He knew he could. All he needed was a distraction.

The bronze girl was standing just to his right. She barely reached his shoulder. Even injured, he could knock her into the water without losing his footing or doing her any real harm.

Drop the girl. Free the boat. Disable the shooter. Kill Nina. Kill Nina. Kill Nina. He took a deep breath and threw his weight at the bronze girl.

She stepped aside as if she'd known he was coming, languidly hooking her heel behind his ankle.

Matthias let out a loud grunt as he landed hard on the stones.

"Matthias—" Nina said, stepping forward. He scrambled backwards, nearly landing himself in the water. If she laid hands on him again, he'd lose his mind. Nina halted, the hurt on her face unmistakable. She had no right.

"Clumsy, this one," the bronze girl said impassively.

"Put him under, Nina," commanded Kaz.

"Don't," Matthias protested, panic surging through him.

"You're dumb enough to capsize the boat."

"Stay away from me, witch," Matthias growled at Nina.

Nina gave him a tight nod. "With pleasure."

She lifted her hands, and Matthias felt his eyelids grow heavy as she dragged him into unconsciousness. "Kill you," he mumbled.

"Sleep well." Her voice was a wolf, dogging his steps. It chased him into the dark.

In a windowless room draped in black and crimson, Matthias listened silently to the strange words coming out of the pale, freakish boy's mouth. Matthias knew monsters, and one glance at Kaz Brekker had told him this was a creature who had spent too long in the dark – he'd brought something back with him when he'd crawled into the light. Matthias could sense it around him. He knew others laughed at Fjerdan superstition, but he trusted his gut. Or he had, until Nina. That had been one of the worst effects of her betrayal, the way he'd been forced to second-guess himself.

That doubt had almost been his undoing at Hellgate, where instinct was everything.

He'd heard Brekker's name in prison, and the words associated with him – criminal prodigy, ruthless, amoral. They called him Dirtyhands because there was no sin he would not commit for the right price. And now this demon was talking about breaking into the Ice Court, about getting Matthias to commit treason. *Again*, Matthias corrected himself. *I'd be committing treason again.*

He kept his eyes on Brekker. He was keenly aware of Nina watching him from the other side of the room. He could still smell her rose perfume in his nose and even in his mouth; the sharp flower scent rested against his tongue, as if he were tasting her.

Matthias had woken bound and tied to a chair in what looked like some kind of gambling parlour. Nina must have brought him out of the stupor she'd placed him in. She was there, along with the bronze girl. Jesper, the long-limbed boy from the boat, sat in a corner with his bony knees drawn up, and a boy with ruddy gold curls doodled aimlessly on a scrap of paper atop a round table made for playing cards, occasionally gnawing on his thumb. The table was covered with a crimson cloth flocked with a repeating pattern of crows and a wheel similar to the one used in the Hellshow arena but with different markings had been propped against a black lacquered wall. Matthias had the feeling that someone – probably Nina – had tended to more of his injuries while he was unconscious. The thought made him sick. Better clean pain than Grisha corruption.

Then Brekker had started talking – about a drug called *jurda parem*, about an impossibly high reward, and about the absurd idea of attempting a raid on the Ice Court. Matthias wasn't sure what might be fact or fiction, but it hardly mattered. When Brekker finally finished, Matthias simply said, "No."

"Believe me when I say this, Helvar: I know getting knocked out and waking up in strange surroundings isn't the friendliest way to start a partnership, but you didn't give us many options, so try to open your mind to the possibilities."

"You could have come to me on your knees, and my answer would be the same."

"You do understand I can have you back at Hellgate in a matter of hours? Once poor Muzzen is in the infirmary, the switch will be easy."

"Do it. I can't wait to tell the warden your ridiculous plans."

"What makes you think you'll be going back with a tongue?"

"Kaz—" Nina protested.

"Do what you want," Matthias said. He wouldn't betray his country again.

"I told you," said Nina.

"Don't pretend to know me, witch," he snarled, his eyes trained on Brekker. He wouldn't look at her. He refused to.

Jesper unfolded himself from the corner. Now that they were out of the Hellgate gloom, Matthias could see he had deep brown Zemeni skin and incongruous grey eyes. He was built like a stork. "Without him, there's no job," said Jesper. "We can't break into the Ice Court blind."

Matthias wanted to laugh. "You can't break into the Ice Court at all." The Ice Court wasn't an ordinary building. It was a compound, Fjerda's ancient stronghold, home to an unbroken succession of kings and queens, repository of their greatest treasures and most sacred religious relics. It was impenetrable.

"Come now, Helvar," said the demon. "Surely there's something you want. The cause is righteous enough for a zealot like you. Fjerda may think they've caught a dragon by the tail, but they won't be able to hold on. Once Bo Yul-Bayur replicates his process, *jurda parem* will enter the market, and it's only a matter of time before others learn to manufacture it, too."

"It will never happen. Yul-Bayur will stand trial, and if he is found guilty he will be put to death."

"Guilty of what?" Nina asked softly.

"Crimes against the people."

"*Which* people?"

He could hear the barely leashed anger in her voice. "Natural people," Matthias replied. "People who live in harmony with the laws of this world instead of twisting them for their own gain."

Nina made a kind of exasperated snorting sound. The others just looked amused, smirking at the poor, backward Fjerdan. Brum had warned Matthias that the world was full of liars, pleasure seekers, faithless heathens. And there seemed to be a concentration of them in this room.

"You're being shortsighted about this, Helvar," said Brekker. "Another team could get to Yul-Bayur first. The Shu. Maybe the Ravkans. All with their own agendas. Border disputes and old rivalries don't matter to the Kerch. All the Merchant Council cares about is trade, and they want to make sure *jurda parem* remains a rumour and nothing more."

"So leading criminals into the heart of Fjerda to steal a valued prisoner is a patriotic act?" Matthias said scornfully.

"I don't suppose the promise of four million *kruge* will sway you either."

Matthias spat. "You can keep your money. Choke on it." Then a thought came to him – vile, barbaric, but the one thing that might allow him to return to Hellgate with peace in his heart even if he didn't have a tongue in his head. He tilted back as far as his bonds would permit and focused all his attention on Brekker. "I'll make a deal with you."

"I'm listening."

"I won't go with you, but I'll give you a plan for the

layout of the Court. That should at least get you past the first checkpoint."

"And what will this valuable information cost me?"

"I don't want your money. I'll give you the plans for nothing." It shamed Matthias to say the words, but he spoke them anyway. "If you let me kill Nina Zenik."

The little bronze girl made a sound of disgust, her contempt for him clear, and the boy at the table stopped doodling, his mouth falling open. Kaz, however, didn't seem surprised. If anything, he looked pleased. Matthias had the uncomfortable sense that the demon had known exactly how this would play out.

"I can give you something better," said Kaz.

What could be better than revenge? "There's nothing else I want."

"I can make you a *drüskelle* again."

"Are you a magician, then? A *wej* sprite who grants wishes? I'm superstitious, not stupid."

"You can be both, you know, but that's hardly the point." Kaz slipped a hand into his dark coat. "Here," he said, and gave a piece of paper to the bronze girl. Another demon. This one walked with soft feet like she'd drifted in from the next world and no one had the good sense to send her back. She brought the paper up to his face for him to read. The document was written in Kerch and Fjerdan. He couldn't read Kerch – he'd only picked up the language in prison – but the Fjerdan was clear enough, and as his eyes moved over the page, Matthias' heart started to pound.

In light of new evidence, Matthias Benedik Helvar is granted full and immediate pardon for all charges of slave trafficking. He is released on this day,_____, with the apologies of the court, and will be provided transport to his homeland or a destination of his choosing with all possible haste and the sincere apologies of this court and the Kerch government.

"What new evidence?"

Kaz leaned back in his chair. "It seems Nina Zenik has recanted her statements. She will face charges of perjury."

Now he did look at her; he couldn't stop it. He'd left bruises on her graceful throat. He told himself to be glad of it.

"Perjury? How long will you serve for that, Zenik?"

"Two months," she said quietly.

"Two months?" Now he did laugh, long and hard. His body twitched with it, as if it were poison constricting his muscles.

The others watched him with some concern.

"Just how crazy is he?" asked Jesper, fingers drumming on the pearl handles of his revolvers.

Brekker shrugged. "He's not what I'd call reliable, but he's all we've got."

Two months. Probably in some cosy prison where she'd charm every guard into bringing her fresh bread and fluffing her pillows. Or maybe she'd just talk them into letting her pay a fine that her rich Grisha keepers back in Ravka could cover for her.

"She can't be trusted, you know," he said to Brekker. "Whatever secrets you hope to gain from Bo Yul-Bayur, she'll turn them over to Ravka."

"Let me worry about that, Helvar. You do your part, and the secrets of Yul-Bayur and *jurda parem* will be in the hands of the people best equipped to make sure they stay rumours."

Two months. Nina would serve her time and return to Ravka four million *kruge* richer, never giving him another thought. But if this pardon was real, then he could go home, too.

Home. He'd imagined breaking out of Hellgate plenty of times, but he'd never really put his mind to the idea of escape. What life was there for him on the outside, with the charge of slaver hanging around his neck? He could never return to Fjerda. Even if he could have borne the disgrace, he'd have lived each day as a fugitive from the Kerch government, a marked man. He knew he could eke out a life for himself in Novyi Zem, but what would have been the point?

This was something different. If the demon Brekker spoke the truth, Matthias would get to go home. The longing for it twisted in his chest – to hear his language spoken, to see his friends again, taste *semla* filled with sweet almond paste, feel the bite of the northern wind as it came roaring over the ice. To return home and be welcomed there without the burden of dishonour. With his name cleared, he could return to his life as a *drüskelle*. And the price would be treason.

"What if Bo Yul-Bayur is dead?" he asked Brekker.

"Van Eck insists he isn't."

But how could the merchant Kaz spoke of truly understand Fjerdan ways? If there hadn't been a trial yet, there would be, and Matthias could easily predict the outcome. His people would never free a man with such terrible knowledge.

"But what if he is, Brekker?"

"You still get your pardon."

Even if their quarry was already ashes on the pyre, Matthias would have his freedom. At what cost, though? He'd made mistakes before. He'd been foolish enough to trust Nina. He'd been weak, and he would carry that shame for the rest of his life. But he'd paid for his stupidity in blood and misery and the stink of Hellgate. And his crimes had been meagre things, the actions of a naive boy. This was so much worse. To reveal the secrets of the Ice Court, to see his homeland once more only to know that every step he took there was an act of treason – could he do such a thing?

Brum would have laughed in their faces, torn that pardon to pieces. But Kaz Brekker was smart. He clearly had resources. What if Matthias said no and against all odds Brekker and his crew still found their way into the Ice Court and stole the Shu scientist? Or what if Brekker was right and another country got there first? It sounded like *parem* was too addictive to be useful to Grisha, but what if the formula fell into Ravkan hands, and they somehow managed to adapt it? To make Ravka's Grisha, its Second Army, even stronger? If he was part of this mission, Matthias could make sure Bo Yul-Bayur never took another breath outside the Ice Court's walls, or he could arrange for some kind of accident on the trip back to Kerch.

Before Nina, before Hellgate, he never would have considered it. Now he found he could make this bargain with himself. He would join the demon's crew, earn his pardon, and when he was a *drüskelle* once more, Nina Zenik would be his first target. He'd hunt her in Kerch, in Ravka, whatever hole or corner of the world she thought would keep her safe. He would run Nina Zenik to ground and make her pay in every way imaginable. Death would be too good. He'd have her thrown into the most miserable cell in the Ice Court, where she'd never be warm again. He'd toy with her as she'd toyed with him. He'd offer her salvation and then deny it. He'd gift her with affection and small kindnesses then snatch them away. He would savour every tear she shed and replace that sweet green flower scent with the salt of her sorrow on his tongue.

Even so, the words were bitter in Matthias' mouth when he said, "I'll do it."

Brekker winked at Nina, and Matthias wanted to knock his teeth in. *When I've dealt Nina her life's share of misery, I'll come for you.* He'd caught witches; how different could it be to slay a demon?

The bronze girl folded up the document and handed it to

Brekker, who slipped it into his breast pocket. Matthias felt like he was watching an old friend, one he'd never hoped to see again, vanish into a crowd, and he was powerless to call out.

"We're going to untie you," said Brekker. "I hope prison hasn't robbed you of all your manners or good sense."

Matthias nodded, and the bronze girl took a knife to the ropes binding him. "I believe you know Nina," Brekker continued. "The lovely girl freeing you is Inej, our thief of secrets and the best in the trade. Jesper Fahey is our sharpshooter, Zemeni-born but try not to hold it against him, and this is Wylan, best demolitions expert in the Barrel."

"Raske is better," Inej said.

The boy looked up, ruddy gold hair flopping in his eyes, and spoke for the first time. "He's not better. He's reckless."

"He knows his trade."

"So do I."

"Barely," Jesper said.

"Wylan is new to the scene," admitted Brekker.

"Of course he's new, he looks like he's about twelve," retorted Matthias.

"I'm sixteen," said Wylan sullenly.

Matthias doubted that. Fifteen at the most. The boy didn't even look as if he'd started shaving. In fact, at eighteen, Matthias suspected that he was the oldest of the bunch. Brekker's eyes were ancient, but he couldn't be any older than Matthias.

For the first time, Matthias really looked at the people around him. *What kind of team is this for a mission so perilous?* Treason wouldn't be an issue if they were all dead. And only he knew exactly how treacherous this endeavour might prove.

"We should be using Raske," Jesper said. "He's good under pressure."

"I don't like it," agreed Inej.

"I didn't ask," said Kaz. "Besides, Wylan isn't just good with the flint and fuss. He's our insurance."

"Against what?" asked Nina.

"Meet Wylan Van Eck," said Kaz Brekker as the boy's cheeks flooded crimson. "Jan Van Eck's son and our guarantee on thirty million *kruge*."

8

JESPER

Jesper stared at Wylan. "Of course you're a Councilman's kid." He burst out laughing. "That explains everything."

He knew he should be angry at Kaz for holding back yet another vital piece of information, but right now, he was just enjoying watching the little revelation of Wylan Van Eck's identity go careening around the room like an ornery colt kicking up dust.

Wylan was red faced and mortified. Nina looked stunned and irritated. The Fjerdan just seemed confused. Kaz appeared utterly pleased with himself. And, of course, Inej didn't look remotely surprised. She gathered Kaz's secrets and kept them as well. Jesper tried to ignore the pang of jealousy he felt at that.

Wylan's mouth opened and closed, his throat working. "You knew?" he asked Kaz miserably.

Kaz leaned back in his chair, one knee bent, his bad leg stretched out before him. "Why do you think I've been keeping you around?"

"I'm good at demo."

"You're passable at demo. You're excellent at hostage."

That was cruel, but that was Kaz. And the Barrel was a far rougher teacher than Kaz could ever be. At least this explained why Kaz had been coddling Wylan and sending jobs his way.

"It doesn't matter," said Jesper. "We should still take Raske and leave this baby merch on lockdown in Ketterdam."

"I don't trust Raske."

"And you trust Wylan Van Eck?" Jesper said incredulously.

"Wylan doesn't know enough people to cause us real trouble."

"Don't I have some say in this?" complained Wylan. "I'm sitting right here."

Kaz raised a brow. "Ever had your pocket picked, Wylan?"

"I . . . not that I know of."

"Been mugged in an alley?"

"No."

"Hung over the side of a bridge with your head in the canal?"

Wylan blinked. "No, but—"

"Ever been beaten until you can't walk?"

"No."

"Why do you think that is?"

"I—"

"It's been three months since you left your daddy's mansion on the Geldstraat. Why do you suppose your sojourn in the Barrel has been so blessed?"

"Lucky, I guess?" Wylan suggested weakly.

Jesper snorted. "Kaz is your luck, merchling. He's had you under Dregs protection – though you're so useless, up until this minute none of us could figure out why."

"It was perplexing," Nina admitted.

"Kaz always has his reasons," murmured Inej.

"Why *did* you move out of your father's house?" Jesper asked.

"It was time," Wylan said tightly.

"Idealist? Romantic? Revolutionary?"

"Idiot?" suggested Nina. "No one chooses to live in the Barrel if he has another option."

"I'm not useless," Wylan said.

"Raske is the better demo man—" Inej began.

"I've been to the Ice Court. With my father. We went to an embassy dinner. I can help with the plans."

"See that? Hidden depths." Kaz tapped his gloved fingers over the crow's head of his cane. "And I don't want our only leverage against Van Eck cooling his heels in Ketterdam while we head north. Wylan goes with us. He's good enough at demo, and he's got a fine hand for sketching, thanks to all those pricey tutors."

Wylan blushed deeper, and Jesper shook his head. "Play piano, too?"

"Flute," said Wylan defensively.

"Perfect."

"And since Wylan has seen the Ice Court with his very own eyes," Kaz continued, "he can help keep you honest, Helvar."

The Fjerdan scowled furiously, and Wylan looked a little ill.

"Don't worry," Nina said. "The glower isn't lethal."

Jesper noted the way Matthias' shoulders bunched every time Nina talked. He didn't know what history they were chewing on, but they'd probably kill each other before they ever got to Fjerda.

Jesper rubbed his eyes. He was low on sleep and exhausted after the excitement of the prison break, and now his thoughts were buzzing and jumping at the possibility of thirty million *kruge*. Even after Per Haskell got his twenty percent, that would leave four million for each of them. What could he do with a pile of scratch that big? Jesper could just imagine his father saying, *Land yourself in a pile of shit twice as big*. Saints, he missed him.

Kaz tapped his cane on the polished wood floor.

"Take out your pen and proper paper, Wylan. Let's put Helvar to work."

Wylan reached into the satchel at his feet and pulled out a slender roll of butcher's paper followed by a metal case that held an expensive-looking pen and ink set.

"How nice," Jesper noted. "A nib for every occasion."

"Start talking," Kaz said to the Fjerdan. "It's time to pay the rent."

Matthias directed his furious gaze at Kaz. Definitely a mighty glower. It was almost fun to watch him pit it against Kaz's shark-like stare.

Finally, the Fjerdan shut his eyes, took a deep breath and said, "The Ice Court is on a bluff overlooking the harbour at Djerholm. It's built in concentric circles, like the rings of a tree." The words came slowly, as if speaking each one was causing him pain. "First, the ringwall, then the outer circle. It's divided into three sectors. Beyond that is the ice moat, then at the centre of everything, the White Island."

Wylan began to sketch. Jesper peered over Wylan's shoulder. "That doesn't look like a tree, it looks like a cake."

"Well, it *is* sort of like a cake," Wylan said defensively. "The whole thing is built on a rise."

Kaz gestured for Matthias to continue.

"The cliffs are unscalable, and the northern road is the only way in or out. You'll have to get through a guarded checkpoint before you even reach the ringwall."

"Two checkpoints," said Wylan. "When I was there, there were two."

"There you have it," Kaz said to Jesper. "Marketable skills. Wylan is watching you, Helvar."

"Why two checkpoints?" Inej asked.

Matthias stared at the black walnut slats of the floor and said, "It's harder to bribe two sets of guards. The security at the Court is always built with multiple fail-safes. If you make it that far—"

"*We*, Helvar. If *we* make it that far," corrected Kaz.

The Fjerdan gave the barest shrug. "If we make it that far, the outer circle is split into three sectors: the prison, the *drüskelle* facilities, and the embassy, each with its own gate in the ringwall. The prison gate is always functioning, but it's kept under constant armed surveillance. Of the two others, only one is ever operational at any given time."

"What determines which gate is used?" asked Jesper.

"The schedule changes each week, and guards are only given their postings the night before."

"Maybe that's a good thing," said Jesper. "If we can figure out which gate isn't running, it won't be manned or guarded—"

"There are always at least four guards on duty even when the gate isn't in use."

"Pretty sure we can handle four guards."

Matthias shook his head. "The gates weigh thousands of pounds and can only be operated from within the guardhouses. And even if you could raise one of them, opening a gate that isn't scheduled for use would trigger Black Protocol. The entire Court would go on lockdown, and you'd give away your location."

A ripple of unease passed through the room. Jesper shifted uncomfortably. If the expressions on the others' faces were any indication, they were all having the same thought: *Just what are we getting into?* Only Kaz seemed unfazed.

"Put it all down," Kaz said, tapping the paper. "Helvar, I expect you to describe the mechanics of the alarm system to Wylan later."

Matthias frowned. "I don't really know how it works. It's some kind of series of cables and bells."

"Tell him all you know. Where will they be keeping Bo Yul-Bayur?"

Slowly, Matthias rose and approached the plans taking shape beneath Wylan's pen. His movements were reluctant, as wary as if Kaz had told him to pet a rattler.

"Probably here," the Fjerdan said, resting his finger on the paper. "The prison sector. The high-security cells are on the topmost floor. It's where they keep the most dangerous criminals. Assassins, terrorists—"

"Grisha?" Nina asked.

"Exactly," he replied grimly.

"You guys are going to make this really fun, aren't you?" asked Jesper. "Usually people don't start hating each other until a week into the job, but you two have a head start."

They cast him twin glares, and Jesper beamed back at them, but Kaz's attention was focused on the plans.

"Bo Yul-Bayur isn't dangerous," he said thoughtfully. "At least not in that way. I don't think they'll keep him locked up with the rabble."

"I think they'll keep him in a grave," said Matthias.

"Operate on the assumption that he isn't dead. He's a valued prisoner, one they don't want falling into the wrong hands before he stands trial. Where would he be?"

Matthias looked at the plan. "The buildings of the outer circle surround the ice moat, and at the moat's centre is the White Island, where the treasury and the Royal Palace are. It's the most secure place in the Ice Court."

"Then that's where Bo Yul-Bayur will be," said Kaz.

Matthias smiled. Actually, it was less a smile than a baring of teeth. *He learned that grin at Hellgate*, thought Jesper.

"Then your quest is pointless," Matthias said. "There is no way a group of foreigners is going to make it to the White Island."

"Don't look so pleased, Helvar. We don't get inside, you don't get your pardon."

Matthias shrugged. "I can't change what is true. The ice

moat is watched from multiple guard towers on the White Island and a lookout atop the Elderclock. It's completely uncrossable except by way of the glass bridge, and there's no way onto the glass bridge without clearance."

"Hringkälla is coming," Nina said.

"Be silent," Matthias snapped at her.

"Pray, don't," said Kaz.

"Hringkälla. It's the Day of Listening, when the new *drüskelle* are initiated on the White Island."

Matthias' knuckles flexed white. "You have no right to speak of those things. They're holy."

"They're facts. The Fjerdan royals throw a huge party with guests from all over the world, and plenty of the entertainment comes straight from Ketterdam."

"Entertainment?" Kaz asked.

"Actors, dancers, a Komedie Brute troupe, and the best talent from the pleasure houses of West Stave."

"I thought Fjerdans didn't go in for that sort of thing," said Jesper.

Inej's lips quirked. "You've never seen Fjerdan soldiers on the Staves?"

"I meant when they're at home," Jesper said.

"It's the one day a year they all stop acting so miserable and actually let themselves have a good time," Nina replied. "Besides, only the *drüskelle* live like monks."

"A good time needn't involve wine and . . . and flesh," Matthias sputtered.

Nina batted her glossy lashes at him. "You wouldn't know a good time if it sidled up to you and stuck a lollipop in your mouth." She looked back at the plans. "The embassy gate will have to be open. Maybe we shouldn't worry about breaking into the Ice Court. Maybe we should just walk in with the performers."

"This isn't the Hellshow," said Kaz. "It won't be that easy."

"Visitors are vetted weeks before they arrive at the Ice

Court," Matthias said. "Anyone entering the embassy will have their papers checked and checked again. Fjerdans aren't fools."

Nina raised a brow. "Not all of them, at least."

"Don't poke the bear, Nina," Kaz said. "We need him friendly. When does this party take place?"

"It's seasonal," Nina said, "on the spring equinox."

"Two weeks from today," Inej noted.

Kaz cocked his head to one side, his eyes focused on something in the distance.

"Scheming face," Jesper whispered to Inej.

She nodded. "Definitely."

"Is the White Rose sending a delegation?" Kaz asked.

Nina shook her head. "I didn't hear anything about it."

"Even if we go straight to Djerholm," Inej said, "we'll need most of a week to travel. There isn't time to secure documents or create cover that will bear up under scrutiny."

"We're not going in through the embassy," said Kaz. "Always hit where the mark isn't looking."

"Who's Mark?" asked Wylan.

Jesper burst out laughing. "Oh, Saints, you are something. The *mark*, the pigeon, the cosy, the fool you're looking to fleece."

Wylan drew himself up. "I may not have had your ... education, but I'm sure I know plenty of words that you don't."

"Also the proper way to fold a napkin and dance a minuet. Oh, and you can play the flute. Marketable skills, merchling. Marketable skills."

"No one dances the minuet any more," grumbled Wylan.

Kaz leaned back. "What's the easiest way to steal a man's wallet?"

"Knife to the throat?" asked Inej.

"Gun to the back?" said Jesper.

"Poison in his cup?" suggested Nina.

"You're all horrible," said Matthias.

Kaz rolled his eyes. "The easiest way to steal a man's wallet is to tell him you're going to steal his watch. You take his attention and direct it where *you* want it to go. Hringkälla is going to do that job for us. The Ice Court will have to divert resources to monitoring guests and protecting the royal family. They can't be looking everywhere at once. It's the perfect opportunity to spring Bo Yul-Bayur." Kaz pointed to the prison gate in the ringwall. "Remember what I told you at Hellgate, Nina?"

"It's hard to keep track of all your wisdom."

"At the prison, they won't care about who's coming in, just anyone trying to get out." His gloved finger slid sideways to the next sector. "At the embassy they won't care who's going out, they'll just be focused on who's trying to get in. We enter through the prison, leave through the embassy. Helvar, is the Elderclock functional?"

Matthias nodded. "It chimes every quarter hour. It's also how the alarm protocols are sounded."

"It's accurate?"

"Of course."

"Quality Fjerdan engineering," Nina said sourly.

Kaz ignored her. "Then we'll use the Elderclock to coordinate our movements."

"Will we enter disguised as guards?" Wylan asked.

Jesper couldn't keep the disdain from his voice. "Only Nina and Matthias speak Fjerdan."

"I speak Fjerdan," Wylan protested.

"Schoolroom Fjerdan, right? I bet you speak Fjerdan about as well as I speak moose."

"Moose is probably your native tongue," mumbled Wylan.

"We enter as we are," Kaz said. "As criminals. The prison is our front door."

"Let me get this straight," said Jesper. "You want us to

let the Fjerdans lock us in jail. Isn't that what we're always trying to avoid?"

"Criminal identities are slippery. It's one of the perks of being a member of the troublemaking class. They'll be counting heads at the prison gate, looking at names and crimes, not checking passports or examining embassy seals."

"Because no one *wants* to go to prison," Jesper said.

Nina rubbed her hands over her arms. "I don't want to be locked up in a Fjerdan cell."

Kaz flicked his sleeve, and two slender rods of metal appeared between his fingers. They danced over his knuckles then vanished once more.

"Lockpicks?" Nina asked.

"You let me take care of the cells," Kaz said.

"Hit where the mark isn't looking," mused Inej.

"That's right," said Kaz. "And the Ice Court is like any other mark, one big white pigeon ready for the plucking."

"Will Yul-Bayur come willingly?" Inej asked.

"Van Eck said the Council gave Yul-Bayur a code word when they first tried to get him out of Shu Han so he'd know who to trust: *Sesh-uyeh*. It will tell him we've been sent by Kerch."

"*Sesh-uyeh*," Wylan repeated, trying the syllables clumsily on his tongue. "What does it mean?"

Nina examined a spot on the floor and said, "Heartsick."

"This can be done," said Kaz, "and we're the ones to do it." Jesper felt the mood shift in the room as possibility took hold. It was a subtle thing, but he'd learned to look for it at the tables – the moment a player came awake to the fact that he might have a winning hand. Anticipation tugged at Jesper, a fizzing mix of fear and excitement that made it hard for him to sit still.

Maybe Matthias sensed it, too, because he folded his huge arms and said, "You have no idea what you're up against."

"But you do, Helvar. I want you working on the plan of

the Ice Court every minute until we sail. No detail is too small or inconsequential. I'll be checking on you regularly."

Inej traced her finger over the rough sketch Wylan had produced, a series of embedded circles. "It really does look like the rings of a tree," she said.

"No," said Kaz. "It looks like a target."

9
KAZ

"We're done here," Kaz told the others. "I'll send word to each of you after I find us a ship, but be ready to sail by tomorrow night."

"So soon?" Inej asked.

"We don't know what kind of weather we'll hit, and there's a long journey ahead of us. Hringkälla is our best shot at Bo Yul-Bayur. I'm not going to risk losing it."

Kaz needed time to think through the plan that was forming in his mind. He could see the basics – where they would enter, how they would leave. But the plan he envisioned would mean that they wouldn't be able to bring much with them. They'd be operating without their usual resources. That meant more variables and a lot more chances for things to go wrong.

Keeping Wylan Van Eck around meant he could at least make sure they got their reward. But it wasn't going to be easy. They hadn't even left Ketterdam, and Wylan already seemed completely out of his depth. He wasn't much younger than Kaz, but somehow he looked like a child –

smooth-skinned, wide-eyed, like a silk-eared puppy in a room full of fighting dogs.

"Keep Wylan out of trouble," he told Jesper as he dismissed them.

"Why me?"

"You're unlucky enough to be in my line of sight, and I don't want any sudden reconciliations between father and son before we set sail."

"You don't need to worry about that," said Wylan.

"I worry about everything, merchling. That's why I'm still alive. And you can keep an eye on Jesper, too."

"On *me*?" Jesper said indignantly.

Kaz slid a blackwood panel aside and unlocked the safe hidden behind it. "Yes, you." He counted out four slender stacks of *kruge* and handed one over to Jesper. "This is for bullets, not bets. Wylan, make sure his feet don't mysteriously find their way into a gambling den on his way to buy ammunition, understood?"

"I don't need a nursemaid," Jesper snapped.

"More like a chaperone, but if you want him to wash your nappies and tuck you in at night, that's your business." He ignored Jesper's stung expression and doled *kruge* out to Wylan for explosives and to Nina for whatever she'd need in her tailoring kit. "Stock up for the journey only," he said. "If this works the way I think it will, we're going to have to enter the Ice Court empty-handed."

He saw a shadow pass over Inej's face. She wouldn't like being without her knives any more than he liked being without his cane.

"I'll need you to get cold weather gear," he told her. "There's a shop on the Wijnstraat that supplies trappers – start there."

"You think to approach from the north?" asked Helvar.

Kaz nodded. "The Djerholm harbour is crawling with

customs agents, and I'm going to bet they'll be tightening security during your big party."

"It isn't a party."

"It sounds like a party," said Jesper.

"It isn't *supposed* to be a party," Helvar amended sullenly.

"What are we going to do with him?" Nina asked, nodding at Matthias. Her voice was disinterested, but the performance was wasted on everyone except Helvar. They'd all seen her tears at Hellgate.

"For the moment, he stays here at the Crow Club. I want you dredging your memory for details, Helvar. Wylan and Jesper will join you later. We'll keep this parlour closed. If anyone playing in the main hall asks, tell them there's a private game going on."

"We have to sleep here?" asked Jesper. "I have things I need to see to at the Slat."

"You'll manage," Kaz said, though he knew asking Jesper to spend the night in a gambling den without placing a bet was a particular kind of cruelty. He turned to the rest of them. "Not a word to anyone. No one is to know you're leaving Kerch. You're working with me on a job at a country house outside the city. That's all."

"Are you going to tell us anything else about your miraculous plan?" Nina asked.

"On the boat. The less you know, the less you can talk."

"And you're leaving Helvar unshackled?"

"Can you behave?" Kaz asked the Fjerdan.

His eyes looked murder, but he nodded.

"We'll be locking this room up tight and posting a guard."

Inej considered the giant Fjerdan. "Maybe two."

"Post Dirix and Rotty, but don't give them too many details. They'll sail out with us, and I can fill them in later. And Wylan, you and I are going to have a chat. I want to know everything about your father's trading company."

Wylan shrugged. "I don't know anything about it. He doesn't include me in those discussions."

"You're telling me you've never snooped around his office? Looked through his documents?"

"No," Wylan said, his chin jutting out slightly. Kaz was surprised to find he actually believed him.

"What did I tell you?" Jesper said cheerfully as he headed through the door. "Useless."

The others started to file out behind him, and Kaz shut the safe, giving the tumbler a spin.

"I'd like a word with you, Brekker," Helvar said. "Alone."

Inej cast Kaz a warning glance. Kaz ignored it. She didn't think he could handle a lump of country muscle like Matthias Helvar? He slid the wall panel closed and gave his leg a shake. It was aching now – too many late nights and too much time with his weight on it.

"Go on, Wraith," he said. "Shut the door behind you."

As soon as the door clicked shut, Matthias lunged for him. Kaz let it happen. He'd been expecting it.

Matthias clamped one filthy hand over Kaz's mouth. The sensation of skin on skin set off a riot of revulsion in Kaz's head, but because he'd been anticipating the attack, he managed to control the sickness that overcame him. Matthias' other hand rooted around in Kaz's coat pockets, first one then the other.

"*Fer esje?*" he grunted angrily in Fjerdan. Then, "Where is it?" in Kerch.

Kaz gave Helvar another moment of frenzied searching, then dropped his elbow and jabbed upwards, forcing Helvar to loosen his grip. Kaz slipped away easily. He smacked Helvar behind the right leg with his cane. The big Fjerdan collapsed. When he tried to shove up again, Kaz kicked him.

"Stay down, you pathetic skiv."

Again, Helvar tried to rise. He was fast, and prison

had made him strong. Kaz cracked him hard on the jaw, then gave the pressure points at Helvar's huge shoulders two lightning-quick jabs with the tip of his cane. The Fjerdan grunted as his arms went limp and useless at his sides.

Kaz flipped the cane in his hand and pressed the carved crow's head against Helvar's throat. "Move again and I'll smash your jaw so badly you'll be drinking your meals for the rest of your life."

The Fjerdan stilled, his blue eyes alight with hate.

"Where is the pardon?" Helvar growled. "I saw you put it in your pocket."

Kaz crouched down beside him and produced the folded document from a pocket that had seemed empty just a moment before. "This?"

The Fjerdan flopped his useless arms, then released a low animal growl as Kaz made the pardon vanish in thin air. It reappeared between his fingers. He turned it once, flashing the text, then ran his hand over it, and showed Helvar the seemingly blank page.

"*Demjin*," muttered Helvar. Kaz didn't speak Fjerdan, but that word he knew. Demon.

Hardly. He'd learned sleight of hand from the cardsharps and monte runners on East Stave, and spent hours practising it in front of a muddy mirror he'd bought with his first week's pay.

Kaz knocked his cane gently against Helvar's jaw. "For every trick you've seen, I know a thousand more. You think a year in Hellgate hardened you up? Taught you to fight? Hellgate would have been paradise to me as a child. You move like an ox – you'd last about two days on the streets where I grew up. This was your one free pass, Helvar. Don't test me again. Nod so I know you understand."

Helvar pressed his lips together and nodded once.

"Good. I think we'll shackle those feet tonight."

Kaz rose, snatched his new hat from the desk where he'd left it, and gave the Fjerdan one last kick to the kidneys for good measure. Sometimes the big ones didn't know when to stay down.

10

INEJ

Over the next day, Inej saw Kaz begin to move the pieces of his scheme into position. She'd been privy to his consultations with every member of the crew, but she knew she was seeing only fragments of his plan. That was the game Kaz always played.

If he had doubts about what they were attempting, they didn't show, and Inej wished she shared his certainty. The Ice Court had been built to withstand an onslaught of armies, assassins, Grisha, and spies. When she'd said as much to Kaz, he'd simply replied, "But it hasn't been built to keep *us* out."

His confidence unnerved her. "What makes you think we can do this? There will be other teams out there, trained soldiers and spies, people with years of experience."

"This isn't a job for trained soldiers and spies. It's a job for thugs and thieves. Van Eck knows it, and that's why he brought us in."

"You can't spend his money if you're dead."

"I'll acquire expensive habits in the afterlife."

"There's a difference between confidence and arrogance."

He'd turned his back on her then, giving each of his gloves a sharp tug. "And when I want a sermon on that, I know who to come to. If you want out, just say so."

Her spine had straightened, her own pride rising to her defence. "Matthias isn't the only irreplaceable member of this crew, Kaz. You need me."

"I need your skills, Inej. That's not the same thing. You may be the best spider crawling around the Barrel, but you're not the only one. You'd do well to remember it if you want to keep your share of the haul."

She hadn't said a word, hadn't wanted to show just how angry he'd made her, but she'd left his office and hadn't said a thing to him since.

Now, as she headed towards the harbour, she wondered what kept her on this path.

She could leave Kerch any time she wanted. She could stow away on a ship bound for Novyi Zem. She could go back to Ravka and search for her family. Hopefully they'd been safe in the west when the civil war broke out, or maybe they'd taken refuge in Shu Han. The Suli caravans had been following the same well-worn roads for years, and she had the skills to steal what she needed to survive until she found them.

That would mean walking out on her debt to the Dregs. Per Haskell would blame Kaz; he'd be forced to carry the price of her indenture, and she'd be leaving him vulnerable without his Wraith to gather secrets. But hadn't he told her that she was easily replaced? If they managed to pull off this heist and return to Kerch with Bo Yul-Bayur safely in tow, her percentage of the haul would be more than enough to buy her way out of her contract with the Dregs. She'd owe Kaz nothing, and there would be no reason for her to stay.

Sunrise was only an hour away, but the streets were crowded as she wended her way from East to West Stave. There was a Suli saying: *The heart is an arrow. It demands aim to land true.* Her father had liked to recite this when she was training on the wire or the swings. *Be decisive,* he'd say. *You have to know where you want to go before you get there.* Her mother had laughed at this. *That's not what that means,* she'd say. *You take the romance out of everything.* He hadn't, though. Her father had adored her mother. Inej remembered him leaving little bouquets of wild geraniums for her mother to find everywhere, in the cupboards, the camp cookpots, the sleeves of her costumes.

Shall I tell you the secret of true love? her father once asked her. *A friend of mine liked to tell me that women love flowers. He had many flirtations, but he never found a wife. Do you know why? Because women may love flowers, but only one woman loves the scent of gardenias in late summer that remind her of her grandmother's porch. Only one woman loves apple blossoms in a blue cup. Only one woman loves wild geraniums.*

That's Mama! Inej had cried.

Yes, Mama loves wild geraniums because no other flower has quite the same colour, and she claims that when she snaps the stem and puts a sprig behind her ear, the whole world smells like summer. Many boys will bring you flowers. But some day you'll meet a boy who will learn your favourite flower, your favourite song, your favourite sweet. And even if he is too poor to give you any of them, it won't matter because he will have taken the time to know you as no one else does. Only that boy earns your heart.

That felt like a hundred years ago. Her father had been wrong. There had been no boys to bring her flowers, only men with stacks of *kruge* and purses full of coin. Would she ever see her father again? Hear her mother singing, listen to her uncle's silly stories? *I'm not sure I have a heart to give any more, Papa.*

The problem was that Inej was no longer certain what she was aiming for. When she'd been little, it had been easy – a smile from her father, the tightrope raised another foot, orange cakes wrapped in white paper. Then it had been getting free of Tante Heleen and the Menagerie, and after that, surviving each day, getting a little stronger with every morning. Now she didn't know what she wanted.

Just this minute, I'll settle for an apology, she decided. *And I won't board the boat without one. Even if Kaz isn't sorry, he can pretend. He at least owes me his best imitation of a human being.*

If she hadn't been running late, she would have looped around West Stave or simply travelled over the rooftops – that was the Ketterdam she loved, empty and quiet, high above the crowds, a moonlit mountain range of gabled peaks and off-kilter chimneys. But tonight she was short on time. Kaz had sent her scouring the shops for two lumps of paraffin at the last minute. He wouldn't even tell her what they were for or why they were so necessary. And snow goggles? She'd had to visit three different outfitters to acquire them. She was so tired she didn't entirely trust herself to make the climb over the gables, not after two nights without sleep and a day spent wrangling supplies for their trek to the Ice Court.

She supposed she was daring herself, too.

She never walked West Stave alone. With the Dregs at her side, she could stroll by the Menagerie without a glance towards the golden bars on the windows. But tonight, her heart was pounding, and she could hear the roar of blood in her ears as the gilded façade came into view. The Menagerie had been built to look like a tiered cage, its first two storeys left open but for the widely spaced golden bars. It was also known as the House of Exotics. If you had a taste for a Shu girl or a Fjerdan giant, a redhead from the Wandering Isle, a dark-skinned Zemeni, the Menagerie was your destination. Each girl was known by her animal name – leopard, mare, fox, raven, ermine, fawn, snake. Suli seers wore the jackal mask when they plied their trade and looked into a person's fate. But what man would want to bed a jackal? So the Suli girl – and the Menagerie always stocked a Suli girl – was known as the lynx. Clients didn't come looking for the girls themselves, just brown Suli skin, the fire of Kaelish hair, the tilt of golden Shu eyes. The animals remained the same, though the girls came and went.

Inej glimpsed peacock feathers in the parlour, and her heart stuttered. It was just a bit of decoration, part of a lavish flower arrangement, but the panic inside her didn't care. It rose up, clutching at her breath. People crowded in on all sides, men in masks, women in veils – or maybe they were men in veils and women in masks. It was impossible to tell. The horns of the Imp. The goggling eyes of the Madman, the sad face of the Scarab Queen wrought in black and gold. Artists loved to paint scenes of West Stave, the boys and girls who worked the brothels, the pleasure seekers dressed as characters of the Komedie Brute. But there was no beauty here, no real merriment or joy, just transactions, people seeking escape or some colourful oblivion, some dream of decadence that they could wake from whenever they wished.

Inej forced herself to look at the Menagerie as she passed. *It's just a place*, she told herself. *Just another house.* How would Kaz see it? Where are the entrances and exits? How do the locks work? Which windows are unbarred? How many guards are posted, and which ones look alert? Just a house full of locks to pick, safes to crack, pigeons to dupe. And she was the predator now, not Heleen in her peacock feathers, not any man who walked these streets.

As soon as she was out of sight of the Menagerie, the tight feeling in her chest and throat began to ease. She'd done it. She'd walked alone on West Stave, right in front of the House of Exotics. Whatever was waiting for her in Fjerda, she could face it.

A hand hooked around her forearm and yanked her off her feet.

Inej regained her balance quickly. She spun on her heel

and tried to pull away, but the grip was too strong.

"Hello, little lynx."

Inej hissed in a breath and tore her arm free. *Tante Heleen.* That was what her girls knew to call Heleen Van Houden or risk the back of her hand. To the rest of the Barrel she was the Peacock, though Inej had always thought she looked less like a bird than a preening cat. Her hair was a thick and luscious gold, her eyes hazel and slightly feline. Her tall, sinuous frame was draped in vibrant blue silk, the plunging neckline accented with iridescent feathers that tickled the signature diamond choker glittering at her neck.

Inej turned to run, but her path was blocked by a huge bruiser, his blue velvet coat stretched tight across his big shoulders. Cobbet, Heleen's favourite enforcer.

"Oh, no you don't, little lynx."

Inej's vision blurred. *Trapped. Trapped. Trapped again.*

"That's not my name," Inej managed to gasp out.

"Stubborn thing."

Heleen grabbed hold of Inej's tunic.

Move, her mind screamed, but she couldn't. Her muscles had locked up; a high whine of terror filled her head.

Heleen ran a single manicured talon along her cheek. "Lynx is your only name," Heleen crooned. "You're still pretty enough to fetch a good price. Getting hard around the eyes though – too much time spent with that little thug Brekker."

A humiliating sound emerged from Inej's throat, a choked wheeze.

"I know what you are, lynx. I know what you're worth down to the cent. Cobbet, maybe we should take her home now."

Black crowded into Inej's vision. "You wouldn't dare. The Dregs—"

"I can bide my time, little lynx. You'll wear my silks again, I promise." She released Inej. "Enjoy your night," she said with a smile, then snapped open her blue fan and whirled away into the crowd, Cobbet trailing after her.

Inej stood frozen, shaking. Then she dove into the crowd, eager to disappear. She wanted to break into a run, but she just kept moving steadily, pushing towards the harbour. As she walked, she released the triggers on the sheaths at her forearms, feeling the grips of her daggers slide into her palms. Sankt Petyr, renowned for his bravery, on the right; the slender, bone-handled blade she'd named for Sankta Alina on the left. She recited the names of her other knives, too. Sankta Marya and Sankta Anastasia strapped to her thighs. Sankt Vladimir hidden in her boot, and Sankta Lizabeta snug at her belt, the blade etched in a pattern of roses. *Protect me, protect me.* She had to believe her Saints saw and understood the things she did to survive.

What was wrong with her? She was the Wraith. She had nothing to fear from Tante Heleen any longer. Per Haskell had bought out her indenture. He'd freed her. She wasn't a slave; she was a valued member of the Dregs, a thief of secrets, the best in the Barrel.

She hurried past the light and music of the Lid, and finally the Ketterdam harbours came into view, the sights and sounds of the Barrel fading as she neared the water. There were no crowds to bump against her here, no cloying perfumes or wild masks. She took a long, deep breath. From this vantage point she could just see the top of one of the Tidemaker towers, where lights always burned. The thick obelisks of black stone were manned day and night by a select group of Grisha who kept the tides permanently high over the landbridge that otherwise would have connected Kerch to Shu Han. Even Kaz had never been able to learn the identities of the Council of Tides, where they lived, or how their loyalty to Kerch had been guaranteed. They watched the harbours, too, and if a signal went up from the harbourmaster or a dockworker, they'd alter the tides and keep anyone from heading out to sea. But on this night, there would be no signal. The right bribes had been paid to the right officials, and their ship should be ready to sail.

Inej broke into a jog, heading for the loading docks at Fifth Harbour. She was very late – she wasn't looking forward to Kaz's disapproving frown when she made it to the pier.

She was glad for the peace of the docks, but they seemed almost too still after the noise and chaos of the Barrel. Here, the rows of crates and cargo containers were stacked high on either side of her – three, sometimes four, on top of one another. They made this part of the docks feel like a labyrinth. A cold sweat broke out at the base of her spine. The run-in with Tante Heleen had left her shaken, and the heft of the daggers in her hands wasn't enough to soothe her rattled nerves. She knew she should get used to carrying a pistol, but the weight threw off her balance, and guns could jam or lock in a bad moment. *Little lynx.* Her blades were reliable. And they made her feel like she'd been born with proper claws.

A light mist was rising off the water, and through it, Inej saw Kaz and the others waiting near the pier. They all wore the nondescript clothes of sailors – roughspun trousers, boots, thick wool coats and hats. Even Kaz had foregone his immaculately cut suit in favour of a bulky wool coat. The thick sheaf of his dark hair was combed back, the sides trimmed short as always. He looked like a dockworker, or a boy setting sail on his first adventure. It was almost as if she were peering through a lens at some other, more pleasant reality.

Behind them, she saw the little schooner Kaz had commandeered, *Ferolind* written in bold script on its side. It would fly the purple Kerch fishes and the colourful flag of the Haanraadt Bay Company. To anyone in Fjerda or on the True Sea, they would simply look like Kerch trappers heading north for skins and furs. Inej quickened her pace. If she hadn't been running late, they probably would have been aboard or even on their way out of the harbour already.

They would keep a minimal crew, all former sailors who had made their way into the ranks of the Dregs through one misfortune or another. Through the mists, she made a quick count of the waiting group. The number was off. They'd brought on four additional members of the Dregs to help sail the schooner since none of them really knew their way around the rigging, but she didn't see any of them. *Maybe they're already on board?* But even as she had the thought, her boot landed on something soft, and she stumbled.

She looked down. In the dim glow of the harbour gaslights, she saw Dirix, one of the Dregs who'd been meant to make the journey with them. There was a knife in his abdomen, and his eyes were glassy.

"Kaz!" she shouted.

But it was too late. The schooner exploded, knocking Inej off her feet and showering the docks in flame.

II

JESPER

Jesper always felt better when people were shooting at him. It wasn't that he liked the idea of dying (in fact, that potential outcome was a definite drawback), but if he was worrying about staying alive, he couldn't be thinking about anything else. That sound – the swift, shocking report of gunfire – called the scattered, irascible, permanently seeking part of his mind into focus like nothing else. It was better than being at the tables and waiting for the flop, better than standing at Makker's Wheel and seeing his number come up. He'd discovered it in his first fight on the Zemeni frontier. His father had been sweating, trembling, barely able to load his revolver. But Jesper had found his calling.

Now he braced his arms on the top of the crate where he'd taken cover and let loose with both barrels. His weapons were Zemeni-made revolvers that could fire six shots in rapid succession, unmatched by anything in Ketterdam. He felt them getting hot in his hands.

Kaz had warned them to anticipate competition, other teams bent on gaining the prize at any cost, but this was early in the job for things to be going so badly. They were surrounded, at least one man down, a burning ship at their backs. They'd lost their transportation to Fjerda, and if the shots raining down on them were any indication, they were seriously outnumbered. He supposed it could have been worse; they could have been on the boat when it exploded.

Jesper crouched down to reload and couldn't quite believe the sight that met his eyes. Wylan Van Eck was actually curled up on the dock, his soft mercher's hands thrown over his head. Jesper heaved a sigh, lay down a few shots for cover and lunged out from behind the sweet security of his crate. He seized Wylan by the collar of his shirt and yanked him back to shelter.

Jesper gave him a little shake. "Pull it together, kid."

"Not a kid," Wylan mumbled, batting Jesper's hands away.

"Fine, you're an elder statesman. Do you know how to shoot?"

Wylan nodded slowly. "Skeet."

Jesper rolled his eyes. He snagged the rifle from his back and shoved it into Wylan's chest. "Great. This is just like shooting clay pigeons, but they make a different sound when you hit one."

Jesper whirled, revolvers raised, as a shape sprang into his peripheral vision, but it was just Kaz.

"Head east to the next dock, board at berth twenty-two," Kaz said.

"What's at berth twenty-two?"

"The real *Ferolind*."

"But—"

"The boat that blew was a decoy."

"You knew?"

"No, I took precautions. It's what I do, Jesper."

"You could have told us we—"

"That would defeat the purpose of a decoy. Get moving." Kaz glanced at Wylan, who stood there cradling the rifle like an infant. "And make sure he gets to the ship in one piece."

Jesper watched Kaz vanish back into the shadows, cane in one hand, pistol in the other. Even on one good leg, he was eerily spry.

Then Jesper gave Wylan another jostle. "Let's go."

"Go?"

"Didn't you hear what Kaz said? We need to make it to berth twenty-two."

Wylan nodded dumbly. His eyes were dazed and wide enough to drink from.

"Just stay behind me and try not to get killed. Ready?"

Wylan shook his head.

"Then forget I asked." He placed Wylan's hand on the rifle's grip. "Come on."

Jesper laid down another series of shots, sketching a wild formation he hoped would disguise their location. One revolver empty, he lunged away from the crate and into the shadows. He half expected Wylan wouldn't follow, but he could hear the merchling behind him, breathing hard, a low whistle in his lungs as they pounded towards the next stack of barrels.

Jesper hissed as a bullet whizzed by his cheek, close enough to leave a burn.

They threw themselves behind the barrels. From this vantage point, he saw Nina wedged into a space between two stacks of crates. She had her arms raised, and as one of their attackers moved into view, she clenched her fist. The boy crumpled to the ground, clutching his chest. She was at a disadvantage in this maze, though. Heartrenders needed to see their targets to bring them down.

Helvar was beside her with his back to the crate, his hands bound. A reasonable precaution, but the Fjerdan was valuable, and Jesper had a moment to wonder why Kaz had left him in such straits before he saw Nina produce a knife from her sleeve and slash through Helvar's bonds. She slapped a pistol into his hands. "Defend yourself," she said with a growl, and then returned her focus to the fight.

Not smart, Jesper thought. *Do not turn your back on an angry Fjerdan.* Helvar looked like he was seriously considering shooting her. Jesper lifted his revolver, prepared to bring the giant down. Then Helvar was standing next to Nina, aiming into the maze of crates beyond. Just like that they were fighting side by side. Had Kaz left Matthias bound with Nina deliberately? Jesper could never tell how much of what Kaz got away with was smarts and planning and how much was dumb luck.

He gave a sharp whistle. Nina glanced over her shoulder, and her gaze found Jesper's. He flashed two fingers, twice, and she gave a quick nod. Had she known berth twenty-two was their real destination? Had Inej? Kaz was at it again, playing with information, keeping one or all of them blind and guessing. Jesper hated it, but he couldn't argue with the fact that they still had a way to get to Fjerda. If they lived to board the second schooner.

He signalled to Wylan, and they continued to make their way past the boats and ships moored along the dock, keeping as low as possible.

"There!" he heard a voice shout from somewhere behind him. They'd been spotted.

"Damn it," Jesper said. "Run!"

They pounded down the dock. There, at berth twenty-two, was a trim-looking schooner with *Ferolind* written on its side. It was almost eerie how much it looked like the other boat. No lanterns had been lit aboard it, but as he and Wylan bolted up the ramp, two sailors emerged.

"You're the first ones here," said Rotty.

"Let's hope we're not the last. Are you armed?"

He nodded. "Brekker told us to stay hidden until—"

"This is until," Jesper said pointing to the men storming towards them on the dock and snatching his rifle back from Wylan. "I need to get to high ground. Keep them back and distracted as long as you can."

"Jesper—" began Wylan.

"No one gets past you. If they take down this schooner, we're done for." The men gunning for them didn't just care about keeping the Dregs from leaving the harbour. They wanted them dead.

Jesper fired at the two men leading the charge down the dock. One fell and the other rolled left and took cover behind the bowsprit of a fishing boat. Jesper squeezed off three more shots, then sprinted up the mast.

Below he could hear more gunfire erupt. Ten feet up, twenty, boots catching in the rigging. He should have stopped to take them off. He was two feet from the crow's nest when he felt a hot blade of pain sear through the flesh of his thigh. His foot slipped and for a moment he dangled above the distant deck with nothing but his slippery palms clinging to the ropes. He forced his legs to work and sought purchase with the toes of his boots. His right leg was nearly worthless from the gunshot, and he had to pull himself up the last few feet with his arms trembling and his heart pounding in his ears. Every one of his senses felt as if it was on fire. Definitely better than a winning streak at the tables.

He didn't stop to rest. He hooked his bad leg in the rigging, ignoring the pain, checked the sight on his rifle, and began picking off anyone in range.

Four million *kruge*, he told himself as he reloaded and found another enemy in his sights. The mist made visibility poor, but this was the skill that had kept him in the Dregs even after his debts had mounted and it had become clear that Jesper loved the cards more than luck loved him. Four million *kruge* would erase his debt and land him in clover for a good long while.

He spotted Nina and Matthias trying to make their way onto the pier, but at least ten men were in their way. Kaz seemed to be running in the opposite direction, and Inej was nowhere to be found, though that didn't mean much when it came to the Wraith. She could be hanging from the sails two feet away from him, and he probably wouldn't know it.

"Jesper!"

The shout came from far below, and it took a moment for Jesper to realise it was Wylan calling to him. He tried to ignore him, taking aim again.

"Jesper!"

I'm going to kill that little idiot. "What do you want?" he shouted down.

"Close your eyes!"

"You can't kiss me from down there, Wylan."

"Just do it!"

"This better be good!" He shut his eyes.

"Are they closed?"

"Damn it, Wylan, yes, they're—"

There was a shrill, shrieking howl, and then bright light bloomed behind Jesper's lids. When it faded, he opened his eyes.

Below, he saw men blundering around, rendered blind by the flash bomb Wylan had set off. But Jesper could see perfectly. *Not bad for a mercher's kid*, he thought to himself, and opened fire.

12

INEJ

Before Inej had ever set foot on the high wire or even a practice rope, her father had taught her to fall – to protect her head and minimise the impact by not fighting her own momentum. Even as the blast from the harbour lifted her off her feet, she was tucking into a roll. She hit hard, but she was up in seconds, pressed against the side of a crate, her ears ringing, her nose singed by the sharp scent of gunpowder.

Inej spared Kaz and the others a single glance, then did what she did best – she vanished. She launched herself up the cargo crates, scaling them like a nimble insect, her rubber-soled feet finding grips and footholds.

The view from above was disturbing. The Dregs were outnumbered, and there were men working their way around their left and right flanks. Kaz had been right to keep their real point of departure a secret from the others. Someone had talked. Inej had tried to keep tabs on the team, but someone else in the gang could have been snooping. Kaz had said it himself: Everything in Ketterdam leaked, including the Slat and the Crow Club.

Someone was firing down from the masts of the new

Ferolind. Hopefully, that meant Jesper had made it to the schooner, and she just had to buy the others enough time to make it there as well.

Inej ran lightly over the tops of the crates, making her way down the row, seeking her targets below. It was easy enough. None of them expected the threat to come from above. She slid to the ground behind two men firing at Nina, and said a silent prayer as she slit one throat, then the next. When the second man dropped, she crouched beside him and rolled up his right sleeve – a tattoo of a hand, its first and second fingers cut off at the knuckle. Black Tips. Was this retribution for Kaz's showdown with Geels, or something more? They shouldn't have been able to raise these kinds of numbers.

She moved on to the next aisle of crates, following a mental map of the other attackers' positions. First, she took down a girl holding a massive, unwieldy rifle, then skewered the man who was supposed to be watching her flank. His tattoo showed five birds in a wedge formation: Razorgulls. Just how many gangs were they up against?

The next corner was blind. Should she scale the cargo containers to check her position or risk what might be waiting for her on the other side? She took a deep breath, sank low, and slipped around the corner in a lunge. Tonight her Saints were kind – two men were firing on the docks with their backs to her. She dispatched them with two quick thrusts of her blades. Six bodies, six lives taken. She was going to have to do a lot of penance, but she'd helped even the odds a bit in the Dregs' favour. Now, she needed to get to the schooner.

She wiped her knives on her leather breeches and returned them to their sheaths, then backed up and took a running start at the nearest cargo container. As her fingers gripped the rim, she felt a piercing pain beneath her arm. She turned in time to see Oomen's ugly face split in a determined grimace. All the intelligence she had gathered on the Black Tips came back to her in a sickening rush – Oomen, Geels' shambling enforcer, the one who could crush skulls with his bare hands.

He yanked her down and grabbed the front of her vest, giving the knife in her side a sharp twist. Inej fought not to black out.

As her hood fell back, he exclaimed, "*Ghezen*! I've got Brekker's Wraith."

"You should have aimed . . . higher," Inej gasped. "Missed my heart."

"Don't want you dead, Wraith," he said. "You're quite the prize. Can't wait to hear all the gossip you've gathered for Dirtyhands, and all *his* secrets, too. I love a good story."

"I can tell you how this one ends," she said on an unsteady breath. "But you're not going to like it."

"That so?" He slammed her up against the crate, and pain crashed through her. Her toes only brushed the ground as blood spurted from the wound at her side. Oomen's forearm was braced against her shoulders, keeping her arms pinned.

"Do you know the secret to fighting a scorpion?"

He laughed. "Talking nonsense, Wraith? Don't die too quick. Need to get you patched up."

She crossed one ankle behind the other and heard a reassuring click. She wore the pads at her knees for crawling and climbing, but there was another reason, too – namely, the tiny steel blades hidden in each of them.

"The secret," she panted, "is to never take your eyes off the scorpion's tail." She brought her knee up, jamming the blade between Oomen's legs.

He shrieked and released her, hands going to his bleeding groin.

She staggered back down the row of crates. She could hear men shouting to each other, the pop of gunfire coming in smatters and bursts now. Who was winning? Had the others made it to the schooner? A wave of dizziness rolled over her.

When she touched her fingers to the wound at her side, they came away wet. Too much blood. Footsteps. Someone was coming. She couldn't climb, not with this wound, not with the amount of blood she'd lost. She remembered her father putting her on the rope ladder the first time. *Climb, Inej.*

The cargo containers were stacked like a pyramid here. If she could make it up just one, she could hide herself on the first level. *Just one.* She could climb or she could stand there and die.

She willed her mind to clarity and hopped up, fingertips latching onto the top of the crate. *Climb, Inej.* She dragged herself over the edge onto the tin roof of the container.

It felt so good to lie there, but she knew she'd left a trail of blood behind her. *One more*, she told herself. *One more and you'll be safe.* She forced herself up to her knees and reached for the next crate.

The surface beneath her began to rock. She heard laughter from below.

"Come out, come out, Wraith! We have secrets to tell!"

Desperately, she reached for the lip of the next crate again and gripped it, fighting through an onslaught of pain as the container under her dropped away. Then she was just hanging, legs dangling helplessly down. They didn't open fire; they wanted her alive.

"Come on down, Wraith!"

She didn't know where the strength came from but she managed to pull herself over the top. She lay on the crate's roof, panting.

Just one more. But she couldn't. Couldn't push to her knees, couldn't reach, couldn't even roll. It hurt too much. *Climb, Inej.*

"I can't, Papa," she whispered. Even now she hated to disappoint him.

Move, she told herself. *This is a stupid place to die.* And yet a voice in her head said there were worse places. She would die here, in freedom, beneath the beginnings of dawn. She'd die after a worthy fight, not because some man had tired of her or required more from her than she could give. Better to die here by her own blade than with her face painted and her body swathed in false silks.

A hand seized her ankle. They'd climbed the crates. Why hadn't she heard them? Was she that far gone? They had her. Someone was turning her onto her back.

She slid the dagger from the sheath at her wrist. In the Barrel, a blade this sharp was known as kind steel. It meant a quick death. Better that than torture at the mercy of the Black Tips or the Razorgulls.

May the Saints receive me. She pressed the tip beneath her breast, between her ribs, an arrow to her heart. Then a hand gripped her wrist painfully, forcing her to drop the blade.

"Not just yet, Inej."

The rasp of stone on stone. Her eyes flew open. *Kaz.*

He bundled her into his arms and leaped down from the crates, landing roughly, his bad leg buckling.

She moaned as they hit the ground.

"Did we win?"

"I'm here, aren't I?"

He must be running. Her body jounced painfully against his chest with every lurching step. He needed his cane.

"I don't want to die."

"I'll do my best to make other arrangements for you."

She closed her eyes.

"Keep talking, Wraith. Don't slip away from me."

"But it's what I do best."

He clutched her tighter. "Just make it to the schooner. Open your damn eyes, Inej."

She tried. Her vision was blurring, but she could make out a pale, shiny scar on Kaz's neck, right beneath his jaw. She remembered the first time she'd seen him at the Menagerie. He paid Tante Heleen for information – stock tips, political pillow talk, anything the Menagerie's clients blabbed about when drunk or giddy on bliss. He never visited Heleen's girls, though plenty would have been happy to take him up to their rooms. They claimed he gave them the shivers, that his hands were permanently stained with blood beneath those black gloves, but she'd recognised the eagerness in their voices and the way they tracked him with their eyes.

One night, as he'd passed her in the parlour, she'd done a foolish thing, a reckless thing. "I can help you," she'd whispered. He'd glanced at her, then proceeded on his way as if she'd said nothing at all. The next morning, she'd been called to Tante Heleen's parlour. She'd been sure another beating was coming or worse, but instead Kaz Brekker had been standing there, leaning on his crow-head cane, waiting to change her life.

"I can help you," she said now.

"Help me with what?"

She couldn't remember. There was something she was supposed to tell him. It didn't matter any more.

"Talk to me, Wraith."

"You came back for me."

"I protect my investments."

Investments. "I'm glad I'm bleeding all over your shirt."

"I'll put it on your tab."

Now she remembered. He owed her an apology. "Say you're sorry."

"For what?"

"Just say it."

She didn't hear his reply. The world had grown very dark indeed.

13

KAZ

"Get us out of here," Kaz shouted as soon as he limped aboard the schooner with Inej in his arms. The sails were already trimmed, and they were on their way out of the harbour in moments, though not nearly as fast as he would have liked. He knew he should have tried to secure some Squallers for the journey, but they were hell to come by.

There was chaos on deck, people shouting and trying to get the schooner into open sea as quickly as possible.

"Specht!" he yelled at the man he'd chosen to captain the vessel, a sailor with a talent for knifework who had fallen on hard times and ended up stuck in the lower ranks of the Dregs. "Get your crew in shape before I start cracking skulls."

Specht saluted – then seemed to catch himself. He wasn't in the navy any longer, and Kaz wasn't a commanding officer.

The pain in Kaz's leg was terrible, the worst it had been since he'd first broken it falling off the roof of a bank near the Geldstraat. It was possible he'd fractured the bone again. Inej's weight wasn't helping, but when Jesper stepped into his path to offer help, Kaz shoved past him.

"Where's Nina?" Kaz snarled.

"Seeing to the wounded below. She already took care of me." Dimly Kaz registered the dried blood on Jesper's thigh. "Wylan got dinged during the fight. Let me help you—"

"Get out of my way," Kaz said, and plunged past him down the ramp that led belowdecks.

He found Nina tending to Wylan in a narrow cabin, her hands drifting over his arm, knitting the flesh of the bullet wound together. It was barely a graze.

"Move," Kaz demanded, and Wylan practically leaped from the table.

"I'm not finished—" began Nina. Then she caught sight of Inej. "Saints," she swore. "What happened?"

"Knife wound."

The cramped cabin was lit by several bright lanterns and a stash of clean bandages had been laid out on a shelf beside a bottle of camphor. Gently, Kaz placed Inej on the table that had been bolted to the deck.

"That's a lot of blood," Nina said on a low breath.

"Help her."

"Kaz, I'm a Heartrender, not a real Healer."

"She'll be dead by the time we find one. Get to work."

"You're in my light."

Kaz stepped back into the passageway. Inej lay perfectly still on the table, her luminous brown skin dull in the swaying lamplight.

He was alive because of Inej. They all were. They'd managed to fight their way out of a corner, but only because she'd prevented them from being surrounded. Kaz knew death. He could feel its presence on the ship now, looming over them, ready to take his Wraith. He was covered in her blood.

"Unless you can be useful, go away," Nina said without looking up at him. "You're making me nervous." He hesitated, then stomped back the way he'd come, stopping to purloin a clean shirt from another cabin. He shouldn't be this shaken up by a dock brawl, even a shoot-out, but he was. Something inside him felt frayed and raw. It was the same feeling he'd had as a boy, in those first desperate days after Jordie's death.

Say you're sorry. That was the last thing Inej had said to him. What had she wanted him to apologise for? There were so many possibilities. A thousand crimes. A thousand stupid jibes.

On deck, he took a deep breath of sea air, watching the harbour and Ketterdam fade from view on the horizon.

"What the hell just happened?" Jesper asked. He was leaning against the railing, his rifle beside him. hair dishevelled, pupils dilated. He seemed almost drunk, or like he'd just rolled out of someone's bed. He always had that look after a fight. Helvar was bent over the railing, vomiting. Not a sailor, apparently. At some point they'd need to shackle his legs again.

"We were ambushed," Wylan said from his perch on the forecastle deck. He had his sleeve pushed up and was running his fingers over the red spot where Nina had seen to his wound.

Jesper shot Wylan a withering glare. "Private tutors from the university, and that's what this kid comes up with? 'We were ambushed'?"

Wylan reddened. "Stop calling me *kid*. We're practically the same age."

"You're not going to like the other names I come up with for you. I *know* we were ambushed. That doesn't explain how they knew we would be there. Maybe Big Bolliger wasn't the only Black Tip spy in the Dregs."

"Geels doesn't have the brains or the resources to bite back this fast or this hard alone," Kaz said.

"You sure? Because it felt like a pretty big bite."

"Let's ask." Kaz limped over to where Rotty had helped him stash Oomen.

I stuck your Wraith, Oomen had giggled when Kaz had spotted him curled up on the ground. *I stuck her good.* Kaz had glanced at the blood on Oomen's thigh and said, *Looks like she got you, too.* But her aim had been off or Oomen wouldn't have been talking to anyone. He'd knocked the enforcer out and had Rotty retrieve him while he went to find Inej.

Now Helvar and Jesper dragged Oomen over to the rail, his hands bound.

"Stand him up."

With one huge hand, Helvar hauled Oomen to his feet.

Oomen grinned, his thatch of coarse white hair flat against his wide forehead.

"Why don't you tell me what brought so many Black Tips out in force tonight?" Kaz said.

"We owed you."

"A public brawl with guns out and thirty men packing? I don't think so."

Oomen snickered. "Geels doesn't like being bested."

"I could fit Geels' brains in the toe of my boot, and Big Bolliger was his only source inside the Dregs."

"Maybe he—"

Kaz interrupted him. "I want you to think real careful now, Oomen. Geels probably thinks you're dead, so there are no rules of barter here. I can do what I want with you."

Oomen spat in his face.

Kaz took a handkerchief from his coat pocket and carefully wiped his face clean. He thought of Inej lying still on the table, her slight weight in his arms.

"Hold him," he told Jesper and the Fjerdan. Kaz flicked his coat sleeve, and an oyster shucking knife appeared in his hand. At any given time he had at least two knives stashed somewhere in his clothes. He didn't even count this one, really – a tidy, wicked little blade.

He made a neat slash across Oomen's eye – from brow to cheekbone – and before Oomen could draw breath to cry out, he made a second cut in the opposite direction, a nearly perfect *X*. Now Oomen was screaming.

Kaz wiped the knife clean, returned it to his sleeve, and drove his gloved fingers into Oomen's eye socket. He shrieked and twitched as Kaz yanked out his eyeball, its base trailing a bloody root. Blood gushed over his face.

Kaz heard Wylan retching. He tossed the eyeball overboard and jammed his spit-soaked handkerchief into the socket where Oomen's eye had been. Then he grabbed Oomen's jaw, his gloves leaving red smears on the enforcer's chin. His actions were smooth, precise, as if he were dealing cards at the Crow Club or picking an easy lock, but his rage felt hot and mad and unfamiliar. Something within him had torn loose.

"Listen to me," he hissed, his face inches from Oomen's. "You have two choices. You tell me what I want to know, and we drop you at our next port with your pockets full of enough coin to get you sewn up and buy you passage back to Kerch. Or I take the other eye, and I repeat this conversation with a blind man."

"It was just a job," babbled Oomen. "Geels got five thousand *kruge* to bring the Black Tips out in force. We pulled in some Razorgulls, too."

"Then why not more men? Why not double your odds?"

"You were supposed to be on the boat when it blew! We were just supposed to take care of the stragglers."

"Who hired you?"

Oomen wavered, sucking on his lip, snot running from his nose.

"Don't make me ask again, Oomen," Kaz said quietly. "Whoever it was can't protect you now."

"He'll kill me."

"And I'll make you wish for death, so you have to weigh those options."

"Pekka Rollins," Oomen sobbed. "It was Pekka Rollins!"

Even through his own shock, Kaz registered the effect of the name on Jesper and Wylan. Helvar didn't know enough to be intimidated.

"Saints," groaned Jesper. "We are so screwed."

"Is Rollins leading the crew himself?" Kaz asked Oomen.

"What crew?"

"To Fjerda."

"I don't know about no crew. We were just supposed to stop you from getting out of the harbour."

"I see."

"I need a medik. Can you take me to a medik now?"

"Of course," said Kaz. "Right this way." He took Oomen by the lapels and hoisted him off his feet, bracing his body against the railing.

"I told you what you wanted!" Oomen screamed, struggling. "I did what you asked!"

Despite Oomen's knobby build, he was deceptively strong – farm strong like Jesper. He'd probably grown up in the fields.

Kaz leaned in so that no one else could hear it when he said, "My Wraith would counsel mercy. But thanks to you, she's not here to plead your case."

Without another word, he tipped Oomen into the sea.

"No!" Wylan shouted, leaning over the railing, his face pale, stunned eyes tracking Oomen in the waves. The enforcer's pleas were still audible as his maimed face faded from view.

"You . . . you said if he helped you—"

"Do you want to go over, too?" asked Kaz.

Wylan took a deep breath as if sucking in courage and sputtered, "You won't throw me overboard. You need me."

Why do people keep saying that? "Maybe," said Kaz. "But I'm not in a very rational mood."

Jesper set his hand on Wylan's shoulder. "Let it go."

"It's not right—"

"Wylan," Jesper said, giving him a little shake. "Maybe your tutors didn't cover this lesson, but you do not argue with a man covered in blood and a knife up his sleeve."

Wylan pressed his lips into a thin line. Kaz couldn't tell if the kid was frightened or furious, and he didn't much care. Helvar stood silent sentinel, observing it all, looking seasick green beneath his blond beard.

Kaz turned to Jesper. "Fit Helvar with some shackles to keep him honest," he said as he headed below. "And get me clean clothes and fresh water."

"Since when am I your valet?"

"Man with a knife, remember?" he said over his shoulder.

"Man with a gun!" Jesper called after him.

Kaz replied with a time-saving gesture that relied heavily on his middle finger and disappeared belowdecks. He wanted a hot bath and a bottle of brandy, but he'd settle for being alone and free of the stink of blood for a while.

Pekka Rollins. The name rattled through his head like gunfire. It always came back to Pekka Rollins, the man who had taken everything from him. The man who now stood between Kaz and the biggest haul any crew had ever attempted. Would Rollins send someone in his place or lead the crew to nab Bo Yul-Bayur himself?

In the dim confines of his cabin, Kaz whispered the words "Brick by brick." Killing Pekka Rollins had always been tempting, but that wasn't enough. Kaz wanted Rollins brought low. He wanted him to suffer the way Kaz had, the way Jordie had. And snatching thirty million *kruge* right out of Pekka Rollins' grubby hands was a very good way to start. Maybe Inej was right. Maybe fate did bother with people like him.

14

NINA

In the cramped little surgeon's cabin, Nina tried to put Inej's body back together, but she hadn't been trained for this type of work.

For the first two years of their education in Ravka's capital, all Grisha Corporalki studied together, took the same classes, performed the same autopsies. But then their training diverged. Healers learned the intricate work of healing wounds, while Heartrenders became soldiers – experts at doing damage, not undoing it. It was a different way of thinking about what was essentially the same power. But the living asked more of you than the dead. A killing stroke took decision, clarity of intent. Healing was slow, deliberate, a rhythm that required thoughtful study of each small choice. The jobs she'd done for Kaz over the last year helped, and in a way so had her work carefully altering moods and tailoring faces at the White Rose.

But looking down at Inej, Nina wished her own school training hadn't been so abbreviated. The Ravkan civil war had erupted when she was still a student at the Little Palace, and she and her classmates had been forced to go into hiding.

When the fighting had ended and the dust had settled, King Nikolai had been anxious to get the few remaining Grisha soldiers trained and in the field, so Nina had spent only six months in advanced classes before she'd been sent out on her first mission. At the time, she'd been thrilled. Now she would have been grateful for even another week of school.

Inej was lithe, all muscle and fine bones, built like an acrobat. The knife had entered beneath her left arm. It had been a very close thing. A little deeper and the blade would have pierced the apex of the heart.

Nina knew that if she simply sealed Inej's skin the way she'd done with Wylan, the girl would just continue to bleed internally, so she'd tried to stop the bleeding from the inside out. She thought she'd managed it well enough, but Inej had lost a lot of blood, and Nina had no idea what to do about that. She'd heard some Healers could match one person's blood to another's, but if it was done incorrectly, it was as good as poisoning the patient. The process was far beyond her.

She finished closing the wound, then covered Inej with a light wool blanket. For now, all Nina could do was monitor her pulse and breathing. As she settled Inej's arms beneath the blanket, Nina saw the scarred flesh on the inside of her forearm. She brushed her thumb gently over the bumps and ridges. It must have been the peacock feather, the tattoo borne by members of the Menagerie, the House of Exotics. Whoever had removed it had done an ugly job of it.

Curious, Nina pushed up Inej's other sleeve. The skin there was smooth and unmarked. Inej hadn't taken on the crow and cup, the tattoo carried by any full member of the Dregs. Alliances shifted this way and that in the Barrel, but your gang was your family, the only protection that mattered. Nina herself bore two tattoos. The one on her left forearm was for the House of the White Rose. The one that counted was on her right: a crow trying to drink from a near empty goblet. It told the world she belonged to the Dregs, that to trifle with her was to risk their vengeance.

Inej had been with the Dregs longer than Nina and yet no tattoo. Strange. She was one of the most valued members of the gang, and it was clear Kaz trusted her – as much as someone like Kaz could. Nina thought of the look on his face when he'd set Inej down on the table. He was the same Kaz – cold, rude, impossible – but beneath all that anger, she thought she'd seen something else, too. Or maybe she was just a romantic.

She had to laugh at herself. She wouldn't wish love on anyone. It was the guest you welcomed and then couldn't be rid of.

Nina brushed Inej's straight black hair back from her face. "Please be okay," she whispered. She hated the frail waver of her voice in the cabin. She didn't sound like a Grisha soldier or a hardened member of the Dregs. She sounded like a little girl who didn't know what she was doing. And that was exactly how she felt. Her training *had* been too short. She'd been sent out on her first mission too soon. Zoya had said as much at the time, but Nina had begged to go, and they'd needed her, so the older Grisha had relented.

Zoya Nazyalensky – a powerful Squaller, gorgeous to the point of absurdity, and capable of reducing Nina's confidence to ash with a single raised brow. Nina had worshipped her. *Reckless, foolish, easily distracted.* Zoya had called her all those things and worse.

"You were right, Zoya. Happy now?"

"Giddy," said Jesper from the doorway.

Nina started and looked up to see him rocking back and forth on the balls of his feet. "Who's Zoya?" he asked.

Nina slumped back in her chair. "No one. A member of the Grisha Triumvirate."

"Fancy. The ones who run the Second Army?"

"What's left of it." Ravka's Grisha soldiers had been

decimated during the war. Some had fled. Most had been killed. Nina rubbed her tired eyes. "Do you know the best way to find Grisha who don't want to be found?"

Jesper scrubbed the back of his neck, touched his hands to his guns, returned to his neck. He always seemed to be in motion. "Never gave it much thought," he said.

"Look for miracles and listen to bedtime stories." Follow the tales of witches and goblins, and unexplained happenings. Sometimes they were just superstition. But often there was truth at the heart of local legends – people who had been born with gifts that their countries didn't understand. Nina had become very good at sniffing out those stories.

"Seems to me if they don't want to be found, you should just let them be."

Nina cast him a dark glance. "The *drüskelle* won't let them be. They hunt Grisha everywhere."

"Are they all charmers like Matthias?"

"And worse."

"I need to find his leg shackles. Kaz gives me all the fun jobs."

"Want to trade?" Nina asked wearily.

The frenetic energy of Jesper's lanky frame seemed to drop away. He went as still as Nina had ever seen him, and his gaze focused on Inej for the first time since he'd entered the little cabin. *He was avoiding it*, Nina realised. *He didn't want to look at her*. The blankets shifted slightly with her shallow breaths. When Jesper spoke, his voice was taut, the strings of an instrument tuned to a too-sharp key.

"She can't die," he said. "Not this way."

Nina peered at Jesper, puzzled. "Not what way?"

"She can't die," he repeated.

Nina felt a surge of frustration. She was torn between wanting to hug Jesper tight and scream at him that she was trying. "Saints, Jesper," she said. "I'm doing my best."

He shifted, and his body seemed to come back alive.

"Sorry," he said a bit sheepishly. He clapped her awkwardly on the shoulder. "You're doing great."

Nina sighed. "Not convincing. Why don't you go chain up a giant blond?"

Jesper saluted and ducked out of the cabin.

Annoying as he was, Nina was almost tempted to call him back. With Jesper gone, there was nothing but Zoya's voice in her head and the reminder that her best wasn't good enough.

Inej's skin felt too cool to the touch. Nina laid a hand on each of the girl's shoulders and tried to improve her blood flow, raising her body temperature very slightly.

She hadn't been completely honest with Jesper. The Grisha Triumvirate hadn't just wanted to save Grisha from Fjerdan witchhunters. They'd sent missions to the Wandering Isle and Novyi Zem because Ravka needed soldiers. They'd sought out Grisha who might be living in secret and tried to convince them to take up residence in Ravka and enter service to the crown.

Nina had been too young to fight in the Ravkan civil war, and she'd been desperate to be part of the rebuilding of the Second Army. It was her gift for languages – Shu, Kaelish, Suli, Fjerdan, even some Zemeni – that finally overcame Zoya's reservations. She agreed to let Nina accompany her and a team of Grisha Examiners to the Wandering Isle, and despite all of Zoya's misgivings, Nina had been a success. Disguised as a traveller, she would slip into taverns and coach houses to eavesdrop on conversations and chat with the locals, then bring the peasant talk back to camp.

If you're going to Maroch Glen, make sure to travel by day. Troubled spirits walk those lands – storms erupt out of nowhere.

The Witch of Fells is real, all right. My second cousin went to her with an outbreak of tsifil *and swears he's never been healthier. What do you mean he's not right in the head? More right than you'll ever be.*

They'd found two Grisha families hiding out in the supposed fairy caves of Istamere, and they'd saved a mother, father, and two boys – Inferni, who could control fire – from a mob in Fenford. They even raided a slaving ship near the port in Leflin. Once the refugees had been sorted, those without powers had been offered safe passage back home. Those whose powers had been confirmed by a Grisha Examiner were offered asylum in Ravka. Only the old Heartrender known as the Witch of Fells chose to remain. "If they want my blood, let them come for it," she'd laughed. "I'll take some of theirs in return."

Nina spoke Kaelish like a native and loved the challenge of taking on a new identity in every town. But for all their triumphs, Zoya hadn't been pleased. "Being good with languages isn't enough," she'd scolded. "You need to learn to be less . . . big. You're too loud, too effusive, too memorable. You take too many risks."

"Zoya," said the Examiner they were travelling with. "Go easy." He was a living amplifier. Dead, his bones would have served to heighten Grisha power, no different from the shark teeth or bear claws that other Grisha wore. But alive, he was invaluable to their mission, trained to use his amplifier gifts to sense Grisha power through touch.

Most of the time, Zoya was protective of him, but now her deep blue eyes flattened to slits. "My teachers didn't go easy on me. If she ends up chased through the woods by a mob of peasants, will you tell them to go easy?"

Nina had stomped off, pride smarting, embarrassed by the tears filling her eyes. Zoya had shouted at her not to go past the ridge, but she'd ignored her, eager to be as far away from the Squaller as she could get – and walked right into a *drüskelle* camp. Six blond boys all speaking Fjerdan, clustered on a cliff above the shore. They'd made no campfire and were dressed as Kaelish peasants, but she'd known what they were right away.

They'd stared at her for a long moment, lit only by silvery moonlight.

"Oh thank goodness," she'd said in lilting Kaelish. "I'm travelling with my family, and I got turned around in the woods. Can one of you help me find the road?"

"I think she's lost," one of them translated in Fjerdan for the others.

Another rose, a lantern in his hand. He was taller than the others, and all her instincts screamed at her to run as he drew closer. *They don't know what you are*, she reminded herself. *You're just a nice Kaelish girl, lost in the woods. Don't do anything stupid. Lead him away from the others, then take him down.*

He raised his lantern, the light shining over both of their faces. His hair was long and burnished gold, and his pale blue eyes glinted like ice beneath a winter sun. *He looks like a painting*, she thought, a Saint wrought in gold leaf on the walls of a church, born to wield a sword of fire.

"What are you doing out here?" he asked in Fjerdan.

She feigned confusion. "I'm sorry," she said in Kaelish. "I don't understand. I'm lost."

He lunged towards her. She didn't stop to think, but simply reacted, raising her hands to attack. He was too quick. Without hesitation, he dropped the lantern and seized her wrists, slamming her hands together, making it impossible for her to use her power.

"*Drüsje*," he said with satisfaction. *Witch*. He had a wolf's smile.

The attack had been a test. A girl lost in the woods cowered; she reached for a knife or a gun. She didn't try to use her hands to stop a man's heart. *Reckless. Impulsive.*

This was why Zoya hadn't wanted to bring her. Properly trained Grisha didn't make these mistakes. Nina had been a fool, but she didn't have to be a traitor. She pleaded with them in Kaelish, not Ravkan, and she didn't cry out for help – not when they bound her hands, not when they threatened her, not when they tossed her in a rowboat like a bag of millet. She wanted to scream her terror, bring Zoya running, beg for someone to save her, but she wouldn't risk the others' lives. The *drüskelle* rowed her to a ship anchored off the coast and threw her into a cage belowdecks full of other captive Grisha. That was when the real horror had begun.

Night blended into day in the dank belly of the ship. The Grisha prisoners' hands were kept tightly bound to keep them from using their power. They were fed tough bread crawling with weevils – only enough to keep them alive – and had to ration fresh water carefully since they never knew when they might have it next. They'd been given no place to relieve themselves, and the stink of bodies and worse was nearly unbearable.

Occasionally the ship would drop anchor, and the *drüskelle* would return with another captive. The Fjerdans would stand outside their cages, eating and drinking, mocking their filthy clothes and the way they smelled. As bad as it was, the fear of what might await them was much more frightening – the inquisitors at the Ice Court, torture, and inevitably death. Nina dreamed of being burned alive on a pyre and woke up screaming. Nightmare and fear and the delirium of hunger tangled together so that she stopped being certain of what was real and what wasn't.

Then one day, the *drüskelle* had crowded into the hold dressed in freshly pressed uniforms of black and silver, the white wolf's head on their sleeves. They'd fallen into orderly ranks and stood at attention as their commander entered. Like all of them, he was tall, but he wore a tidy beard, and his long blond hair showed grey at the temples. He walked the length of the hold, then came to a halt in front of the prisoners.

"How many?" he asked.

"Fifteen," replied the burnished gold boy who had captured her. It was the first time she had seen him in the hold.

The commanding officer cleared his throat and clasped his hands behind his back. "I am Jarl Brum."

A tremor of fear passed through Nina, and she felt it reverberate through the Grisha in the cell, a warning call none of them were free to heed.

In school, Nina had been obsessed with the *drüskelle*. They'd been the creatures of her nightmares with their white wolves and their cruel knives and the horses they bred for battle with Grisha. It was why she'd studied to perfect her Fjerdan and her knowledge of their culture. It had been a way of preparing herself for them, for the battle to come. And Jarl Brum was the worst of them.

He was a legend, the monster waiting in the dark. The *drüskelle* had existed for hundreds of years, but under Brum's leadership, their force had doubled in size and become infinitely more deadly. He had changed their training, developed new techniques for rooting out Grisha in Fjerda, infiltrated Ravka's borders, and begun pursuing rogue Grisha in other lands, even hunting down slaving ships, 'liberating' Grisha captives with the sole purpose of clapping them back in chains and sending them to Fjerda for trial and execution. She'd imagined facing Brum one day as an avenging warrior or a clever spy. She hadn't pictured herself confronting him caged and starving, hands bound, dressed in rags.

Brum must have known the effect his name would have. He waited a long moment before he said in excellent Kaelish, "What stands before you is the next generation of *drüskelle*, the holy order charged with protecting the sovereign nation of Fjerda by eradicating your kind. They will bring you to Fjerda to face trial and so earn the rank of officer. They are the strongest and best of our kind."

Bullies, Nina thought.

"When we reach Fjerda, you will be interrogated and tried for your crimes."

"Please," said one of the prisoners. "I've done nothing. I'm a farmer. I've done you no harm."

"You are an insult to Djel," Brum replied. "A blight on this earth. You speak peace, but what of your children to whom you may pass on this demonic power? What about their children? I save my mercy for the helpless men and women mowed down by Grisha abominations."

He faced the *drüskelle*. "Good work, lads," he said in Fjerdan. "We sail for Djerholm immediately."

The *drüskelle* seemed ready to burst with pride. As soon as Brum exited the hold, they were knocking each other affectionately on the shoulders, laughing in relief and satisfaction.

"Good work is right," one said in Fjerdan. "Fifteen Grisha to deliver to the Ice Court!"

"If this doesn't earn us our teeth—"

"You know it will."

"Good, I'm sick of shaving every morning."

"I'm going to grow a beard down to my navel."

Then one of them reached through the bars and snatched Nina up by her hair. "I like this one, still nice and round. Maybe we should open that cage door and hose her down."

The boy with the burnished hair smacked his comrade's hand away. "What's wrong with you?" he said, the first time he'd spoken since Brum had vanished. The brief rush of gratitude she'd felt withered when he said, "Would you fornicate with a dog?"

"What does the dog look like?"

The others roared with laughter as they headed above. The golden one who'd likened her to an animal was the last to go, and just as he was about to step into the passage, she said in crisp, perfect Fjerdan, "What crimes?"

He stilled, and when he'd looked back at her, his blue eyes had been bright with hate. She refused to flinch.

"How do you come to speak my language? Did you serve on Ravka's northern border?"

"I'm Kaelish," she lied, "and I can speak any language."

"More witchcraft."

"If by witchcraft, you mean the arcane practice of reading. Your commander said we'd be tried for our crimes. I want you to tell me just what crime I've committed."

"You'll be tried for espionage and crimes against the people."

"We are not criminals," said a Fabrikator in halting Fjerdan from his place on the floor. He'd been there the longest and was too weak to rise. "We are ordinary people – farmers, teachers."

Not me, Nina thought grimly. *I'm a soldier.*

"You'll have a trial," said the *drüskelle*. "You'll be treated more fairly than your kind deserve."

"How many Grisha are ever found innocent?" Nina asked.

The Fabrikator groaned. "Don't provoke him. You will not sway his mind."

But she gripped the bars with her bound hands and said, "How many? How many have you sent to the pyre?"

He turned his back on her.

"Wait!"

He ignored her.

"Wait! Please! Just . . . just some fresh water. Would you treat your dogs like this?"

He paused, his hand on the door. "I shouldn't have said that. Dogs know loyalty, at least. Fidelity to the pack. It is an insult to the dog to call you one."

I'm going to feed you to a pack of hungry hounds, Nina thought. But all she said was, "Water. Please."

He vanished into the passage. She heard him climb the ladder, and the hatch closed with a loud bang.

"Don't waste your breath on him," the Fabrikator counselled. "He will show you no kindness."

But a short while later the *drüskelle* returned with a tin cup and a bucket of clean water. He'd set it down inside the cell and slammed the bars shut without a word. Nina helped the Fabrikator drink, then gulped down a cup herself. Her hands were shaking so badly, half of it sloshed down her blouse. The Fjerdan turned away, and with pleasure, Nina saw she'd embarrassed him.

"I'd kill for a bath," she taunted. "You could wash me."

"Don't talk to me," he growled, already stalking towards the door.

He hadn't returned, and they'd gone without fresh water for the next three days. But when the storm hit, that tin cup had saved her life.

Nina's chin dipped, and she jerked awake. Had she nodded off?

Matthias was standing in the passage outside the cabin. He filled the doorway, far too tall to be comfortable belowdecks. How long had he been watching her? Quickly, Nina checked Inej's pulse and breathing, relieved to find that she seemed to be stable for now.

"Was I sleeping?" she asked.

"Dozing."

She stretched, trying to blink away her exhaustion. "But not snoring?" He said nothing, just watched her with those ice chip eyes. "They let you have a razor?"

His shackled hands went to his freshly shaved jaw. "Jesper did it." Jesper must have seen to Matthias' hair, too. The tufts of blond that had grown raggedly from his scalp had been trimmed down. It was still too short, bare golden fuzz over skin that showed cuts and bruises from his last fight in Hellgate.

He must be happy to be free of the beard, though, Nina thought. Until a *drüskelle* had accomplished a mission on his own and been granted officer status, he was required to remain clean-shaven. If Matthias had brought Nina to face trial at the Ice Court, he would have been granted that permission. He would have worn the silver wolf's head that marked an officer of the *drüskelle*. It made her sick to think of it. *Congratulations on your recent advancement to murderer of rank.* The thought helped remind her just who she was dealing with. She sat up straighter, chin lifting.

"*Hje marden*, Matthias?" she asked.

"Don't," he said.

"You'd prefer I spoke Kerch?"

"I don't want to hear my language from your mouth." His eyes flicked to her lips, and she felt an unwelcome flush.

With vindictive pleasure, she said in Fjerdan, "But you always liked the way I spoke your tongue. You said it sounded pure." It was true. He'd loved her accent – the vowels of a princess, courtesy of her teachers at the Little Palace.

"Don't press me, Nina," he said. Matthias' Kerch was ugly, brutal, the guttural accent of thieves and murderers that he'd met in prison. "That pardon is a dream that's hard to hold on to. The memory of your pulse fading beneath my fingers is far easier to bring to mind."

"Try me," she said, her anger flaring. She was sick of his threats. "My hands aren't pinned now, Helvar." She curled her fingertips, and Matthias gasped as his heart began to race.

"Witch," he spat, clutching his chest.

"Surely you can do better than that. You must have a hundred names for me by now."

"A thousand," he grunted as sweat broke out on his brow.

She relaxed her fingers, feeling suddenly embarrassed. What was she doing? Punishing him? Toying with him? He had every right to hate her.

"Go away, Matthias. I have a patient to see to." She focused on checking Inej's body temperature.

"Will she live?"

"Do you care?"

"Of course I care. She's a human being."

She heard the unspoken end to that sentence. She's a human being – *unlike you*. The Fjerdans didn't believe the Grisha were human. They weren't even on par with animals, but something low and demonic, a blight on the world, an abomination.

She lifted a shoulder. "I don't know, really. I did my best, but my gifts lie elsewhere."

"Kaz asked you if the White Rose would send a delegation to Hringkälla."

"You know the White Rose?"

"West Stave is a favourite subject of conversation in Hellgate."

Nina paused. Then, without saying a word, she pushed up the sleeve of her shirt. Two roses intertwined on the inside of her forearm. She could have explained what she'd done there, that she'd never made her living on her back, but it was none of his business what she did or didn't do. Let him believe what he liked.

"You chose to work there?"

"*Chose* is a bit of a stretch, but yes."

"Why? Why would you remain in Kerch?"

She rubbed her eyes. "I couldn't leave you in Hellgate."

"You *put* me in Hellgate."

"It was a mistake, Matthias."

Rage ignited in his eyes, the calm veneer dropping away. "A *mistake*? I saved your life, and you accused me of being a slaver."

"Yes," Nina said. "And I've spent most of this last year trying to find a way to set things right."

"Has a true word ever left your lips?"

She sagged back wearily in her chair. "I've never lied to you. I never will."

"The first words you said to me were a lie. Spoken in Kaelish, as I recall."

"Spoken right before you captured me and stuffed me in a cage. Was that the time for speaking truths?"

"I shouldn't blame you. You can't help yourself. It's your nature to dissemble." He peered at her neck. "Your bruises are gone."

"I removed them. Does that bother you?"

Matthias said nothing, but she saw a glimmer of shame move over his face. Matthias had always fought his own decency. To become a *drüskelle*, he'd had to kill the good things inside him. But the boy he should have been was always there, and she'd begun to see the truth of him in the days they'd spent together after the shipwreck. She wanted to believe that boy was still there, locked away, despite her betrayal and whatever he'd endured at Hellgate.

Looking at him now, she couldn't be sure. Maybe this was the truth of him, and the image she'd held on to this last year had been an illusion.

"I need to see to Inej," she said, eager to have him gone.

He didn't leave. Instead he said, "Did you think of me at all, Nina? Did I trouble your sleep?"

She shrugged. "A Corporalnik can sleep whenever she likes." Though she couldn't control her dreams.

"Sleep is a luxury at Hellgate. It's a danger. But when I slept, I dreamed of you."

Her head snapped up.

"That's right," he said. "Every time I closed my eyes."

"What happened in the dreams?" she asked, eager for an answer, but fearing it, too.

"Horrible things. The worst kinds of torture. You drowned me slowly. You burned my heart from my chest. You blinded me."

"I was a monster."

"A monster, a maiden, a sylph of the ice. You kissed me, whispered stories in my ear. You sang to me and held me as I slept. Your laugh chased me into waking."

"You always hated my laugh."

"I loved your laugh, Nina. And your fierce warrior's heart. I might have loved you, too."

Might have. Once. Before she had betrayed him. Those words carved an ache into her chest.

She knew she shouldn't speak, but she couldn't help herself. "And what did you do, Matthias? What did you do to me in your dreams?"

The ship listed gently. The lanterns swayed. His eyes were blue fire. "Everything," he said, as he turned to go. "Everything."

15

MATTHIAS

When he emerged on deck, Matthias had to head straight for the railing. All of these canal rats and slum dwellers had easily found their sea legs, used to hopping from boat to boat on the waterways of Ketterdam. Only the soft one, Wylan, seemed to be struggling. He looked as poorly as Matthias felt.

It was better in the fresh air, where he could keep an eye on the horizon. He'd managed sea voyages as a *drüskelle*, but he'd always felt more comfortable on land, on the ice. It was humiliating to have these foreigners see him vomit over the railing for the third time in as many hours.

At least Nina wasn't here to witness that particular shame. He kept thinking of her in that cabin, ministering to the bronze girl, all concern and kindness. And fatigue. She'd looked so weary. *It was a mistake*, she'd said. To have him branded as a slaver, tossed onto a Kerch ship, and thrown in jail? She claimed she'd tried to set things right. But even if that were true, what did it matter? Her kind had no honour. She'd proven that.

Someone had brewed coffee, and he saw the crew drinking

it from copper mugs with ceramic lids. The thought to bring Nina a cup entered his head, and he crushed it. He didn't need to tend to her or tell Brekker that she could use relief. He clenched his fingers, looking at the scabbed knuckles. She had seeded such weakness in him.

Brekker gestured Matthias over to where he, Jesper, and Wylan had gathered on the forecastle deck to examine plans of the Ice Court away from the eyes and ears of the crew. The sight of those drawings was like a knife to his heart. The walls, the gates, the guards. They should have dissuaded these fools, but apparently he was as much a fool as the rest of them.

"Why aren't there names on anything?" Brekker asked, gesturing at the plans.

"I don't know Fjerdan, and we need the details right," Wylan said. "Helvar should do it." He drew back when he saw Matthias' expression. "I'm just doing my job. Stop glaring at me."

"No," Matthias growled.

"Here," Kaz said, tossing him a tiny, clear disk that winked in the sun. The demon had propped himself on a barrel and was leaning against the mast, his bad leg elevated on a coil of rope, that cursed walking stick resting on his lap. Matthias liked to imagine breaking it into splinters and feeding them to Brekker one by one.

"What is it?"

"One of Raske's new inventions."

Wylan's head popped up. "I thought he did demo work."

"He does everything," said Jesper.

"Wedge it between your back teeth," Kaz said as he handed the disks to the others. "But don't bite dow—"

Wylan started to sputter and cough, clawing at his mouth. A transparent film had spread over his lips; it bulged like a frog's gullet as he tried to breathe, eyes darting left and right in panic.

Jesper started laughing, and Kaz just shook his head. "I told you not to bite down, Wylan. Breathe through your nose."

The boy took deep inhales, nostrils flaring.

"Easy," said Jesper. "You're going to make yourself pass out."

"What is this?" asked Matthias, still holding the tiny disk in his palm.

Kaz pushed his deep into his mouth, wiggling it between his teeth. "*Baleen*. I'd planned to save these, but after that ambush, I don't know what kind of trouble we may run into on the open sea. If you go over and can't come up for air, wiggle it free and bite down. It will buy you ten minutes of breathing time. Less if you panic," he said with a meaningful look at Wylan. He gave the boy another piece of *baleen*. "Be careful with that one." Then he tapped the Ice Court plans.

"Names, Helvar. All of them."

Reluctantly, Matthias picked up the pen and ink Wylan had laid out and began to scratch in the names of the buildings and surrounding roads. Somehow doing it himself felt even more treasonous. Part of him wondered if he could simply find a way to separate from the group once they got there, reveal their location, and thereby win his way back into the good graces of his government. Would anyone at the Ice Court even recognise him? He was probably believed to be dead, drowned in the shipwreck that had killed his closest friends and Commander Brum. He had no proof of his true identity. He would be a stranger who had no business in the Ice Court, and by the time he got anyone to listen—

"You're holding back," Brekker said, his dark eyes trained on Matthias.

Matthias ignored the shiver that passed through him. Sometimes it was like the demon could read minds. "I'm telling you what I know."

"Your conscience is interfering with your memory. Remember the terms of our deal, Helvar."

"All right," Matthias said, his anger rising. "You want my expertise? Your plan won't work."

"You don't even know my plan."

"In through the prison, out through the embassy?"

"As a start."

"It can't be done. The prison sector is completely isolated from the rest of the Ice Court. It isn't connected to the embassy. There's no way to reach it from there."

"It has a roof, doesn't it?"

"You can't get to the roof," Matthias said with satisfaction. "The *drüskelle* spend three months working with Grisha prisoners and guards as part of our training. I've been in the prison, and there's no access to the roof for exactly that reason – if someone manages to get out of his cell, we don't want him running around the Ice Court. The prison is totally sealed off from the other two sectors in the outer circle. Once you're in, you're in."

"There's always a way out." Kaz pulled the prison plan from the stack. "Five floors, right? Processing area, and four levels of cells. So what's here? In the basement?"

"Nothing. A laundry and the incinerator."

"The incinerator."

"Yes, where they burn the convicts' clothes when they arrive. It's a plague precaution but—" As soon as the words left Matthias'mouth he understood what Brekker had in mind. "Sweet Djel, you want us to climb six storeys up an incinerator shaft?"

"When does the incinerator run?"

"If I remember right, early morning, but even without the heat, we—"

"He doesn't mean for *us* to climb it," said Nina, emerging from belowdecks.

Kaz sat up straighter. "Who's watching Inej?"

"Rotty," she said. "I'll go back in a minute. I just needed some air. And don't feign concern for Inej when you're planning to send her climbing up six storeys of chimney with only a rope and a prayer."

"The Wraith can manage it."

"The *Wraith* is a sixteen-year-old girl currently lying unconscious on a table. She may not even survive the night."

"She will," said Kaz, and something savage flashed in his eyes. Matthias suspected that Brekker would drag the girl back from hell himself if he had to.

Jesper picked up his rifle, running a soft cloth over it. "Why are we talking about scaling chimneys when we've got a bigger problem?"

"And what's that?" Kaz asked, though Matthias had the distinct impression he knew.

"We have no business going after Bo Yul-Bayur if Pekka Rollins is involved."

"Who is Pekka Rollins?" Matthias asked, turning the ridiculous syllables over in his mouth. Kerch names had no dignity to them. He knew that the man was a gang leader and that he lined his pockets with proceeds from the Hellshow. That was bad enough, but Matthias sensed there was more.

Wylan shuddered, pulling at the gummy substance on his lips. "Only the biggest, baddest operator in all of Ketterdam. He has money we don't have, connections we don't have, and probably a head start."

Jesper nodded. "For once, Wylan is making sense. If by some miracle we do manage to spring Bo Yul-Bayur before Rollins does, once he finds out we're the ones who beat him to it, we're all dead men."

"Pekka Rollins is a Barrel boss," Kaz said. "No more, no less. Stop making him out to be some kind of immortal."

There's something else going on here, thought Matthias. Brekker had lost the thrum of violence that seemed to drive him earlier, when he'd murdered Oomen. But there was still a lingering intensity in his words. Matthias felt sure that Kaz Brekker hated Pekka Rollins, and it wasn't just because he'd blown up their ship and hired thugs to shoot at them. This had the feel of old wounds and bad blood.

Jesper leaned back and said, "You think Per Haskell is going to back you when he finds out you crossed Pekka Rollins? You think the old man wants that war?"

Kaz shook his head, and Matthias saw real frustration there. "Pekka Rollins didn't come into this world dressed in velvet and rolling in *kruge*. You're still thinking small. The way Per Haskell does, the way men like Rollins want you to. We pull off this job and divvy up that haul, *we'll* be the legends of the Barrel. We'll be the crew that *beat* Pekka Rollins."

"Maybe we should forget approaching from the north," said Wylan. "If Pekka's crew has a head start, we should head straight to Djerholm."

"The harbour will be crawling with security," Kaz said. "Not to mention all the usual customs agents and lawmen."

"The south? Through Ravka?"

"That border is locked down tight," Nina said.

"It's a big border," said Matthias.

"But there's no way to know where it's most vulnerable," she replied. "Unless you have some magical knowledge about which watchtowers and outposts are active. Besides, if we enter from Ravka, we have to contend with Ravkans *and* Fjerdans."

What she said made sense, but it unnerved him. In Fjerda women didn't talk this way, didn't speak of military or strategic matters. But Nina had always been like that.

"We enter from the north as planned," Kaz said.

Jesper knocked his head against the hull and cast his eyes heavenward. "Fine. But if Pekka Rollins kills us all, I'm going to get Wylan's ghost to teach my ghost how to play the flute just so that I can annoy the hell out of your ghost."

Brekker's lips quirked. "I'll just hire Matthias' ghost to kick your ghost's ass."

"My ghost won't associate with your ghost," Matthias said primly, and then wondered if the sea air was rotting his brain.

PART 3

HEARTSICK

16

INEJ

$\mathcal{E}$verything hurt. And why was the room moving?

Inej came awake slowly, her thoughts jumbled. She remembered the thrust of Oomen's knife, climbing the crates, people shouting as she dangled from the tips of her fingers. *Come on down, Wraith.* But Kaz had returned for her, to rescue his investment. They must have made it onto the *Ferolind*.

She tried to roll over, but the pain was too intense, so she settled for turning her head. Nina was drowsing on a stool tucked into the corner by the table, Inej's hand grasped loosely in her own.

"Nina," she croaked. Her throat felt like it was coated in wool.

Nina jolted awake. "I'm up!" she blurted, then peered blearily at Inej. "You're awake." She sat up straighter. "Oh, Saints, you're awake!"

And then Nina burst out crying.

Inej tried to sit up, but could barely lift her head.

"No, no," Nina said. "Don't try to move, just rest."

"Are you okay?"

Nina started to laugh through her tears. "I'm fine. You're the one who got stabbed. I don't know what's wrong with me. It's just so much easier to kill people than take care of them." Inej blinked, and then they both started laughing. "Owwww," groaned Inej. "Don't make me laugh. That feels awful."

Nina winced. "How *do* you feel?"

"Sore, but not terrible. Thirsty."

Nina offered her a tin cup full of cold water. "It's fresh. We had rain yesterday."

Inej sipped carefully, letting Nina hold her head up. "How long was I out?"

"Three days, almost four. Jesper is driving us all crazy. I don't think I've seen him sit still for more than two minutes together." She stood up abruptly. "I need to tell Kaz you're awake! We thought—"

"Wait," Inej said, grabbing for Nina's hand. "Just . . . can we not tell him right away?"

Nina sat back down, her face puzzled. "Sure, but—"

"Just for tonight." She paused. "Is it night?"

"Yes. Just past midnight, actually."

"Do we know who came after us at the harbour?"

"Pekka Rollins. He hired the Black Tips and the Razorgulls to keep us from getting out of Fifth Harbour."

"How did he know where we were leaving from?"

"We're not sure yet."

"I saw Oomen—"

"Oomen's dead. Kaz killed him."

"He did?"

"Kaz killed a lot of people. Rotty saw him go after the Black Tips who had you up on the crates. I believe his exact words were, 'There was enough blood to paint a barn red.'"

Inej closed her eyes. "So much death." They were

surrounded by it in the Barrel. But this was the closest it had ever come to her.

"He was afraid for you."

"Kaz isn't afraid of anything."

"You should have seen his face when he brought you to me."

"I'm a very valuable investment."

Nina's jaw dropped. "Tell me he didn't say that."

"Of course he did. Well, not the valuable part."

"Idiot."

"How's Matthias?"

"Also an idiot. Do you think you can eat?"

Inej shook her head. She didn't feel hungry at all.

"Try," urged Nina. "There wasn't much of you to begin with."

"I just want to rest for now."

"Of course," Nina said. "I'll turn down the lantern."

Inej reached for her again. "Don't. I don't want to go back to sleep yet."

"I could read to you if I had anything to read. There's a Heartrender at the Little Palace who can recite epic poetry for hours. Then you'd wish you had died."

Inej laughed then winced. "Just stay."

"All right," said Nina. "Since you want to talk. Tell me why you don't have the cup and crow on your arm."

"Starting with the easy questions?"

Nina crossed her legs and planted her chin in her hands. "Waiting."

Inej was quiet for a while. "You saw my scars." Nina nodded. "When Kaz got Per Haskell to pay off my indenture with the Menagerie, the first thing I did was have the peacock feather tattoo removed."

"Whoever took care of it did a pretty rough job."

"He wasn't a Corporalnik or even a medik." Just one of the half-knowledgeable butchers who plied their trade among the desperate of the Barrel. He'd offered her a slug of whisky, then simply hacked away at the skin, leaving a puckered spill of wounds down her forearm. She hadn't cared. The pain was liberation. They had loved to talk about her skin at the House of Exotics. It was like coffee with sweet milk. It was like burnished caramel. It was like satin. She welcomed every cut of the knife and the scars it left behind. "Kaz told me I didn't have to do anything but make myself useful."

Kaz had taught her to crack a safe, pick a pocket, wield a knife. He'd gifted her with her first blade, the one she called Sankt Petyr – not as pretty as wild geraniums, but more practical, she supposed.

Maybe I'll use it on you, she'd said.

He'd sighed. *If only you were that bloodthirsty*. She hadn't been able to tell if he was kidding.

Now she shifted slightly on the table. There was pain, but it wasn't too bad. Given how deep the knife had gone, her Saints must have been guiding Nina's hand.

"Kaz said if I proved myself I could join the Dregs when I was ready. And I did. But I didn't take the tattoo."

Nina's brows rose. "I didn't think it was optional."

"Technically it isn't. I know some people don't understand, but Kaz told me . . . he said it was my choice, that he wouldn't be the one to mark me again."

But he had, in his own way – despite her best intentions. Feeling anything for Kaz Brekker was the worst kind of foolishness. She knew that. But he'd been the one to rescue her, to see her potential. He'd bet on her, and that meant something – even if he'd done it for his own selfish reasons. He'd even dubbed her the Wraith.

I don't like it, she'd said. *It makes me sound like a corpse.*

A phantom, he corrected.

Didn't you say I was to be your spider? Why not stick with that?

Because there are plenty of spiders in the Barrel. Besides, you want your enemies to be afraid. Not think they can squash you with the toe of one boot.

My enemies?

Our *enemies.*

He'd helped her build a legend to wear as armour, something bigger and more frightening than the girl she'd been. Inej sighed. She didn't want to think about Kaz any more.

"Talk," she said to Nina.

"Your eyelids are drooping. You should sleep."

"Don't like boats. Bad memories."

"Me too."

"Sing something, then."

Nina laughed. "Remember what I said about wishing you were dead? You do *not* want me to sing."

"Please?"

"I only know Ravkan folk tunes and Kerch drinking songs."

"Drinking song. Something rowdy, please."

Nina snorted. "Only for you, Wraith." She cleared her throat and began. "*Mighty young captain, bold on the sea. Soldier and sailor and free of disease—*"

Inej started to giggle and clutched her side. "You're right. You couldn't carry a tune in a bucket."

"I *told* you that."

"Go on."

Nina's voice really was terrible. But it helped to keep Inej on this boat, in this moment. She didn't want to think about the last time she'd been at sea, but the memories were hard to fight.

She wasn't even supposed to be in the wagon the morning the slavers took her. She'd been fourteen, and her family had been summering on the coast of West Ravka, enjoying the seaside and performing in a carnival on the outskirts of

Os Kervo. She should have been helping her father mend the nets. But she'd been feeling lazy, and she'd allowed herself another few minutes to sleep in, drowsing beneath the thin cotton covers and listening to the rush and sigh of the waves.

When a man had appeared silhouetted in the door to the caravan, she hadn't even known to run. She'd simply said, "Five more minutes, Papa."

Then they had her by the legs and were dragging her out of the wagon. She banged her head hard on the ground. There were four of them, big men, seafarers. When she tried to scream, they gagged her. They bound her hands and wrists, and one of them threw her over his shoulder as they plunged into a longboat they'd moored in the cove.

Later, Inej learned that the coast was a popular location for slavers. They'd spotted the Suli caravan from their ship and rowed in after dawn when the camp was all but deserted.

The rest of the journey was a blur. She was thrown into a cargo hold with a group of other children – some older, some younger, mostly girls but a few boys, too. She was the only Suli, but a few spoke Ravkan, and they told their own stories of being taken. One had been snatched from his father's shipyard; another had been playing in the tidepools and had strayed too far from her friends. One had been sold by her older brother to pay off his gambling debts. The sailors spoke a language she didn't know, but one of the other children claimed they were being taken to the largest of Kerch's outer islands, where they would be auctioned to private owners or pleasure houses in Ketterdam and Novyi Zem. People came from all over the world to bid. Inej had thought slaving was illegal in Kerch, but apparently it still happened.

She never saw the auction block. When they'd finally dropped anchor, Inej was led on deck and handed over to one of the most beautiful women she'd ever seen, a tall blonde with hazel eyes and piles of golden hair.

The woman had held her lantern up and examined every inch of Inej – her teeth, her breasts, even her feet. She'd tugged on the matted hair on Inej's head. "This will have to be shaved." Then she'd stepped back. "Pretty," she said. "Scrawny and flat as a pan, but her skin is flawless."

She'd turned away to barter with the sailors as Inej stood there, clutching her bound hands over her chest, her blouse still open, her skirt still hiked around her waist. Inej could see the glint of moonlight off the waves of the cove. *Jump*, she'd thought. *Whatever waits at the bottom of the sea is better than where this woman is taking you.* But she hadn't had the courage.

The girl she'd become would have jumped without a second thought, and maybe taken one of the slavers down with her. Or maybe she was kidding herself. She'd frozen when Tante Heleen had accosted her in West Stave. She'd been no stronger, no braver, just the same frightened Suli girl who'd been paralysed and humiliated on the deck of that ship.

Nina was still singing, something about a sailor who'd abandoned his sweetheart.

"Teach me the chorus," Inej said.

"You should rest."

"Chorus."

So Nina taught her the words, and they sang together, fumbling through the verses, hopelessly out of key, until the lanterns burned low.

JESPER

Jesper felt about ready to hurl himself overboard just for a change in routine. *Six more days.* Six more days on this boat – if they were lucky and the wind was good – and then they should make land. Fjerda's western coast was all perilous rock and steep cliffs. It could only be safely approached at Djerholm and Elling, and since security at both harbours was tight, they'd been forced to travel all the way to the northern whaling ports. He was secretly hoping they'd be attacked by pirates, but the little ship was too small to be carrying valuable cargo. They were an unworthy target and they passed unmolested through the busiest trade routes of the True Sea, flying neutral Kerch colours. Soon, they were in the cold waters of the north, moving into the Isenvee.

Jesper prowled the deck, climbed the rigging, tried to get the crew to play cards with him, cleaned his guns. He missed land and good food and better lager. He missed the city. If he'd wanted wide open spaces and silence, he would have stayed on the frontier and become the farmer his father had hoped for. There was little to do on the ship but study the layout of the Ice Court, listen to Matthias grumbling, and annoy Wylan, who could always be found labouring over his attempts to reconstruct the possible mechanisms of the ringwall gates.

Kaz had been impressed with the sketches.

"You think like a lockpick," he'd told Wylan.

"I do not."

"I mean you can see space along three axes."

"I'm not a criminal," Wylan protested.

Kaz had cast him an almost pitying look. "No, you're a flautist who fell in with bad company."

Jesper sat down next to Wylan. "Just learn to take a compliment. Kaz doesn't hand them out often."

"It's not a compliment. I'm nothing like him. I don't belong here."

"No arguments from me."

"And you don't belong here, either."

"I beg your pardon, merchling?"

"We don't need a sharpshooter for Kaz's plan, so what's your job – other than stalking around making everyone antsy?"

He shrugged. "Kaz trusts me."

Wylan snorted and picked up his pen. "Sure about that?"

Jesper shifted uncomfortably. Of course he wasn't sure about it. He spent far too much of his time guessing at Kaz Brekker's thoughts. And if he *had* earned some small part of Kaz's trust, did he deserve it?

He tapped his thumbs against his revolvers and said, "When the bullets start flying, you may find I'm nice to have around. Those pretty pictures aren't going to keep you alive."

"We need these plans. And in case you've forgotten, one of my flash bombs helped get us out of the Ketterdam harbour."

Jesper blew out a breath. "Brilliant strategy."

"It worked, didn't it?"

"You blinded our guys right along with the Black Tips."

"It was a calculated risk."

"It was cross-your-fingers-and-hope-for-the-best. Believe me, I know the difference."

"So I've heard."

"Meaning?"

"Meaning everyone knows you can't keep away from a fight or a wager, no matter the odds."

Jesper squinted up at the sails. "If you aren't born with every advantage, you learn to take your chances."

"I wasn't—" Wylan left off and set down his pen. "Why do you think you know everything about me?"

"I know plenty, merchling."

"How nice for you. I feel like I'll never know enough."

"About what?"

"About anything," Wylan muttered.

Against his better judgement, Jesper was intrigued. "Like what?" he pressed.

"Well, like those guns," he said gesturing to Jesper's revolvers. "They have an unusual firing mechanism, don't they? If I could take them apart—"

"Don't even think about it."

Wylan shrugged. "Or what about the ice moat?" he said, tapping the plan of the Ice Court. Matthias had said the moat wasn't solid, only a slick, wafer-thin layer of ice over frigid water, thoroughly exposed and impossible to cross.

"What about it?"

"Where does all the water come from? The Court is on a hill, so where's the aquifer or aqueduct to bring the water up?"

"Does it matter? There's a bridge. We don't need to cross the ice moat."

"But aren't you curious?"

"Saints, no. Get me a system for winning at Three Man

Bramble or Makker's Wheel. *That* I'm curious about."

Wylan had turned back to his work, his disappointment obvious.

For some reason, Jesper felt a little disappointed, too.

Jesper checked on Inej every morning and every night. The idea that the ambush on the docks might simply be the end of her had shaken him. Despite Nina's efforts, he'd been fairly sure the Wraith wasn't long for this world.

But one morning, Jesper arrived to find Inej sitting up, clothed in breeches, quilted vest, and hooded tunic.

Nina was bent over, struggling to get the Suli girl's feet into her strange rubber-soled slippers.

"Inej!" Jesper crowed. "You're not dead!"

She smiled faintly. "No more than anyone."

"If you're spouting depressing Suli wisdom, then you must be feeling better."

"Don't just stand there," Nina groused. "Help me get these things on her feet."

"If you would just let me—" Inej began.

"Do not bend," Nina snapped. "Do not leap. Do not move abruptly. If you don't promise to take it easy, I'll slow your heart and keep you in a coma until I can be sure you've recovered fully."

"Nina Zenik, as soon as I figure out where you've put my knives, we're going to have words."

"The first ones had better be '*Thank you, oh great Nina, for dedicating every waking moment of this miserable journey to saving my sorry life.*'"

Jesper expected Inej to laugh and was startled when she took Nina's face between her hands and said, "Thank you for keeping me in this world when fate seemed determined to drag me to the next. I owe you a life debt."

Nina blushed deeply. "I was teasing, Inej." She paused. "I think we've both had enough of debts."

"This is one I'm glad to bear."

"Okay, okay. When we're back in Ketterdam, take me out for waffles."

Now Inej did laugh. She dropped her hands and appeared to speculate. "Dessert for a life? I'm not sure that seems equitable."

"I expect really good waffles."

"I know just the place," said Jesper. "They have this apple syrup—"

"You're not invited," Nina said. "Now come help me get her standing."

"I can stand on my own," Inej grumbled as she slid off the table and rose to her feet.

"Humour me."

With a sigh, Inej gripped the arm that Jesper offered, and they made their way out of the cabin and up to the deck, Nina trailing behind them.

"This is foolishness," Inej said. "I'm fine."

"*You* are," replied Jesper, "but I may keel over at any moment, so pay attention."

Once they were on deck, Inej squeezed his arm to get him to halt. She tilted her head back, breathing deeply. It was a stone grey day, the sea a bleak slate broken up by whitecaps, the sky pleated with thick ripples of cloud. A hard wind filled the sails, carrying the little boat over the waves.

"It feels good to be this kind of cold," she murmured.

"This kind?"

"Wind in your hair, sea spray on your skin. The cold of the living."

"Two turns around the deck," Nina warned. "Then back to bed." She went to join Wylan at the stern. It didn't escape Jesper that she'd moved to the point on the ship furthest from Matthias.

"Have they been like that the whole time?" Inej asked, looking between Nina and the Fjerdan.

Jesper nodded. "It's like watching two bobcats circle each other."

Inej made a little humming noise. "But what do they mean to do when they pounce?"

"Claw each other to death?"

Inej rolled her eyes. "No wonder you do so badly at the tables."

Jesper steered her towards the rail, where they could make an approximation of a promenade without getting in anyone's way. "I'd threaten to toss you into the drink, but Kaz is watching."

Inej nodded. She didn't look up to where Kaz stood beside Specht at the wheel. But Jesper did and gave him a cheery wave. Kaz's expression didn't change.

"Would it kill him to smile every once in a while?" Jesper asked.

"Very possibly."

Every crew member called greetings and well wishes, and Jesper could sense Inej perking up with every cheer of "The Wraith returns!" Even Matthias gave her an awkward bow and said, "I understand you're the reason we made it out of the harbour alive."

"I suspect there were a lot of reasons," said Inej.

"I'm a reason," Jesper offered helpfully.

"All the same," said Matthias, ignoring him. "Thank you."

They moved on, and Jesper saw a pleased grin playing over Inej's lips.

"Surprised?" he asked.

"A bit," she admitted. "I spend so much time with Kaz. I guess—"

"It's a novelty to feel appreciated."

She released a little chuckle and pressed a hand to her side. "Still hurts to laugh."

"They're glad you're alive. *I'm* glad."

"I should hope so. I think I just never quite felt like I fit in with the Dregs."

"Well, you don't."

"Thanks."

"We're a crew with limited interests, and you don't gamble, swear, or drink to excess. But here's the secret to popularity: risk death to save your compatriots from being blown to bits in an ambush. Great way to make friends."

"As long as I don't have to start going to parties."

When they reached the foredeck, Inej leaned on the railing and looked out at the horizon. "Did he come to see me at all?"

Jesper knew she meant Kaz. "Every day."

Inej turned her dark eyes on him, then shook her head. "You can't read people, *and* you can't bluff."

Jesper sighed. He hated disappointing anyone. "No," he admitted.

She nodded and looked back at the ocean.

"I don't think he likes sickbeds," Jesper said.

"Who does?"

"I mean, I think it was hard for him to be around you that way. That first day when you were hurt . . . he went a little crazy." It cost Jesper something to admit that. Would Kaz have gone off on that kind of a mad-dog tear if it had been Jesper with a knife stuck in his side?

"Of course he did. This is a six-person job, and apparently he needs me to scale an incinerator shaft. If I die, the plan falls apart."

Jesper didn't argue. He couldn't pretend to understand Kaz or what drove him. "Tell me something. What was the big falling out between Wylan and his father?"

Inej cast a quick glance up at Kaz, then looked over her shoulder to make sure none of the crew was lurking nearby. Kaz had been clear that information even remotely related to the job must be kept among the six of them. "I don't know exactly," she said. "Three months ago Wylan turned up at a flophouse near the Slat. He was using a different surname, but Kaz keeps tabs on everyone new to the Barrel, so he had me do some snooping."

"And?"

Inej shrugged. "The servants at the Van Eck house are paid well enough that they're hard to bribe. The information I got didn't add up to much. There were rumours Wylan had been caught in a sweaty romp with one of his tutors."

"Really?" said Jesper incredulously. *Hidden depths indeed.*

"Just a rumour. And it's not as if Wylan left home to take up residence with a lover."

"So why did Papa Van Eck kick him out?"

"I don't think he did. Van Eck writes to Wylan every week, and Wylan doesn't even open the letters."

"What do they say?"

Inej leaned back carefully on the railing. "You're assuming I read them."

"You didn't?"

"Of course I did." Then she frowned, remembering. "They just said the same thing again and again: *If you're reading this, then you know how much I wish to have you home. Or I pray that you read these words and think of all you've left behind.*"

Jesper looked over to where Wylan was chatting with Nina. "The mysterious merchling. I wonder what Van Eck did that was bad enough to send Wylan to slum it with us."

"Now you tell *me* something, Jesper. What brought you on this mission? You know how risky this job is, what the chances are that we'll come back. I know you love a challenge, but this is a stretch, even for you."

Jesper looked at the grey swells of the sea, marching to the horizon in endless formation. He'd never liked the ocean, the sense of the unknown beneath his feet, that something hungry and full of teeth might be waiting to drag him under. And that was how he felt every day now, even on land.

"I'm in debt, Inej."

"You're always in debt."

"No. It's bad this time. I borrowed money from the wrong people. You know my father has a farm?"

"In Novyi Zem."

"Yes, in the west. It just started turning a profit this year."

"Oh, Jesper, you didn't."

"I needed the loan. . . . I told him it's so I can finish my degree at the university."

She stared at him. "He thinks you're a student?"

"That's why I came to Ketterdam. My first week in the city I went down to East Stave with some other students. I put a few *kruge* on the table. It was a whim. I didn't even know the rules of Makker's Wheel. But when the dealer gave the wheel a spin, I'd never heard a more beautiful sound. I won, and I kept winning. It was the best night of my life."

"And you've been chasing it ever since."

He nodded. "I should have stayed in the library. I won. I lost. I lost some more. I needed money so I started taking on work with the gangs. Two guys jumped me in an alley one night. Kaz took them down, and we started doing jobs together."

"He probably hired those boys to attack you so you'd feel indebted to him."

"He wouldn't—" Jesper stopped short, and then he laughed. "Of course he would." Jesper flexed his knuckles, concentrated on the lines of his palms. "Kaz is . . . I don't know, he's like nobody else I've ever known. He surprises me."

"Yes. Like a hive of bees in your dresser drawer."

Jesper barked a laugh. "Just like that."

"So what are we doing here?"

Jesper turned back to the sea, feeling his cheeks heat.

"Hoping for honey, I guess. And praying not to get stung."

Inej bumped her shoulder against his. "Then at least we're both the same kind of stupid."

"I don't know what your excuse is, Wraith. I'm the one who can never walk away from a bad hand."

She looped her arm in his. "That makes you a rotten gambler, Jesper. But an excellent friend."

"You're too good for him, you know."

"I know. So are you."

"Shall we walk?"

"Yes," Inej said, falling into step beside him. "And then I need you to distract Nina, so I can go search for my knives."

"No problem. I'll just bring up Helvar." Jesper glanced back at the wheel as they set off down the opposite side of the deck. Kaz hadn't moved. He was still watching them, his eyes hard, his face as unreadable as ever.

18

KAZ

It took two days after she emerged from the surgeon's cabin for Kaz to make himself approach Inej. She was sitting by herself, legs crossed, back to the hull of the ship, sipping a cup of tea.

Kaz limped over to her. "I want to show you something."

"I'm well, thank you for asking," she said, looking up at him. "How are you?"

He felt his lips twist. "Splendid." Awkwardly, he lowered himself down beside her and set aside his cane.

"Is your leg bad?"

"It's fine. Here." He spread Wylan's drawing of the prison sector between them. Most of Wylan's plans showed the Ice Court from above, but the prison elevation was a side view, a cross-section showing the building's floors stacked on top of one another.

"I've seen it," Inej said. She ran her finger from the basement up to the roof in a straight line. "Six storeys up a chimney."

"Can you do it?"

Her dark brows rose. "Is there another option?"

"No."

"So if I say I can't make that climb, will you tell Specht to turn the boat around and take us back to Ketterdam?"

"I'll find another option," said Kaz. "I don't know what, but I'm not giving up that haul."

"You know I can do it, Kaz, and you know I'm not going to refuse. So why ask?"

Because I've been looking for an excuse to talk to you for two days.

"I want to make sure you know what you'll be dealing with and that you're studying the plans."

"Will there be a test?"

"Yes," said Kaz. "If you fail, we'll all end up stuck inside a Fjerdan prison."

"Mmm," she said and took a sip of her tea. "And I'll end up dead." She closed her eyes and leaned her head back against the hull. "I'm worried about the escape route to the harbour. I don't like that there's only one way out."

Kaz settled back against the hull, too. "Me neither," he conceded, stretching out his bad leg. "But that's why the Fjerdans built it that way."

"Do you trust Specht?"

Kaz cast her a sideways glance. "Is there a reason I shouldn't?"

"Not at all, but if the *Ferolind* isn't waiting for us in the harbour . . ."

"I trust him enough."

"He owes you?"

Kaz nodded. He glanced around then said, "The navy threw him out for insubordination, and refused him his pension. He has a sister to support near Belendt. I got him his money."

"That was good of you."

Kaz narrowed his eyes. "I'm not some character out of a children's story who plays harmless pranks and steals from the rich to give to the poor. There was money to be made and information to be had. Specht knows the navy's routes like the back of his hand."

"Never something for nothing, Kaz," she said, her gaze steady. "I know. Still, if the *Ferolind* is intercepted, we'll have no way out of Djerholm."

"I'll get us out. You know that."

Tell me you know that. He needed her to say it. This job wasn't like anything he'd attempted before. Every doubt she'd raised was a legitimate one, and only echoed the fears in his own head. He'd snapped at her before they'd left Ketterdam, told her he'd get a new spider for the job if she didn't think he could pull it off. He needed to know that she believed he could do this, that he could take them into the Ice Court and bring them out feeling whole and righteous the way he'd done with other crews on other jobs. He needed to know she believed in him.

But all she said was, "I hear Pekka Rollins was the one gunning for us in the harbour."

Kaz felt a surge of disappointment. "So?"

"Don't think I haven't noticed the way you go after him, Kaz."

"He's just another boss, one more Barrel thug."

"No, he isn't. When you go after the other gangs, it's business. But with Pekka Rollins it's personal."

Later, he wasn't sure why he said it. He'd never told anyone, never spoken the words aloud. But now Kaz kept his eyes on the sails above them and said, "Pekka Rollins killed my brother."

He didn't have to see Inej's face to sense her shock. "You had a brother?"

"I had a lot of things," he muttered.

"I'm sorry."

Had he wanted her sympathy? Was that why he'd told her?

"Kaz—" She hesitated. What would she do now? Try to

lay a comforting hand on his arm? Tell him she understood?

"I'll pray for him," Inej said. "For peace in the next world if not in this one."

He turned his head. They were sitting close together, their shoulders nearly touching. Her eyes were so brown they were almost black, and for once her hair was down. She always wore it tied back in a ruthlessly tight coil. Even the idea of being this near someone should have set his skin crawling. Instead he thought, *What happens if I move closer?*

"I don't want your prayers," he said.

"What do you want, then?"

The old answers came easily to mind. *Money. Vengeance. Jordie's voice in my head silenced forever.* But a different reply roared to life inside him, loud, insistent, and unwelcome. *You, Inej. You.*

He shrugged and turned away. "To die buried under the weight of my own gold."

Inej sighed. "Then I'll pray you get all you ask for."

"More prayers," he asked. "And what do you want, Wraith?" he asked.

"To turn my back on Ketterdam and never hear that name again."

Good. He'd need to find a new spider, but he'd be rid of this distraction.

"Your share of thirty million *kruge* can grant that wish." He pushed to his feet. "So save your prayers for good weather and stupid guards. Just leave me out of it."

Kaz limped to the bow, annoyed with himself and angry with Inej. Why had he sought her out? Why had he told her about Jordie? He'd been irritable and unfocused for days. He was used to having his Wraith around – feeding the crows outside his window, sharpening her knives while he worked at his desk, chastising him with her Suli proverbs.

He didn't want Inej. He just wanted their routine back.

Kaz leaned against the ship's railing. He wished he hadn't said anything about his brother. Even those few words raised the memories, clamouring for attention. What had he said to Geels at the Exchange? *I'm the kind of bastard they only manufacture in the Barrel.* One more lie, one more piece of the myth he'd built for himself.

After their father died, crushed beneath a plough with his insides strewn across a field like a trail of damp red blossoms, Jordie had sold the farm. Not for much. The debts and liens had seen to that. But it was enough to see them safe to Ketterdam and to keep them in modest comfort for a good while.

Kaz had been nine, still missing Da and frightened of travelling from the only home he'd ever known. He'd held tight to his big brother's hand as they journeyed through miles of sweet, rolling countryside, until they reached one of the major waterways and hopped a bogboat that carried produce to Ketterdam.

"What will happen when we get there?" he'd asked Jordie.

"I'll get a job as a runner at the Exchange, then a clerk. I'll become a stockholder and then a proper merchant, and then I'll make my fortune."

"What about me?"

"You will go to school."

"Why won't you go to school?"

Jordie had scoffed. "I'm too old for school. Too smart, too."

The first few days in the city were all Jordie had promised. They'd walked along the great curve of the harbours known as the Lid, then down East Stave to see all the gambling palaces. They didn't venture too far south, where they'd been warned the streets grew dangerous. They let rooms in a tidy little boarding house not far from the Exchange and tried every new food they saw, stuffing themselves sick on quince candy. Kaz liked the little omelette stands where you could choose what you liked to put in them.

Each morning, Jordie went to the Exchange to look for work and told Kaz to stay in his room. Ketterdam wasn't safe for children on their own. There were thieves and pickpockets and even men who would snap up little boys and sell them to the highest bidder. So Kaz stayed inside. He pushed a chair up to the basin and climbed on it so he could see himself in the mirror as he tried to make coins disappear, just as he'd seen a magician do, performing in front of one of the gambling halls. Kaz could have watched him for hours, but eventually Jordie had dragged him away. The card tricks had been good, but the disappearing coin kept him up at night. How had the magician done it? It had been there one moment, gone the next.

The disaster began with a wind-up dog.

Jordie had come home hungry and irritable, frustrated after another wasted day. "They say they have no jobs, but they mean they have no jobs for a boy like me. Everyone there is someone's cousin or brother or best friend's son."

Kaz hadn't been in a mood to try to cheer him up. He was grouchy after so many hours indoors with nothing but coins and cards to keep him company. He wanted to go down to East Stave to find the magician.

In the years after, Kaz would always wonder what might have happened if Jordie hadn't indulged him, if they'd gone to the harbour to look at boats instead, or if they'd simply been walking on the other side of the canal. He wanted to believe that might have made the difference, but the older he got, the more he doubted it would have mattered at all.

They'd passed the green riot of the Emerald Palace, and right next door, in front of the Gold Strike, there'd been a boy selling little mechanical dogs. The toys wound up with a bronze key and waddled on stiff legs, tin ears flapping. Kaz had crouched down, turning all the keys, trying to get all the dogs waddling at the same time, and the boy selling them had struck up a conversation with Jordie. As it turned out, he was from Lij, not two towns over from where Kaz and Jordie had been raised, and he knew a man with jobs open for runners – not at the Exchange, but at an office just down the street. Jordie should come by the next morning, he said, and they could go chat with him together. He'd been hoping to land a job as a runner, too.

On the way home, Jordie had bought them each a hot chocolate, not just one to share.

"Our luck is changing," he'd said as they curled their hands around the steaming cups, feet dangling over a little bridge, the lights of the Stave playing over the water. Kaz had looked down at their reflections on the bright surface of the canal and thought, *I feel lucky now.*

The boy who sold the mechanical dogs was named Filip and the man he knew was Jakob Hertzoon, a minor mercher who owned a small coffeehouse near the Exchange, where he arranged for low-level investors to split stakes in trade voyages passing through Kerch.

"You should see this place," Jordie had crowed to Kaz upon arriving home late that night. "There are people there at every hour, talking and trading news, buying and selling shares and futures, ordinary people – butchers and bakers and dockworkers. Mister Hertzoon says any man can become rich. All he needs is luck and the right friends."

The next week was like a happy dream. Jordie and Filip worked for Mister Hertzoon as runners, carrying messages to and from the dock and occasionally placing orders for him at the Exchange or other trading offices. While they were working, Kaz was allowed to stay at the coffeehouse. The man who filled drink orders from behind the bar would let him sit up on the counter and practise his magic tricks, and gave Kaz all the hot chocolate he could drink.

They were invited to the Hertzoon home for dinner, a

grand house on the Zelverstraat with a blue front door and white lace curtains in the windows. Mister Hertzoon was a big man with a ruddy, friendly face and tufty grey sideburns. His wife, Margit, pinched Kaz's cheeks and fed him *hutspot* made with smoked sausage, and he'd played in the kitchen with their daughter, Saskia. She was ten years old, and Kaz thought she was the most beautiful girl he'd ever seen. He and Jordie stayed late into the night singing songs while Margit played the piano, their big silver dog thumping its tail in hapless rhythm. It was the best Kaz had felt since his father died. Mister Hertzoon even let Jordie put tiny sums down on company stocks. Jordie wanted to invest more, but Mister Hertzoon always advised caution. "Small steps, lad. Small steps."

Things got even better when Mister Hertzoon's friend returned from Novyi Zem. He was the captain of a Kerch trader, and it seemed he had crossed paths with a sugar farmer in a Zemeni port. The farmer had been in his cups, moaning about how his and his neighbours' cane fields had been flooded. Right now sugar prices were low, but when people found out how hard it would be to get sugar in the coming months, prices would soar. Mister Hertzoon's friend intended to buy up all the sugar he could before the news reached Ketterdam.

"That seems like cheating," Kaz had whispered to Jordie.

"It isn't cheating," Jordie had snorted. "It's just good business. And how are ordinary people supposed to move up in the world without a little extra help?"

Mister Hertzoon had Jordie and Filip place the orders with three separate offices to make sure such a large purchase didn't garner unwanted attention. News of the failed crop came in, and sitting in the coffeehouse, the boys had watched the prices on the chalkboard rise, trying to contain their glee.

When Mister Hertzoon thought the shares had gone as

high as they could go, he sent Jordie and Filip to sell out and collect. They'd returned to the coffeehouse, and Mister Hertzoon had handed both of them their profits straight from his safe.

"What did I tell you?" Jordie said to Kaz as they headed out into the Ketterdam night. "Luck and good friends!"

Only a few days later, Mister Hertzoon told them of another tip he'd received from his friend the captain, who'd had similar word on the next crop of *jurda*. "The rains are hitting everyone hard this year," Mister Hertzoon said. "But this time, not only the fields were destroyed, but the warehouses down by the docks in Eames. This is going to be big money, and I intend to go in heavy."

"Then we should, too," said Filip.

Mister Hertzoon had frowned. "I'm afraid this isn't a deal for you, boys. The minimum investment is far too high for either of you. But there will be more trades to come!"

Filip had been furious. He'd yelled at Mister Hertzoon, told him it wasn't fair. He said Mister Hertzoon was just like the merchants at the Exchange, hoarding all the riches for himself, and called Mister Hertzoon names that had made Kaz cringe. When he'd stormed out, everyone at the coffeehouse had stared at Mister Hertzoon's red, embarrassed face.

He'd gone back to his office and slouched down in his chair. "I . . . I can't help the way business is done. The men running the trade want only big investors, people who can support the risk."

Jordie and Kaz had stood there, unsure of what to do.

"Are you angry with me, too?" asked Mister Hertzoon.

Of course not, they assured him. Filip was the one who was being unfair.

"I understand why he's angry," said Mister Hertzoon. "Opportunities like this one don't come along often, but there's nothing to be done."

"I have money," said Jordie.

Mister Hertzoon had smiled indulgently. "Jordie, you're a good lad, and some day I have no doubt you'll be a king of the Exchange, but you don't have the kind of funds these investors require."

Jordie's chin had gone up. "I do. From the sale of my father's farm."

"And I expect it's all you and Kaz have to live on. That's not something to be risked on a trade, no matter how certain the outcome. A child your age has no business—"

"I'm not a child. If it's a good opportunity, I want to take it."

Kaz would always remember that moment, when he'd seen greed take hold of his brother, an invisible hand guiding him onward, the lever at work.

Mister Hertzoon had taken a lot of convincing. They'd all gone back to the Zelverstraat house and discussed it well into the night. Kaz had fallen asleep with his head on the silver dog's side and Saskia's red ribbon clutched in his hand.

When Jordie finally roused him, the candles had burned low, and it was already morning. Mister Hertzoon had asked his business partner to come over and draw up a contract for a loan from Jordie. Because of his age, Jordie would loan Mister Hertzoon the money, and Mister Hertzoon would place the trade. Margit gave them milk tea and warm pancakes with sour cream and jam. Then they'd all walked to the bank that held the funds from the sale of the farm and Jordie signed them over.

Mister Hertzoon insisted on escorting them back to their boarding house, and he'd hugged them at the door. He handed the loan agreement to Jordie and warned him to keep it safe. "Now, Jordie," he said. "There is only a small chance that this trade will go bad, but there is always a chance. If it does, I'm relying on you not to use that document to call in your loan. We both must take the risk together. I am trusting you."

Jordie had beamed. "The deal is the deal," he said.

"The deal is the deal," said Mister Hertzoon proudly, and they shook hands like proper merchants. Mister Hertzoon handed Jordie a thick roll of *kruge*. "For a fine dinner to celebrate. Come back to the coffeehouse a week from today, and we'll watch the prices rise together."

That week they'd played *ridderspel* and *spijker* at the arcades on the Lid. They'd bought Jordie a fine new coat and Kaz a new pair of soft leather boots. They'd eaten waffles and fried potatoes, and Jordie had purchased every novel he craved at a bookshop on Wijnstraat. When the week was over, they'd walked hand in hand to the coffeehouse.

It was empty. The front door was locked and bolted. When they pressed their faces to the dark windows, they saw that everything was gone – the tables and chairs and big copper urns, the chalkboard where the figures for the day's trades had been posted.

"Do we have the wrong corner?" asked Kaz.

But they knew they didn't. In nervous silence, they walked to the house on Zelverstraat. No one answered their knock on the bright blue door.

"They've just gone out for a while," said Jordie. They waited on the steps for hours, until the sun began to set. No one came or went. No candles were lit in the windows.

Finally, Jordie worked up the courage to knock on a neighbour's door. "Yes?" said the maid who answered in her little white cap.

"Do you know where the family next door has gone? The Hertzoons?"

The maid's brow furrowed. "I think they were just visiting for a time from Zierfoort."

"No," Jordie said. "They've lived here for years. They—"

The maid shook her head. "That house stood empty for

nearly a year after the last family moved away. It was only rented a few weeks ago."

"But—"

She'd closed the door in his face.

Kaz and Jordie said nothing to each other, not on the walk home or as they climbed the stairs to their little room in the boarding house. They sat in the growing gloom for a long time. Voices floated back to them from the canal below as people went about their evening business.

"Something happened to them," Jordie said at last. "There was an accident or an emergency. He'll write soon. He'll send for us."

That night, Kaz took Saskia's red ribbon from beneath his pillow. He rolled it into a neat spiral and clutched it in his palm. He lay in bed and tried to pray, but all he could think about was the magician's coin: there and then gone.

19

MATTHIAS

It was too much. He hadn't anticipated how difficult it would be to see his homeland for the first time in so long. He'd had over a week aboard the *Ferolind* to prepare, but his head had been full of the path he'd chosen, of Nina, of the cruel magic that had taken him from his prison cell and placed him on a boat speeding north beneath a limitless sky, still bound not just by shackles but by the burden of what he was about to do.

He got his first glimpse of the northern coast late in the afternoon, but Specht decided to wait until dusk to make land in hopes the twilight would lend them some cover. There were whaling villages along the shore, and no one was eager to be spotted. Despite their cover as trappers, the Dregs were still a conspicuous group.

They spent the night on the ship. At dawn the next morning, Nina had found him assembling the cold weather gear Jesper and Inej had distributed. Matthias was impressed by Inej's resilience. Though she still had circles beneath her eyes, she moved without stiffness, and if she was in pain, she hid it well.

Nina held up a key. "Kaz sent me to remove your shackles."

"Are you going to lock me in again at night?"

"That's up to Kaz. And you, I suppose. Have a seat."

"Just give me the key."

Nina cleared her throat. "He also wants me to tailor you."

"What? Why?" The thought of Nina altering his appearance with her witchcraft was intolerable.

"We're in Fjerda now. He wants you looking a little less . . . like yourself, just in case."

"Do you know how big this country is? The chance that—"

"The odds of you being recognised will be considerably higher at the Ice Court, and I can't make changes to your appearance all at once."

"Why?"

"I'm not that good a Tailor. It's part of all Corporalki training now, but I just don't have an affinity for it."

Matthias snorted.

"What?" she asked.

"I've never heard you admit you're not good at something."

"Well, it happens so rarely."

He was horrified to find his lips curling in a smile, but it was easy enough to quell when he thought of his face being changed. "What does Brekker want you to do to me?"

"Nothing radical. I'll change your eye colour, your hair – what you have of it. It won't be permanent."

"I don't want this." *I don't want you near me.*

"It won't take long, and it will be painless, but if you want to argue about it with Kaz . . ."

"Fine," he said, steeling himself. It was pointless to argue with Brekker, not when he could simply taunt Matthias with the promise of the pardon. Matthias picked up a bucket, flipped it over, and sat down. "Can I have the key now?"

She handed it over to him and he unshackled his wristsas

she rooted around in a box she'd brought over. It had a handle and several little drawers stuffed with powders and pigments in tiny jars. She extracted a pot of something black from a drawer.

"What is it?"

"Black antimony." She stepped close to him, tilting his chin back with the tip of her finger. "Unclench your jaw, Matthias. You're going to grind your teeth down to nothing."

He crossed his arms.

She started shaking some of the antimony over his scalp and gave a rueful sigh. "Why does the brave *drüskelle* Matthias Helvar eat no meat?" she asked in a theatrical voice as she worked. "'Tis a sad story indeed, my child. His teeth were winnowed away by a vexatious Grisha, and now he can eat only pudding."

"Stop that," he grumbled.

"What? Keep your head tilted back."

"What are you doing?"

"Darkening your brows and lashes. You know, the way girls do before a party." He must have grimaced because she burst out laughing. "The look on your face!"

She leaned in, the waves of her brown hair brushing against his cheeks as she bled the colour from the antimony into his brows. Her hand cupped his cheek.

"Shut your eyes," she murmured. Her thumbs moved over his lashes, and he realised he was holding his breath.

"You don't smell like roses any more," he said, then wanted to kick himself. He shouldn't be noticing her scent.

"I probably smell like boat."

No, she smelled sweet, perfect like. . . "Toffee?"

Her eyes slid away guiltily. "Kaz said to pack what we needed for the journey. A girl has to eat." She reached into her pocket and drew out a bag of toffees. "Want one?"

Yes. "No."

She shrugged and popped one in her mouth. Her eyes

rolled back, and she sighed happily. "So good."

It was a humiliating epiphany, but he knew he could have watched her eat all day. This was one of the things he'd liked best about Nina – she *savoured* everything, whether it was a toffee or cold water from a stream or dried reindeer meat.

"Eyes now," she said around the candy as she pulled a tiny bottle from her case. "You'll have to keep them open."

"What is that?" he asked nervously.

"A tincture developed by a Grisha named Genya Safin. It's the safest way to change eye colour."

Again she leaned in. Her cheeks were rosy from the cold, her mouth slightly open. Her lips were bare inches from his. If he sat up straighter, they'd be kissing.

"You have to look at me," she instructed.

I am. He shifted his gaze to hers. *Do you remember this shore, Nina?* he wanted to ask, though he knew she must.

"What colour are you making my eyes?"

"Shhh. This is difficult." She dabbed the drops onto her fingers and held them close to his eyes.

"Why can't you just put them in?"

"Why can't you stop talking? Do you want me to blind you?"

He stopped talking.

Finally, she drew back, gaze roving over his features. "Brownish," she said. Then she winked. "Like toffee."

"What do you intend to do about Bo Yul-Bayur?"

She straightened and stepped away, her expression shuttering. "What do you mean?"

He was sorry to see her easy manner go, but that didn't matter. He glanced over his shoulder to make sure no one was listening. "You know exactly what I mean. I don't believe for a second you'll let these people hand Bo Yul-Bayur over to the Kerch Merchant Council."

She put the bottle back in one of the little drawers. "We'll have to do this at least two more times before we get to the Ice Court so I can deepen the colour. Get your things together. Kaz wants us ready to leave on the hour." She snapped the top of the case closed and picked up the shackles. Then she was gone.

By the time they bid their goodbyes to the ship's crew, the sky had turned from pink to gold.

"See you in Djerholm harbour," Specht called. "No mourners."

"No funerals," the others replied. Strange people.

Brekker had been frustratingly tight-lipped about how exactly they were going to reach Bo Yul-Bayur and then get out of the Ice Court with the scientist in tow, but he'd been clear that once they had their prize, the *Ferolind* was their escape route. It had papers bearing the Kerch seal and indicating that all fees and applications had been made for representatives of the Haanraadt Bay Company to transport furs and goods from Fjerda to Zierfoort, a port city in south Kerch.

They began the march from the rocky shore up the cliff side. Spring was coming, but ice was still thick on the ground, and it was a tough climb. When they reached the top of the cliff, they stopped to catch their breath. The *Ferolind* was still visible on the horizon, its sails full of the wind that whipped at their cheeks.

"Saints," said Inej. "We're actually doing this."

"I've spent every minute of every miserable day wishing to be off that ship," said Jesper. "So why do I suddenly miss it?"

Wylan stamped his boots. "Maybe because it already feels like our feet are going to freeze off."

"When we get our money, you can burn *kruge* to keep

you warm," said Kaz. "Let's go." He'd left his crow's head cane aboard the *Ferolind* and substituted a less conspicuous walking stick. Jesper had mournfully left behind his prized pearl-handled revolvers in favour of a pair of unornamented guns, and Inej had done the same with her extraordinary set of knives and daggers, keeping only those she could bear to part with when they entered the prison. Practical choices, but Matthias knew that talismans had their power.

Jesper consulted his compass, and they turned south, seeking a path that would lead them to the main trading road. "I'm going to pay someone to burn my *kruge* for me."

Kaz fell into step beside him. "Why don't you pay someone else to pay someone to burn your *kruge* for you? That's what the big players do."

"You know what the really big bosses do? They pay someone to pay someone to . . ."

Their voices trailed off as they tromped ahead, and Matthias and the others followed after. But he noticed that each of them cast a final backwards glance at the vanishing *Ferolind*. The schooner was a part of Kerch, a piece of home for them, and that last familiar thing was drifting further away with every moment.

Matthias felt some small measure of sympathy, but as they trekked through the morning, he had to admit he enjoyed seeing the canal rats shiver and struggle a bit for once. They thought they knew cold, but the white north had a way of forcing strangers to reevaluate their terms. They stumbled and staggered, awkward in their new boots, trying to find the trick of walking in hard-crusted snow, and soon Matthias was in the lead, setting the pace, though Jesper kept a steady eye on his compass.

"Put your . . ." Matthias paused and had to gesture to Wylan. He didn't know the Kerch word for 'goggles' or even 'snow', for that matter. They weren't terms that came up in prison. "Keep your eyes covered, or you could damage them permanently." Men went blind this far north; they lost lips, ears, noses, hands, and feet. The land was barren and brutal, and that was all most people saw. But to Matthias it was beautiful. The ice bore the spirit of Djel. It had colour and shape and even a scent if you knew to seek it out.

He pushed ahead, feeling almost at peace, as if here Djel could hear him and ease his troubled mind. The ice brought back memories of childhood, of hunting with his father. They'd lived further south, near Halmhend, but in the winters that part of Fjerda didn't look much different from this, a world of white and grey, broken by groves of black-limbed trees and jutting clusters of rock that seemed to have risen up from nowhere, shipwrecks on a bare ocean floor.

The first day trekking was like a cleansing – little talk, the white hush of the north welcoming Matthias back without judgement. He'd expected more complaints, but even Wylan had simply put his head down and walked. *They're all survivors*, Matthias understood. *They adapt.* When the sun began to set, they ate their rations of dried beef and hardtack and collapsed into their tents without a word.

But the next morning brought an end to the quiet and Matthias' fragile sense of peace. Now that they were off the ship and away from its crew, Kaz was ready to dig into the details of the plan.

"If we get this right, we're going to be in and out of the Ice Court before the Fjerdans ever know their prize scientist is gone," Kaz said as they shouldered their packs and continued to push south. "When we enter the prison, we'll be taken to the holding area beneath the men's and women's cellblocks to await charges. If Matthias is right and the procedures are still the same, the patrols only pass through the holding cells three times a day for head counts. Once we're out of the cells, we should have at least six hours to cross to the embassy, locate Yul-Bayur on the White Island, and get him down to the harbour before they realise anyone is missing."

"What about the other prisoners in the holding cells?" Matthias asked.

"We have that covered."

Matthias scowled, but he wasn't particularly surprised. Once they were in those holding cells, Kaz and the others would be at their most vulnerable. It would take only a word to the guards for Matthias to put an end to all their scheming. That was what Brum would do, what an honourable man would choose. Some part of Matthias had believed that coming back to Fjerda would return him to his senses, give him the strength to forsake this mad quest; instead it had only made his longing for home, for the life he'd once lived among his *drüskelle* brothers more acute.

"Once we're out of the cells," Kaz continued, "Matthias and Jesper will secure rope from the stables while Wylan and I get Nina and Inej out of the women's holding area. The basement is our meet. That's where the incinerator is, and no one should be in the laundry after the prison shuts down for the night. While Inej makes the climb, Wylan and I scour the laundry for anything he can use for demo. And just in case the Fjerdans decided to stash Bo Yul-Bayur in the prison and make life easy on us, Nina, Matthias, and Jesper will search the top level cells."

"Nina and Matthias?" Jesper asked. "Far be it from me to doubt anyone's professionalism, but is that really the ideal pairing?"

Matthias bit down on his anger. Jesper was right, but he hated being discussed in this way.

"Matthias knows prison procedure, and Nina can handle any guards without a noisy fight. Your job is to keep them from killing each other."

"Because I'm the diplomat of the group?"

"There is no diplomat of the group. Now listen," Kaz said. "The rest of the prison isn't like the holding area. Patrols in the cellblock rotate every two hours, and we don't want to risk anyone sounding an alarm, so be smart. We coordinate everything to the chiming of the Elderclock. We're out of the cells right after six bells, we're up the incinerator and on the roof by eight bells. No exceptions."

"And then what?" asked Wylan.

"We cross to the embassy sector roof and get access to the glass bridge through there."

"We'll be on the other side of the checkpoints," said Matthias, unable to keep a hint of admiration from his voice. "The guards on the bridge will assume we passed through the embassy gate and had our papers scrutinised there."

Wylan frowned. "In prison uniforms?"

"Phase two," said Jesper. "The fake."

"That's right," said Kaz. "Inej, Nina, Matthias, and I will *borrow* a change of clothes from one of the delegations – and a little something extra for our friend Bo Yul-Bayur when we find him – and stroll across the glass bridge. We locate Yul-Bayur and get him back to the embassy. Nina, if there's time, you'll tailor him as much as possible, but as long as we don't trigger any alarms, no one is going to notice one more Shu among the guests."

Unless Matthias managed to get to the scientist first. If he was dead when the others found him, Kaz couldn't hold Matthias responsible. He'd still get his pardon. And if he never managed to separate from the group? A shipboard accident might still befall Yul-Bayur on the journey back.

"So what I'm getting from this," said Jesper, "is that I'm stuck with Wylan."

"Unless you've suddenly acquired an encyclopedic knowledge of the White Island, the ability to pick locks, scale unscalable walls, or flirt confidential information out of high level officials, yes. Besides, I want two sets of hands making bombs."

Jesper looked mournfully at his guns. "Such potential wasted."

Nina crossed her arms. "Let's say this all works. How do we get out?"

"We walk," Kaz said. "That's the beauty of this plan. Remember what I said about guiding the mark's attention? At the embassy gate, all eyes will be focused on guests coming into the Ice Court. People leaving aren't a security risk."

"Then why the bombs?" asked Wylan.

"Precautions. There are seven miles of road between the Ice Court and the harbour. If someone notices Bo Yul-Bayur is missing, we're going to have to cover that territory fast." He drew a line in the snow with his walking stick. "The main road crosses a gorge. We blow the bridge, no one can follow."

Matthias put his head in his hands, imagining the havoc these low creatures were about to wreak on his country's capital.

"It's one prisoner, Helvar," said Kaz.

"And a bridge," Wylan put in helpfully.

"And anything we have to blow up in between," added Jesper.

"Everyone shut up," Matthias growled.

Jesper shrugged. "Fjerdans."

"I don't like any of this," said Nina.

Kaz raised a brow. "Well, at least you and Helvar found something to agree on."

Further south they travelled, the coast long gone, the ice broken more and more by slashes of forest, glimpses of black earth and animal tracks, proof of the living world, the heart of Djel beating always. The questions from the others were ceaseless.

"How many guard towers are on the White Island again?"

"Do you think Yul-Bayur will be in the palace?"

"There are guard barracks on the White Island. What if he's in the barracks?"

Jesper and Wylan debated which kinds of explosives might be assembled from the prison laundry supplies and if they could get their hands on some gunpowder in the embassy sector. Nina tried to help Inej estimate what her pace would have to be to scale the incinerator shaft with enough time to secure the rope and get the others to the top.

They drilled each other constantly on the architecture and procedures of the Court, the layout of the ringwall's three gatehouses, each built around a courtyard.

"First checkpoint?"

"Four guards."

"Second checkpoint?"

"Eight guards."

"Ringwall gates?"

"Four when the gate is nonoperational."

They were like a maddening chorus of crows, squawking in Matthias' ear: *Traitor, traitor, traitor.*

"Yellow Protocol?" asked Kaz.

"Sector disturbance," said Inej.

"Red Protocol?"

"Sector breach."

"Black Protocol?"

"We're all doomed?" said Jesper.

"That about covers it," Matthias said, pulling his hood tighter and trudging ahead. They'd even made him imitate the different patterns of the bells. A necessity, but he'd felt like a fool chanting, "*Bing bong bing bing bong.* No, wait, *bing bing bong bing bing.*"

"When I'm rich," Jesper said behind him. "I'm going somewhere I never have to see snow again. What about you, Wylan?"

"I don't know exactly."

"I think you should buy a golden piano—"

"Flute."

"And play concerts on a pleasure barge. You can park it in the canal right outside your father's house."

"Nina can sing," Inej put in.

"We'll duet," Nina amended. "Your father will have to move."

She did have a terrible singing voice. He hated that he knew that, but he couldn't resist glancing over his shoulder. Nina's hood had fallen back, and the thick waves of her hair had escaped her collar.

Why do I keep doing that? he thought in a rush of frustration. It had happened aboard the ship, too. He'd tell himself to ignore her, and the next thing he knew his eyes would be seeking her out.

But it was foolish to pretend that she wasn't in his mind. He and Nina had walked this same territory together. If his calculations were right, they'd washed up only a few miles from where the *Ferolind* had put into shore. It had started with a storm, and in a way, that storm had never ended. Nina had blown into his life with the wind and rain and set his world spinning. He'd been off balance ever since.

The storm had come out of nowhere, tossing the ship like a toy on the waves. The sea had played along until it had tired of the game, and dragged their boat under in a tangle of rope and sail and screaming men.

Matthias remembered the darkness of the water, the terrible cold, the silence of the deep. The next thing he knew, he was spitting up salt water, gasping for breath. Someone had an arm around his chest, and they were moving through the water. The cold was unbearable, yet somehow he was bearing it.

"Wake up, you miserable lump of muscle." Clean Fjerdan, pure, spoken like a noble. He turned his head and was shocked to see that the young witch they'd captured on the southern coast of the Wandering Isle had hold of him and was muttering to herself in Ravkan. He'd *known* she wasn't really Kaelish. Somehow she'd got free of her bonds and the cages. Every part of him went into a panic, and if he'd been less shocked or numb, he would have struggled.

"Move," she told him in Fjerdan, panting. "Saints, what do they feed you? You weigh about as much as a haycart."

She was struggling badly, swimming for both of them. She'd saved his life. Why?

He shifted in her arms, kicking his legs to help drive them forward. To his surprise, he heard her give a low sob. "Thank the Saints," she said. "Swim, you giant oaf."

"Where are we?" he asked.

"I don't know," she replied, and he could hear the terror in her voice.

He kicked away from her.

"Don't!" she cried. "Don't let go!"

But he shoved hard, breaking her hold. The moment he left her arms, the cold rushed in. The pain was sharp and sudden, and his limbs went sluggish. She'd been using her sick magic to keep him warm. He reached for her in the dark.

"*Drüsje?*" he called, ashamed of the fear in his voice. It was the Fjerdan word for witch, but he had no name for her.

"*Drüskelle!*" she shouted, and then he felt his fingers brush against hers in the black water. He grabbed hold and drew her to him. Her body didn't feel warm exactly, but as soon as they made contact, the pain in his own limbs receded. He was gripped by gratitude and revulsion.

"We have to find land," she gasped. "I can't swim and keep both of our hearts beating."

"I'll swim," he said. "You ... I'll swim." He clasped her

back to his chest, his arm looped under hers and across her body, the way she'd been holding him only moments ago, as if she were drowning. And she was, they both were, or they would be soon if they didn't freeze to death first.

He kicked his legs steadily, trying not to expend too much energy, but they both knew it was probably futile. They hadn't been far from land when the storm had hit, but it was completely dark. They might be headed towards the coastline or further out to sea.

There was no sound but their breathing, the slosh of the water, the roll of the waves. He kept them moving – though they might well have been paddling in a circle – and she kept both of them breathing. Which one of them would give out first, he didn't know.

"Why did you save me?" he asked finally.

"Stop wasting energy. Don't talk."

"Why did you do it?"

"Because you're a human being," she said angrily.

Lies. If they did make land, she'd need a Fjerdan to help her survive, someone who knew the land, though clearly she knew the language. Of course she did. They were all deceivers and spies, trained to prey on people like him, people without their unnatural gifts. They were predators.

He continued to kick, but the muscles in his legs were tiring, and he could feel the cold creeping in on him.

"Giving up already, witch?"

He felt her shake off her exhaustion, and blood rushed back into his fingers and toes.

"I'll match your pace, *drüskelle*. If we die, it will be your burden to bear in the next life."

He had to smile a little at that. She certainly didn't lack for spine. That much had been clear even when she was caged.

That was the way they went on that night, taunting each other whenever one of them faltered. They knew only the sea, the ice, the occasional splash that might have been a wave or something hungry moving towards them in the water.

"Look," the witch whispered when dawn came, rosy and blithe. There, in the distance, he could just make out a jutting promontory of ice and the blessed black slash of a dark gravel shore. Land.

They wasted no time on relief or celebration. The witch tilted her head back, resting it against his shoulder as he drove forward, inch by miserable inch, each wave pulling them back, as if the sea was unwilling to relinquish its hold. At last, their feet touched bottom, and they were half swimming, half crawling to shore. They broke apart, and Matthias' body flooded with misery as he dragged himself over the black rocks to the dead and frozen land.

Walking was impossible at first. Both of them moved in fits and starts, trying to get their limbs to obey, shuddering with cold. Finally he made it to his feet. He thought about just walking off, finding shelter without her. She was on her hands and knees, head bent, her hair a wet and tangled mess covering her face. He had the distinct sense that she was going to lie down and simply not get back up.

He took one step, then another. Then he turned back. Whatever her reasons, she'd saved his life last night, not once, but again and again. That was a blood debt.

He staggered back to her and offered his hand.

When she looked up at him, the expression on her face was a bleak map of loathing and fatigue. In it, he saw the shame that came with gratitude, and he knew that in this brief moment, she was his mirror. She didn't want to owe him anything, either.

He could make the decision for her. He owed her that much. He reached down and yanked her to her feet, and they limped together off the beach.

They headed what Matthias hoped was west. The sun

could play tricks on your senses this far north and they had no compass with which to navigate. It was almost dark, and Matthias had begun to feel the stirrings of real panic when they finally spotted the first of the whaling camps. It was deserted – the outposts were only active in the spring – and little more than a round lodge made of bone, sod, and animal skins. But shelter meant they might at least survive the night.

The door had no lock. They practically fell through it.

"Thank you," she groaned as she collapsed beside the circular hearth.

He said nothing. Finding the camp had been mere luck. If they'd washed up even a few miles further up the coast they would have been done for.

The whalers had left peat and dry kindling in the hearth. Matthias laboured over the fire, trying to get it to do more than smoke. He was clumsy and tired and hungry enough that he would have gladly gnawed the leather off his boot. When he heard a rustling behind him, he turned and almost dropped the piece of driftwood he'd been using to coax the little flames.

"What are you doing?" he barked.

She had glanced over her shoulder – her very bare shoulder – and said, "Is there something I'm supposed to be doing?"

"Put your clothes back on!"

She rolled her eyes. "I'm not going to freeze to death to preserve your sense of modesty."

He gave the fire a stern jab, but she ignored him and stripped off the rest of her clothes – tunic, trousers, even her underthings – then wrapped herself in one of the grimy reindeer skins that had been piled near the door.

"Saints, this smells," she grumbled, shuffling over and assembling a nest of the few other pelts and blankets beside the fire. Every time she moved, the reindeer cloak parted, revealing a flash of round calf, white skin, the shadow between her breasts. It was deliberate. He knew it. She was trying to rattle him. He needed to focus on the fire. He'd almost died, and if he didn't get a fire started, he still might. If only she would stop making so much damn noise. The driftwood snapped in his hands.

Nina snorted and lay down in the nest of pelts, propping herself on one elbow. "For Saint's sake, *drüskelle*, what's wrong with you? I just wanted to be warm. I promise not to ravish you in your sleep."

"I'm not afraid of you," he said irritably.

Her grin was vicious. "Then you're as stupid as you look."

He stayed crouching beside the fire. He knew he was meant to lie down next to her. The sun had set, and the temperature was dropping. He was struggling to keep his teeth from chattering, and they would need each other's warmth to get through the night. It shouldn't have concerned him, but he didn't want to be near her. *Because she's a killer*, he told himself. *That's why. She's a killer and a witch.*

He forced himself to rise and stride towards the blankets. But Nina held out a hand to stop him.

"Don't even think about getting near me in those clothes. You're soaked through."

"You can keep our blood flowing."

"I'm exhausted," she said angrily. "And once I fall asleep, all we'll have is that fire to keep us warm. I can see you shaking from here. Are all Fjerdans this prudish?"

No. Maybe. He didn't really know. The *drüskelle* were a holy order. They were meant to live chastely until they took wives – good Fjerdan wives who didn't run around yelling at people and taking their clothes off.

"Are all Grisha so immodest?" he asked defensively.

"Boys and girls train side by side together in the First and Second Armies. There isn't a lot of room for maidenly blushing."

"It's not natural for women to fight."

"It's not natural for someone to be as stupid as he is tall, and yet there you stand. Did you really swim all those miles just to die in this hut?"

"It's a lodge, and you don't know that we swam miles."

Nina blew out an exasperated breath and curled up on her side, burrowing as close as she could get to the fire. "I'm too tired to argue." She closed her eyes. "I can't believe your face is going to be the last thing I see before I die."

He felt like she was daring him. Matthias stood there feeling foolish and hating her for making him feel that way. He turned his back on her and quickly sloughed off his sodden clothes, spreading them beside the fire. He glanced once at her to make sure she wasn't looking then strode to the blankets and wriggled in behind her, still trying to keep his distance.

"Closer, *drüskelle*," she crooned, taunting.

He threw an arm over her, hooking her back against his chest. She let out a startled *oof* and shifted uneasily.

"Stop moving," he muttered. He'd been close to girls – not many, it was true – but none of them had been like her. She was indecently round.

"You're cold and clammy," she complained with a shiver. "It's like lying next to a burly squid."

"You told me to get closer!"

"Ease up a bit," she instructed and when he did, she flipped over to face him.

"What are you doing?" he asked, pulling back in a panic.

"Relax, *drüskelle*. This isn't where I have my way with you."

His blue eyes narrowed. "I hate the way you talk." Did he imagine the hurt that flashed across her face? As if his words could have any effect on this witch.

She confirmed he'd been imagining things when she said, "Do you think I care what you like or don't like?"

She laid her hands on his chest, focusing on his heart. He shouldn't let her do this, shouldn't show his weakness, but as his blood began to flow and his body warmed, the relief and ease that coursed through him felt too good to resist.

He let himself relax slightly, grudgingly, beneath her palms. She flipped over and pulled his arm back around her. "You're welcome, you big idiot."

He'd lied. He did like the way she talked.

He still did. He could hear her yammering to Inej somewhere behind him, trying to teach her Fjerdan words. "No, Hring-kaaalle. You have to hang on the last syllable a bit."

"Hringalah?" tried Inej.

"Better but – here, it's like Kerch is a gazelle. It hops from word to word," she pantomimed. "Fjerdan is like gulls, all swoops and dives." Her hands became birds riding currents on the air. At that moment, she looked up and caught him staring.

He cleared his throat. "Do not eat the snow," he counselled. "It will only dehydrate you and lower your body temperature." He plunged forward, eager to be up the next hill with some distance between them. But as he came over the rise, he halted dead in his tracks.

He turned round, holding out his arms. "Stop! You don't want to—"

But it was too late. Nina clapped her hands over her mouth. Inej made some kind of warding sign in the air. Jesper shook his head, and Wylan gagged. Kaz stood like a stone, his expression inscrutable.

The pyre had been made on a bluff. Whoever was responsible had tried to build the fire in the shelter of a rock outcropping, but it hadn't been enough to keep the flames from dying out in the wind. Three stakes had been driven into the icy ground, and three charred bodies were bound to them, their blackened, cracked skin still smouldering.

"*Ghezen*," swore Wylan. "What is this?"

"This is what Fjerdans do to Grisha." Nina said. Her face was slack, her green eyes staring.

"It's what criminals do," said Matthias, his insides churning. "The pyres have been illegal since—"

Nina whirled on him and shoved his chest hard. "Don't you dare," she seethed, fury burning like a halo around her. "Tell me the last time someone was prosecuted for putting a Grisha to the flames. Do you even call it murder when you put down dogs?"

"Nina—"

"Do you have a different name for killing when you wear a uniform to do it?"

They heard it then – a moan, like a creaking wind.

"Saints," Jesper said. "One of them is alive."

The sound came again, thin and keening, from the black hulk of the body on the far right. It was impossible to tell if the shape was male or female. Its hair had burned away, its clothing fused to its limbs. Black flakes of skin had peeled away in places, showing raw flesh.

A sob tore from Nina's throat. She raised her hands but she was shaking too badly to use her power to end the creature's suffering. She turned her tear-filled eyes to the others. "I . . . Please, someone . . ."

Jesper moved first. Two shots rang out, and the body fell silent. Jesper returned his pistols to their holsters.

"Damn it, Jesper," Kaz growled. "You just announced our presence for miles."

"So they think we're a hunting party."

"You should have let Inej do it."

"I didn't want to do it," Inej said quietly. "Thank you, Jesper."

Kaz's jaw ticked, but he said nothing more.

"Thank you," Nina choked out. She plunged ahead over the frozen ground, following the shape of the path through the snow. She was weeping, stumbling over the terrain. Matthias followed. There were few landmarks here, and it was easy to get turned around.

"Nina, you mustn't stray from the group—"

"That's what you're going back to, Helvar," she said harshly. "That's the country you long to serve. Does it make you proud?"

"I've never sent a Grisha to the pyre. Grisha are given a fair trial—"

She turned on him, goggles up, tears frozen on her cheeks.

"Then why has a Grisha never been found innocent at the end of your supposedly fair trials?"

"I—"

"Because our crime is *existing*. Our crime is what we are."

Matthias went quiet, and when he spoke he was caught between shame for what he was about to say and the need to speak the words, the words he'd been raised on, the words that still rang true for him. "Nina, has it ever occurred to you that maybe . . . you weren't *meant* to exist?"

Nina's eyes glinted green fire. She took a step towards him, and he could feel the rage radiating off her. "Maybe you're the ones who shouldn't exist, Helvar. Weak and soft, with your short lives and your sad little prejudices. You worship woodsprites and ice spirits who can't be bothered to show themselves, but you see real power, and you can't wait to stamp it out."

"Don't mock what you don't understand."

"My *mockery* offends you? My people would welcome your laughter in place of this barbarity." A look of supreme satisfaction crossed her face. "Ravka is rebuilding. So is the Second Army, and when they do, I hope they give you the fair trial you deserve. I hope they put the *drüskelle* in shackles and make them stand to hear their crimes enumerated so the world will have an accounting of your evils."

"If you're so desperate to see Ravka rise, why aren't you there now?"

"I want you to have your pardon, Helvar. I want you to be here when the Second Army marches north and overruns every inch of this wasteland. I hope they burn your fields and salt the earth. I hope they send your friends and your family to the pyre."

"They already did, Zenik. My mother, my father, my baby sister. Inferni soldiers, your precious, persecuted Grisha, burned our village to the ground. I have nothing left to lose."

Nina's laugh was bitter. "Maybe your stay in Hellgate was too short, Matthias. There's always more to lose."

20

NINA

I *can smell them.* Nina batted at her hair and clothes as she lurched through the snow, trying not to retch. She couldn't stop seeing those bodies, the angry red flesh peeking through their burned black casings like banked coals. It felt as if she was coated in their ashes, in the stink of burning flesh. She couldn't take a full breath.

Being around Matthias made it easy to forget what he really was, what he really thought of her. She'd tailored him again just this morning, enduring his glowers and grumbling. No, *enjoying* them, grateful for the excuse to be near him, ridiculously pleased every time she brought him close to a laugh. *Saints, why do I care?* Why did one smile from Matthias Helvar feel like fifty from someone else? She'd felt his heart race when she'd tipped his head back to work on his eyes. She'd thought about kissing him. She'd wanted to kiss him, and she was pretty sure he'd been thinking the same thing. *Or maybe he was thinking about strangling me again.*

She hadn't forgotten what he'd said aboard the *Ferolind*, when he'd asked what she intended to do about Bo Yul-

Bayur, if she truly meant to hand the scientist over to the Kerch. If she sabotaged Kaz's mission, would it cost Matthias his pardon? She couldn't do that. No matter what he was, she owed him his freedom.

Three weeks she'd travelled with Matthias after the shipwreck. They hadn't had a compass, hadn't known where they were going. They hadn't even known where on the northern shore they'd washed up. They'd spent long days slogging through the snow, freezing nights in whatever rudimentary shelter they could assemble or in the deserted huts of whaling camps when they were lucky enough to come across them. They'd eaten roasted seaweed and whatever grasses or tubers they could find. When they'd found a stash of dried reindeer meat at the bottom of a travel pack in one of the camps, it had been like some kind of miracle. They'd gnawed on it in mute bliss, feeling nearly drunk on its flavour.

After the first night, they'd slept in all the dry clothes and blankets they could find but on opposite sides of the fire. If they didn't have wood or kindling, they curled against one another, barely touching, but by morning, they'd be pressed together, breathing in tandem, cocooned in muzzy sleep, a single crescent moon.

Every morning he complained that she was impossible to wake.

"It's like trying to raise a corpse."

"The dead request five more minutes," she would say, and bury her head in the furs.

He'd stomp around, packing their few things as loudly as possible, grumbling to himself. "Lazy, ridiculous, selfish . . ." until she finally roused herself and set about preparing for the day.

"What's the first thing you're going to do when you get home?" she asked him on one of their endless days trekking through the snow, hoping to find some sign of civilization.

"Sleep," he said. "Bathe. Pray for my lost friends."

"Oh yes, the other thugs and killers. How did you become a *drüskelle*, anyway?"

"*Your* friends slaughtered my family in a Grisha raid," he'd said coldly. "Brum took me in and gave me something to fight for."

Nina hadn't wanted to believe that, but she knew it was possible. Battles happened, innocent lives were lost in the cross fire. It was equally disturbing to think of that monster Brum as some kind of father figure.

It didn't seem right to argue or to apologise, so she said the first thing that popped into her head.

"*Jer molle pe oonet. Enel mörd je nej afva trohem verretn.*" I have been made to protect you. Only in death will I be kept from this oath.

Matthias had stared at her in shock. "That's the *drüskelle* oath to Fjerda. How do you know those words?"

"I tried to learn as much about Fjerda as I could."

"Why?"

She'd wavered, then said, "So I wouldn't fear you."

"You don't seem afraid."

"Are you afraid of me?" she'd asked.

"No," he'd said, and he'd sounded almost surprised. He'd claimed before that he didn't fear her. This time she believed him. She tried to remind herself that wasn't a good thing.

They'd walked on for a while, and then he'd asked, "What's the first thing you're going to do?"

"Eat."

"Eat what?"

"Everything. Stuffed cabbage, potato dumplings, blackcurrant cakes, blini with lemon zest. I can't wait to see Zoya's face when I come walking into the Little Palace."

"Zoya Nazyalensky?"

Nina had stopped short. "You know her?"

"We all know of her. She's a powerful witch."

It had hit her then: For the *drüskelle*, Zoya was a little like Jarl Brum – cruel, inhuman, the thing that waited in the dark with death in her hands. Zoya was this boy's monster. The thought left her uneasy.

"How did you get out of the cages?"

Nina blinked. "What?"

"On the ship. You were bound and in cages."

"The water cup. The handle broke and the lip was jagged beneath. We used it to cut through our bonds. Once our hands were free . . ." Nina trailed off awkwardly.

Matthias' brow lowered. "You were planning to attack us."

"We were going to make our move that night."

"But then the storm hit."

"Yes."

A Squaller and a Fabrikator had smashed a hole right through the deck, and they'd swum free. But had any of them survived the icy waters? Had they managed to make their way to land? She shivered. If they hadn't discovered the cup's secret, she would have drowned in a cage.

"What do *drüskelle* eat?" she asked, picking up her pace. "Other than Grisha babies?"

"We don't eat babies!"

"Dolphin blubber? Reindeer hooves?"

She saw his mouth twist and wondered if he was nauseous or if maybe, possibly, he was trying not to laugh.

"We eat a lot of fish. Herring. Salt cod. And yes, reindeer, but not the hooves."

"How about cake?"

"What about it?"

"I'm very keen on cake. I'm wondering if we can find some common ground."

He shrugged.

"Oh, come on, *drüskelle*," she said. They still hadn't exchanged names, and she wasn't sure they should.

Eventually, if they survived, they would reach a town or village. She didn't know what would happen then, but the less he knew about her the better, in any case. "You're not giving up Fjerdan government secrets. I just want to know why you don't like cake."

"I do like cake, but we're not permitted sweets."

"Anyone? Or just *drüskelle?*"

"*Drüskelle.* It's considered an indulgence. Like alcohol or—"

"Girls?"

His cheeks reddened, and he trudged forward. It was just so easy to make him uncomfortable.

"If you're not allowed sugar or alcohol, you'd probably really love *pomdrakon.*"

He hadn't taken the bait at first, just walked on, but finally the quiet proved too much for him. "What's *pomdrakon?*"

"Dragonbowl," Nina said eagerly. "First you soak raisins in brandy, and then you turn off the lights and set them on fire."

"Why?"

"To make it hard to grab them."

"What do you do once you have them?"

"You eat them."

"Don't they burn your tongue?"

"Sure but—"

"Then why would you—"

"Because it's *fun*, dummy. You know, 'fun'? There's a word for it in Fjerdan so you must be familiar with the term."

"I have plenty of fun."

"All right, what do you do for fun?"

And that was the way they went on, sniping at each other, just like that first night in the water, keeping each other alive, refusing to acknowledge that they were growing weaker, that if they didn't find a real town soon, they weren't going to last much longer. There were days when their hunger and the glare off the northern ice had them moving in circles, backtracking, faltering over their own steps, but they never spoke of it, never said the word *lost*, as if they both knew that would somehow be admitting defeat.

"Why don't Fjerdans let girls fight?" she asked him one night as they'd lain curled beneath a lean-to, the cold palpable through the skins they'd laid on the ground.

"They don't want to fight."

"How do you know? Have you ever asked one?"

"Fjerdan women are to be venerated, protected."

"That's probably a wise policy."

He'd known her well enough by then to be surprised. "It is?"

"Think how embarrassing it would be for you when you got trounced by a Fjerdan girl."

He snorted.

"I'd love to see you get beaten by a girl," she said happily.

"Not in this lifetime."

"Well, I guess I won't get to *see* it. I'll just get to live the moment when I knock you on your ass."

This time he did laugh, a proper laugh that she could feel through her back.

"Saints, Fjerdan, I didn't know you could laugh. Careful now, take it slow."

"I enjoy your arrogance, *drüsje*."

Now she laughed. "That may be the worst compliment I've received."

"Do you never doubt yourself?"

"All the time," she'd said as she slid into sleep. "I just don't show it."

The next morning, they picked their way across an ice field splintered by jagged crevasses, keeping to the solid expanses between the deadly rifts, and arguing about Nina's sleeping habits.

"How can you call yourself a soldier? You'd sleep until noon if I let you."

"What does that have to do with anything?"

"Discipline. Routine. Does it mean nothing to you? Djel, I can't wait to have a bed to myself again."

"Right," said Nina. "I can feel just how much you hate sleeping next to me. I feel it every morning."

Matthias flushed bright scarlet. "Why do you have to say things like that?"

"Because I like it when you turn red."

"It's disgusting. You don't need to make everything lewd."

"If you would just relax—"

"I don't want to relax."

"Why? What are you so afraid will happen? Afraid you might start to like me?"

He said nothing.

Despite her fatigue, she trotted ahead of him. "That's it, isn't it? You don't want to like a Grisha. You're scared that if you laugh at my jokes or answer my questions, you might start thinking I'm human. Would that be so terrible?"

"I do like you."

"What was that?"

"I do like you," he said angrily.

She'd beamed, feeling a well of pleasure erupt through her. "Now, really, is that so bad?"

"Yes!" he roared.

"Why?"

"Because you're horrible. You're loud and lewd and . . . treacherous. Brum warned us that Grisha could be charming."

"Oh, I see. I'm the wicked Grisha seductress. I have beguiled you with my Grisha wiles!"

She poked him in the chest.

"Stop that."

"No. I'm beguiling you."

"Quit it."

She danced around him in the snow, poking his chest, his stomach, his side. "Goodness! You're very solid. This is strenuous work." He started to laugh. "It's working! The beguiling has begun. The Fjerdan has fallen. You are powerless to resist me. You—"

Nina's voice broke off in a scream as the ice gave way beneath her feet. She threw her hands out blindly, reaching for something, anything that might stop her fall, fingers scraping over ice and rock.

The *drüskelle* grabbed her arm, and she cried out as it was nearly wrenched from its socket.

She hung there, suspended over nothing, the grip of his fingers the only thing between her and the dark mouth of the ice. For a moment, looking into his eyes, she was certain he was going to let go.

"Please," she said, tears sliding over her cheeks.

He dragged her up over the edge, and slowly they crawled onto more solid ground. They lay on their backs, panting.

"I was afraid . . . I was afraid you were going to let me go," she managed.

There was a long pause and then he said, "I thought about it. Just for a second."

Nina huffed out a little laugh. "It's okay," she said at last. "I would have thought about it, too."

He got to his feet and offered her his hand. "I'm Matthias."

"Nina," she said, taking it. "Nice to make your acquaintance."

The shipwreck had been more than a year ago, but it felt as if no time had passed at all. Part of Nina wanted to go back to the moment before everything had gone wrong, to those long days on the ice when they'd managed to be Nina and

Matthias instead of Grisha and witchhunter. But the more she thought about it, the more surely she knew there had never been a moment like that. Those three weeks were a lie that she and Matthias had built to survive. The truth was the pyre.

"Nina," Matthias said, jogging up behind her now. "Nina, you need to stay with the others."

"Leave me alone."

When he took her arm, she whirled and clenched her fist, cutting off the air to his throat. An ordinary man would have released her, but Matthias was a trained *drüskelle*. He seized her other arm and clamped it to her body, bundling her tight to him so she couldn't use her hands. "Stop," he said softly.

She struggled against his hold, glaring up at him. "Let me go."

"I can't. Not while you're a threat."

"I will always be a threat to you, Matthias."

The corner of his mouth pulled up in a rueful smile. His eyes were almost sorrowful. "I know."

Slowly, he released her. She stepped back.

"What will I see when I get to the Ice Court?" she demanded.

"You're frightened."

"Yes," she said, chin jutting up defiantly. There was no point denying it.

"Nina—"

"Tell me. I need to know. Torture chambers? A pyre blazing from a rooftop?"

"They don't use pyres at the Court any more."

"Then what? Drawing and quartering? Firing squads? Does the Royal Palace have a view of the gallows?

"I've had enough of your judgements, Nina. This has to stop."

"He's right. You can't go on this way." Jesper was standing

in the snow with the others. How long had they been there? Had they seen her attack Matthias?

"Stay out of this," Nina snapped.

"If you two keep fighting, you're going to get us all killed, and I have a lot more card games I need to lose."

"You must find a way to make peace," said Inej. "At least for a while."

"This is not your concern," Matthias growled.

Kaz stepped forward, his expression dangerous. "It is very much our concern. And watch your tone."

Matthias threw up his hands. "You've all been taken in by her. This is what she does. She makes you think she's your friend and then—"

Inej crossed her arms. "Then what?"

"Let it go, Inej."

"No, Nina," Matthias said. "Tell them. You said you were my friend once. Do you remember?" He turned to the others. "We travelled together for three weeks. I saved her life. We saved each other. When we got to Elling, we . . . I could have revealed her to the soldiers we saw there at any time. But I didn't." Matthias started pacing, his voice rising, as if the memories were getting the better of him. "I borrowed money. I arranged lodging. I was willing to betray everything I believed in for the sake of her safety. When I saw her down to the docks so we could try to book passage, there was a Kerch trader there, ready to set sail." Matthias was there again, standing on the docks with her, she could see it in his eyes. "Ask her what she did then, this honourable ally, this girl who stands in judgement of me and my kind."

No one said a word, but they were watching, waiting.

"*Tell them*, Nina," he demanded. "They should know how you treat your friends."

Nina swallowed, then forced herself to meet their gazes. "I told the Kerch that he was a slaver and that he'd taken me prisoner. I threw myself on their mercy and begged them to help me. I had a seal I'd taken from a slaving ship we'd raided near the Wandering Isle. I used it as proof."

She couldn't bear to look at them. Kaz knew, of course. She'd had to tell him the charges she'd made and tried to recant when she was begging for his assistance. But Kaz had never probed, never asked why, never chastised her. In a way, telling Kaz had been a comfort. There could be no judgement from a boy known as Dirtyhands.

But now the truth was there for everyone to see. Privately, the Kerch knew slaves moved in and out of the ports of Ketterdam, and most indentures were really slaves by another name. But publicly, they reviled it and were obligated to prosecute all slavers. Nina had known exactly what would happen when she'd branded Matthias with that charge.

"I didn't understand what was happening," said Matthias. "I didn't speak Kerch, but Nina certainly did. They seized me and put me in chains. They tossed me in the brig and kept me there in the dark for weeks while we crossed the sea. The next time I saw daylight was when they led me off the ship in Ketterdam."

"I had no choice," Nina said, the ache of tears pressing at her throat. "You don't know—"

"Just tell me one thing," he said. There was anger in his voice, but she could hear something else, too, a kind of pleading. "If you could go back, if you could undo what you did to me, would you?"

Nina made herself face them. She had her reasons, but did they matter? And who were they to judge her? She straightened her spine, lifted her chin. She was a member of the Dregs, an employee of the White Rose, and occasionally a foolish girl, but before anything else she was a Grisha and a soldier. "No," she said clearly, her voice echoing off the endless ice. "I'd do it all over again."

A sudden rumble shook the ground. Nina nearly lost her footing, and she saw Kaz brace himself with his walking stick. They exchanged puzzled glances.

"Are there fault lines this far north?" Wylan asked.

Matthias frowned. "Not that I know of, but—"

A slab of earth shot up from beneath Matthias' feet, knocking him to the ground. Another erupted to Nina's right, sending her sprawling. All around them, crooked monoliths of earth and ice burst upwards, as if the ground was coming to life. A harsh wind whipped at their faces, snow spinning in flurries.

"What the hell is this?" cried Jesper.

"Some of kind of earthquake!" shouted Inej.

"No," said Nina, pointing to a dark spot that seemed to be floating in the sky, unaffected by the howling wind. "We're under attack."

Nina crawled on hands and knees, seeking some kind of shelter. She thought she might well have lost her mind. There was someone in the air, hovering in the sky high above her. She was watching someone fly.

Grisha Squallers could control current. She'd even seen them play at tossing each other into the air at the Little Palace, but the level of finesse and power it took to maintain controlled flight was unthinkable – at least it had been, until now. *Jurda parem*. She hadn't quite believed Kaz. Maybe she'd even suspected him of outright lying to her about what he'd seen just to get her to do the job. But unless she'd taken a blow to the head she didn't remember, this was real.

The Squaller turned in the air, stirring the storm into a frenzy, sending ice flying until it stung her cheeks. She could barely see. She fell backwards as another slab of rock and ice shot from the ground. They were being corralled, pushed closer together to make a single target.

"I need a distraction!" shouted Jesper from somewhere in the storm.

She heard a tinny *plink*.

"Get down," cried Wylan. Nina flattened her body to the snow. A *boom* sounded overhead, and an explosion lit the sky just to the right of the Squaller. The winds around them dropped as the Squaller was thrown off course and forced to focus on righting himself. It took the briefest second, but it was enough time for Jesper to aim his rifle and fire.

A shot rang out, and the Squaller was hurtling towards the earth. Another slab of ice slid into place. They were being trapped like animals in a pen, ready for the slaughter. Jesper aimed between the slabs at a distant stand of trees, and Nina realised there was another Grisha there, a boy with dark hair. Before Jesper could get off a shot, the Grisha rammed a fist upwards, and Jesper was thrown off his feet by a shaft of earth. He rolled as he fell and fired from the ground.

The boy in the distance cried out and dropped to one knee, but his arms were still raised, and the ground still rumbled and rocked beneath them. Jesper fired again and missed. Nina lifted her hands and tried to focus on the Grisha's heart, but he was well out of her range.

She saw Inej signal to Kaz. Without a word, he positioned himself against the nearest slab and cupped his hands at his knee. The ground buckled and swayed, but he held steady as she launched herself from the cradle of his fingers in a graceful arc. She vanished over the slab without a sound. A moment later, the ground went still.

"Trust the Wraith," said Jesper.

They stood, dazed, the air strangely hushed after the chaos that had come before.

"Wylan," Jesper panted, pushing to his feet. "Get us out of here."

Wylan nodded, pulled a putty-coloured lump from his pack, and gently placed it against the nearest rock. "Everybody down," he instructed.

They crouched together in a cluster as far away as the

enclosure would permit. Wylan slapped his hand against the explosive and dove away, careening into Matthias and Jesper as they all covered their ears.

Nothing happened.

"Are you kidding me?" said Jesper.

Boom. The slab exploded. Ice and bits of rock rained down over their heads.

Wylan was covered in dust and wearing a slightly dazed, deliriously happy expression. Nina started to laugh. "*Try* to look like you knew it would work."

They stumbled out of the corral of slabs.

Kaz gestured to Jesper. "Perimeter. Let's make sure there aren't more surprises." They set off in opposite directions.

Nina and the others found Inej standing over the body of the trembling Grisha. He wore clothes of olive drab, and his eyes were glassy. Blood spilled from the bullet wound in his upper thigh, and a knife jutted from the right side of his chest. Inej must have thrown it when she'd escaped from the enclosure.

Nina kneeled beside him.

"I need a little more," the Grisha mumbled. "Just a little more." He grabbed at Nina's hand, and only then did she recognise him.

"Nestor?"

He twitched at the sound of his name, but he didn't seem to know her.

"Nestor, it's me, Nina." She had been at school with him back at the Little Palace. They'd been sent to Keramzin together during the war. At King Nikolai's coronation, they'd stolen a bottle of champagne and got sick by the lake. He was a Fabrikator, one of the Durasts who worked with metal, glass, and fibers. It didn't make sense. Fabrikators made textiles, weapons. He shouldn't have been capable of what she'd just witnessed.

"Please," he begged, his face crumpling. "I need more."

"*Parem?*"

"Yes," he sobbed. "Yes. Please."

"I can heal your wound, Nestor, if you stay still." He was in bad shape, but if she could stop the bleeding . . .

"I don't want your help," he said angrily, trying to push away from her.

She tried calming him, lowering his pulse, but she was afraid of stopping his heart. "Please, Nestor. Please be still."

He was screaming now, fighting her.

"Hold him down," she said.

Matthias moved to help, and Nestor threw up his arms.

The ground rose in a rippling sheet, thrusting Nina and the others back.

"Nestor, please! Let us help you."

He stood up, staggering on his wounded leg, pulling at the knife buried in his chest. "Where are they?" he screamed. "Where did they go?"

"Who?"

"The Shu!" he wailed. "Where did they go? Come back!" He took a wobbling step, then another. "Come back!" He fell face forwards into the snow. He didn't move again.

Nina rushed to his side and turned him over. There was snow in his eyes and his mouth. She placed her hands on his chest, trying to restore his heartbeat, but it was no good. If he hadn't been ravaged by the drug, he might have survived his wounds. But his body was weak, the skin tight to his bones and so pale it seemed transparent.

This isn't right, Nina thought miserably. Practising the Small Science made a Grisha healthier, stronger. It was one of the things she loved most about her power. But the body had limits. It was as if the drug had caused Nestor's power to outpace his body. It had simply used him up.

Kaz and Jesper returned, panting.

"Anything?" asked Matthias.

Jesper nodded. "A party of people heading south."

"He was calling out for the Shu," Nina said.

"We knew the Shu would send a team to retrieve Bo Yul-Bayur," said Kaz.

Jesper looked down at Nestor's motionless body. "But we didn't know they'd send Grisha. How can we be sure they aren't mercenaries?"

Kaz held up a coin emblazoned with a horse on one side and two crossed keys on the other. "This was in the Squaller's pocket," he said, tossing it to Jesper. "It's a Shu *wen ye*. The Coin of Passage. This is a government mission."

"How did they find us?" Inej asked.

"Maybe Jesper's gunshots drew them," said Kaz.

Jesper bristled and pointed at Nina and Matthias. "Or maybe they heard these two shouting at each other. They could have been following us for miles."

Nina tried to make sense of what she was hearing. Shu didn't use Grisha as soldiers, and they weren't like the Fjerdans; they didn't see Grisha power as unnatural or repulsive. They were fascinated by it. But they still viewed the Grisha as less than human. The Shu government had been capturing and experimenting on Grisha for years in an attempt to locate the source of their power. They would never use Grisha as mercenaries. Or at least that had been the case before. Maybe *parem* had changed the game.

"I don't understand," said Nina. "If they have *jurda parem*, why go after Bo Yul-Bayur?"

"It's possible they have a stash of it, but can't reproduce his process," Kaz said. "That's what the Merchant Council seemed to think. Or maybe they just want to make sure Yul-Bayur doesn't give the formula to anyone else."

"Do you think they'll use drugged Grisha to try to break into the Ice Court?" Inej asked.

"If they have more of them," said Kaz. "That's what I would do."

Matthias shook his head. "If they'd had a Heartrender, we'd all be dead."

"It was still a close thing," replied Inej.

Jesper shouldered his rifle. "Wylan earned his keep."

Wylan gave a little jump at the sound of his name. "I did?"

"Well, you made a down payment."

"Let's move," said Kaz.

"We need to bury them," Nina said.

"The ground's too hard, and we don't have the time. The Shu team is still moving towards Djerholm. We don't know how many other Grisha they may have, and Pekka's team could already be inside."

"We can't just leave them for the wolves," she said, her throat tight.

"Do you want to build them a pyre?"

"Go to hell, Brekker."

"Do your job, Zenik," he shot back. "I didn't bring you to Fjerda to perform funeral rites."

She lifted her hands. "How about I crack your skull open like a robin's egg?"

"You don't want a look at what's inside my head, Nina dear."

She took a step forward, but Matthias moved in front of her.

"Stop," he said. "I'll do it. I'll help you dig the grave." Nina stared at him. He took a pick from his gear and handed it to her, then took another from Jesper's pack. "Head due south from here," he said to the others. "I know the terrain, and I'll make sure we catch up to you by nightfall. We'll move faster on our own."

Kaz looked at him steadily. "Just remember that pardon, Helvar."

"Are we sure it's a good idea to leave them alone?" Wylan asked as they moved down the slope.

"No," replied Inej.

"But we're still doing it?"

"We trust them now or we trust them later," Kaz said.

"Are we going to talk about Matthias' little revelation about Nina's loyalties?" asked Jesper.

Nina could just make out Kaz's reply: "Pretty sure most of us don't have 'stalwart' or 'true' checked off on our résumés." For all that she wanted to pummel Kaz, she couldn't help being a bit grateful, too.

Matthias walked a few steps away from Nestor's body. He heaved the pick into the icy earth, wrenched it free, plunged it in again.

"Here?" Nina asked.

"Do you want him elsewhere?"

"I . . . I don't know." She gazed out at the fields of white, marked by sparse groves of birch. "It all looks the same to me."

"You know our gods?"

"Some," she said.

"But you know Djel."

"The wellspring."

Matthias nodded. "The Fjerdans believe all the world is connected through its waters – the seas, the ice, the rivers and streams, the rain and storms. All feed Djel and are fed by him. When we die, we call it *felöt-objer*, taking root. We become as roots of the ash tree, drinking from Djel wherever we are laid."

"Is that why you burn Grisha instead of burying them?"

He paused, then gave a brief nod.

"But you'll help me lay Nestor and the Squaller to rest here?"

He nodded again.

She took hold of the other pick and attempted to match his swing. The ground was hard and unyielding. Every time the pick struck the earth it sent a rattling jolt up her arms.

"Nestor shouldn't have been able to do that," she said, her thoughts still churning. "No Grisha can use power that way. It's all wrong."

He was quiet for a moment, and then he said, "Do you understand a little better now? What it's like to face a power so alien? To face an enemy with such unnatural strength?"

Nina tightened her hold on the pick. Nestor in the grip of *parem* had seemed like a perversion of everything she loved about her power. Was that what Matthias and the other Fjerdans saw in Grisha? Power beyond explanation, the natural world undone?

"Maybe." It was the most she could offer.

"You said you had no choice at the harbour in Elling," he said without looking at her. His pick rose and fell, the rhythm unbroken. "Was it because I was *drüskelle*? Were you planning it all along?"

Nina remembered their last real day together, the elation they'd felt when they'd crested a steep hill and seen the port town spread out below. She'd been shocked to hear Matthias say, "I am almost sorry, Nina."

"Almost?"

"I'm too hungry to really be sorry."

"At last, you succumb to my influence. But how are we going to eat without any money?" she asked as they headed down the hill. "I may have to sell your pretty hair to a wig shop for cash."

"Don't get ideas," he'd said with a laugh. His laughter had come more easily as they'd travelled, as if he were becoming fluent in a new language. "If this is Elling, I should be able to find us lodging."

She'd stopped then, the truth of their situation returning to her with terrible clarity. She was deep in enemy territory with no allies but a *drüskelle* who'd thrown her in a cage only a few weeks earlier. But before she could speak, Matthias had said, "I owe you my life, Nina Zenik. We will get you safely home."

She'd been surprised at how easy it was to trust him. And he'd trusted her, too.

Now she swung her pick, felt the impact reverberate up her arms and into her shoulders, and said, "There were Grisha in Elling."

He halted midswing. "What?"

"They were spies doing reconnaissance work in the port. They saw me enter the main square with you and recognised me from the Little Palace. One of them recognised you, too, Matthias. He knew you from a skirmish near the border."

Matthias remained still.

"They waylaid me when you went to speak to the manager of the boarding house," Nina continued. "I convinced them I was under cover there, too. They wanted to take you prisoner, but I told them that you weren't alone, that it would be too risky to try to capture you right away. I promised I would bring you to them the next day."

"Why didn't you just tell me?"

Nina tossed down her pick. "Tell you there were Grisha spies in Elling? You might have made your peace with me, but you can't expect me to believe you wouldn't have revealed them."

He looked away, a muscle twitching in his jaw, and she knew she'd spoken truth.

"That morning," he said, "on the docks—"

"I had to get us both away from Elling as fast as I could. I thought if I could just find us a vessel to stow away on. . . but the Grisha must have been watching the boarding house and seen us leave. When they showed up on the docks, I knew they were coming for you, Matthias. If they'd captured you, you would have been taken to Ravka, interrogated, maybe executed. I spotted the Kerch trader. You know their laws on slaving."

"Of course I do," he said bitterly.

"I made the charge. I begged them to save me. I knew they'd have to take you into custody, and bring us safely to Kerch. I didn't know – Matthias, I didn't know they'd throw you in Hellgate."

His eyes were hard when he faced her, his knuckles white on the handle of his pick. "Why didn't you speak up? Why didn't you tell the truth when we arrived in Ketterdam?"

"I tried. I swear it. I tried to recant. They wouldn't let me see a judge. They wouldn't let me see you. I couldn't explain the seal from the slaver or why I'd made the charges, not without revealing Ravka's intelligence operations. I would have compromised Grisha still in the field. I would have been sentencing them to death."

"So you left me to rot in Hellgate."

"I could have gone home to Ravka. Saints, I wanted to. But I stayed in Ketterdam. I gave up my wages for bribes, petitioned the Court—"

"You did everything but tell the truth."

She'd meant to be gentle, apologetic, to tell him that she'd thought of him every night and every day. But the image of the pyre was still fresh in her mind. "I was trying to protect my people, people you've spent your life trying to exterminate."

He gave a rueful laugh, turning the pick over in his hands. *"Wanden olstrum end kendesorum."*

It was the first part of a Fjerdan saying, *The water hears and understands.* It sounded kind enough, but Matthias knew that Nina would be familiar with the rest of it.

"Isen ne bejstrum," she finished. The water hears and understands. The ice does not forgive.

"And what will you do now, Nina? Will you betray the people you call friends again, for the sake of the Grisha?"

"What?"

"You can't tell me you intend to let Bo Yul-Bayur live."

He knew her well. With every new thing she'd learned of *jurda parem*, she'd been more certain that the only way to protect Grisha was to end the scientist's life. She thought of Nestor begging with his last breath for his Shu masters to return. "I can't bear the thought of my people being slaves," she admitted. "But we have a debt to settle, Matthias. The pardon is my penance, and I won't be the person who keeps you from your freedom again."

"I don't want the pardon."

She stared at him. "But—"

"Maybe your people would become slaves. Or maybe they would become an unstoppable force. If Yul-Bayur lives and the secret of *jurda parem* becomes known, anything is possible."

For a long moment, they held each other's gaze. The sun was beginning to set, light falling in golden shafts across the snow. She could see the blond of Matthias' lashes peeking through the black antimony she had used to stain them. She'd have to tailor him again soon.

In those days after the shipwreck, she and Matthias had formed an uneasy truce. What had grown up between them had been something fiercer than affection – an understanding that they were both soldiers, that in another life, they might have been allies instead of enemies. She felt that now.

"It would mean betraying the others," she said. "They won't get their pay from the Merchant Council."

"True."

"And Kaz will kill us both."

"If he learns the truth."

"Have you tried lying to Kaz Brekker?"

Matthias shrugged. "Then we die as we lived."

Nina looked at Nestor's emaciated form. "For a cause."

"We are of one mind in this," said Matthias. "Bo Yul-

Bayur will not leave the Ice Court alive."

"The deal is the deal," she said in Kerch, the language of trade, a tongue that belonged to neither of them.

"The deal is the deal," he replied.

Matthias swung his pick and brought it down in a hard arc, a kind of declaration. She hefted her pick and did the same. Without another word, they returned to the work of the grave, falling into a determined rhythm.

Kaz was right about one thing at least. She and Matthias had finally found something to agree on.

PART 4

THE TRICK TO FALLING

21

INEJ

Inej felt as though she and Kaz had become twin soldiers, marching on, pretending they were fine, hiding their wounds and bruises from the rest of the crew.

It took two more days of travel to reach the cliffs that overlooked Djerholm, but the going was easier as they moved south and towards the coast. The weather warmed, the ground thawed, and she began to see signs of spring. Inej had thought Djerholm would look like Ketterdam – a canvas of black, grey, and brown, tangled streets dense with mist and coalsmoke, ships of every kind in the harbour, pulsing with the rush and bustle of trade. Djerholm's harbour was crowded with ships, but its tidy streets marched to the water in orderly fashion, and the houses were painted such colours – red, blue, yellow, pink – as if in defiance of the wild white land and the long winters this far north. Even the warehouses by the quay were wrought in cheerful colours. It looked the way she'd imagined cities as a child, everything candy-hued and in its proper place.

Was the *Ferolind* already waiting at the docks, snug in its berth, flying its Kerch flag and the distinctive orange and green parti-colour of the Haanraadt Bay Company? If the plan went the way Kaz hoped, tomorrow night they would stroll down the Djerholm quay with Bo Yul-Bayur in tow, hop on their ship, and be far out to sea before anyone in Fjerda was the wiser. She preferred not to think of what tomorrow night might look like if the plan went wrong.

Inej glanced up to where the Ice Court stood like a great white sentinel on a massive cliff overlooking the harbour. Matthias had called the cliffs unscalable, and Inej had to admit that they would present a challenge even for the Wraith. They seemed impossibly high, and from a distance, their white lime surface looked clean and bright as ice.

"Cannon," said Jesper.

Kaz squinted up at the big guns pointed out at the bay. "I've broken into banks, warehouses, mansions, museums, vaults, a rare book library, and once the bedchamber of a visiting Kaelish diplomat whose wife had a passion for emeralds. But I've never had a cannon shot at me."

"There's something to be said for novelty," offered Jesper.

Inej pressed her lips together. "Hopefully, it won't come to that."

"Those guns are there to stop invading armadas," Jesper said confidently. "Good luck hitting a skinny little schooner cutting through the waves bound for fortune and glory."

"I'll quote you on that when a cannonball lands in my lap," said Nina.

They slipped easily into the traffic of travellers and traders where the cliff road met the northern road that led to Upper Djerholm. The upper town was a rambling extension of the city below, a sprawling collection of shops, markets, and inns that served the guards and staff who worked at the Ice Court as well as visitors. Luckily, the crowds were heavy and motley enough that one more group of foreigners could go unnoticed, and Inej found herself breathing a bit easier. She'd worried that she and Jesper might be dangerously conspicuous in the Fjerdan capital's sea of blonds. Maybe the crew from the Shu Han was relying on the jumbled crowd for cover, too.

Signs of Hringkälla celebrations were everywhere. The shops had created elaborate displays of pepper cookies baked in the shape of wolves, some hanging like ornaments from large, twisting trees, and the bridge spanning the river gorge had been festooned with ribbons in Fjerdan silver. One way into the Ice Court and one way out. Would they cross this bridge as visitors tomorrow?

"What are they?" Wylan asked, pausing in front of a peddler's cart laden with wreaths made of the same twisting branches and silver ribbons.

"Ash trees," replied Matthias. "Sacred to Djel."

"There's supposed to be one in the middle of the White Island," said Nina, ignoring the warning look the Fjerdan cast her. "It's where the *drüskelle* gather for the listening ceremony."

Kaz tapped his walking stick on the ground. "Why is this the first I'm hearing of it?"

"The ash is sustained by the spirit of Djel," said Matthias. "It's where we may best hear his voice."

Kaz's eyes flickered. "Not what I asked. Why isn't it on our plans?"

"Because it's the holiest place in all of Fjerda and not essential to our mission."

"I say what's essential. Anything else you decided to leave out in your great wisdom?"

"The Ice Court is a vast structure," Matthias said, turning away. "I can't label every crack and corner."

"Then let's hope nothing is lurking in those corners," Kaz replied.

Upper Djerholm had no real centre, but the bulk of its taverns, inns, and market stalls were clustered around the base of the hill leading to the Ice Court. Kaz steered them seemingly aimlessly through the streets until he found a run-down tavern called the Gestinge.

"Here?" Jesper complained, peering into the dank main room. The whole place stank of garlic and fish.

Kaz just gave a significant glance upwards and said, "Terrace."

"What's a *gestinge?*" Inej wondered aloud.

"It means 'paradise'," said Matthias. Even he looked skeptical.

Nina helped secure them a table on the tavern's rooftop terrace. It was mostly empty, the weather still too cold to attract many patrons. Or maybe they'd been scared away by the food – herring in rancid oil, stale black bread, and some kind of butter that looked distinctly mossy.

Jesper looked down at his plate and moaned. "Kaz, if you want me dead, I prefer a bullet to poison."

Nina scrunched her nose. "When I don't want to eat, you know there's a problem."

"We're here for the view, not the food."

From their table, they had a clear, if distant, view of the Ice Court's outer gate and the first guardhouse. It was built into a white arch formed by two monumental stone wolves on their hind legs, and spanned the road leading up the hill to the Court. Inej and the others watched the traffic come and go through the gates as they picked at their lunches, waiting for a sign of the prison wagons. Inej's appetite had finally returned, and she'd been eating as much as possible to build her strength, but the skin atop the soup she'd ordered wasn't helping.

There was no coffee to be had so they ordered tea and little glasses of clear *brännvin* that burned going down but helped to keep them warm as a wind picked up, stirring the silvery ribbons tied to the ash boughs lining the street below.

"We're going to start looking conspicuous soon," said

Nina. "This isn't the kind of place people like to linger."

"Maybe they don't have anyone to take to jail," suggested Wylan.

"There's always someone to take to jail," Kaz replied, then bobbed his chin towards the road. "Look."

A boxy wagon was rolling to a stop at the guardhouse. Its roof and high sides were covered in black canvas, and it was drawn by four stout horses. The door at the back was heavy iron, bolted and padlocked.

Kaz reached into his coat pocket. "Here," he said and handed Jesper a slender book with an elaborate cover.

"Are we going to read to each other?"

"Just flip it open to the back."

Jesper opened the book and peered at the last page, puzzled. "So?"

"Hold it up so we don't have to look at your ugly face."

"My face has character. Besides – oh!"

"An excellent read, isn't it?"

"Who knew I had a taste for literature?"

Jesper passed it to Wylan, who took it tentatively. "What does it say?"

"Just look," said Jesper.

Wylan frowned and held it up, then he grinned. "Where did you get this?"

Matthias had his turn and released a surprised grunt.

"It's called a backless book," said Kaz as Inej took the volume from Nina and held it up. The pages were full of ordinary sermons, but the ornate back cover hid two lenses that acted as a long glass. Kaz had told her to keep an eye out for women using similarly made mirrored compacts at the Crow Club. They could read the hand a player was holding from across the room, then signal to a partner at the table.

"Clever," Inej remarked as she peered through. To the barmaid and the other patrons on the terrace, it looked as if they were handing a book around, discussing some interesting passage. Instead Inej had a close view of the gatehouse and the wagon parked in front of it.

The gate between the rampant wolves was wrought iron, bearing the symbol of the sacred ash and bordered by a high, spiked fence that circled the Ice Court's grounds.

"Four guards," she noted, just as Matthias had said. Two were stationed on each side of the gatehouse, and one of them was chatting with the driver of the prison wagon, who handed him a packet of documents.

"They're the first line of defence," said Matthias. "They'll check paperwork and confirm identities, flag anyone they think requires closer scrutiny. By this time tomorrow the line going through the gates will be full of Hringkälla guests and backed up all the way to the gorge."

"By then we'll be inside," Kaz said.

"How often do the wagons run?" asked Jesper.

"It depends," said Matthias. "Usually in the morning. Sometimes in the afternoon. But I can't imagine they'll want prisoners arriving at the same time as guests."

"Then we have to be on the early wagon," Kaz said.

Inej lifted the backless book again. The wagon driver wore a grey uniform similar to the ones worn by the guards at the gate but absent any sash or decoration. He swung down from his seat and came around to unlock the iron door.

"Saints," Inej said as the door swung open. Ten prisoners were seated along benches that ran the wagon's length, their wrists and feet shackled, black sacks over their heads.

Inej handed the book back to Matthias, and as it made the rounds, Inej felt the group's apprehension rise. Only Kaz seemed unfazed.

"Hooded, chained, and shackled?" said Jesper. "You're sure we can't go in as entertainers? I hear Wylan really kills it on the flute."

"We go in as we are," said Kaz, "as criminals."

Nina peered through the lenses of the book. "They're doing a head count."

Matthias nodded. "If procedure hasn't changed, they'll do a quick head count at the first checkpoint, then a second count at the next checkpoint, where they'll search the interior and undercarriage for any contraband."

Nina passed the book to Inej. "The driver is going to notice six more prisoners when he opens the door."

"If only I'd thought of that," Kaz said drily. "I can tell you've never picked a pocket."

"And I can tell you've never given enough thought to your haircut."

Kaz frowned and ran a self-conscious hand along the side of his head. "There's nothing wrong with my haircut that can't be fixed by four million *kruge*."

Jesper cocked his head to one side, grey eyes alight. "We're going to use a bunk biscuit, aren't we?"

"Exactly."

"I don't know that word, *bunkbiscuit*," said Matthias, running the syllables together.

Nina gave Kaz a sour look. "Neither do I. We're not as streetwise as you, Dirtyhands."

"Nor will you ever be," Kaz said easily. "Remember our friend Mark?" Wylan winced. "Let's say the mark is a tourist walking through the Barrel. He's heard it's a good place to get rolled, so he keeps patting his wallet, making sure it's there, congratulating himself on just how alert and cautious he's being. No fool he. Of course every time he pats his back pocket or the front of his coat, what is he doing? He's telling every thief on the Stave exactly where he keeps his scrub."

"Saints," grumbled Nina. "I've probably done that."

"Everyone does," said Inej.

Jesper lifted a brow. "Not everyone."

"That's only because you never have anything *in* your wallet," Nina shot back.

"Mean."

"Factual."

"Facts are for the unimaginative," Jesper said with a dismissive wave.

"Now, a bad thief," continued Kaz, "one who doesn't know his way around, just makes the grab and tries to run for it. Good way to get pinched by the *stadwatch*. But a proper thief – like myself – nabs the wallet and puts something else in its place."

"A biscuit?"

"Bunk biscuit is just a name. It can be a rock, a bar of soap, even an old roll if it's the right size. A proper thief can tell the weight of a wallet just by the way it changes the hang of a man's coat. He makes the switch, and the poor mark keeps tapping his pocket, happy as can be. It's not until he tries to pay for an omelette or lay his stake at a table that he realises he's been done for a sucker. By then the thief is somewhere safe, counting up his scrub."

Wylan shifted unhappily in his chair. "Duping innocent people isn't something to be proud of."

"It is if you do it well." Kaz gave a nod to the prison wagon, now rumbling its way up the road towards the Ice Court and the second checkpoint. "We're going to be the biscuit."

"Hold on," said Nina. "The door locks on the outside. How do we get in and get the door locked again?"

"That's only a problem if you don't know a proper thief. Leave the locks to me."

Jesper stretched out his long legs. "So we have to unlock, unchain, and incapacitate six prisoners, take their places, and somehow get the wagon sealed tight again without the guards or the other prisoners being the wiser?"

"That's right."

"Any other impossible feats you'd like us to accomplish?"

The barest smile flickered over Kaz's lips. "I'll make you a list."

Proper thievery aside, Inej would have liked a proper night's sleep in a proper bed, but there would be no comfortable stay at an inn, not if they were going to find their way onto a prison wagon and into the Ice Court before Hringkälla began. There was too much to do.

Nina was sent out to chat up the locals and try to discover the best place to lay their ambush for the wagon. After the horrors of Gestinge's herring, they'd demanded Kaz provide something edible, and were waiting for Nina in a crowded bakery, nursing hot cups of coffee mixed with chocolate, the wreckage of demolished rolls and cookies spread over their table in little piles of buttery crumbs. Inej noted that Matthias' mug sat untouched before him, slowly cooling as he stared out the window.

"This must be hard for you," she said quietly. "To be here but not really be home."

He looked down at his cup. "You have no idea."

"I think I do. I haven't seen my home in a long time."

Kaz turned away and began chatting with Jesper. He seemed to do that whenever she mentioned going back to Ravka. Of course, Inej couldn't be certain she'd find her parents there. Suli were travellers. For them, 'home' really just meant family.

"Are you worried about Nina being out there?" Inej asked.

"No."

"She's very good at this, you know. She's a natural actress."

"I'm aware," he said grimly. "She can be anything to anyone."

"She's best when she's Nina."

"And who is that?"

"I suspect you know better than any of us."

He crossed his huge arms. "She's brave," he said grudgingly.

"And funny."

"Foolish. Every last thing needn't be a joke."

"Bold," Inej said.

"Loud."

"So why do your eyes keep searching the crowd for her?"

"They do *not*," Matthias protested. She had to laugh at the ferocity of his scowl. He drew a finger through a pile of crumbs. "Nina is everything you say. It's too much."

"Mmm," Inej murmured, taking a sip from her mug. "Maybe you're just not enough."

Before he could reply, the bell on the bakery door jingled, and Nina sailed inside, cheeks rosy, brown hair in a gorgeous tangle, and declared, "Someone needs to start feeding me sweet rolls immediately."

For all Matthias' grumbling, Inej didn't think she imagined the relief on his face.

It had taken Nina less than an hour to discover that most of the prison wagons passed by a roadhouse known as the Warden's Waystation on the route to the Ice Court. Inej and the others had to trek almost two miles out of Upper Djerholm to locate the tavern. It was too crowded with farmers and local labourers to be useful, so they headed further up the road, and by the time they found a spot with enough cover and a stand of trees large enough to suit their purpose, Inej felt close to collapse. She thanked her Saints for Jesper's seemingly limitless energy. He cheerfully volunteered to continue on and be the lookout. When the prison cart rolled by, he'd signal the rest of the crew with a flare, then sprint back to join them.

Nina took a few minutes to tailor Jesper's forearm, hiding

the Dregs' tattoo and leaving a blotchy patch of skin over it. She would see to Kaz's tattoos and her own that night. It was possible no one at the prison would recognise Ketterdam gang or brothel markings, but there was no reason to take the chance.

"No mourners," Jesper called as he loped off into the twilight, long legs eating up the distance easily.

"No funerals," they replied. Inej sent a real prayer along with him, too. She knew Jesper was well armed and could take care of himself, but between his lanky frame and Zemeni skin, he was just too noticeable for comfort.

They camped in a dry gully bordered by a tangle of shrubs, and took shifts dozing on the hard rock ground and keeping watch. Despite her fatigue, Inej hadn't thought she would be able to sleep, but the next thing she knew, the sun was high above them, a bright pocket of glare in an overcast sky. It had to be past noon. Nina was beside her with a piece of one of the pepper wolf cookies she'd bought in Upper Djerholm. Inej saw that someone had made a low fire, and the sticky remnants of a block of melted paraffin were visible in its ashes.

"Where are the others?" she asked, looking around the empty gully.

"In the road. Kaz said we should let you sleep."

Inej rubbed her eyes. She supposed it was a concession to her injuries. Maybe she hadn't hidden her exhaustion well at all. A sudden, crackling *snap snap snap* from the road had her on her feet with knives drawn in seconds.

"Easy," Nina said. "It's just Wylan."

Jesper must have already raised the signal. Inej took the cookie from Nina and hurried up to where Kaz and Matthias were watching Wylan fuss with something at the base of a thick red fir. Another series of pops sounded, and tiny puffs of white smoke burst from the tree's trunk where it met the ground. For a moment it looked as if nothing would happen, then the roots loosed themselves from the soil, curling and withering.

"What was that?" asked Inej.

"Salt concentrate," said Nina.

Inej cocked her head to the side. "Is Matthias . . . praying?"

"Saying a blessing. Fjerdans do it whenever they cut down a tree."

"Every time?"

"The blessings depend on how you intend to use the wood. One for houses, one for bridges." She paused. "One for kindling."

It took less than a minute for them to pull the tree down so that its trunk lay blocking the road. With the roots intact, it looked as if it had simply been felled by disease.

"Once the wagon stops, the tree will buy us about fifteen minutes and not much more," Kaz said. "Move quickly. The prisoners should be hooded, but they'll be able to hear, so not a word. We can't afford to arouse suspicion. For all they know, this is a routine stop, and we want to keep it that way."

As Inej waited in the gully with the others, she considered all the things that might go wrong. The prisoners might not be wearing hoods. The guards might have one of their own in the back of the wagon. And if their crew succeeded? Well, then they'd be captives on their way into the Ice Court. That didn't seem like a particularly promising outcome, either.

Just when she started to wonder if Jesper had been wrong and sent up the flare too early, a prison wagon rumbled into view. It rolled past them, then came to a halt in front of the tree. She could hear the driver cursing to his companion.

They both slid down from the box seat and made their way over to the tree. For a long minute, they stood there staring at it. The larger guard took off his hat and scratched his belly.

"How lazy can they be?" Kaz muttered.

Finally, they seemed to accept that the tree wasn't going to move on its own. They strolled back to the wagon to retrieve a heavy coil of rope and unhitched one of the horses to help drag the tree out of the road.

"Be ready," Kaz said. He skittered over the top of the gully to the back end of the cart. He'd left his walking stick behind in the ditch, and whatever pain he might have been feeling, he disguised it well. He slipped his lockpicks from the lining of his coat and cradled the padlock gently, almost lovingly. In seconds, it sprang open, and he shoved the bolt to the side. He glanced around to where the men were tying ropes around the tree and then opened the door.

Inej tensed, waiting for the signal. It didn't come. Kaz was just standing there, staring into the wagon.

"What's happening?" whispered Wylan.

"Maybe they aren't hooded?" she replied. From the side, she couldn't see. "I'll go." They couldn't all bunch up around the back of the cart at once.

Inej climbed out of the gully and came up behind Kaz. He was still standing there, perfectly still. She touched his shoulder briefly, and he flinched. Kaz Brekker *flinched*. What was going on? She couldn't ask him and risk giving anything away to the listening prisoners. She peered into the wagon.

The prisoners were all cuffed and had black sacks over their heads. But there were considerably more of them than in the wagon they'd seen at the checkpoint. Instead of being seated and chained to the benches at the sides, they were standing, pressed up against one another. Their feet and hands had been shackled, and they all wore iron collars that had been clipped to hooks in the wagon's roof. Whenever one started to slump or lean too heavily, his or her breath would be cut off. It wasn't pretty, though they were so tightly packed together it didn't look like anyone could actually fall and choke.

Inej gave Kaz another little nudge. His face was pale, almost waxen, but at least this time he didn't just stand there. He pushed himself up into the wagon, his movements jerky and awkward, and began unlocking the prisoners' collars.

Inej signalled to Matthias, who leaped out of the gully to join them.

"What's happening?" one of the prisoners asked in Ravkan, his voice frightened.

"*Tig!*" Matthias growled harshly in Fjerdan. A rustle went through the prisoners in the truck, as if they were all coming to attention. Without meaning to, Inej had straightened her spine, too. With that word, Matthias' whole demeanour had changed, as if with a single sharp command he'd stepped back into the uniform of a *drüskelle*. Inej eyed him nervously. She'd started to feel comfortable with Matthias. An easy habit to fall into, but unwise.

Kaz unlocked six sets of hand and foot shackles. One by one, Inej and Matthias unloaded the six prisoners closest to the door. There wasn't time to consider height or build or even if they'd freed men or women. They led them to the edge of the gully, all while keeping an eye on the progress of the guards on the road. "What's happening?" one of the captives dared to ask. But another quick "*Tig!*" from Matthias silenced him.

Once they were out of view, Nina dropped their pulses, sending them into unconsciousness. Only then did Wylan remove the prisoners' hoods: four men, one of them quite old, a middle-aged woman, and a Shu boy. It definitely wasn't ideal, but hopefully the guards wouldn't fret too much over accuracy. After all, how much trouble could a group of chained and shackled convicts be?

Nina injected the prisoners with a sleeping solution to prolong their rest, and Wylan helped roll them into the gully behind the trees.

"Are we just going to leave them there?" Wylan whispered

to Inej as they hurried back to the wagon with the prisoners' hoods in hand.

Inej's eyes were trained on the guards moving the tree, and she didn't look at him when she said, "They'll wake soon enough and make a run for it. They might even get to the coast and freedom. We're doing them a favour."

"It doesn't look like a favour. It looks like leaving them in a ditch."

"Quiet," she ordered. This wasn't the time or the place for moral quibbling. If Wylan didn't know the difference between being in chains and out of them, he was about to find out.

Inej cupped her hand to her mouth and gave a low, soft bird call. They had four, maybe five minutes left before the guards cleared the road. Thankfully, the guards were raising quite a noise shouting encouragement at the horse and yelling to one another.

Matthias locked Wylan into place first, then Nina. Inej saw him stiffen as Nina lifted her hair to accept the collar, revealing the white curve of her neck. As he fastened it around her throat, Nina met his eyes over her shoulder, and the look they exchanged could have melted miles of northern ice. Matthias moved away hurriedly. Inej almost laughed. So that was all it took to send the *drüskelle* scurrying and bring the boy back.

Jesper was next, panting from his run back to the crossroads. He winked at her as she placed the sack over his head. They could hear the guards calling back and forth.

Inej locked Matthias' collar and stood on tiptoe to place the hood on his head. But when she moved to pull Nina's hood down, the Grisha fluttered her eyes rapidly, bobbing her head towards the wagon door. She still wanted to know how Kaz was going to lock them in.

"Watch," Inej mouthed.

Kaz signalled to Inej, and she leaped down. She shut the

wagon door, fastened the padlock, and slid the bolt home. A second later the opposite side of the door pushed open. Kaz had simply removed the hinges. It was a trick they'd used plenty of times when a lock was too complicated to pick quickly or they wanted to make a theft look like an inside job. *Ideal for faking suicides*, Kaz had once told her, and she'd never been sure if he was sincere.

Inej took a last look at the road. The men had finished with the tree. The big one was dusting off his hands and slapping the horse's back. The other was already approaching the front of the wagon. Inej gripped the lip of the door and swung herself up, squeezing inside. Immediately, Kaz started replacing the hinges. Inej shoved a hood over Nina's surprised face, then took her place beside Jesper.

But even in the dim light, she could tell Kaz was moving too slowly, his gloved fingers clumsier than she'd ever seen them. What was wrong with him? And why had he frozen at the wagon door? Something had made him hesitate, but what?

She heard the *ping* of metal as Kaz dropped one of the screws. She peered at the wagon floor and kicked it back to him, trying to ignore the pounding of her heart.

Kaz crouched down to replace the second hinge. He was breathing hard. She knew he was working in low light, by touch alone, in those cursed leather gloves he always insisted on wearing, but Inej didn't think that was why he seemed so agitated. She heard footsteps on the right side of the wagon, one guard shouting to another. *Come on, Kaz.* She hadn't taken the time to sweep away their footprints. What if the guard noticed? What if he pulled on the door, and it simply fell off its hinges, revealing Kaz Brekker, unhooded and unchained?

She heard another *ping*. Kaz cursed once under his breath. Suddenly, the door shook as the guard gave the chained padlock a rattle. Kaz braced his hand against the hinge. The crack of light beneath the door widened. Inej sucked in a breath.

The hinges held.

Another shout in Fjerdan, more footsteps. Then the crack of the reins and the cart surged forward, rumbling over the road. Inej let herself exhale. Her throat had gone completely dry.

Kaz took his place beside her. He shoved a hood over her head, and the musty smell filled her nostrils. He would put his own hood on next, then lock himself in. Easy enough, a cheap magician's trick, and Kaz knew them all. His arm pressed along hers from shoulder to elbow as he locked the collar around his neck. Bodies shifted against Inej's back and side, crowding up against her.

For now they were safe. But despite the rattle of the wagon's wheels, Inej could tell Kaz's breathing had got worse – shallow, rapid pants like an animal caught in a trap. It was a sound she'd never thought to hear from him.

It was because she was listening so closely that she knew the exact moment when Kaz Brekker, Dirtyhands, the bastard of the Barrel and the deadliest boy in Ketterdam, fainted.

22

KAZ

The money Mister Hertzoon had left with Kaz and Jordie ran out the following week. Jordie tried to return his new coat, but the shop wouldn't take it, and Kaz's boots had clearly been worn.

When they brought the loan agreement Mister Hertzoon had signed to the bank, they found that – for all its official-looking seals – it was worthless paper. No one knew of Mister Hertzoon or his business partner.

They were evicted from the boarding house two days later, and had to find a bridge to sleep under, but were soon rousted by the *stadwatch*. After that, they wandered aimlessly until morning. Jordie insisted that they go back to the coffeehouse. They sat for a long time in the park across the street. When night came, and the watch began its rounds, Kaz and Jordie headed south, into the streets of the lower Barrel, where the police did not bother to patrol.

They slept beneath a set of stairs in an alley behind a tavern, tucked between a discarded stove and bags of kitchen refuse. No one bothered them that night, but the next they were discovered by a gang of boys who told them they were in Razorgull territory. They gave Jordie a thrashing and knocked Kaz into the canal, but not before they took his boots.

Jordie fished Kaz out of the water and gave him his dry coat.

"I'm hungry," Kaz said.

"I'm not," Jordie replied. And for some reason that had struck Kaz as funny, and they'd both started laughing. Jordie wrapped his arms around Kaz and said, "The city is winning so far. But you'll see who wins in the end."

The next morning, Jordie woke with a fever.

In years to come people would call the outbreak of firepox that struck Ketterdam the Queen's Lady Plague, after the ship believed to have brought the contagion to the city. It hit the crowded slums of the Barrel hardest. Bodies piled up in the streets, and sickboats moved through the canals, using long shovels and hooks to tumble corpses onto their platforms and haul them out to the Reaper's Barge for burning.

Kaz's fever came on two days after Jordie's. They had no money for medicine or a medik, so they huddled together in a pile of broken-up wooden boxes that they dubbed the Nest.

No one came to roust them. The gangs had all been laid low by disease.

When the fever reached full fire, Kaz dreamed he had returned to the farm, and when he knocked on the door, he saw Dream Jordie and Dream Kaz already there, sitting at the kitchen table. They peered at him through the window, but they wouldn't let him in, so he wandered through the meadow, afraid to lie down in the tall grass.

When he woke, he couldn't smell hay or clover or apples, only coalsmoke, and the spongy rotting vegetable stink of garbage. Jordie was lying next to him, staring at the sky. "Don't leave me," Kaz wanted to say, but he was too tired.

So he laid his head on Jordie's chest. It felt wrong already, cold and hard.

He thought he was dreaming when the bodymen rolled him onto the sickboat. He felt himself falling, and then he was caught in a tangle of bodies. He tried to scream, but he was too weak. They were everywhere, legs and arms and stiff bellies, rotting limbs and blue-lipped faces covered in firepox sores. He floated in and out of consciousness, unsure of what was real or fever dream as the flatboat moved out to sea. When they tumbled him into the shallows of the Reaper's Barge, he somehow found the strength to cry out.

"I'm alive," he shouted, as loud as he could. But he was so small, and the boat was already drifting back to harbour.

Kaz tried to pull Jordie from the water. His body was covered in the little blooming sores that gave the firepox its name, his skin white and bruised. Kaz thought of the little wind-up dog, of drinking hot chocolate on the bridge. He thought that heaven would look like the kitchen of the house on Zelverstraat and smell like *hutspot* cooking in the Hertzoons' oven. He still had Saskia's red ribbon. He could give it back to her. They would make candies out of quince paste. Margit would play the piano, and he could fall asleep by the fire. He closed his eyes and waited to die.

Kaz expected to wake in the next world, warm and safe, his belly full, Jordie beside him. Instead, he woke surrounded by corpses. He was lying in the shallows of the Reaper's Barge, his clothes soaked through, skin wrinkled from the damp. Jordie's body was beside him, barely recognisable, white and swollen with rot, floating on the surface like some kind of gruesome deep sea fish.

Kaz's vision had cleared, and the rash had receded. His fever had broken. He'd forgotten his hunger, but he was thirsty enough that he thought he would go mad.

All that day and night, he waited in the pile of bodies, looking out at the harbour, hoping the flatboat would return. They had to come to set the fires that would burn the corpses, but when? Did the bodymen collect every day? Every other day? He was weak and dehydrated. He knew he wouldn't last much longer. The coast seemed so far away, and he knew he was too weak to swim the distance. He had survived the fever, but he might well die out here on the Reaper's Barge. Did he care? There was nothing waiting for him in the city except more hunger and dark alleys and the damp of the canals. Even as he thought it, he knew it wasn't true. Vengeance was waiting, vengeance for Jordie and maybe for himself, too. But he would have to go to meet it.

When night came, and the tide changed direction, Kaz forced himself to lay hands on Jordie's body. He was too frail to swim on his own, but with Jordie's help, he could float. He held tight to his brother and kicked towards the lights of Ketterdam. Together, they drifted, Jordie's distended body acting as a raft. Kaz kept kicking, trying not to think of his brother, of the taut, bloated feel of Jordie's flesh beneath his hands; he tried not to think of anything but the rhythm of his legs moving through the sea. He'd heard there were sharks in these waters, but he knew they wouldn't touch him. He was a monster now, too.

He kept kicking, and when dawn came, he looked up to find himself at the east end of the Lid. The harbour was nearly deserted; the plague had caused shipping in and out of Kerch to grind to a halt.

The last hundred yards were hard. The tide had turned once more, and it was working against him. But Kaz had hope now, hope and fury, twin flames burning inside him. They guided him to the dock and up the ladder. When he reached the top, he flopped down on his back on the wooden slats, then forced himself to roll over. Jordie's body was caught in the current, bumping against the pylon below. His eyes were still open, and for a moment, Kaz thought his brother was staring back at him. But Jordie didn't speak, he didn't blink, his gaze didn't shift as the tide dragged him free of the pylon and began to carry him out to sea.

I should close his eyes, thought Kaz. But he knew if he climbed down the ladder and waded back into the sea, he would never find his way out again. He'd simply let himself drown, and that wasn't possible any more. He had to live. Someone had to pay.

In the prison wagon, Kaz woke to a sharp jab against his thigh. He was ice cold and in darkness. There were bodies all around him, pressing against his back, his sides. He was drowning in corpses.

"Kaz." A whisper.

He shuddered.

Another jab to his thigh.

"Kaz." Inej's voice. He managed a deep breath through his nose. He felt her pull away from him. Somehow, in the cramped confines of the wagon, she managed to give him space. His heart was pounding.

"Keep talking," he rasped.

"What?"

"Just keep talking."

"We're passing through the prison gate. We made it past the first two checkpoints."

That brought him fully to his senses. They'd gone through two checkpoints. That meant they'd been counted. Someone had opened that door – not once but twice – maybe even laid hands on him, and he hadn't woken. He could have been robbed, killed. He'd imagined his death a thousand ways, but never sleeping through it.

He forced himself to breathe deeply, despite the smell of bodies. He'd kept his gloves on, something the guards might have easily taken note of, and a frustrating concession to his weakness, but if he hadn't, he felt fairly sure he'd have gone completely mad.

Behind him, he could hear the other prisoners murmuring to one another in different languages. Despite the fears the darkness woke in him, he gave thanks for it. He could only hope that the rest of his crew, hooded and burdened by their own anxiety, hadn't noticed anything strange about his behaviour. He'd been sluggish, slow to react when they'd ambushed the wagon, but that was all, and he could make up some excuse to account for it.

He hated that Inej had seen him this way, that anyone had, but on the heels of that thought came another: *Better it should be her.* In his bones, he knew that she would never speak of it to anyone, that she would never use this knowledge against him. She relied on his reputation. She wouldn't want him to look weak. But there was more to it than that, wasn't there? Inej would never betray him. He knew it. Kaz felt ill. Though he'd trusted her with his life countless times, it felt much more frightening to trust her with this shame.

The wagon came to a halt. The bolt slid back, and the doors flew open.

He heard Fjerdan being spoken, then scraping noises and a *thunk*. His collar was unlocked, and he was led from the wagon down some kind of ramp with the other prisoners. He heard what sounded like a gate creaking open, and they were herded forward, shuffling along in their shackles.

He squinted as his hood was suddenly yanked free. They were standing in a large courtyard. The massive gate set into the ringwall was already being lowered closed, and it struck the stones with an ominous series of clanks and groans. When Kaz looked up, he saw guards stationed all along the roof of the courtyard, rifles aimed down at the prisoners. The guards below were moving along the rows of shackled captives, trying to match them to the driver's paperwork by name or description.

Matthias had described the layout of the Ice Court in detail, but he'd said little about the way it actually looked. Kaz had expected something old and damp – grim grey stone, battle-hard. Instead, he was surrounded by marble so white it almost glowed blue. He felt as if he'd wandered into some dream-like version of the harsh lands they'd travelled in the north. It was impossible to tell what might be glass or ice or stone.

"If this isn't Fabrikator craft, then I'm the queen of the woodsprites," muttered Nina in Kerch.

"*Tig!*" one of the guards commanded. He slammed his rifle into her gut, and she doubled over in pain. Matthias kept his head turned, but Kaz didn't miss the tension in his frame.

The Fjerdan guards were gesturing over their papers, trying to make the numbers and identities of the prisoners match up to the group before them. This was the first real moment of exposure, one Kaz would have no control over. It would have been too time-consuming and dangerous to pick and choose the prisoners they'd replaced. It was a calculated risk, but now Kaz could only wait and hope that laziness and bureaucracy would do the rest.

As the guards moved down the line, Inej helped Nina to her feet.

"You okay?" Inej asked, and Kaz felt himself drawn towards her voice like water rolling downhill.

Slowly, Nina unbent herself and stood upright. "I'm fine," she whispered. "But I don't think we have to worry about Pekka Rollins' team any more."

Kaz tracked Nina's gaze to the top of the ringwall, high above the courtyard, where five men had been impaled on spikes like meat skewered for roasting, backs bent, limbs dangling. Kaz had to squint, but he recognised Eroll Aerts,

Rollins' best lockpick and safecracker. The bruises and welts from the beating they'd given him before his death were deep purple in the morning light, and Kaz could just make out a black mark on his arm – Aerts' Dime Lion tattoo.

He scanned the other faces – some were too swollen and distorted in death to identify. Could one of them be Rollins? Kaz knew he should be glad another team had been taken out, but Rollins was no fool, and the thought that his crew hadn't made it past the Ice Court gates was more than a little nerve-racking. Besides, if Rollins had met his death at the end of a Fjerdan pike . . . No, Kaz refused that possibility. Pekka Rollins belonged to him.

The guards were arguing with the wagon driver now, and one of them was pointing at Inej.

"What's happening?" he whispered to Nina.

"They're claiming the papers are out of order, that they have a Suli girl instead of a Shu boy."

"And the driver?" asked Inej.

"He just keeps telling them it's not his problem."

"That's the way," Kaz murmured encouragingly.

Kaz watched them go back and forth. That was the beauty of all these fail-safes and layers of security. The guards always thought they could rely on someone else to catch a mistake or fix a problem. Laziness wasn't as reliable as greed, but it still made a fine lever. And they were talking about prisoners – chained, surrounded on all sides, and about to be dumped into cells. Harmless.

Finally, one of the prison guards sighed and signalled to his cohorts. "*Diveskemen.*"

"Go on," Nina translated, and then continued as the guard spoke. "Take them to the east block and let the next shift sort them out."

Kaz allowed himself the briefest sigh of relief.

As anticipated, guards split the group into men and women, then led both rows, chains jangling, through a nearly round archway fashioned in the shape of a wolf's open mouth.

They entered a chamber where an old woman sat with her hands chained, flanked by guards. Her eyes were vacant. As each prisoner approached, the woman gripped his or her wrist.

A human amplifier. Kaz knew Nina had worked with them when she'd been scouring the Wandering Isle for Grisha to join the Second Army. They could sense Grisha power by touch, and he'd seen them hired on at high stakes card games to make sure none of the players were Grisha. Someone who could tamper with another player's pulse or even raise the temperature in a room had an unfair advantage. But the Fjerdans used them for a different purpose – to make sure no Grisha breached their walls without being identified.

Kaz watched Nina approach. He could see her trembling as she held out her arm. The woman clamped her fingers around Nina's wrist. Her eyelids stuttered briefly. Then she dropped Nina's hand and waved her along.

Had she known and not cared? Or had the paraffin they'd used to encase Nina's forearms worked?

As they were led through an arch on the left, Kaz glimpsed Inej disappearing into the opposite arch with the other female prisoners. He felt a twinge in his chest, and with a disturbing jolt, he realised it was panic. She'd been the one to wake him from his stupor in the cart. Her voice had brought him back from the dark; it had been the tether he gripped and used to drag himself back to some semblance of sanity.

The male prisoners were led clanking up a dark flight of stairs to a metal walkway. On their left was the smooth white bulk of the ringwall. To their right the walkway overlooked a vast glass enclosure, nearly a quarter mile long and tall enough to comfortably fit a trading ship. It was lit by a huge iron lantern that hung from the ceiling like a glowing cocoon. Looking down, Kaz saw rows of heavily armoured wagons capped by domed gun turrets. Their wheels were large and linked by a thick tread. On each wagon, a massive gun barrel – somewhere between the shape of a rifle and a cannon – jutted out into the space where a team of horses would ordinarily be hitched.

"What are those things?" he whispered.

"*Torvegen*," Matthias said under his breath. "They don't need horses to pull them. They were still perfecting the design when I left."

"No horses?"

"Tanks," murmured Jesper. "I saw prototypes when I was working with a gunsmith in Novyi Zem. Multiple guns in the turret, and that big barrel out in front? Serious firepower."

There were also gravity-fed heavy artillery guns in the enclosure, racks full of rifles, ammunition, and the little black bombs that Ravkans called *grenatye*. On the walls behind the glass, older weapons had been arranged in an elaborate display – axes, spears, longbows. Above it all hung a banner in silver and white: STRYMAKT FJERDAN.

When Kaz glanced at Matthias, the big man muttered, "Fjerdan might."

Kaz peered through the thick glass. He knew defences, and Nina had been right, this glass was another piece of Fabrikator work – bulletproof and impenetrable. Coming or going from the prison, captives would see weapons, armaments, machines of war – all a brutal reminder of the power of the Fjerdan state.

Go on and flex, Kaz thought. *Doesn't matter how big the gun is if you don't know where to point it.*

On the other side of the enclosure, he saw a second walkway, where the female prisoners were being marched.

Inej will be fine. He had to stay sharp. They were in enemy territory now, a place of steep risk, the kind of fix you didn't walk out of if you didn't keep your wits about you. Had Pekka's team made it this far before they'd been found out? And where was Pekka Rollins himself? Had he stayed safe and secure in Kerch, or was he a prisoner of the Fjerdans as well?

None of it mattered. For now, Kaz had to focus on the plan and finding Yul-Bayur. He glanced at the others. Wylan looked as if he was ready to wet himself. Helvar appeared grim as always. Jesper just grinned and whispered, "Well, we've managed to get ourselves locked into the most secure prison in the world. We're either geniuses or the dumbest sons of bitches to ever breathe air."

"We'll know soon enough."

They were led into another white room, this one equipped with tin tubs and hoses.

The guard gabbled something in Fjerdan, and Kaz saw Matthias and some of the others start to strip down. He swallowed the bile that rose in his throat. He refused to vomit.

He could do this, he had to do this. He thought of Jordie. What would Jordie say if his little brother lost their chance at justice because he couldn't conquer some stupid sickness inside him? But it only brought back the memory of Jordie's cold flesh, the way it had grown loose in the salt water, the bodies crowding around him in the flatboat. His vision started to blur.

Get it together, Brekker, he scolded himself harshly. It didn't help. He was going to faint again, and this would all be over. Inej had once offered to teach him how to fall. "The trick is not getting knocked down," he'd told her with a laugh. "No, Kaz," she'd said, "the trick is in getting back up." More Suli platitudes, but somehow even the memory of her voice helped. He was better than this. He had to be. Not just for Jordie, but for his crew. He'd brought these people here. He'd brought Inej here. It was his job to bring them out again.

The trick is in getting back up. He kept her voice in his head, repeating those words, again and again, as he stripped off his boots, his clothes, and finally his gloves.

He saw that Jesper was staring at his hands. "What were you expecting?" Kaz growled.

"Claws, at least," Jesper said, shifting his gaze to his own bony bare feet. "Possibly a spiny thumb."

The guard returned from dumping their clothes in a bin that would no doubt be taken to the incinerator. He tilted Kaz's head back roughly and forced his mouth open, feeling around with fat fingers. Black spots bloomed in Kaz's sight as he fought to remain conscious. The guard's fingers passed over the spot between Kaz's teeth where he'd wedged the *baleen*, then pinched and prodded the interior of his cheeks.

"*Ondetjärn!*" the guard exclaimed. "*Fellenjuret!*" he shouted again as he pulled two slender pieces of metal from Kaz's mouth. The lockpicks hit the stone floor with a *plink-plink*. The guard shouted something at him in Fjerdan and cuffed him hard across the face. Kaz fell to his knees, but forced himself back up. He registered Wylan's panicked expression, but it was all he could do to stay on his feet as the guard shoved him into line for an ice-cold shower.

When he emerged, soaked and shaking, another guard handed him colourless, prison-issue trousers and a tunic from the stack beside him. Kaz pulled them on, then limped to the holding area with the rest of the prisoners. In that moment, he would have given up half his share of the thirty million *kruge* for the familiar heft of his cane.

The holding cells looked much more like the prison he had anticipated – no white stone or glass displays, just dank grey rock and iron bars.

They were herded into an already crowded cell. Helvar sat down with his back to the wall, surveying the pacing men, eyes slitted. Kaz rested against the iron bars, watching the guards depart. He could sense the movements of the bodies behind him. There was space enough, but they still felt too close. *Just a little longer*, Kaz told himself. His hands felt impossibly bare.

Kaz waited. He knew what was coming. He'd sussed out the others as soon as they entered the cell, and he knew it would be the burly Kaelish with the birthmark who came for him. He was twitchy, nervous, and he'd taken obvious notice of Kaz's limp.

"Hey, cripple," the Kaelish said in Fjerdan. He tried again in Kerch, his lilt heavy. "Hey, crip." He needn't have bothered. Kaz knew the word for cripple in plenty of languages.

The next second, Kaz felt the air move as the Kaelish reached for him. He stepped left, and the Kaelish lurched forward, carried by his own momentum. Kaz helped him along, seizing the man's arm and driving it through the space between bars, all the way up to the shoulder. The Kaelish let out a loud grunt as his face smashed up against the iron bars.

Kaz braced the man's forearm against the metal. He threw his weight against his opponent's body, and felt a satisfying pop as the Kaelish's arm dislocated from his shoulder. As the man opened his lips to scream, Kaz covered his mouth with one hand and pinched his nose shut with the other. The feel of bare flesh on his fingers made him want to gag.

"Shhhhhh," he said, using his grip on the man's nose to steer him backwards to the bench against the wall. The other prisoners scattered to clear a path.

The man sat down hard, eyes watering, breathless. Kaz kept his hold on his nose and mouth. The Kaelish trembled beneath his grasp.

"You want me to put it back?" Kaz asked.

The Kaelish whimpered.

"Do you?"

He whimpered louder as the prisoners looked on.

"You scream, and I'll make sure it never works right again, understand?"

He released the man's mouth and shoved his arm back into its socket. The Kaelish rolled over on his side, curled up on the bench, and began to weep.

Kaz wiped his hands on his trousers and returned to his spot by the bars. He could feel the others watching, but now he knew he would be left in peace.

Helvar came up beside him. "Was that really necessary?"

"No." But it had been – to make sure they were left alone to do what needed to be done, and to remember that he wasn't helpless.

23

JESPER

Jesper wanted to pace, but he'd staked out this spot on the bench, and he intended to keep it. It felt like little quakes of anxiety and excitement were vibrating under his skin, and Wylan seated next to him drumming frenetically on his kneecaps wasn't helping him settle. He didn't think he could handle much more waiting. First the boat, then all that hiking, and now he was stuck in a cell until the guards came by to make their evening head count.

Only his father had understood his restless energy. He'd tried to get Jesper to use it up on the farm, but the work had been too monotonous. University was supposed to be the thing that gave him direction, but instead he'd wandered down a different path. He cringed at what his father would say if he learned his son had died in a Fjerdan prison. Then again, how would he ever know? That was too depressing to dwell on.

How much time had passed? What if they couldn't even hear the Elderclock in here? The guards were supposed to make the head count at six bells. Then Jesper and the others would have until midnight to get the job done.

They hoped. Matthias had only spent three months at the prison. Protocols could have changed. He might have got something wrong. *Or maybe the Fjerdan just wants us behind bars before he rats us out.*

But Matthias was sitting silently on the far side of the cell near Kaz. Jesper hadn't been able to miss Kaz's little skirmish with the Kaelish. Kaz was usually unshakeable during a job, but now he was on edge, and Jesper didn't know why. Part of him wanted to ask, though he knew that was the stupid part, the hopeful farmboy who picked the worst possible person to care about, who searched for signs in things that he knew deep down meant nothing – when Kaz chose him for a job, when Kaz played along with one of his jokes. He could have kicked himself. He'd finally seen the infamous Kaz Brekker without a stitch of clothing, and he'd been too worried about ending up on a pike to pay proper attention.

But if Jesper was anxious, Wylan looked as if he might actually throw up.

"What are we supposed to do now?" Wylan whispered. "What good is a lockpick without his picks?"

"Be quiet."

"And what good are you? A sharpshooter without his guns. You're completely extraneous to this mission."

"It's not a mission; it's a job."

"Matthias calls it a mission."

"He's military, you're not. And I'm already in jail, so don't tempt me to commit homicide."

"You aren't going to kill me, and I'm not going to pretend everything is okay. We're stuck in here."

"You're definitely better suited to a gilded cage than to a real one."

"I left my father's house."

"Yeah, you gave up a life of luxury so you could slum it with us sobs in the Barrel. That doesn't make you interesting, Wylan, just stupid."

"You don't know anything about it."

"So tell me," Jesper said, turning to him. "We have time. What makes a good little merch boy leave home to keep company with criminals?"

"You act like you were born in the Barrel like Kaz, but you're not even Kerch. You chose this life, too."

"I like cities."

"They don't have cities in Novyi Zem?"

"Not like Ketterdam. Have you ever even been anywhere but home, the Barrel, and fancy embassy dinners?"

Wylan looked away. "Yes."

"Where? The suburbs for peach season?"

"The races at Caryeva. The Shu oil fields. The *jurda* farms near Shriftport. Weddle. Elling."

"Really?"

"My father used to take me everywhere with him."

"Until?"

"Until what?"

"*Until.* My father took me everywhere *until* I contracted terrible seasickness, *until* I vomited at a royal wedding, *until* I tried to hump the ambassador's leg."

"The leg was asking for it."

Jesper released a bark of laughter. "Finally, a little spine."

"I have plenty of spine," Wylan grumbled. "And look where it got—"

He was interrupted by a guard's voice shouting in Fjerdan just as the Elderclock began to chime six bells. At least the Fjerdans were punctual.

The guard spoke again in Shu and then in Kerch. "On your feet."

"*Shimkopper*," the guard demanded. They all looked at him blankly. "The piss bucket," he tried in Kerch. "Where is . . . to empty?" He pantomimed.

There were shrugs and confused glances.

The guard's gloomy sulk made it clear he couldn't care less. He shoved a bucket of fresh water into the cell and slammed the bars shut.

Jesper pushed to the front and took a big gulp from the cup tied to its handle. Most of it splashed on his shirt. When he handed the cup to Wylan, he made sure it soaked him as well.

"What are you doing?" Wylan protested.

"Patience, Wylan. And do try to follow along."

Jesper hiked up his pants and felt around the thin skin over his ankle.

"Tell me what's happen—"

"Be quiet. I need to concentrate." It was true. He really didn't want the pellet buried beneath his skin to open up while it was still inside him.

He felt along the thin stitches Nina had placed there. It hurt like hell when he popped them open and slid the pellet out. It was about the size of a raisin and slick with his blood. Nina would be using her powers to split open her own skin right now. Jesper wondered if it hurt any less than the stitches.

"Pull your shirt up over your mouth," he told Wylan.

"What?"

"Stop being dense. You're cuter when you're smart."

Wylan's cheeks went pink. He scowled and pulled his collar up.

Jesper reached under the bench where he'd hidden the waste bucket and pulled it out.

"A storm's coming," Jesper said loudly in Kerch. He saw Matthias and Kaz draw their collars up. He turned his face away, pulled his shirt over his mouth, and dropped the pellet into the bucket.

There was a sizzling whoosh as a cloud of mist bloomed from the water. In seconds it had blanketed the cells, turning the air a milky green.

Wylan's eyes were panicked above his hiked-up collar. Jesper was tempted to pretend to faint, but he settled for the effect of men toppling to the ground all around him.

Jesper waited for a count of sixty, then dropped his collar and took a tentative breath. The air still smelled sickly sweet and would leave them woozy for a bit, but the worst of it had dispersed. When the guards came through for the next head count, the prisoners would have bad headaches but not much to tell. And hopefully by then they'd be long gone.

"Was that chloro gas?"

"Definitely cuter when you're smart. Yes, the pellet's an enzyme-based casing filled with chloro powder. It's harmless unless it comes into contact with any amount of ammonia. Which it just did."

"The urine in the bucket . . . but what was the point? We're still stuck in here."

"Jesper," Kaz said waving him over to the bars. "The clock is ticking."

Jesper rolled his shoulders as he approached. This kind of work usually took a lot of time, particularly because he'd never had real training. He placed his hands on either side of a single bar and concentrated on locating the purest particles of ore.

"What is he doing?" asked Matthias.

"Performing an ancient Zemeni ritual," Kaz said.

"Really?"

"No."

A murky haze was forming between Jesper's hands.

Wylan gasped. "Is that iron ore?"

Jesper nodded as he felt sweat break out on his brow.

"Can you dissolve the bars?"

"Don't be an idiot," Jesper grunted. "Do you see how thick they are?" In fact, the bar he was working on looked unchanged, but he'd pulled enough iron from it that the cloud between his hands was nearly black. He bent his fingertips, and the particles spun, whirring into a tightening spiral that grew narrower and denser.

Jesper dropped his hands, and a slender needle fell to the floor with a musical *ping*.

Wylan snatched it up, holding it so the light gleamed over its dull surface.

"You're a Fabrikator," Matthias said grimly.

"Just barely."

"You either are or you aren't," said Wylan.

"I am." He jabbed a finger at Wylan. "And you're going to keep your mouth shut about it when we get back to Ketterdam."

"But why would you lie about—"

"I like walking the streets free," said Jesper. "I like not worrying about being snatched up by a slaver or put to death by some skiv like our friend Helvar here. Besides, I have other skills that bring me more pleasure and profit than this. *Lots* of other skills."

Wylan coughed. Flirting with him might actually be more fun than annoying him, but it was a close call.

"Does Nina know you're Grisha?"

"No and she's not finding out. I don't need lectures about joining the Second Army and the glorious Ravkan cause."

"Do it again," Kaz interrupted. "And hurry."

Jesper repeated his effort on another bar.

"If this was the plan, what was the point to trying to smuggle in those lockpicks?" Wylan asked.

Kaz folded his arms. "Ever hear about the dying man whose medik told him he'd been miraculously cured? He danced into the street and was trampled to death by a horse. You have to let the mark feel like he's won. Were the guards studying Matthias and wondering if he looked familiar? Were they looking for trouble when Jesper went into the showers with paraffin sloughing off his arms? No, they were too busy congratulating themselves on catching me. They thought they'd neutralised the threat."

When Jesper finished, Kaz took the two slender lockpicks between his fingers. It was strange to see him work without his gloves, but in moments, the lock clicked open, and they were free. Once they were out, Kaz used his picks to lock the door behind them.

"You know your assignments," he whispered. "Wylan and I will get Nina and Inej out. Jesper, you and Matthias—"

"I know, nab as much rope as we can find."

"Be in the basement by the half chime."

They split. The wheels were in motion.

According to Wylan's plans, the stables were adjacent to the gatehouse courtyard, so they would have to backtrack through the holding area. In theory, this section of the prison was only supposed to be active when prisoners were being processed in or out, but they still had to be careful. It would only take one wayward guard to ruin their plans. The scariest part was traversing the walkway through the glass enclosure, a long, brightly lit stretch that left them completely exposed. There was nothing to do except cross their fingers and make a run for it. Then they headed down the stairs and to the left of the chamber where that poor old Grisha amplifier had tested him. Jesper suppressed a shudder. Even though paraffin on his arms always worked at the gambling dens, his heart had still been hammering as he faced her. She'd been thin as a husk and as empty. That was what happened to Grisha who got found in the wrong place at the wrong time – a life sentence of slavery or worse.

When Jesper pushed open the door to the stables, he felt some small thing inside him relax. The smell of the hay, the shift of animals in their stalls, the nickering of the horses brought back memories of Novyi Zem. In Ketterdam, the canals rendered most coaches and wagons unnecessary. Horses were a luxury, an indulgence to show that you had the space to keep them and the wealth to care for them. He hadn't realised how much he missed simply being around animals.

But there was no time for nostalgia or to stop and stroke a velvety nose. He strode past the stalls and into the tack room. Matthias hoisted a massive coil of rope over each shoulder. He looked surprised when Jesper managed two as well.

"Grew up on a farm," Jesper explained.

"You don't look it."

"Sure, I'm skinny," he said as they hurried back through the stables, "but I stay drier in the rain."

"How?"

"Less falls on me."

"Are all of Kaz's associates as strange as this crew?" Matthias asked.

"Oh, you should meet the rest of the Dregs. They make us look like Fjerdans."

They passed through the showers and, instead of continuing to the holding area, turned down a tight flight of stairs and the long dark hall that led to the basement. They were under the main prison now, five storeys of cellblock, prisoners, and guards stacked on top of them.

Jesper had expected the rest of the crew to be collecting demo supplies in the big laundry room already. But all he saw were giant tin tubs, long tables for folding, and clothes left to dry overnight on racks taller than he was.

They found Wylan and Inej in the refuse room. It was smaller than the laundry and stank of garbage. Two big rolling bins full of discarded clothes were pushed against one wall, waiting to be burned. Jesper felt the heat emanating from the incinerator as soon as they entered.

"We have a problem," Wylan said.

"How bad?" Jesper asked, dumping his coils of rope on the floor.

Inej gestured to a pair of big metal doors set into what looked like a giant chimney that jutted out from the wall and stretched all the way up to the ceiling. "I think they ran the incinerator this afternoon."

"You said they ran it in the mornings," he said to Matthias.

"They used to."

When Jesper grabbed the doors' leather-covered handles and pulled them open, he was hit by a blast of searing air. It carried the black and acrid smell of coal – and something else, a chemical smell, maybe something they added to make the fires burn hotter. It wasn't unpleasant. This was where all the refuse from the prisons was disposed of – kitchen leavings, buckets of human filth, the clothing stripped from prisoners, but whatever the Fjerdans had added to the fuel burned hot enough to sear any foulness away. He leaned in, already beginning to sweat. Far below, he saw the incinerator coals, banked but still pulsing with an angry red glow.

"Wylan, give me a shirt from one of the bins," Jesper said.

He tore off one of the sleeves and tossed it into the shaft. It fell soundlessly, caught flame mid-air, and had begun to burn away to nothing before it ever had the chance to reach the coals.

He shut the doors and tossed the remnants of the shirt back in the bin. "Well, demo is out," he said. "We can't take explosives in there. Can you still make the climb?" he asked Inej.

"Maybe. I don't know."

"What does Kaz say? Where *is* Kaz? And where's Nina?"

"Kaz doesn't know about the incinerator yet," said Inej. "He and Nina went to search the upper cells."

Matthias' glower went dark as a rain-heavy sky ready to split. "Jesper and I were supposed to go with Nina."

"Kaz didn't want to wait."

"We were on time," said Matthias angrily. "What is he up to?"

Jesper wondered the same thing. "He's going to limp up and down all those flights of stairs, dodging patrols?"

"I may have tried to point that out to him," Inej said. "Always surprising, remember?"

"Like a hive of bees. I really hope we're not all about to get stung."

"Inej," Wylan called from one of the rolling bins. "These are our clothes."

He reached in and, one after the other, pulled out Inej's little leather slippers.

Her face broke into a dazzling smile. Finally, a bit of luck. Kaz didn't have his cane. Jesper didn't have his guns. And Inej didn't have her knives. But at least she had those magic slippers.

"What do you say, Wraith? Can you make the climb?"

"I can."

Jesper took the shoes from Wylan. "If I didn't think these might be crawling with disease, I would kiss them and then you."

24

NINA

Nina trailed Kaz up the stairs. Flight upon steep flight of stone and flickering gaslight. She watched him closely. He was setting a good pace, but his gait was stiff. Why had he insisted on being the one to make this climb? It couldn't be a question of time, so maybe it was what Kaz always intended. Maybe he'd meant to keep some bit of information from Matthias. Or he was just determined to keep them all guessing.

They paused at every landing, listening for patrols. The prison was full of sounds, and it was hard not to jump at every one of them – voices floating down the stairwell, the metallic clang of doors opening and closing. Nina thought of the violent chaos of Hellgate, bribes changing hands, blood staining the sand, a world away from this sterile place. The Fjerdans could certainly be counted on to keep things orderly.

On their way up the fourth flight, voices and bootsteps suddenly burst into the stairwell. Hurriedly, Nina and Kaz backtracked to the third floor landing and slipped through the door leading to the cells. The prisoner in the cell nearest to them started to shout. Nina quickly raised a hand and squeezed his airway shut. He stared at her, eyes bulging, clawing at his neck. She dropped his pulse, sending him into unconsciousness as she released the pressure on his larynx, allowing him to breathe. They needed him quiet, not dead.

The noises grew as the guards clambered down the stairs, loud Fjerdan reverberating off the walls. Nina held her breath, watching the door, hands ready. Kaz had no weapon, but he'd dropped into a fighting stance, waiting to see if the door would crash open. Instead, the guards continued on past the landing, down to the next floor.

When the sounds had faded, Kaz signalled to her, and they slipped back out the door, closing it as silently as possible behind them, and continued their ascent.

Seven bells struck as they reached the top floor. One hour had passed since they'd knocked out the prisoners in the holding area. They had forty-five minutes to search the high-security cells, meet back at the landing, and get to the basement. Kaz gestured for her to take the corridor on the left while he took the right.

The door creaked loudly as Nina stepped inside. The lanterns were spaced far apart here, and the shadows between them looked deep enough to fall into. She told herself to be grateful for the cover, but she couldn't deny it was eerie. The cells were different, too, with doors of solid steel instead of iron bars. A viewing grate was lodged into each of them at eye level. Well, eye level for a Fjerdan. Nina was tall, but she still had to stand on tiptoe to peek into them.

Most of the prisoners were asleep or resting, curled into corners or flat on their backs with an arm thrown over their eyes to block out the dim lamplight that filtered through the grate. Others sat propped against the walls, staring listlessly at nothing. Occasionally she found someone pacing back and forth and had to step away quickly. None of them were Shu.

"*Ajor?*" one called after her in Fjerdan. She ignored him and moved on, heart thudding.

What if Bo Yul-Bayur really was in these cells? She knew it was unlikely, and yet. . . she could kill him in his cell, put him in a deep, painless sleep, and simply stop his heart. She'd tell Kaz she hadn't found him. And what if Kaz located Bo Yul-Bayur? She might have to wait until they were out of the Ice Court to find a solution, but she could at least count on Matthias to help her. What a strange, grim bargain they'd struck.

But as she worked her way back and forth along the corridors, the tiny hope that the scientist might be there withered away to nothing. *One more row of cells*, she thought, *then back down to the basement with nothing to show for it.* Except when she entered the final corridor, she saw it was shorter than the others. Where there should have been more cells there was a steel door, bright light shining beneath it.

A flutter of unease passed through her as she approached, but she made herself push the door open. She had to squint against the brightness. The light was harsh – as clear as daylight but with none of its warmth – and she couldn't locate its source. She heard the door whooshing closed behind her. At the last moment she whirled and grabbed it by the edge. Something told her this door would need a key to unlock it from the inside. She looked for anything she might use to prop it open, and had to settle for tearing off a piece from the bottom of her prison trousers and stuffing it in the lock.

This place felt wrong. The walls, floor, and ceiling were a white so clean it hurt to look at. Half of one wall was made up of panels of smooth, perfect glass. *Fabrikatormade.* Just like the glass enclosure surrounding that vile display of weaponry. No Fjerdan craftsman could make surfaces so pristine. Grisha power had been used to create this glass, she felt sure of it. There were rogue Grisha who served no country and who might consider hiring themselves out to the Fjerdan government. But would they survive such a commission? Slave labour seemed more likely.

Nina took one step, then another. She glanced back over her shoulder. If a guard entered the corridor behind her, she'd have nowhere to hide. *So move, Nina.*

She peered inside the first window. The cell was as white as the hallway and illuminated by that same sustained, bright light. The room was empty and devoid of any kind of furniture – no bench, no basin, no bucket. The only break in all that whiteness was a drain at the very centre of the floor, surrounded by reddish stains.

She continued to the next cell. It was identical and equally empty, as was the next, and the next. But here something caught her eye, a coin lying next to the drain – no, not a coin, a button. A tiny silver button emblazoned with a wing, the symbol of a Grisha Squaller. She felt a chill creep over her arms. Had these cells been crafted by Grisha slaves for Grisha prisoners? Had the glass, the walls, the floor been made to withstand Fabrikator manipulation? The rooms were devoid of metal. There was no plumbing, no pipes to carry water that a Tidemaker might abuse. And Nina suspected that the glass she was peering through was mirrored on the other side, so that a Heartrender in the cell wouldn't be able to locate a target. These were cells designed to hold Grisha. Designed to hold her.

She whirled on her heel. Bo Yul-Bayur wasn't here, and she wanted out of this place right now. She snatched the fabric from the lock and blew through the door, not stopping to make sure it closed behind her. The corridor of iron cells was even darker after the brightness that had come before, and she stumbled as she raced back the way she'd come. Nina knew she was being incautious, but she couldn't get the image of those white rooms out of her head. *The drain. The stains around it. Had Grisha been tortured there? Made to confess their crimes against the people?*

She'd studied the Fjerdans – their leaders, their language. She'd even dreamed of entering the Ice Court as a spy just like this, of striking at the heart of this nation that hated her so much. But now that she was here, she just wanted to be gone. She'd grown used to Ketterdam, to the adventures that came with her involvement with the Dregs, to her easy life at the White Rose. But even there, had she ever felt safe? In a city where she couldn't walk down the streets without fear? *I want to go home.* The longing for it hit her hard, a physical ache. *I want to go back to Ravka.*

The Elderclock began to chime a soft three-quarter-hour. She was late. Still, she forced her steps to slow before she opened the door into the stairway. There was no one there, not even Kaz. She ducked her head into the opposite passage to see if he was coming. Nothing – iron doors, deep shadow, no sign of Kaz.

Nina waited, unsure of what to do. They'd been meant to meet on the landing with fifteen minutes to spare before the hour. What if he was in some kind of trouble? She hesitated, then plunged down the corridor Kaz had been responsible for searching. She raced past the cells, the hallways snaking back and forth, but Kaz was nowhere to be found.

Enough, thought Nina when she reached the end of the second corridor. Either Kaz had abandoned her and was already downstairs with the others, or he'd been caught and dragged off somewhere. Either way, she had to get to the incinerator. Once she found the others they could figure out what to do.

She sped back through the halls and threw open the door to the landing. Two guards stood chatting at the head of the stairs. For a moment, they stared at her, open-mouthed.

"*Sten!*" one shouted in Fjerdan, ordering her to halt as they fumbled for their guns. Nina threw out both hands, fingers forming fists, and watched the guards topple backwards. One fell flat on the landing, but the other tumbled down the stairs, his rifle firing, sending bullets pinging against the stone walls, the sound echoing down the stairwell. Kaz was going to kill her. She was going to kill Kaz.

Nina hurtled past the guards' bodies, down one flight, two flights. On the third floor landing a door flew open as a guard burst into the stairwell. Nina twisted her hands in the air, and the guard's neck broke with an audible *snap*. She was plunging down the next flight before his body struck the ground.

That was when the Elderclock began to chime. Not the steady tolling of the hour, but a shrill clamour, high and percussive – a sound of alarm.

25

INEJ

Inej looked up, into the dark. High above her floated a small, grey patch of evening sky. Six levels to climb in the dark with her hands slippery from sweat and the fires of hell burning below, with the rope weighing her down and no net to catch her. *Climb, Inej.*

Bare hands were best for climbing, but the incinerator walls were far too hot to permit that. So Wylan and Jesper had helped her fish Kaz's gloves from the laundry bins. She hesitated briefly. Kaz would tell her to just put the gloves on, to do whatever it took to get the job done. And yet, she felt curiously guilty as she slid the supple black leather over her hands, as if she had crept into his rooms without his permission, read his letters, lain down in his bed. The gloves were unlined, with the slenderest slashes hidden in the fingertips. *For sleight of hand,* she realised, *so that he can keep contact with coins or cards or finesse the workings of a lock. Touch without touch.*

There was no time to acclimatise herself to the oversized feel of the gloves. Besides, she'd climbed with covered hands plenty of times when the Ketterdam winters had turned her fingers numb. She flexed her toes in her little leather slippers, revelling in the familiar feel of them on her feet, bouncing on her nubbly rubber soles, fearless and eager. The heat was nothing, mere discomfort. The weight of seventy feet of rope coiled around her body? She was the Wraith. She'd suffered worse. She launched herself up into the chimney with pure confidence.

When her fingers made contact with the stone, she hissed in a breath. Even through the leather, she could feel the dense heat of the bricks. Without the gloves, her skin would have started to blister right away. But there was nothing to do except hold on. She climbed – hand then foot, then hand again, seeking the next small crack, the next divot in the soot-slick walls.

Sweat coursed down her back. They'd doused the rope and her clothes in water, but it didn't seem to be doing much good. Her whole body felt flushed, suffused with blood as if she were being slowly cooked in her own skin.

Her feet pulsed with heat. They felt heavy, clumsy, as if they belonged to someone else. She tried to centre herself. She trusted her body. She knew her own strength and exactly what she could do. Another hand up, forcing her limbs to cooperate, seeking a rhythm, but finding only an awkward syncopation that left her muscles trembling with every upwards gain. She reached for the next hold, digging in. *Climb, Inej.*

Her foot slipped. Her toes lost contact with the wall, and her stomach lurched as she felt the pull of her weight and the rope. She gripped the stone, digging into the cracks, Kaz's gloves bunching around her damp fingers. Again, her toes sought purchase, but only slid over the bricks. Then her other foot began to slip, too. She sucked in a gust of searing air. Something was wrong. She risked a glance down. Far below, she saw the red glow of the coals, but it was what she saw on her feet that shocked her heart into a panicked gallop. They were a gummy mess. The soles of her shoes – her perfect, beloved shoes – were melting.

It's all right, she told herself. *Just change your grip. Put your weight in your shoulders. The rubber will cool as you go higher. It will help you grip.* But her feet felt like they were on fire. Seeing what was happening had somehow made it worse, as if the rubber was fusing with her flesh.

Inej blinked the sweat from her eyes and hauled herself up a few more inches. From somewhere above, she heard the chime of the Elderclock. The half hour? Or quarter till? She had to move faster. She should be on the roof by now, attaching the rope.

She pushed higher and her foot skidded down the brick. She dropped, her whole body stuttering against the wall as she scrambled for purchase. There was no one to save her. No Kaz to come to her rescue, no net waiting to break her fall, only the fire ready to claim her.

Inej canted her head back, seeking that patch of sky. It still seemed impossibly distant. How far was it? Twenty feet? Thirty? It might as well have been miles. She was going to die here, slowly, horribly on the coals. They were all going to die – Kaz, Nina, Jesper, Matthias, Wylan – and it was her fault.

No. No, it wasn't.

She hefted herself up another foot – *Kaz brought us here* – and then another. She forced herself to find the next hold. Kaz and his greed. She didn't feel guilty. She wasn't sorry. She was just mad. Mad at Kaz for attempting this insane job, furious with herself for agreeing to it.

And why had she? To pay off her debt? Or because despite all good sense and better intentions, she'd let herself feel something for the bastard of the Barrel?

When Inej entered Tante Heleen's salon on that long ago night, Kaz Brekker had been waiting, dressed in darkest grey, leaning on his crow's head cane. The salon was furnished in gold and teal, one wall patterned entirely in peacock feathers. Inej hated every inch of the Menagerie – the parlour where she and the other girls were forced to coo and bat their lashes at prospective clients, her bedroom that had been made up to look like some farcical version of a Suli caravan, festooned in purple silk and redolent with incense – but Tante Heleen's salon was the worst. It was the room for beatings, for Heleen's worst rages.

Inej had tried to escape when she'd first arrived in Ketterdam. She'd got two blocks from the Menagerie, still in her silks, dazed by the light and chaos of West Stave, running without direction, before Cobbet had clamped a meaty hand on the nape of her neck and hauled her back. Heleen took her into the salon and beat her badly enough that she hadn't been able to work for a week. For the month after, Heleen had kept her in golden chains, not even letting her go down to the parlour. When she'd finally unlocked the shackles, Heleen had said, "You owe me for a month of lost income. Run again, and I'll have you thrown in Hellgate for breach of contract."

That night, she'd entered the salon with dread, and when she'd seen Kaz Brekker there, her dread only doubled. Dirtyhands must have informed on her. He'd told Tante Heleen that she'd spoken out of turn, that she'd been trying to make trouble.

But Heleen had leaned back in her silken chair and said, "Well, little lynx, it seems you're someone else's problem now. Apparently Per Haskell has a taste for Suli girls. He's purchased your indenture for a very tidy sum."

Inej swallowed. "I'm moving to a different house?"

Heleen waved a hand. "Haskell does own a pleasure house – if you can call it that – somewhere in the lower

Barrel, but you'd be a waste of his money there – though you'd certainly learn just how kind Tante Heleen has been to you. No, Haskell wants you for his very own."

Who was Per Haskell? *Does it matter?* said a voice inside her. *He's a man who buys women. That's all you need to know.*

Inej's distress must have been obvious because Tante Heleen laughed lightly. "Don't worry. He's old, *disgustingly* old, but he seems harmless enough. Of course, one never knows." She lifted a shoulder. "Perhaps he'll share you with his errand boy, Mister Brekker."

Kaz turned his cold eyes on Tante Heleen. "Are we done?" It was the first time Inej had heard him speak, and she was startled by the rough burn of his voice.

Heleen sniffed, adjusting the neckline of her shimmering blue gown. "We are indeed, you little wretch." She heated a stick of peacock blue wax and affixed her seal to the document before her. Then, she rose and examined her reflection in the looking glass that hung above the mantel. Inej watched Heleen straighten the diamond choker on her neck, the jewels glinting brightly. Through the din of confusion in her head, Inej thought, *They look like stolen stars.*

"Goodbye, little lynx," said Tante Heleen. "I doubt you'll last more than a month in that part of the Barrel." She glanced at Kaz. "Don't be surprised if she runs. She's faster than she looks. But maybe Per Haskell will enjoy that, too. See yourselves out."

She swept from the room in a billow of silk and honeyed perfume, leaving a stunned Inej in her wake.

Slowly, Kaz crossed the room and shut the door. Inej tensed for whatever was to come next, fingers twisting in her silks.

"Per Haskell runs the Dregs," Kaz said. "You've heard of us?"

"They're your gang."

"Yes, and Haskell is my boss. Yours, too, if you like."

She summoned her courage and said, "And if I don't like?"

"I withdraw the offer and go back home looking like a fool. You stay here with that monster Heleen."

Inej's hands flew to her mouth. "She listens," Inej whispered, terrified.

"Let her listen. The Barrel has all kinds of monsters in it, and some of them are very beautiful indeed. I pay Heleen for information. In fact, I pay her too much for information. But I know exactly what she is. I asked Per Haskell to pay off your indenture. Do you know why?"

"You like Suli girls?"

"I don't know enough Suli girls to say." He moved to the desk and picked up the document, tucking it in his coat. "The other night, when you spoke to me—"

"I meant no offence, I—"

"You wanted to offer me information. Perhaps in return for help? A letter to your parents? Some extra pay?"

Inej cringed. That was exactly what she'd wanted. She'd overheard gossip about a silk trade and had thought to make some kind of exchange. It was foolish, brash.

"Is Inej Ghafa your real name?"

A strange sound escaped Inej's throat, part sob, part laugh, a weak, embarrassing sound, but it had been months since she'd heard her own name, her family name. "Yes," she managed.

"Is that what you prefer to be called?"

"Of course," she said, then added, "Is Kaz Brekker *your* real name?"

"Real enough. Last night, when you approached me, I didn't know you were anywhere near me until you spoke."

Inej frowned. She'd wanted to be silent so she had been. What did that matter?

"Bells on your ankles," Kaz said, gesturing to her costume, "but I didn't hear you. Purple silks and spots painted on your shoulders, but I didn't see you. And I see *everything*."

She shrugged, and he cocked his head to one side. "Were you trained as a dancer?"

"An acrobat." She paused. "My whole family are acrobats."

"High wire?"

"And swings. Juggling. Tumbling."

"Did you work with a net?"

"Only when I was very little."

"Good. There aren't any nets in Ketterdam. Have you ever been in a fight?"

She shook her head.

"Killed someone?"

Her eyes widened. "No."

"Ever think about it?"

She paused and then crossed her arms. "Every night."

"That's a start."

"I don't want to kill people, not really."

"That's a solid policy until people want to kill you. And in our line of work that happens a lot."

"*Our* line of work?"

"I want you to join the Dregs."

"Doing what?"

"Gathering information. I need a spider to climb the walls of Ketterdam's houses and businesses, to listen at windows and in the eaves. I need someone who can be invisible, who can become a ghost. Do you think you could do that?"

I'm already a ghost, she thought. *I died in the hold of a slaver ship.*

"I think so."

"This city is full of rich men and women. You're going to learn their habits, their comings and goings, the dirty things they do at night, the crimes they try to cover by day, their shoe sizes, their safe combinations, the toy they loved best as a child. And I'm going to use that information to take away their money."

"What happens when you take their money and you become a rich man?"

Kaz's mouth had quirked slightly at that. "Then you can steal my secrets, too."

"This is why you bought me?"

The humour vanished from his face. "Per Haskell didn't buy you. He paid off your indenture. That means you owe him money. A lot of it. But it's a real contract. Here," he said, removing Heleen's document from his coat. "I want you to see something."

"I don't read Kerch."

"It doesn't matter. See these numbers? This is the price Heleen claims you borrowed from her for transport from Ravka. This is the money you've earned in her employ. And this is what you still owe her."

"But . . . but that's not possible. It's more now than when I got here."

"That's right. She charged you for room, board, grooming."

"She *bought* me," Inej said, her anger rising despite herself. "I couldn't even read what I was signing."

"Slavery is illegal in Kerch. Indentures are not. I know this contract is a sham and any thinking judge would, too. Unfortunately, Heleen has many thinking judges in her pocket. Per Haskell is offering you a loan – no more, no less. Your contract will be in Ravkan. You'll pay interest, but it won't break you. And as long as you pay him a certain percentage every month, you'll be free to come and go as you please."

Inej shook her head. None of this seemed possible.

"Inej, let me be very clear with you. If you skip out on your contract, Haskell will send people after you, people who make Tante Heleen look like a doting grandmother. And I won't stop him. I'm putting my neck on the line for this little arrangement. It's not a position I enjoy."

"If this is true," Inej said slowly. "Then I'm free to say no."

"Of course. But you're obviously dangerous," he said. "I'd prefer you never became dangerous to me."

Dangerous. She wanted to clutch the word to her. She was fairly sure this boy was demented or just hopelessly deluded, but she liked that word, and unless she was mistaken, he was offering to let her walk out of this house tonight.

"This isn't . . . it isn't a trick, is it?" Her voice was smaller than she wanted it to be.

The shadow of something dark moved across Kaz's face. "If it were a trick, I'd promise you safety. I'd offer you happiness. I don't know if that exists in the Barrel, but you'll find none of it with me."

For some reason, those words had comforted her. Better terrible truths than kind lies.

"All right," she said. "How do we begin?"

"Let's start by getting out of here and finding you some proper clothes. Oh, and Inej," he said as he led her out of the salon. "Don't ever sneak up on me again."

The truth was she'd tried to sneak up on Kaz plenty of times since then. She'd never managed it. It was as if once Kaz had seen her, he'd understood how to keep seeing her.

She'd trusted Kaz Brekker that night. She'd become the dangerous girl he'd sensed lurking inside her. But she'd made the mistake of continuing to trust him, of believing in the legend he'd built around himself. That myth had brought her here to this sweltering darkness, balanced between life and death like the last leaf clinging to an autumn branch. In the end, Kaz Brekker was a just a boy, and she'd let him lead her to this fate.

She couldn't even blame him. She'd let herself be led

because she hadn't known where she'd wanted to go. *The heart is an arrow*. Four million *kruge*, freedom, a chance to return home. She'd said she wanted these things. But in her heart, she couldn't bear the thought of returning to her parents. Could she tell her mother and father the truth? Would they understand all she'd done to survive, not just at the Menagerie, but every day since? Could she lay her head in her mother's lap and be forgiven? What would they see when they looked at her?

Climb, Inej. But where was there to go? What life was waiting for her after all she'd suffered? Her back ached. Her hands were bleeding. The muscles in her legs shook with invisible tremors, and her skin felt ready to peel away from her body. Every breath of black air seared her lungs. She couldn't breathe deeply. She couldn't even focus on that grey patch of sky. The sweat kept beading down her forehead and stinging her eyes. If she gave up, she'd be giving up for all of them – for Jesper and Wylan, for Nina and her Fjerdan, for Kaz. She couldn't do that.

It isn't up to you any longer, little lynx, Tante Heleen's voice crooned in her head. *How long have you been holding on to nothing?*

The heat of the incinerator wrapped around Inej like a living thing, a desert dragon in his den, hiding from the ice, waiting for her. She knew her body's limits, and she knew she had no more to give. She'd made a bad wager. It was as simple as that. The autumn leaf might cling to its branch, but it was already dead. The only question was when it would fall.

Let go, Inej. Her father had taught her to climb, to trust the rope, the swing, and finally, to trust in her own skill, to believe that if she leaped, she would reach the other side. Would he be waiting for her there? She thought of her knives, hidden away aboard the *Ferolind* – maybe they could go to some other girl who dreamed of being dangerous. She whispered their names: Petyr, Marya, Anastasia, Vladimir, Lizabeta, Sankta Alina, martyred before she could turn eighteen. *Let go, Inej.* Should she jump now or simply wait for her body to give out?

Inej felt wetness on her cheeks. Was she crying? Now? After everything she'd done and had done to her?

Then she heard it, a soft patter, a gentle drum that had no real rhythm. She felt it on her cheeks and face. She heard the hiss as it struck the coals below. *Rain.* Cool and forgiving. Inej tilted her head back. Somewhere, she heard bells ringing the three-quarter hour, but she didn't care. She only heard the music of the rain as it washed away the sweat and soot, the coalsmoke of Ketterdam, the face paint of the Menagerie, as it bathed the jute strands of the rope, and hardened the rubber on her suffering feet. It felt like a blessing, though she knew Kaz would just call it weather.

She had to move now, quickly, before the stones grew slick and the rain became an enemy. She forced her muscles to flex, her fingers to seek, and pulled herself up one foot, then another, again and again, murmuring prayers of gratitude to her Saints. Here was the rhythm that had eluded her before, buried in the whispered cadence of their names.

But even as she gave thanks, she knew that the rain was not enough. She wanted a storm – thunder, wind, a deluge. She wanted it to crash through Ketterdam's pleasure houses, lifting roofs and tearing doors off their hinges. She wanted it to raise the seas, take hold of every slaving ship, shatter their masts, and smash their hulls against unforgiving shores. *I want to call that storm*, she thought. And four million *kruge* might be enough to do it. Enough for her own ship – something small and fierce and laden with firepower. Something like her. She would hunt the slavers and their buyers. They would learn to fear her, and they would know her by her name. *The heart is an arrow. It demands aim to land true.* She clung to the wall, but it was purpose she grasped at long last, and that carried her upwards.

She was not a lynx or a spider or even the Wraith. She was Inej Ghafa, and her future was waiting above.

26

KAZ

Kaz sped through the upper cells, sparing brief seconds for a glance through each grate. Bo Yul-Bayur would not be here. And he didn't have much time.

Part of him felt unhinged. He had no cane. His feet were bare. He was in strange clothes, his hands pale and ungloved. He didn't feel like himself at all. No, that wasn't quite true. He felt like the Kaz he'd been in the weeks after Jordie had died, like a wild animal, fighting to survive.

Kaz spotted a Shu prisoner lurking at the back of one of the cells.

"*Sesh-uyeh*," Kaz whispered. The man stared at him blankly. "Yul-Bayur?" Nothing. The man started shouting at him in Shu, and Kaz hurried away, past the rest of the cells, then slipped out to the landing and charged down to the next level as fast as he could manage. He knew he was being reckless, selfish, but wasn't that why they called him Dirtyhands? No job too risky. No deed too low. Dirtyhands would see the rough work done.

He wasn't sure what was driving him. It was possible Pekka Rollins wasn't here. It was possible he was dead. But

Kaz didn't believe it. *I'd know. Somehow I'd know.* "Your death belongs to me," he whispered.

The swim back from the Reaper's Barge had been Kaz's rebirth. The child he'd been had died of firepox. The fever had burned away every gentle thing inside him.

Survival wasn't nearly as hard as he'd thought once he left decency behind. The first rule was to find someone smaller and weaker and take what he had. Though – small and weak as Kaz was – that was no easy task. He shuffled up from the harbour, keeping to the alleys, heading towards the neighbourhood where the Hertzoons had lived. When he spotted a sweetshop, he waited outside, then waylaid a chubby little schoolboy lagging behind his friends. Kaz knocked him down, emptied his pockets, and took his bag of liquorice.

"Give me your trousers," he'd said.

"They're too big for you," the boy had cried.

Kaz bit him. The boy gave up his trousers. Kaz rolled them in a ball and threw them in the canal, then ran as fast as his weak legs would take him. He didn't want the trousers; he just wanted the boy to wait before he went wailing for help. He knew the schoolboy would huddle in that alley for a long while, weighing the shame of appearing half-dressed in the street with the need to get home and tell what had happened.

Kaz stopped running when he reached the darkest alley he could find in the Barrel. He crammed all the liquorice into his mouth at once, swallowing it in painful gulps, and promptly vomited it up. He took the money and bought a hot roll of white bread. He was barefoot and filthy. The baker gave him a second roll just to stay away.

When he felt a bit stronger, a bit less shaky, he walked to East Stave. He found the dingiest gambling den, one with no sign and just a single lonely barker out front.

"I want a job," he said at the door.

"Don't have any, nub."

"I'm good with numbers."

The man laughed. "Can you clean a pisspot?"

"Yes."

"Well, too bad. We already have a boy who cleans the pisspots."

Kaz waited all night until he saw a boy about his age leave the premises. He followed him for two blocks, then hit him in the head with a rock. He sat down on the boy's legs and pulled off his shoes, then slashed the soles of his feet with a piece of broken bottle. The boy would recover, but he wouldn't be working anytime soon. Touching the bare flesh of his ankles had filled Kaz with revulsion. He kept seeing the white bodies of the Reaper's Barge, feeling the ripe bloat of Jordie's skin beneath his hands.

The next evening, he returned to the den.

"I want a job," he said. And he had one.

From there he'd worked and scraped and saved. He'd trailed the professional thieves of the Barrel and learned how to pick pockets and how to cut the laces on a lady's purse. He did his first stint in jail, and then a second. He quickly earned a reputation for being willing to take any job a man needed done, and the name Dirtyhands soon followed. He was an unskilled fighter, but a tenacious one.

"You have no finesse," a gambler at the Silver Garter once said to him. "No technique."

"Sure I do," Kaz had responded. "I practise the art of 'pull his shirt over his head and punch till you see blood.'"

He still went by Kaz, as he always had, but he stole the name Brekker off a piece of machinery he'd seen on the docks. Rietveld, his family name, was abandoned, cut away like a rotten limb. It was a country name, his last tie to Jordie and his father and the boy he'd been. But he didn't want Jakob Hertzoon to see him coming.

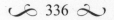

He found out that the con Hertzoon had run on him and Jordie was a common one. The coffeehouse and the house on Zelverstraat had been nothing more than stage sets, used to fleece fools from the country. Filip with his mechanical dogs had been the roper, used to draw Jordie in, while Margit, Saskia, and the clerks at the trade office had all been shills in on the scam. Even one of the bank officers had to have been in on it, passing information to Hertzoon about their customers and tipping him off to newcomers from the country opening accounts. Hertzoon had probably been running the con on multiple marks at once. Jordie's little fortune wasn't enough to justify such a set-up.

But the cruelest discovery was Kaz's gift for cards. It might have made him and Jordie rich. Once he learned a game, it took him mere hours to master it, and then he simply couldn't be beaten. He could remember every hand that had been played, each bet that was made. He could keep track of the deal for up to five decks. And if there was something he couldn't recall, he made up for it by cheating. He'd never lost his love for sleight of hand, and he graduated from palming coins to cards, cups, wallets, and watches. A good magician wasn't much different from a proper thief. Before long, he was banned from play in every gambling hall on East Stave.

In each place he went, in each bar and flophouse and brothel and squat, he asked after Jakob Hertzoon, but if anyone knew the name, they refused to admit it.

Then, one day, Kaz was crossing a bridge over East Stave when he saw a man with florid cheeks and tufty sideburns entering a gin shop. He wasn't wearing staid mercher black any longer, but garish striped trousers and a maroon paisley vest. His velvet coat was bottle green.

Kaz pushed through the crowd, mind buzzing, heart racing, unsure of what he meant to do, but at the door to the shop, a giant bruiser in a bowler hat stopped him with one meaty hand.

"Shop's closed."

"I can see it's open." Kaz's voice sounded wrong to him – reedy, unfamiliar.

"You'll have to wait."

"I need to see Jakob Hertzoon."

"Who?"

Kaz felt like he was about to climb out of his skin. He pointed through the window. "Jakob *fucking* Hertzoon. I want to talk to him."

The bruiser had looked at Kaz as if he were deranged. "Get your head straight, lad," he'd said. "That ain't no Hertzoon. That's Pekka Rollins. Want to get anywhere in the Barrel, you'd best learn his name."

Kaz knew Pekka Rollins' name. Everyone did. He'd just never seen the man.

At that moment, Rollins turned towards the window. Kaz waited for acknowledgement – a smirk, a sneer, some spark of recognition. But Rollins' eyes passed right over him. One more mark. One more cull. Why would he remember?

Kaz had been courted by any number of gangs who liked his way with his fists and the cards. He'd always said no. He'd come to the Barrel to find Hertzoon and punish him, not to join some makeshift family. But learning that his real target was Pekka Rollins changed everything. That night, he lay awake on the floor of the squat he'd holed up in and thought of what he wanted, of what would finally make things right for Jordie. Pekka Rollins had taken everything from Kaz. If Kaz intended to do the same to Rollins, he would need to become his equal and then his better, and he couldn't do it alone. He needed a gang, and not just any gang, but one that needed him. The next day he'd walked into the Slat and asked Per Haskell if he could use another soldier. He'd known even then, though: he'd start as a grunt, but the Dregs would become his army.

Had all of those steps brought him here tonight? To these dark corridors? It was hardly the vengeance he'd dreamed of.

The rows of cells stretched on and on, infinite, impossible. There was no way he would find Rollins in time. But it was only impossible until it wasn't, until he sighted that big frame, that florid face through the grate in an iron door. It was only impossible until he was standing in front of Pekka Rollins' cell.

He was on his side, sleeping. Someone had given him a bad beating. Kaz watched the rise and fall of his chest.

How many times had Kaz seen Pekka since that first glimpse in the gin shop? Never once had there been a flicker of recognition. Kaz wasn't a boy any longer; there was no reason Pekka should be able to see the child he'd swindled in his features. But it made him furious every time their paths had crossed. It wasn't right. Pekka's face – Hertzoon's face – was indelible in Kaz's mind, carved there by a jagged blade.

Kaz hung back now, feeling the delicate weight of his lockpicks like an insect cradled in his palm. Wasn't this what he wanted? To see Pekka brought low, humiliated, miserable and hopeless, the best of his crew dead on pikes. Maybe this could be enough. Maybe all he needed now was for Pekka to know exactly who he was, exactly what he'd done. He could stage a little trial of his own, pass sentence, and mete it out, too.

The Elderclock began to chime the three-quarter-hour. He should go. There wasn't much time left to get to the basement. Nina would be waiting for him. They all would.

But he needed this. He'd fought for this. It wasn't the way he'd imagined, but maybe it made no difference. If Pekka Rollins was put to death by some nameless Fjerdan executioner, then none of this would matter. Kaz would have four million *kruge*, but Jordie would never have his revenge.

The lock on the door gave up easily to Kaz's picks.

Pekka's eyes opened, and he smiled. He hadn't been sleeping at all.

"Hello, Brekker," Rollins said. "Come to gloat?"

"Not exactly," Kaz replied.

He let the door slam shut behind him.

PART 5

THE ICE DOES NOT FORGIVE

27

JESPER

EIGHT BELLS

Where the hell is Kaz? Jesper bounced from foot to foot in front of the incinerator, the dim clang of alarm bells filling his ears, rattling his thoughts. Yellow Protocol? Red Protocol? He couldn't remember which was which. Their whole plan had been built around never hearing the sound of an alarm.

Inej had secured a rope to the roof and dropped down a line for them to climb. Jesper had sent the rest of the rope up with Wylan and Matthias, along with a pair of shears he'd located in the laundry, and a crude grappling hook he'd fashioned from the metal slats of a washboard. Then he'd cleaned the spatter of rain and moisture from the floor of the refuse room, and made sure there were no scraps of rope or other signs of their presence. There was nothing left to do but wait – and panic when the alarm started to ring.

He heard people shouting to each other, a hail of stomping boots through the ceiling above. Any minute, some intuitive guards might venture down to the basement. If they found Jesper by the incinerator, the route to the roof would be obvious. He'd be damning not only himself but the others as well.

Come on, Kaz. I'm waiting on you. They all were. Nina had come charging into the room only minutes before, gasping for breath.

"Go!" she'd cried. "What are you waiting for?"

"You!" Jesper shot back. But when he asked her where Kaz was, Nina's face had crumpled.

"I hoped he was with you."

She'd vanished up the rope, grunting with effort, leaving Jesper standing below, frozen with indecision. Had the guards captured Kaz? Was he somewhere in the prison fighting for his life?

He's Kaz Brekker. Even if they locked him up, Kaz could escape any cell, any pair of shackles. Jesper could leave the rope for him, pray the rain and the cooling incinerator was enough to keep the bottom of it from burning away. But if he just kept standing here like a podge, he'd give away their escape route, and they'd all be doomed. There was nothing to do but climb.

Jesper grabbed the rope just as Kaz hurtled through the door. His shirt was covered in blood, his dark hair a wild mess.

"Hurry," he said without preamble.

A thousand questions crowded into Jesper's head, but he didn't stop to ask them. He swung out over the coals and started to climb. Rain was still falling in a light patter from above, and he felt the rope tremble as Kaz took hold beneath him. When Jesper looked down, he saw Kaz bracing himself to sling the incinerator doors closed behind them.

Jesper put hand over hand, pulling himself up from knot to knot, his arms beginning to ache, the rope cutting into his palms, bracing his feet against the wall of the incinerator when he needed to, then recoiling at the heat of the bricks. How had Inej made this climb with nothing to hold on to?

 344

High above, the Elderclock's alarm bells still clanged like a drawer full of angry pots and pans. What had gone wrong? Why had Kaz and Nina been separated? And how were they going to get out of this?

Jesper shook his head, trying to blink the rain from his eyes, muscles bunching in his back as he rose higher.

"Thank the Saints," he gasped when Matthias and Wylan grabbed his shoulders and hauled him up the last few feet. He tumbled over the lip of the chimney and onto the roof, drenched and trembling like a half-drowned kitten. "Kaz is on the rope."

Matthias and Wylan seized the rope to pull him up. Jesper wasn't sure how much Wylan was actually helping, but he was certainly working hard. They dragged Kaz out of the shaft. He flopped onto his back, gulping air. "Where's Inej?" he gasped. "Where's Nina?"

"Already on the embassy roof," said Matthias.

"Leave this rope and take the rest," Kaz said. "Let's move."

Matthias and Wylan tossed the incinerator rope into a grimy heap and grabbed two clean coils. Jesper took one and forced himself to his feet. He followed Kaz to the lip of the roof where Inej had secured a tether that ran from the top of the prison to the embassy sector roof below. Someone had rigged up a sling for those without the Wraith's particular gift for flouting gravity.

"Thank the Saints, Djel, and your Aunt Eva," Jesper said gratefully, and slid down the rope, followed by the others.

The roof of the embassy was curved, probably to keep the snow off, but it was a bit like walking on the humped back of an enormous whale. It was also decidedly more . . . porous than the prison roof. It was pocked with multiple points of entry – vents, chimneys, small glass domes designed to let in the light. Nina and Inej were tucked up against the base of the biggest dome, a filigreed skylight that overlooked the embassy's entry rotunda. It didn't offer much shelter from the dwindling rain, but should any of the guards on the ringwall turn their attention away from the approach road and onto the rooftops of the Court, the crew would be hidden from view.

Nina had Inej's feet in her lap.

"I can't get all the rubber off her heels," she said, as she saw them approaching.

"Help her," said Kaz.

"Me?" Jesper said. "You don't mean—"

"Do it."

Jesper crawled over to get a better look at Inej's blistered feet, keenly aware of Kaz tracking his movements. Kaz's reaction the last time Inej was injured had been more than a little disturbing, though this wasn't nearly as bad as a stab wound – and this time Kaz didn't have the Black Tips to blame. Jesper focused on the particles of rubber, trying to draw them away from Inej's flesh the same way he'd extracted ore from the prison bars.

Inej knew his secret, but Nina was gaping at him. "You're a Fabrikator?"

"Would you believe me if I said no?"

"Why didn't you tell me?"

"You never asked?" he said lamely.

"Jesper—"

"Just leave it alone, Nina." She pressed her lips together, but he knew this wasn't the last he'd hear of it. He made himself refocus on Inej's feet. "Saints," he said.

Inej grimaced. "That bad?"

"No, you just have really ugly feet."

"Ugly feet that got you on this roof."

"But are we stuck here?" asked Nina. The Elderclock ceased its ringing, and in the silence that followed, she shut her eyes in relief. "Finally."

"What happened at the prison?" Wylan said, that panicked crackle back in his voice. "What triggered the alarm?"

"I ran into two guards," said Nina.

Jesper glanced up from his work. "You didn't put them down?"

"I did. But one of them got off a few shots. Another guard came running. That was when the bells started."

"Damn. So that's what set off the alarm?"

"Maybe," said Nina. "Where were you, Kaz? I wouldn't have been in the stairwell if I hadn't wasted time looking for you. Why didn't you meet me on the landing?"

Kaz was peering down through the glass of the dome. "I decided to search the cells on the fifth floor, too."

They all stared at him. Jesper felt his temper beginning to fray.

"What the hell is this?" he said. "You take off before Matthias and I get back, then you just decide to expand your search and leave Nina thinking you're in trouble?"

"There was something I needed to take care of."

"Not good enough."

"I had a hunch," Kaz said. "I followed it."

Nina's expression was pure disbelief. "A *hunch*?"

"I made a mistake," growled Kaz. "All right?"

"No," said Inej calmly. "You owe us an explanation."

After a moment, Kaz said, "I went looking for Pekka Rollins." A look passed between Kaz and Inej that Jesper didn't understand; there was knowledge in it that he'd been locked out of.

"For Saints' sake, why?" asked Nina.

"I wanted to know who in the Dregs leaked information to him."

Jesper waited. "And?"

"I couldn't find him."

"What about the blood on your shirt?" Matthias asked.

"Run in with a guard."

Jesper didn't believe it.

Kaz ran a hand over his eyes. "I screwed up. I made a bad

call, and I deserve the blame for it. But that doesn't change our situation."

"What *is* our situation?" Nina asked Matthias. "What will they do now?"

"The alarm was Yellow Protocol, a sector disturbance."

Jesper pushed at his temples. "I don't remember what that means."

"My guess is that they think someone's attempting a prison break. That sector is already sealed off from the rest of the Ice Court, so they'll authorise a search, probably try to figure out who's missing from the cells."

"They'll find the people we knocked out in the women's and men's holding areas," said Wylan. "We need to get out of here. Forget Bo Yul-Bayur."

Matthias cut a dismissive hand through the air. "It's too late. If the guards think there's a prison break in progress, the checkpoints will be on high alert. They're not going to let anyone just walk through."

"We could still try," said Jesper. "We get Inej's feet patched up—"

She flexed them, then stood, testing her bare soles on the gravel. "They feel all right. My calluses are gone, though."

"I'll give you an address where you can mail your complaints," Nina said with a wink.

"Okay, the Wraith is ambulatory," Jesper said, rubbing a sleeve over his damp face. The rain had faded away to a light mist. "We find a cosy room to bash some partygoers on the head and waltz out of this place decked in their finest."

"Past the embassy gate and two checkpoints?" Matthias said skeptically.

"They don't know anyone escaped the prison sector. They saw Nina and Kaz so they know people are out of their cells, but the guards at the checkpoints are going to be looking for hoodlums in prison clothes, not sweet-smelling diplos in fancy dress. We have to do this before they get wise to the fact that six people are on the loose in the outer circle."

"Forget it," said Nina. "I came here to find Bo Yul-Bayur, and I'm not leaving without him."

"What's the point?" said Wylan. "Even if you manage to get to the White Island and find Yul-Bayur, we'll have no way out. Jesper's right: We should go now while we still have a chance."

Nina folded her arms. "If I have to cross to the White Island alone, I will."

"That may not be an option," said Matthias. "Look."

They gathered around the base of the glass dome. The rotunda below was a mass of people, drinking, laughing, greeting each other, a kind of raucous party before the celebrations on the White Island.

As they watched, a group of new guards pushed into the room, trying to form the crowd into lines.

"They're adding another checkpoint," Matthias said. "They're going to review everyone's identification again before they allow people access to the glass bridge."

"Because of Yellow Protocol?" asked Jesper.

"Probably. A precaution."

It was like seeing the last bit of their luck drain from a glass.

"Then that decides it," said Jesper. "We cut our losses and try to get out now."

"I know a way," Inej said quietly. They all turned to look at her. The yellow light from the dome pooled in her dark eyes. "We can get through that checkpoint and onto the White Island." She pointed below to where two groups of people had entered the rotunda from the gatehouse courtyard and were shaking the mist from their clothes. The girls from the House of the Blue Iris were easily identified by the colour of their gowns and the flowers displayed in their hair and at their necklines. And no one could mistake the men of the Anvil – extensive tattoos on proud display, arms bare despite the chilly weather. "The West Stave delegations have started to arrive. We can get in."

"Inej—" said Kaz.

"Nina and I can get inside," she continued. Her back was straight, her tone steady. She looked like someone facing the firing squad and saying damn the blindfolds. "We enter with the Menagerie."

28

INEJ

EIGHT BELLS AND HALF CHIME

Kaz was watching her intently, his bitter coffee eyes glittering in the light from the dome.

"You know those costumes," she said. "Heavy cloaks, hoods. That's all the Fjerdans will see. A Zemeni fawn. A Kaelish mare." She swallowed and forced the next words past her lips. "A Suli lynx." Not people, not even really girls, just lovely objects to be collected. *I've always wanted to tumble a Zemeni girl*, a customer would whisper. *A Kaelish girl with red hair. A Suli girl with burnt caramel skin.*

"It's a risk," said Kaz.

"What job isn't?"

"Kaz, how are you and Matthias going to get through?" asked Nina. "We might need you for locks, and if things go bad on the island, I don't want to be stranded. I doubt you can pass yourselves off as members of the Menagerie."

"That shouldn't be a problem," said Kaz. "Helvar's been holding out on us."

"Have you?" asked Inej.

"It's not—" Matthias dragged a hand over his cropped hair. "How do you know these things, *demjin*?" he growled at Kaz.

"Logic. The whole Ice Court is a masterpiece of fail-safes and doubled systems. That glass bridge is impressive, but in an emergency, there would have to be another way to get reinforcements to the White Island and get the royal family out."

"Yes," said Matthias in exasperation. "There's another way to the White Island. But it's messy." He glanced at Nina. "And it certainly can't be done in a gown."

"Hold on," Jesper interrupted. "Who cares if you can all get onto the White Island? Let's say Nina sparkles Yul-Bayur's location out of some Fjerdan higher-up, and you get him back here. We'll be trapped. By then, the prison guards will have completed their search and are going to know six inmates got out of the sector somehow. Any chance we have of making it through the embassy gates and the checkpoints will be gone."

Kaz peered past the dome to the embassy's open courtyard and the ringwall gatehouse beyond.

"Wylan, how hard would it be to disable one of these gates?"

"To get it open?"

"No, to keep it closed."

"You mean break it?" Wylan shrugged. "I don't think it would be too difficult. I couldn't see the mechanism when we entered the prison gate, but from the layout, I'm guessing it's pretty standard."

"Pulleys, cogs, some really big screws?"

"Well, yes, and a sizeable winch. The cables wrap around it like a big spool, and the guards just turn it with some kind of handle or wheel."

"I know how a winch works. Can you take one apart?"

"I think so, but it's the alarm system the cables are

attached to that's complicated. I doubt I could do it without triggering Black Protocol."

"Good," said Kaz. "Then that's what we'll do."

Jesper held up a hand. "I'm sorry, isn't Black Protocol the thing we want to avoid at all costs?"

"I do seem to remember something about certain doom," said Nina.

"Not if we use it against them. Tonight, most of the Court's security is concentrated on the White Island and right here at the embassy. When Black Protocol sounds, the glass bridge will shut down, trapping all those guards on the island along with the guests."

"But what about Matthias' route off the island?" asked Nina.

"They can't move a major force that way," Matthias conceded. "At least not quickly."

Kaz gazed out at the White Island, head tilted, eyes slightly unfocused.

"Scheming face," Inej murmured.

Jesper nodded. "Definitely."

She was going to miss that look.

"Three gates in the ringwall," Kaz said. "The prison gate is already locked up tight because of Yellow Protocol. The embassy gate is a bottleneck crammed with guests – the Fjerdans aren't going to get troops through there. Jesper, that just leaves the gate in the *drüskelle* sector for you and Wylan to handle. You use it to engage Black Protocol, then wreck it. Break it badly enough that any guards who manage to mobilise can't get out to follow us."

"I'm all for locking the Fjerdans in their own 'fortress'," said Jesper. "Truly. But how do *we* get out? Once we trigger Black Protocol, you guys will be trapped on that island, and we'll be trapped in the outer circle. We have no weapons and no demo materials."

Kaz's grin was sharp as a razor. "Thank goodness we're

proper thieves. We're going to do a little shopping – and it's all going on Fjerda's tab. Inej," he said, "let's start with something shiny."

Beside the big glass dome, Kaz laid out the details of what he had in mind. If the old plan had been daring, it had at least been built on stealth. The new plan was audacious, maybe even mad. They wouldn't just be announcing their presence to the Fjerdans, they'd be trumpeting it. Again, the crew would be separated, and again, they would time their movements to the chiming of the Elderclock, but now there would be even less room for error.

Inej searched her heart, expecting to find caution there, fear. But all she felt was ready. This wasn't a job she was performing to pay off her debt to Per Haskell. It wasn't a task to be accomplished for Kaz or the Dregs. *She* wanted this – the money, the dream it would help to secure.

While Kaz explained, and Jesper used the laundry shears to portion out pieces of rope, Wylan helped Inej and Nina prepare. To pass as members of the Menagerie, they would need tattoos. They started with Nina. Using one of Kaz's lockpicks and copper pyrite Jesper had extracted from the roof, Wylan traced his best imitation of the Menagerie feather on Nina's arm, following Inej's description and making corrections as needed. Then Nina sank the ink into her own flesh. A Corporalnik didn't need a tattoo needle. Nina did her best to smoothe the scars on Inej's forearm. The work wasn't perfect, but they were short on time and Nina's calling wasn't as a tailor. Wylan sketched a second peacock feather over Inej's skin.

Nina paused, "You're sure?"

Inej took a deep breath. "It's warpaint," she said, both to Nina and herself. "It's my mark to take."

"It's also temporary," Nina promised. "I'll remove it as soon as we're in the harbour."

The harbour. Inej thought of the *Ferolind* with its cheerful flags, and tried to hold that image in her head as she watched the peacock feather sink into her skin.

The finished tattoos wouldn't bear up under any kind of close scrutiny, but hopefully they would do.

Finally, they stood. Inej had predicted that the Menagerie would arrive late – Tante Heleen loved to make an entrance – but they still needed to be in position and ready to move when the time came.

And yet, they hesitated. The knowledge that they might never see each other again, that some of them – maybe all of them – might not survive this night hung heavy in the air. A gambler, a convict, a wayward son, a lost Grisha, a Suli girl who had become a killer, a boy from the Barrel who had become something worse.

Inej looked at her strange crew, barefoot and shivering in their soot-stained prison uniforms, their features limned by the golden light of the dome, softened by the mist that hung in the air.

What bound them together? Greed? Desperation? Was it just the knowledge that if one or all of them disappeared tonight, no one would come looking? Inej's mother and father might still shed tears for the daughter they'd lost, but if Inej died tonight, there would be no one to grieve for the girl she was now. She had no family, no parents or siblings, only people to fight beside. Maybe that was something to be grateful for, too.

It was Jesper who spoke first. "No mourners," he said with a grin.

"No funerals," they replied in unison. Even Matthias muttered the words softly.

"If any of you survive, make sure I have an open casket," Jesper said as he hefted two slender coils of rope over his shoulder and signalled for Wylan to follow him across the roof. "The world deserves a few more moments with this face."

Inej was only slightly surprised to see the intensity of the look that passed between Matthias and Nina. Something had changed between them after the battle with the Shu, but Inej couldn't be sure what.

Matthias cleared his throat and gave Nina an awkward little bow. "A word?" he asked.

Nina returned the bow with considerably more panache, and let him lead her away. Inej was glad; she wanted a moment with Kaz.

"I have something for you," she said as she pulled his leather gloves from the sleeve of her prison tunic.

He stared at them. "How—"

"I got them from the discarded clothes. Before I made the climb."

"Six storeys in the dark."

She nodded. She wasn't going to wait for thanks. Not for the climb, or the gloves, or for anything ever again.

He pulled the gloves on slowly, and she watched his pale, vulnerable hands disappear beneath the leather. They were trickster hands – long, graceful fingers made for prying open locks, hiding coins, making things vanish.

"When we get back to Ketterdam, I'm taking my share, and I'm leaving the Dregs."

He looked away. "You should. You were always too good for the Barrel."

It was time to go. "Saints' speed, Kaz."

Kaz snagged her wrist. "Inej." His gloved thumb moved over her pulse, traced the top of the feather tattoo. "If we don't make it out, I want you to know . . ."

She waited. She felt hope rustling its wings inside her, ready to take flight at the right words from Kaz. She willed that hope into stillness. Those words would never come. *The heart is an arrow.*

She reached up and touched his cheek. She thought he might flinch again, even knock her hand away. In nearly two years of battling side by side with Kaz, of late-night scheming, impossible heists, clandestine errands, and harried meals of fried potatoes and *hutspot* gobbled down as they rushed from one place to another, this was the first time she had touched him skin to skin, without the barrier of gloves or coat or shirtsleeve. She let her hand cup his cheek. His skin was cool and damp from the rain. He stayed still, but she saw a tremor pass through him, as if he were waging a war with himself.

"If we don't survive this night, I will die unafraid, Kaz. Can you say the same?"

His eyes were nearly black, the pupils dilated. She could see it took every last bit of his terrible will for him to remain still beneath her touch. And yet, he did not pull away. She knew it was the best he could offer. It was not enough.

She dropped her hand. He took a deep breath.

Kaz had said he didn't want her prayers and she wouldn't speak them, but she wished him safe nonetheless. She had her aim now, her heart had direction, and though it hurt to know that path led away from him, she could endure it.

Inej joined Nina at the edge of the dome to await the arrival of the Menagerie. The dome was wide and shallow, all silver filigree and glass. Inej saw there was a mosaic on the floor of the vast rotunda below. It appeared in brief flashes between partygoers – two wolves chasing each other, destined to move in circles for as long as the Ice Court stood.

The guests entering through the grand archway were being shepherded into rooms off the rotunda in small groups to be searched for weapons. Inej saw guards emerge with little piles of brooches, porcupine quills, even sashes that Inej assumed must contain metal or wire.

"You don't have to do this, you know," said Nina. "You don't have to put those silks on again."

"I've done worse."

"I know. You scaled six storeys of hell for us."

"That's not what I meant."

Nina paused. "I know that, too." She hesitated, then said, "Is the haul so important to you?" Inej was surprised to hear what sounded like guilt in Nina's voice.

The Elderclock began to chime nine bells. Inej looked down at the wolves chasing each other around the rotunda floor. "I'm not sure why I began this," she admitted. "But I know why I have to finish. I know why fate brought me here, why it placed me in the path of this prize."

She was being vague, but she wasn't yet ready to speak the dream that had ignited in her heart – a crew of her own, a ship under her command, a crusade. It felt like something that was meant to be kept secret, a new seed that might grow to something extraordinary if it wasn't forced to bloom too soon. She didn't even know how to sail. And yet a part of her wanted to tell Nina all of it. If Nina didn't choose to go back to Ravka, a Heartrender would be an excellent addition to her crew.

"They're here," Nina said.

The girls of the Menagerie entered through the rotunda doors in a wedge formation, their gowns glittering in the candlelight, the hoods of their capes shadowing their faces. Each hood was fashioned to represent an animal – a Zemeni fawn with soft ears and delicate white spots, a Kaelish mare with an auburn topknot, a Shu serpent with beaded red scales, a Ravkan fox, a leopard from the Southern Colonies, a raven, an ermine, and of course the Suli lynx. The tall blonde girl who played the role of the Fjerdan wolf in silvery furs was notably absent.

They were met by uniformed female guards.

"I don't see her," said Nina.

"Just wait. The Peacock will enter last."

And sure enough, there she was: Heleen Van Houden, shimmering in teal satin, an elaborate ruff of peacock feathers framing her golden head.

"Subtle," said Nina.

"Subtle doesn't sell in the Barrel."

Inej gave a high, trilling whistle. Jesper's whistle came back from somewhere in the distance. *This is it*, Inej thought. She'd shoved, and now the boulder was rolling down the hill. Who knew what damage it might do and what might be built on the rubble?

Nina squinted down through the glass. "How does she keep from collapsing under the weight of those diamonds? They can't possibly be real."

"Oh, they're real," said Inej. Those jewels had been purchased with the sweat and blood and sorrow of girls like her.

The guards divided the members of the Menagerie into three groups, while Heleen was escorted separately. The Peacock would never be expected to turn out her clothes and lift her skirts in front of her girls.

"Them," Inej said, pointing to the group that included the Suli lynx and Kaelish mare. They were heading to the doors on the left of the rotunda.

As Nina tracked the group with her eyes, Inej moved over the roof, following their trajectory.

"Which door?" she called.

"Third on the right," Nina said. Inej moved to the nearest air duct and lifted the grate. It would be a tight squeeze for Nina, but they'd manage. She slid down into the ventilation duct, crouching and moving along the narrow shaft between rooms. Behind her, she heard a grunt and then a loud *whump* as Nina hit the bottom of the shaft like a sack of laundry. Inej winced. Hopefully the noises of the crowd below would lend them cover. Or maybe the Ice Court had really big rats.

They crawled along, peering in vents as they went. Finally, they were looking down into some kind of small meeting room that had been commandeered for the purpose of guards searching guests.

The Exotics had removed their capes and laid them on the long oval table. One of the blonde guards was patting the girls down, feeling along the seams and hems of their costumes, and even poking fingers into their hair, while the other guard kept watch with her hand resting on her rifle. She looked ill at ease with the gun. Inej knew Fjerdans didn't let women serve in the army in a combat capacity. Maybe the female guards had been conscripted from some other unit.

Inej and Nina waited until the guards had finished searching the girls, their capes, and their little beaded purses.

"*Ven tidder*," one of the guards said as they exited the room to let the Menagerie girls set themselves to rights.

"Five minutes," translated Nina in a whisper.

"Go," said Inej.

"I need you to move."

"Why?"

"Because I need a clear line of sight, and right now all I can see is your ass."

Inej wiggled forwards so Nina had a better view through the vent, and a moment later, she heard four soft thuds as the Menagerie girls collapsed on the dark blue carpet.

Quickly, she wrenched the grate loose and dropped onto the shiny surface of the table. Nina tumbled down after her, landing in a heap.

"Sorry," she moaned as she dragged herself upright.

Inej almost laughed. "You're very graceful in battle, just not when you're plummeting."

"Missed that day in school."

They stripped the Suli and Kaelish girls down to their underclothes, then bound all the girls' wrists and ankles with cords from the curtains and gagged them with torn pieces of their prison clothes.

"Clock is ticking," said Inej.

"Sorry," Nina whispered to the Kaelish girl. Inej knew that ordinarily Nina would have used pigments to alter her own hair colour, but there simply wasn't time. Nina bled the girl's bright red colour directly from the strands of her hair into Nina's own, leaving the poor Kaelish with a mop of white waves that looked vaguely rusty in places, and Nina with hair that wasn't quite Kaelish red. Nina's eyes were green and not blue, but that kind of tailoring couldn't be rushed, so they'd have to do. She took white powder from the girl's beaded bag and did her best to pale her skin.

As Nina worked, Inej dragged the other girls into a tall silverwood cabinet on the far wall, arranging their limbs so that there would be room for the Kaelish. She felt a stab of guilt as she made sure the Suli girl's gag was secure. Tante Heleen must have bought her to replace Inej; she had the same bronze skin, the same thick sheaf of dark hair. She was built differently, though, soft and curving instead of lean and angular. Maybe she'd come to Tante Heleen of her own free will. Maybe she'd chosen this life. Inej hoped that was true.

"Saints protect you," Inej whispered to the unconscious girl.

A rap came at the door and a voice spoke in Fjerdan.

"They need the room for the next girls," Nina whispered.

Inej and Nina shoved the Kaelish into the cupboard and managed to get the doors closed and locked, then yanked on their costumes. Inej was glad she didn't have time to dwell on the unwelcome familiarity of the silks on her skin, the horrible tinkling of the bells on her anklets. They swept on their capes and took a quick glance in the mirror.

Neither of the costumes fit properly. Inej's purple silks were far too loose, and as for Nina . . .

"What the hell is this supposed to be?" she said, looking down at herself. The plunging gown barely covered her substantial cleavage and clung tightly to her buttocks. It had been wrought to look like blue-green scales, giving way to a shimmering chiffon fan.

"Maybe a mermaid?" suggested Inej. "Or a wave?"

"I thought I was a horse."

"Well they weren't going to put you in a dress of hooves."

Nina smoothed her hands over the ridiculous costume. "I'm about to be very popular."

"I wonder what Matthias would have to say about that outfit."

"He wouldn't approve."

"He doesn't approve of anything about you. But when you laugh, he perks up like a tulip in fresh water."

Nina snorted. "Matthias the tulip."

"The big, brooding, yellow tulip."

"Are you ready?" Nina asked as they pulled their hoods far down over their faces.

"Yes." Inej said, and she meant it. "We'll need a distraction. They're going to notice four girls went in and only two are coming out."

"Leave it to me. And watch your hem."

As soon as they opened the door to the hallway, the guards were waving them over impatiently. Beneath her cape, Nina flicked her fingers hard. One of the guards bleated as her nose began to gush blood down the front of her uniform in absurdly forceful gouts. The other guard recoiled, but in the next instant, she clutched her stomach. Nina was twisting her wrist in a roiling motion, sending waves of nausea through the woman's system.

"Your hem," Nina repeated calmly.

Inej barely had time to gather up her cape before the guard bent double and heaved her dinner over the tiled floor. The guests in the hallway shrieked and shoved at each other, trying to get away from the mess. Nina and Inej sailed by, emitting appropriate squeals of disgust.

"The nosebleed probably would have done the trick," whispered Inej.

"Best to be thorough."

"If I didn't know any better, I'd think you liked making Fjerdans suffer."

They kept their heads down and entered the swell of people filling the rotunda, ignoring the Zemeni fawn who tried to direct them to the other side of the room. It was essential that they not get too close to any of the real Menagerie girls. Inej only wished the cloaks weren't so easy to track through a crowd.

"This one," Inej said, steering Nina into a line far from the other members of the Menagerie. It seemed to be moving a bit faster. But when they reached the front of the line, Inej wondered if she'd chosen poorly. This guard seemed even more stern-faced and humourless than the others. He held his hand out for Nina's papers and scrutinised them with cold blue eyes.

"This description says you have freckles," he said in Kerch.

"I do," said Nina smoothly. "They're just not visible right now. Want to see?"

"No," the Fjerdan said icily. "You're taller than described here."

"Boots," Nina said. "I like to be able to look a man in the eye. You have very pretty eyes."

He looked at the paper, then took in her ensemble.

"You're heavier than it says on this paper, I'll wager."

She shrugged artfully, the scales of her neckline slipping lower. "I like to eat when I'm in the mood," she said, puckering her lips shamelessly. "And I'm always in the mood."

Inej struggled to keep a straight face. If Nina resorted to eyelash batting, she knew she would lose the fight and burst out laughing. But the Fjerdan seemed to be eating it up. Maybe Nina had a stupefying effect on all stalwart northerners.

"Move along," he said gruffly. Then added, "I . . . I may be at the party later."

Nina ran a finger down his arm. "I'll save you a dance."

He grinned like a fool, then cleared his throat, and his stern expression fell back into place. *Saints*, Inej thought, *it must be exhausting to be so stolid all the time*. He glanced cursorily at Inej's papers, his mind still clearly on the prospect of unwrapping Nina's layers of blue-green chiffon. He waved her past, but as Inej stepped forwards she stumbled.

"Wait," said the guard.

She stopped. Nina looked back over her shoulder.

"What's wrong with your shoes?"

"Just a bit big," said Inej. "They stretched more than expected."

"Show me your arms," the guard said.

"Why?"

"Just do it," the guard said harshly.

Inej pulled her arms free of the cloak and held them out, displaying the lumpy peacock feather tattoo.

A guard in captain's stripes wandered over. "What is it?"

"She's Suli, for sure, and she has the Menagerie tattoo, but it doesn't look quite right."

Inej shrugged. "I got a bad burn as a child."

The captain gestured to a group of annoyed-looking partygoers gathered near the entry and surrounded by guards. "Anyone suspicious goes over there. Put her with them, and we'll take her back to the checkpoint to have her papers reviewed."

"I'll miss the party," said Inej.

The guard ignored her, seizing her arm and pulling her back towards the entry as the other people in line stared and whispered. Her heart began to pound.

Nina's face was frightened, pale even beneath her powder, but there was nothing Inej could say to reassure her. She gave her the briefest nod. *Go*, she thought silently. *It's up to you now.*

29

MATTHIAS

NINE BELLS

"**W**hat if I say no, Brekker?" It was mere posturing, Matthias knew that. The time for protest had long passed. They were already jogging down the gentle slope of the embassy roof towards the *drüskelle* sector, Wylan panting from exertion, Jesper loping along with ease, and Brekker keeping pace despite his crooked gait and lack of cane. But Matthias disliked how well this low thief could read him. "What if I don't give you this last bit of myself and my honour?"

"You will, Helvar. Nina is on her way to the White Island right now. Are you really going to leave her stranded?"

"You presume a great deal."

"Seems like the perfect amount to me."

"These are the law courts, right?" Jesper said as they raced over the roof, catching glimpses of the elegant courtyards below, each built around a burbling fountain and dotted with rustling ice willows. "I guess if you're going to be sentenced to death, this isn't a bad place for it."

"Water everywhere," said Wylan. "Do the fountains symbolise Djel?"

"The wellspring," mused Kaz, "where all sins are washed clean."

"Or where they drown you and make you confess," Wylan said.

Jesper snorted. "Wylan, your thoughts have taken a very dark turn. I fear the Dregs may be a bad influence."

They used a doubled segment of rope and the grappling hook to cross to the roof of the *drüskelle* sector. Wylan had to be looped into a sling, but Jesper and Kaz moved easily across the rope, hand over hand, with unnerving speed. Matthias approached with more caution, and though he didn't show it, he did not like the way the rope creaked and bowed with his own weight.

The others pulled him onto the stone of the *drüskelle* roof, and as Matthias stood, he was struck by a wave of vertigo. More than any place in the Ice Court, more than any place in the world, this felt like home to him. But it was home turned on its head, his life viewed at the wrong angle. Peering into the dark, he saw the massive pyramid skylights that marked the roof. He had the disconcerting sense that if he looked through the glass he would see himself running drills in the training rooms, seated at the long table in the dining hall.

In the distance, he heard the wolves barking and yapping in their kennel by the gatehouse, wondering where their masters had gone for the night. Would they recognise him if he approached with an outstretched hand? He wasn't sure he recognised himself. On the northern ice, his choices had seemed clear. But now his thoughts were muddied with these thugs and thieves, with Inej's courage and Jesper's daring, and with Nina, always Nina. He couldn't deny the relief he'd felt when she'd emerged from the incinerator shaft, dishevelled and gasping, frightened but alive. When he and Wylan had pulled her out of the flue, he'd had to force himself to let her go.

No, he would not look through those skylights. He could afford no more weakness, especially on this night. It was time to move forwards.

They reached the lip of the roof overlooking the ice moat. From here it looked solid, its surface polished bright as a mirror and illuminated by the guard towers on the White Island. But the moat's waters were ever shifting, concealed only by a wafer-thin skin of frost.

Kaz secured another coil of rope to the roof's edge and prepared to rappel down to the shore.

"You know what to do," he said to Jesper and Wylan. "Eleven bells and not before."

"When have I ever been early?" asked Jesper.

Kaz braced himself for the descent and vanished over the side. Matthias followed, hands gripping the rope, bare feet pressed against the wall. When he glanced up, he saw Wylan and Jesper gazing down at him. But the next time he looked, they were gone.

The shore surrounding the ice moat was little more than a slender, slippery rind of white stone. Kaz perched there, pressed against the wall and frowning out at the moat.

"How do we cross? I don't see anything."

"Because you are not worthy."

"I'm also not near-sighted. There's nothing there."

Matthias began edging along the wall, running his hand over the stone at hip level. "On Hringkälla the *drüskelle* finish our initiation," he said. "We go from aspirant to novice *drüskelle* in the ceremony at the sacred ash."

"Where the tree talks to you."

Matthias resisted the urge to shove him into the water. "Where we hope to hear the voice of Djel. But that's the final step. First, we have to cross the ice moat undetected. If we are judged worthy, Djel shows us the path."

In truth, elder *drüskelle* simply passed the secret of the crossing along to aspirants they wished to see enter the order; it was a way of culling the weak or those who had simply not meshed successfully with the group. If you'd made friends, if you'd proven yourself, then one of the brothers would take you aside and tell you that on the night of the initiation, you should go to the shore of the ice moat and run your hand along the wall of the *drüskelle* sector. At its centre, you would find an etching of a wolf that marked the location of another glass bridge – not grand and arching like the one that spanned the moat from the embassy wing, but flat, level, and only a few feet wide. It lay just under the frozen skin of the surface, invisible if you didn't know to look for it. Commander Brum himself had been the one to tell Matthias how to find the secret bridge, as well as the trick for crossing it undetected.

It took Matthias two passes along the wall before his fingers found the carved lines of the wolf. He rested his hand there briefly, feeling the traditions that connected him to the order of *drüskelle*, as old as the Ice Court itself.

"Here," he said.

Kaz shuffled over and squinted across the moat. He leaned out and Matthias yanked him back.

He pointed to the guard towers on the top of the wall surrounding the White Island. "You'll be visible," he said. "Use this."

He scraped his hand along the wall and his palm came away white. The night of his initiation, Matthias had rubbed his clothes and hair with the same chalky powder. Camouflaged from the view of the guards in their towers, he'd crossed the slender path to the island to meet his brothers.

Now he and Kaz did the same, though Matthias noticed Kaz tucked his gloves neatly away first. Inej must have returned them.

Matthias stepped onto the secret bridge, then heard Kaz hiss when the icy waters of the moat closed over his feet.

"Chilly, Brekker?"

"If only we had time for a swim. Get moving."

Despite his taunts to Kaz, by the time they were halfway to the island, Matthias' feet had gone almost completely numb, and he was keenly aware of the guard towers high above the moat. *Drüskelle* would have come this way earlier tonight. He'd never heard of any aspirant being spotted or shot at on the bridge, but anything was possible.

"All this to be a witchhunter?" Kaz said behind him. "The Dregs need a better initiation."

"This is only one part of Hringkälla."

"Yes, I know, then a tree tells you the secret handshake."

"I feel sorry for you, Brekker. There is nothing sacred in your life."

There was a long pause, and then Kaz said, "You're wrong."

The outer wall of the White Island loomed up before them, covered in a rippling pattern of scales. It took a moment to locate the ridge of scales that hid the gate. Only a short while ago, *drüskelle* would have been gathered in this niche of the wall to welcome their new brothers ashore, but now it was empty, the iron grating chained. Kaz made quick work of the lock, and soon they were in a slender passage that would lead them to the gardens that backed the barracks of the royal guard.

"Were you always good at locks?"

"No."

"How did you learn?"

"The way you learn about anything. Take it apart."

"And the magic tricks?"

Kaz snorted. "So you don't think I'm a demon any more?"

"I know you're a demon, but your tricks are human."

"Some people see a magic trick and say, 'Impossible!' They clap their hands, turn over their money, and forget about it ten minutes later. Other people ask how it worked. They go home, get into bed, toss and turn, wondering how it was done. It takes them a good night's sleep to forget all about it. And then there are the ones who stay awake, running through the trick again and again, looking for that skip in perception, the crack in the illusion that will explain how their eyes got duped; they're the kind who won't rest until they've mastered that little bit of mystery for themselves. I'm that kind."

"You love trickery."

"I love puzzles. Trickery is just my native tongue."

"The gardens," Matthias said, pointing to the hedges up ahead. "We can follow them all the way round to the ballroom."

Just as they were about to emerge from the passage, two guards rounded the corner – both in black and silver *drüskelle* uniforms, both carrying rifles.

"*Perjenger!*" one of them shouted in surprise. Prisoners. "*Sten!*"

Without thinking, Matthias said, "*Desjenet, Djel comenden!*" Stand down, Djel wills it so. They were the words of a *drüskelle* commanding officer, and he delivered them with all the authority he'd ever learned to muster.

The soldiers exchanged a confused glance. That moment of hesitation was enough. Matthias grabbed the first soldier's rifle and head-butted him hard. The *drüskelle* collapsed.

Kaz slammed into the other soldier, knocking him over. The *drüskelle* kept hold of his rifle, but Kaz slipped behind him and brought his forearm across the soldier's throat, applying pressure until the soldier's eyes shut, and his head fell forwards as he slipped into unconsciousness.

Kaz rolled the body off him and stood.

The reality of the situation struck Matthias suddenly. Kaz hadn't picked up the rifle. Matthias had a gun in his hands, and Kaz Brekker was unarmed. They were standing over the bodies of two unconscious *drüskelle*, men who were supposed to be Matthias' brothers. *I can shoot him*, Matthias thought. *Doom Nina and the rest of them with a single act.* Again, Matthias had the strange sense of his life viewed the wrong way up. He was dressed in prison clothes, an intruder in the place he'd once called home. *Who am I now?*

He looked at Kaz Brekker, a boy whose only cause was himself. Still, he was a survivor, and his own kind of soldier. He had honoured his bargain with Matthias. At any point, he might have decided that Matthias had served his purpose – once he'd helped them draw up the plans, once they'd got past the holding cells, once Matthias had revealed the secret bridge. And whoever he'd become, Matthias was not going to shoot someone unarmed. He'd not yet sunk so far.

Matthias lowered his weapon.

A faint smile touched Kaz's lips. "I wasn't sure what you'd do if it came down to this."

"Neither was I," Matthias admitted. Kaz lifted a brow, and the truth struck Matthias with the force of a blow. "It was a test. You *chose* not to pick up the rifle."

"I needed to be sure you were really with us. All of us."

"How did you know I wouldn't shoot?"

"Because, Matthias, you stink of decency."

"You're mad."

"Do you know the secret to gambling, Helvar?" Kaz brought his good foot down on the butt of the fallen soldier's rifle. The gun flipped up. Kaz had it in his hands and pointed at Matthias in the space of a breath. He'd never been in any danger at all. "Cheat. Now let's clean up and get those uniforms on. We have a party to go to."

"One day you'll run out of tricks, *demjin.*"

"You'd better hope it's not today."

We'll see what this night brings, Matthias thought as he bent to the task. *Trickery is not my native tongue, but I may learn to speak it yet.*

30

JESPER

NINE BELLS AND QUARTER CHIME

Jesper knew he should be mad at Kaz – for going after Pekka Rollins and blowing their first plan to bits, and for pushing them into deeper danger with this new scheme. But as he and Wylan crept along the *drüskelle* roof towards the gatehouse, he was too damn happy to be mad. His heart was pounding, and adrenaline crackled through his body in delicious spikes. It was a little like a party he'd once gone to on West Stave. Someone had filled a city fountain with champagne, and it had taken about two seconds for Jesper to dive in with boots off and gullet open. Now it was risk filling up his nose and mouth, making him feel giddy and invincible. He loved it, and he hated himself for loving it. He should be thinking about the job, the money, getting out from under his debt, making sure his father didn't suffer for his antics. But when Jesper's mind even brushed up against those thoughts, everything in him recoiled. Trying not to die was the best possible distraction.

Even so, Jesper was more conscious of the sounds they made now that they were away from the crowds and chaos of the embassy. This night belonged to the *drüskelle*. Hringkälla was their holiday, and they were all safely ensconced on the White Island. This building was probably the safest place for him and Wylan to be at the moment. But the silence here seemed weighted, sinister. There were no willows or fountains here, as there had been at the embassy. Like the prison, this part of the Ice Court wasn't intended for public eyes. Jesper caught himself nervously wiggling the *baleen* wedged between his teeth with his tongue and forced himself to stop before he triggered it. He was fairly sure Wylan would never let him forget a blunder like that.

A large pyramid-shaped skylight looked down on what seemed to be a training room, its floor emblazoned with the *drüskelle* wolf's head, the shelves lined with weapons. Through the next glass pyramid, he glimpsed a big dining hall. One wall was taken up by a massive hearth, a wolf's head carved into the stone above it. The opposite wall was adorned by an enormous banner with no discernible pattern, a patchwork of slender strips of cloth – mostly red and blue, but some purple, too. It took Jesper a moment to understand what he was seeing.

"Saints," he said, feeling a little sick. "Grisha colours."

Wylan squinted. "The banner?"

"Red for Corporalki. Blue for Etherealki. Purple for Materialki. Those are pieces of the *kefta* that Grisha wear in battle. They're trophies."

"There are so many."

Hundreds. Thousands. *I would have worn purple*, Jesper thought, *if I'd joined the Second Army.* He reached for the fizzy elation that had been bubbling through him moments before. He'd been willing, even eager to risk capture and execution as a thief and hired gun. Why was it worse to think about being hunted as a Grisha?

"Let's keep moving."

Just like the prison and the embassy, the gatehouse in

the *drüskelle* sector was built around a courtyard so anyone entering could be observed and fired upon from above. But with the gate out of operation, the courtyard battlements were as deserted as the rest of the building. Here, slabs of sleek black stone were inlaid with the silver wolf's head, the surfaces lit with eerie blue flame. It was the one part of the Ice Court he'd seen that wasn't white or grey. Even the gate was some kind of black metal that looked impossibly heavy.

A guard was visible below, leaning against the gatehouse arch, a rifle slung over his shoulder.

"Only one?" asked Wylan.

"Matthias said four guards for non-operational gates."

"Maybe Yellow Protocol is working in our favour," said Wylan. "They could have been sent to the prison sector or—"

"Or maybe there are twelve big Fjerdans keeping warm inside."

As he and Wylan watched, the guard opened a tin of *jurda* and shoved a wad of the dried orange blossoms into his mouth. He looked bored and irritated, probably frustrated to be stationed far from the fun of the Hringkälla festivities.

I don't blame you, Jesper thought. *But your life's about to get a lot more exciting.*

At least the guard was wearing an ordinary uniform instead of *drüskelle* black, Jesper considered, still unable to shake the image of that banner from his mind. His mother was Zemeni, but his father had the Kaelish blood that had given Jesper his grey eyes, and he'd never quite shaken the superstitions of the Wandering Isle. When Jesper had started to show his power, his father had been heartbroken. He'd encouraged Jesper to keep it hidden. "I'm afraid for you," he'd said. "The world can be cruel to your kind." But Jesper had always wondered if maybe his father had been a little afraid *of* him, too.

What if I'd gone to Ravka instead of Kerch? Jesper

thought. *What if I'd joined the Second Army?* Did they even let Fabrikators fight, or were they kept walled up in workshops? Ravka was more stable now, rebuilding. There was no compulsory draft for Grisha. He could go, visit, maybe learn to use his power better, leave the gambling dens of Ketterdam behind. If they succeeded in delivering Bo Yul-Bayur to the Merchant Council, anything might be possible. He gave himself a shake. What was he thinking? He needed a dose of imminent peril to get his head straight.

He rose out of his crouch. "I'm going in."

"What's the plan?"

"You'll see."

"Let me help."

"You can help by shutting up and staying out of the way. Here," Jesper said as he hooked the rope over the side of the roof, letting it drop down behind a row of stone slabs lining the walkway. "Wait until I've immobilised the guards, then lower yourself down."

"Jesper—"

Jesper took off across the roof, keeping low as he gave the lip overlooking the courtyard a wide berth. He positioned himself on the wall behind the guard.

As noiselessly as he could, he secured another section of rope to the roof and slowly began to rappel down the wall. The guard was almost directly beneath him. Jesper was no Wraith, but if he could just make the drop silently and sneak up behind the guard he could keep things quiet.

He tensed, ready to drop. Another guard strode out of the gatehouse, clapping his hands in the cold and talking loudly, then a third appeared. Jesper froze. He was dangling over three armed guards, halfway down a wall, completely exposed. This was why Kaz did the planning. Sweat broke out on his brow. He couldn't take three guards at once. And what if there were more in the gatehouse, ready to ring the alarm?

"Wait," said one of the guards. "Did you hear something?"

Don't look up. Oh, Saints, don't look up.

The guards moved in a slow circle, rifles raised. One of them craned his head back, scanning the roof. He began to turn.

A strange, sweet sound pierced the air.

"Skerden Fjerda, kende hjertzeeeeeng, lendten isen en de waaaanden."

Fjerdan words Jesper didn't understand crested over the courtyard in a shimmering, perfect tenor that seemed to catch upon the black stone battlements.

Wylan.

The guards whirled, rifles pointed at the walkway that led to the courtyard, seeking the source of the sound.

"Olander?" one called.

"Nilson?" said another.

Their guns were raised, but their voices were more bemused and curious than aggressive.

What the hell is he doing?

A silhouette appeared in the walkway arch, lurching left and right.

"Skerden Fjerda, kende hjertzeeeeeng," Wylan sang, doing a surprisingly convincing impression of a drunk but very talented Fjerdan.

The guards burst out laughing, joining in on the song. *"Lendten isen . . ."*

Jesper leaped down. He seized the closest Fjerdan, snapped his neck, and grabbed his rifle. As the next guard turned, Jesper slammed the butt of the rifle into his face with a nasty crunch. The third guard raised his weapon, but Wylan snagged his arms from behind in an awkward hold. The rifle dropped from the guard's hands, clattering against the stone. Before he could cry out, Jesper lunged forwards and rammed the butt of his rifle into the guard's gut, then finished him with two strikes to the jaw.

He reached down and tossed one of the rifles to Wylan. They stood over the guards' bodies, panting, weapons raised, waiting for more Fjerdan soldiers to flood out of the gatehouse. No one came. Maybe the fourth guard had been pulled away for Yellow Protocol.

"Is that how you shut up and stay out of the way?" Jesper whispered as they dragged the guards' bodies out of view behind one of the stone slabs.

"Is that how you say thank you?" Wylan retorted.

"What the hell was that song?"

"National anthem," Wylan said smugly. "Schoolroom Fjerdan, remember?"

Jesper shook his head. "I'm impressed. With you *and* your tutors."

They liberated two of the guards' uniforms, leaving their own prison clothes in a tidy bundle, then bound the hands and feet of the guards who still had pulses and gagged them with torn pieces of their prison clothes. Wylan's uniform was far too big, and Jesper's sleeves and pants looked ridiculously short, but at least the boots were a reasonable fit.

Wylan gestured to the guards. "Is it safe to leave them, you know—"

"Alive? I'm not big on killing unconscious men."

"We could wake them up."

"Pretty ruthless, merchling. Have you ever killed anyone?"

"I'd never even seen a dead body before I came to the Barrel," Wylan admitted.

"It's not something to be embarrassed about," Jesper said, surprising himself a little. But he meant it. Wylan needed to learn to take care of himself, but it would be nice if he could do it without getting on friendly terms with death. "Make sure the gags are tight."

They took the extra precaution of securing the bound

guards to the base of a stone slab. The poor nubs would probably be discovered before they managed to get loose.

"Let's go," Jesper said, and they crossed the courtyard to the gatehouse. There were doors to the right and left of the arch.

They took the right side, climbing the stairs cautiously. Though Jesper didn't think anyone would be lying in wait, some guard might be charged with protecting the gate mechanism at all cost. But the room above the arch was empty, lit only by a lantern set on a low table where a book lay open next to a little pile of whole walnuts and cracked shells. The walls were lined with racks of rifles – very expensive rifles – and Jesper assumed the boxes on the shelves were filled with ammunition. No dust anywhere. Tidy Fjerdans.

Most of the room was taken up by a long winch, handles at each end, thick loops of chain spooled around it. Near each handle, the chains extended in taut spokes through slots in the stone.

Wylan cocked his head to the side. "Huh."

"I don't like that sound. What's wrong?"

"I was expecting rope or cables, not steel chains. If we're going to make sure the Fjerdans can't get the gate open, we're going to have to cut through the metal."

"But then how do we trigger Black Protocol?"

"That's the problem."

The Elderclock began to sound ten bells.

"I'll weaken the links," said Jesper. "Look for a file or anything with an edge."

Wylan held up the shears from the laundry.

"Good enough," said Jesper. It would have to be.

We have time, he told himself as he focused on the chain. *We can still get this done.* Jesper hoped the others hadn't met with any surprises.

Maybe Matthias was wrong about the White Island.

Maybe the shears would snap in Wylan's hands. Maybe Inej would fail. Or Nina. Or Kaz.

Or me. Maybe I'll fail.

Six people, but a thousand ways this insane plan could go wrong.

NINE BELLS AND HALF CHIME

Nina dared one more glance over her shoulder, watching the guards drag Inej away. *She's smart, deadly. Inej can take care of herself.*

The thought brought Nina little comfort, but she had to keep moving. She and Inej had clearly been together, and she wanted to be gone before the guard who had stopped Inej extended his suspicions to her. Besides, there was nothing she could do for Inej now, not without giving herself away and ruining everything. She ducked through the hordes of partygoers and shucked off the conspicuous horsehair cloak, letting it trail behind her, then allowing it to drop and be trampled by the crowd. Her costume would still turn heads, but at least now she didn't have to worry about a big red topknot giving away her location.

The glass bridge rose before her in a gleaming arc, shimmering in the blue flames of the lanterns on its spires. All around her people laughed and clung to one another as they climbed higher above the ice moat, its surface shining below, a near-perfect mirror. The effect was disconcerting, dizzying; her too-tight beaded slippers seemed to float in mid-air. The people beside her looked as if they were walking on nothing at all.

Again she had the unpleasant understanding that this place must have been built by Fabrikator craft in some distant past. Fjerdans claimed the construction of the Ice Court was the work of a god or of Sënj Egmond, one of the Saints they claimed had Fjerdan blood. But in Ravka, people had begun to rethink the miracles of the Saints. Had they been true miracles or simply the work of talented Grisha? Was this bridge a gift from Djel? An ancient product of slave labour? Or had the Ice Court been built in a time before Grisha had come to be viewed as monsters by the Fjerdans?

At the highest point of the arch, she got her first real view of the White Island and the inner ring. From a distance, she'd seen the island was protected by another wall. But from this vantage point she saw the wall had been crafted in the shape of a leviathan, a giant ice dragon circling the island and swallowing its own tail. She shivered. Wolves, dragons, what was next? In Ravkan stories, monsters waited to be woken by the call of heroes. *Well*, she thought, *we're certainly not heroes. Let's hope this one stays asleep.*

The descent on the bridge was even more dizzying, and Nina was relieved when her feet struck solid white marble once more. White cherry trees and silvery buttonwood hedges lined the marble walkway, and security on this side of the bridge seemed decidedly more relaxed. The guards who stood at attention wore elaborate white uniforms accented with silver fur and less than intimidating silver lace. But Nina remembered what Matthias had said: As you moved deeper into the rings, security actually tightened – it just became less visible. She looked at the partygoers moving with her up the slippery stairs and through the cleft between the dragon's tail and mouth. How many were truly guests, noblemen, entertainers? And how many were Fjerdan soldiers or *drüskelle* in disguise?

They passed through an open stone court and the palace doors into a vaulted entry several storeys high. The palace was made of the same clean, white, unadorned stone as the Ice Court walls, and the whole place felt as if it had been hollowed out of a glacier. Nina couldn't tell if it was nerves, imagination, or if the place really was cold, but her skin puckered with gooseflesh, and she had to fight to keep her teeth from chattering.

She entered a vast circular ballroom packed with people dancing and drinking beneath a glistening pack of wolves hewn from ice. There had to be at least thirty massive sculptures of running, leaping beasts, their flanks gleaming slickly in the silvery light, jaws open, their slowly melting muzzles dripping occasionally onto the crowd below. Music from an unseen orchestra was barely audible over the gabble of conversation.

The Elderclock began to chime ten bells. It had taken her too long to get across that stupid glass bridge. She needed a better view of the room. As she headed for a swooping white stone staircase, she caught sight of two familiar figures in the shadows of a nearby alcove. Kaz and Matthias. They'd made it. And they were in *drüskelle* uniforms. Nina suppressed a shiver. Seeing Matthias in those colours settled a different kind of cold into her bones. What had he thought when he put it on? She let her eyes meet his briefly, but his gaze was unreadable. Still, seeing Kaz beside him gave her some comfort. She wasn't alone, and they were still on schedule.

She didn't risk so much as a nod of acknowledgement, but continued up the stairs to the balcony on the second floor where she could get a better look at the flow of the crowd. It was a trick she'd learned in school from Zoya Nazyalensky. There were patterns in the way people moved, the way they clustered around power. They thought they were drifting, milling aimlessly, but really they were being drawn towards people of status. Not surprisingly, there was a large concentration eddying around the Fjerdan queen and her attendants. *Strange*, Nina thought, observing their white gowns. In Ravka, white was a servant's colour. But that crown wasn't anything to sniff at – twisting spines of diamonds that looked like branches glowing with new frost.

The royals were too well-protected to be of use to her, but not far away she saw another whirl of activity around a group in military dress. If anyone knew Yul-Bayur's location on the island, it would be someone highly ranked in Fjerda's military.

"Nice view, isn't it?"

Nina nearly jumped as a man sidled up beside her. Some spy she made. She hadn't even noticed him approaching.

He grinned at her and placed a hand at the small of her back. "You know, there are rooms here set aside for a little fun. And you look like more than a little fun." His hand slid lower.

Nina plunged his heart rate, and he dropped like a stone, conking his head on the banister. He'd wake up in about ten minutes with a bad headache and possibly a minor concussion.

"Is he all right?" asked a passing couple.

"Too much to drink," said Nina airily.

She slipped quickly down the stairs and into the crowd, moving steadily towards where a group of soldiers garbed in silver-and-white military dress surrounded a portly man with a luxuriant moustache. If the constellation of medals on his chest was any indication, he had to be a general or close to it. Should she target him directly? She needed someone of high-enough rank to have access to privileged information – someone drunk enough to make ill-considered decisions, but not so drunk that he couldn't take her where she needed to go. By the ruddy look of the general's cheeks and the way he was swaying on his feet, he looked as if he might be too far gone to do anything but take a nap facedown in a potted plant.

Nina could feel the minutes ticking down. It was time to make her bid. She nabbed a glass of champagne then moved carefully around the circle. As a soldier separated from the group, she took a step backwards, directly into his path. He slammed into her. He was light enough on his feet that it wasn't much of a hit, but she gave a sharp cry and lurched forwards, spilling her champagne. Instantly, several strong arms reached out to brace her fall.

"You clod," said the general. "You nearly knocked her from her feet."

And on the first try, Nina thought to herself. *Never mind. I am an excellent spy.*

The poor soldier's cheeks were bright red. "Apologies, miss."

"I'm sorry," she said in Kerch, feigning confusion and keeping to the language of the Menagerie. "I don't speak Fjerdan."

"Deep apologies," he attempted in Kerch. Then made a valiant attempt at Kaelish, "Much sorry."

"Oh no, it was my fault entirely," Nina said breathlessly.

"Ahlgren, stop slaughtering her language and fetch her a fresh glass of champagne." The soldier bowed and hurried off. "Are you quite all right? Shall I find you a seat?" the general asked in excellent Kerch.

"He just startled me," Nina said with a smile, leaning on the general's arm.

"I think it might be best to get you off your feet."

Nina restrained an arch of her brow. *I just bet. But first I need to find out what you know.*

"And miss the party?"

"You look pale. Some rest in one of the upper rooms will help."

Saints, he doesn't waste any time, does he? Before Nina could insist that she was perfectly well but might like to take a turn on the terrace, a warm voice said, "Really, General Eklund, the best way to garner a woman's goodwill is not to tell her she looks sickly."

The general scowled, his moustache bristling, but then he seemed to snap to attention.

"So true, so true," he laughed nervously.

Nina turned, and the floor seemed to drop from beneath her feet. *No,* she thought, her heart stuttering in panic. *It can't be. He drowned. He's supposed to be at the bottom of the ocean.*

But if Jarl Brum was dead, he made a very lively corpse.

32

JESPER

TEN BELLS AND HALF CHIME

Jesper's clothes were covered in tiny slivers and shavings of steel. His stolen uniform was soaked with sweat, his arms ached, and the headache that had burrowed into his left temple felt as if it was setting up permanent residence there. For nearly a half hour, he had been focusing on a single link in the chain that ran from the left end of the winch into one of the slots in the stone wall, using his power to weaken the metal as Wylan sawed away at it with the laundry shears. At first they'd been cautious, worried they'd snap the link and disable the gate before it was time to raise it, but the steel was stronger than either of them had anticipated, and their progress was frustratingly slow. When the three-quarters chime rang, Jesper's panic took over.

"Let's just raise the gate," he said with a frustrated growl. "We sound Black Protocol, and then shoot at the winch until it gives up."

Wylan flipped his curls from his forehead and spared him a quick glance. Jesper could see the blood on his hands where blisters had formed and then burst as he hacked away at the link. "You really love guns so much?"

Jesper shrugged. "I don't love killing people."

"Then what is it about them?"

Jesper refocused on the link. "I don't know. The sound. The way the world narrows to just you and the target. I worked with a gunsmith in Novyi Zem who knew I was a Fabrikator. We came up with some crazy stuff."

"For killing people."

"You build bombs, merchling. Spare me your judgement."

"My name is Wylan. And you're right. I don't have any business criticising you."

"Don't start doing that."

"What?"

"Agreeing with me," said Jesper. "Sure path to destruction."

"I don't like the idea of killing people, either. I don't even like chemistry."

"What do you like?"

"Music. Numbers. Equations. They're not like words. They . . . they don't get mixed up."

"If only you could talk to girls in equations."

There was a long silence, and then, eyes trained on the notch they'd created in the link, Wylan said, "Just girls?"

Jesper restrained a grin. "No. Not just girls." It really was a shame they were all probably going to die tonight. Then the Elderclock began to toll eleven bells. His eyes met Wylan's. They were out of time.

Jesper leaped to his feet, trying to dust some of the metal bits from his face and shirt. Would the chain hold long enough? Too long? They'd just have to find out. "Get in position."

Wylan took his spot at the right handle of the winch, and Jesper grabbed the handle on the left.

"Prepared to hear the sound of certain doom?" he asked.

"You've never heard my father mad."

"That sense of humour is getting progressively more

Barrel-appropriate. If we survive, I'll teach you to swear. On my count," said Jesper. "Let's let the Ice Court know the Dregs have come to call."

He counted down from three and they began to turn the winch, carefully matching each other's pace, eyes on the weakened link. Jesper had expected some thunderous noise, but except for a few creaks and clanks, the machinery was silent.

Slowly, the ringwall gate began to rise. Five inches. Ten inches.

Maybe nothing will happen, thought Jesper. *Maybe Matthias was lying, or all this stuff about Black Protocol is a fake to keep people from even trying to open the gates.*

Then the bells of the Elderclock rang out, loud and panicked, high and demanding, an escalating tide of echoes, climbing one on top of another, booming over the White Island, the ice moat, the wall. The bells of Black Protocol had begun to sound. There was no turning back now. They released the handles of the winch in unison, letting the gate thunder down, but still the link didn't give.

"Come on," Jesper said, coaxing the stubborn metal. A better Fabrikator probably could have made quick work of it. A Fabrikator on *parem* probably could have turned the chain into a set of steak knives and had time for a cup of coffee. But Jesper was neither of those things, and he'd run out of finesse. He grabbed hold of the chain, hanging from it, using all his weight to try to put pressure on the link. Wylan did the same, and for a moment they hung, pulling on the chain like a couple of crazed squirrels who hadn't mastered climbing. Any minute now guards would be storming into the courtyard, and they'd have to leave off this insanity to defend themselves. The gate would still be operational. They'd have failed.

"Maybe you should try singing at it," Jesper said hopelessly.

And then, with a final shiver of protest, the link snapped.

Jesper and Wylan fell to the floor as the chain zipped through their hands, one end vanishing through the slot, the other sending the winch handles spinning.

"We did it!" Jesper shouted over the din of the bells, caught somewhere between excitement and terror. "I'll cover you. Deal with the winch!"

Jesper picked up his rifle, braced himself at a slit in the stone wall overlooking the courtyard, and prepared for all hell to break loose.

33

INEJ

TEN BELLS AND HALF CHIME

"Just how long are we going to be kept waiting?" a man in wine-coloured velvet asked. The guards ignored him, but the other guests clustered by the entry with Inej grumbled their frustration. "I came here at great expense," he continued, "and it was not so I could spend all my time hovering by the front door."

The guard closest to them recited in a bored monotone, "The men at the checkpoint are dealing with other guests. As soon as they're free, you'll be taken back through the ringwall and detained at the checkpoint until your identification can be cleared."

"*Detained*," said the man in velvet. "Like criminals!"

Inej had heard variations on the same exchange for the better part of an hour. She glanced out at the courtyard that led to the embassy's ringwall gate. If she was going to make this plan work, she had to be smart, stay calm. Except this wasn't quite the plan, and she definitely didn't feel calm. The certainty and optimism she'd felt only a short while ago had all but evaporated. She waited as the minutes ticked by, eyes scanning the crowd. But when the three-quarters chime sounded, she knew she could wait no longer. She had to act now.

"I've had enough," Inej said loudly. "Take us to the checkpoint or let us go."

"The guards manning the checkpoint—"

Inej thrust herself to the front of the group and said, "We're all sick of that speech. Take us to the gate and get on with it."

"Be silent," commanded the guard. "You are guests here."

Inej jabbed a finger into his chest. "So treat us like guests," she said, mustering her best Nina imitation. "I demand to be taken to the gate immediately, you big blond lump."

The guard grabbed her arm. "You're so desperate to go to the gate? Let's go. You won't be coming back through."

"I only—"

Then another voice echoed across the rotunda. "Stop! You there, I said stop!"

Inej smelled her perfume – lilies, rich and creamy, a dense golden smell. She wanted to gag. Heleen Van Houden, owner and proprietor of the Menagerie, the House of Exotics, where the world was yours for a price, was pushing her way through the crowd.

Hadn't she said Tante Heleen loved to make an entrance?

The guard came to a startled halt as Heleen shoved in front of him. "Madam, your girl will be returned to you at night's end. Her papers—"

"She is *not* my girl," Heleen said, her eyes slitting viciously. Inej stood perfectly still, but not even she could vanish with nowhere to go. "That is the Wraith, right hand of Kaz Brekker and one of the most notorious criminals in Ketterdam."

The people around them turned to stare.

"How dare you come here under the auspices of my House?" Heleen hissed. "The house that clothed you and fed you? And where is Adjala?"

Inej opened her mouth, but panic rose up, tightening her throat, choking the words before they could come out. Her tongue felt useless and numb. Once more, she was looking into the eyes of the woman who had beaten her, threatened her, bought her once, and then sold her again and again.

Heleen grabbed Inej by the shoulders and shook her. *"Where is my girl?"*

Inej looked down at the fingers digging into her flesh. For a brief second, every horror came back to her, and she truly was a wraith, a ghost taking flight from a body that had given her only pain. *No.* A body that had given her strength. A body that had carried her over the rooftops of Ketterdam, that had served her in battle, that had brought her up six storeys in the dark of a soot-stained chimney.

Inej seized Heleen's wrist and twisted it hard to the right. Heleen yelped, her knees buckling as the guards surged forwards.

"I threw your girl in the ice moat," Inej snarled, barely recognising her own voice. Her other hand seized Heleen's throat, squeezing. "And she's better off there than with you."

Then strong arms were tugging at her, pulling her off the older woman, hauling her back.

Inej panted, heart racing. *I could have killed her*, she thought. *I felt her pulse beneath my palm. I should have killed her.*

Heleen got to her feet, whimpering and coughing as onlookers moved to help her. "If she's here, then Brekker is as well!" she shrieked.

At that moment, as if in agreement, the bells of the Black Protocol began to sound, loud and insistent. There was a stunned second of inertia. Then the entire rotunda seemed to explode into action as guards rushed to their posts and commanders began calling orders.

One of the guards, clearly the captain, said something in Fjerdan. The only word Inej recognised was *prison*. He grabbed the silk of her cape and shouted in Kerch, "Who is on your team? What is your target?"

"I will not speak," said Inej.

"You'll sing if we want you to," spat the guard.

Heleen's laugh was low and rich with pleasure. "I'll see you hanged. And Brekker, too."

"The bridge is closed," someone declared. "No one else is getting on or off the island tonight!" Angry guests turned to anyone who would listen, demanding explanations.

The guards dragged Inej through the courtyard, past gaping onlookers, and out of the ringwall gate as the bells continued to toll. They did not bother with gentleness or diplomacy now.

"I told you you'd wear my silks again, little lynx," Heleen called from the courtyard. The gate was already lowering, as the guards sealed it in accordance with Black Protocol. "You'll hang in them now."

The gate slammed closed, but Inej could swear that she still heard Heleen's laughter.

34
NINA

TEN BELLS AND HALF CHIME

Nina prayed her panic didn't show. Did Brum recognise her? He looked exactly the same: long gold hair touched by grey at the temples, the lean jaw marked by a tidy beard, the *drüskelle* uniform – black and silver, the right sleeve emblazoned with the silver wolf's head. It had been more than a year since she'd seen him, but she would never forget that face or the resolute blue of his eyes.

The last time she'd found herself in Jarl Brum's company he'd been strutting for Matthias and his *drüskelle* brethren in the hold of a ship. *Matthias.* Had he seen Brum, his old mentor, alive and talking to Nina? Was he watching them right now? She resisted the urge to scour the crowd for some sign of him and Kaz.

Still, the ship's hold had been dark, and she'd been one of a group of prisoners – filthy and frightened. Now she was clean, perfumed. Her hair was a different colour; her skin was powdered. She was suddenly grateful for her absurd costume. Brum was a man, after all. Hopefully, Inej was right, and he would just see a redheaded Kaelish with a very low neckline.

She curtseyed deeply and looked up at him through her lashes. "A pleasure."

His gaze roved over her figure. "It just might be. You're from the House of Exotics, are you not? *Kep ye nom?*"

"*Nomme* Fianna," she replied in Kaelish. Was he testing her? "But you can call me anything you like."

"I thought Kaelish girls with the Menagerie wore the red mare cloak."

She plumped her lips into a sulk. "Our Zemeni stepped on it and tore the hem. I think she did it on purpose."

"Cursed girl. Shall we find her and punish her?"

Nina forced a giggle. "How would you set about it?"

"They say the punishment should fit the crime, but I feel it should suit the criminal. Were you my prisoner, I'd make it my business to learn your likes and dislikes – and your fears, of course."

"I am fearless," she said with a wink.

"Truly? How intriguing. Fjerdans value courage greatly. How are you finding our country?"

"It's a magical place," Nina gushed. *If you like ice and more ice.* She steeled herself. If he knew who she was, then she might as well find out now. And if he didn't, well, then she still needed to locate Bo Yul-Bayur – and what a pleasure it would be to trick the legendary Jarl Brum out of the information. She drew closer. "Do you know where I'd truly like to visit?"

He matched her conspiratorial tone. "I'd love to know all your secrets."

"Ravka."

The *drüskelle's* lip curled. "Ravka? A land of blasphemers and barbarism."

"True, but to see a Grisha? Can you imagine the thrill?"

"I assure you. It's hardly a thrill."

"You only say that because you wear the sign of the wolf. This means you are a . . . *drüskelle*, yes?" she asked, pretending to struggle with the Fjerdan word.

"I am their commander."

Nina widened her eyes. "Then you must have bested many Grisha in battle."

"There is little honour in a fight with such a creature. I'd rather face a thousand honest men with swords than one of those deceitful witches with unnatural powers."

And when you arrive with your repeating rifles and your tanks, when you set upon children and helpless villages, should we not use the weapons we possess? Nina bit down hard on her inner cheek.

"There are Grisha in Kerch, are there not?" Brum asked.

"So I've heard, but I've never seen one at the Menagerie or in the Barrel. At least not that I know of." Could she risk a mention of *jurda parem*? How would the girl she was pretending to be have such knowledge? She leaned into him, curling her lips into a wicked, slightly guilty smile, and hoping she looked eager for excitement rather than information. "I know they're dreadful, but . . . they do make me shiver. I've heard their powers have no limits."

"Well . . ." the *drüskelle* hemmed.

Nina could see he was debating something with himself. Best to stage a strategic retreat. She shrugged. "But perhaps that's not your area of expertise." She glanced over his shoulder and caught the eye of a young nobleman in pale grey silk.

"Would you like to see a Grisha tonight?"

Her gaze snapped back to Brum. *All I need is a mirror.* Did Brum have Grisha prisoners stashed somewhere? What she wanted was to hear all about Bo Yul-Bayur and *jurda parem*, but this might be a start. And if she could get Brum alone . . .

She swatted his chest. "You're teasing."

"Would your mistress notice if you slipped away?"

"That's why we're here, no? To slip away?"

He offered his arm. "Then shall we?"

She smiled and looped her hand over his forearm. He patted it gently. "Good girl."

She wanted to gag. *Maybe I'll make you impotent*, Nina thought grimly, as he led her out of the ballroom and through a terraced forest of ice sculptures – a wolf with a screaming double eagle in its jaws, a serpent wrapped around a bear.

"How . . . primal," she murmured.

Brum chuckled and patted her hand again. "We are a culture of warriors."

Would it be so dreadful to just kill him now? She considered as they strolled. *Make it look like a heart attack? Leave him here in the cold?* But she could endure Jarl Brum leering down the front of her dress for a little while longer if it meant keeping *jurda parem* from the world.

Besides, if Bo Yul-Bayur was on this Saintsforsaken island, Brum was the one to get her to him. The guards at the ballroom doors had let them past with little more than a raised brow and a smirk.

Directly ahead of them, Nina saw a vast, silvery tree at the centre of a circular courtyard, its boughs spreading over the stones in a sparkling canopy. *The sacred ash*, Nina realised. Then they must be in the middle of the island. The courtyard was surrounded on both sides by arched colonnades. If Matthias' and Wylan's drawings had been correct, the building directly beyond it was the treasury.

Instead of leading her across the courtyard, Brum turned left onto a path that hugged the side of the colonnade. As he did, Nina glimpsed a group of people in hooded black coats moving towards the tree.

"Who are they?" asked Nina, though she suspected she knew.

"*Drüskelle.*"

"Shouldn't you be with them?"

"This is a ceremony for the young brothers to be welcomed by the old, not for captains and officers."

"Did you go through it?"

"Every *drüskelle* in history has been inducted into the order through the same ceremony since Djel anointed the first of us."

Nina forced herself not to roll her eyes. *Sure, a giant, gushing spring chose some guy to hunt innocent people down and murder them. That seems likely.*

"That's what Hringkälla celebrates," continued Brum. "And every year if there are worthy initiates, the *drüskelle* gather at the sacred ash, where they may once more hear the voice of god."

Djel says you're a fanatic, drunk on your own power. Come back next year.

"People forget this is a holy night," Brum muttered. "They come to the palace to drink and dance and fornicate."

Nina had to bite her tongue. Given Brum's interest in the dip of her neckline, she doubted his thoughts were particularly holy.

"Are those things so very bad?" she asked teasingly.

Brum smiled and squeezed her arm. "Not in moderation."

"Moderation isn't one of my specialities."

"I can see that," he said. "I like the look of a woman who enjoys herself."

I'd enjoy choking you slowly, she thought as she ran her fingers over his arm. Looking at Brum, she knew she didn't just blame him for the things he'd done to her people; it was what he'd done to Matthias as well. He'd taken a brave, miserable boy and fed him on hate. He'd silenced Matthias' conscience with prejudice and the promise of a divine calling that was probably nothing more than the wind moving through the branches of an ancient tree.

They reached the far side of the colonnade. With a start, she realised Brum had deliberately led her around

the courtyard. Maybe he hadn't wanted to bring a whore through a sacred space. *Hypocrite.*

"Where are we going?" she asked.

"The treasury."

"Are you going to woo me with jewels?"

"I didn't think girls like you needed wooing. Isn't that the point?"

Nina laughed. "Well, every girl likes a little attention."

"Then that's what you shall have. And the thrill you were seeking, too."

Was it possible Yul-Bayur was in the treasury? Kaz had said he'd be in the most secure place in the Ice Court. That might mean the palace, but it might just as easily mean the treasury. Why not here? It was another circular structure wrought in glowing white stone, but the treasury had no windows, no whimsical decoration or dragon's scales. It looked like a tomb. Instead of ordinary guards, two *drüskelle* stood watch by the heavy door.

Suddenly, the full weight of what she was doing hit her. She was alone with one of the deadliest men in Fjerda, a man who would gladly torture and murder her if he knew what she truly was. The plan had been to find someone to give her information on Bo Yul-Bayur's location, not to get cosy with the highest-ranking *drüskelle* on the White Island. Her eyes scanned the surrounding trees and paths, the hedge maze pushed up against the treasury's east side, hoping to see some shadow move, to know that someone was there with her and that she wasn't completely on her own. Kaz had sworn he could get her off this island, but Kaz's first plan had gone to pieces – maybe this one would, too.

The soldiers didn't blink as Nina and Brum passed, merely offered a tight salute. Brum pulled a chain from his neck; a strange circular disk hung from it. He slid the disk into a nearly invisible indentation in the door and gave it a turn. Nina eyed the lock warily. This might be beyond even Kaz Brekker's skill.

The barrel-vaulted entry was cold and bare, lit by the same harsh light as the Grisha cells in the prison wing. No gaslight, no candles. Nothing for Squallers or Inferni to manipulate.

She squinted. "Where are we?"

"The old treasury. The vault was moved years ago. This was converted into a laboratory."

Laboratory. The word formed a cold knot beneath Nina's ribs. "Why?"

"Such an inquisitive little thing."

I'm nearly as tall as you, she thought.

"The treasury was already secure and well-positioned on the White Island, so it was a logical choice for such a facility."

The words were innocuous, but that knot of fear tightened, a cold fist now, pressing against her chest. She matched Brum's steps down the vaulted hall, past smooth white doors, each with a small glass window set into it.

"Here we are," Brum said, stopping in front of a door that seemed identical to the others.

Nina peered through the glass. The cell was just like the ones on the top level of the prison, but the observation panel was on the other side – a large mirror that took up half of the opposite wall. Inside, she saw a young boy in a bedraggled blue *kefta* pacing restlessly, gabbling to himself, scratching at his arms. His eyes were hollows, his hair lank. He looked just like Nestor before he'd died. *Grisha don't get sick*, she thought. But this was a different kind of sickness.

"He doesn't look very menacing."

Brum moved up behind her. His breath brushed against her ear when he said, "Oh, believe me, he is."

Nina's skin crawled, but she made herself lean into him slightly. "What is he here for?"

"The future."

Nina turned and laid her hands on his chest.

"Are there more?"

He blew out an impatient breath and led her to the next door. A girl lay on her side, her tangled hair covering her face. She was dressed in a dirty shift, and she had bruises all over her arms. Brum gave a sharp rap on the little window, startling Nina.

"Look alive," Brum taunted, but the girl didn't move. Brum's finger hovered over a brass button embedded next to the window. "If you really want a show, I could press this button."

"What does it do?"

"Beautiful things. Miraculous, really."

Nina thought she knew; the button would dose the girl with *jurda parem* somehow. For Nina's entertainment. She tugged Brum away. "It's all right."

"I thought you wanted to see a Grisha use her powers."

"Oh, I do, but she doesn't look like much fun. Are there more?"

"Close to thirty."

Nina flinched. The Second Army had been nearly obliterated in Ravka's civil war. She couldn't bear to think that there were thirty Grisha here. "And are they all in that state?"

He shrugged and steered her down a corridor. "Some are better. Some are worse. If I find you a lively one, what will be my reward?"

"It would be easier to show you," she purred.

Nina had had enough of seeing starving, frightened Grisha. She needed Yul-Bayur. Brum must know where he was. The treasury was nearly deserted. They hadn't seen a single guard inside. If she could get Brum into an empty corridor far enough from the entrance that the guards couldn't hear them ... Could she torture a hardened *drüskelle*? Could she make him talk? She thought she just might be able to. She'd seal his nose, put pressure on his larynx. A few minutes gasping for breath might soften him up.

"Maybe we could find a quiet corner?" Nina suggested.

Brum preened, his chest puffing out. "This way, *dirre*," he said using the Kaelish word for sweetheart.

He led her down a deserted hall, unlocking the door with his circular key.

"This should do," he said with a bow. "A bit of privacy and a bit of charm."

Nina winked and sashayed past him. She'd expected some kind of office or retiring room for the guards. But there was no desk, no cot. The room was completely bare – except for the drain at the centre of the floor.

She whirled in time to see the cell door slam shut.

"No!" she shouted, hands scrabbling over the surface of the door. It had no handle.

Brum's face appeared in the window. His expression was smug, his eyes cold. "I may have exaggerated the charm, but there is plenty of privacy, Nina."

She recoiled.

"That is your name, isn't it?" he said. "Did you really think I wouldn't recognise you? I remember your stubborn little face from the slaving ship, and we have files on every one of Ravka's active Grisha. I make it my business to know them all – even the ones I hope have been swallowed by the sea."

Nina lifted her hands.

"Go ahead," he said. "Burst my eyes in their sockets. Crush my heart in my chest. That door won't unlock, and in the time it takes you to tamper with my pulse, I'll press this button." She couldn't see the brass button, but she could imagine his finger hovering over it. "Do you know what it does? You've seen the effects of *jurda parem*. Would you like to feel them, too? It is effective as a powder, but even more so as a gas."

Nina froze.

"Smart girl." His grin lifted the hair on her arms. *I will not beg*, she told herself. But she knew she would. Once the drug was in her system, she wouldn't be able to stop it. She took a breath of clean air. A futile gesture, even childish, but she was determined to hold it as long as she could.

Then Brum paused. "No. This vengeance is not mine to take. There is someone else who owes you so much more." He vanished from the window and a moment later, Matthias' face filled the glass. He looked back at her, his eyes hard.

"How?" Nina whispered, not even sure if they could hear her through the door.

"Did you really believe I'd turn against my nation?" Matthias' voice was thick with disgust. "That I'd give up the cause I devoted my life to? I came to warn Brum as soon as I could."

"But you said—"

"Country before self, Zenik. It's something you've never understood."

Nina pressed a hand to her mouth.

"I may never be *drüskelle* again," he said. "I may live always with the charge of 'slaver' around my neck, but I'll find another way to serve Fjerda. And I'll get to see you dosed with *jurda parem*. I'll get to see you mow down your own kind and beg for the next fix. I'll get to see you betray the people you love as you asked me to betray my own."

"Matthias—"

He slammed his fist against the window. "Do not speak my name." Then he smiled, a smile as cold and unforgiving as the northern sea. "Welcome to the Ice Court, Nina Zenik. Now our debt is paid."

From somewhere outside, the bells of Black Protocol began to ring.

35

MATTHIAS

ELEVEN BELLS

"She's beautiful," Brum said, "in an exaggerated way. You were strong not to be lured by her."

I was lured, though, thought Matthias. *And it wasn't just her beauty.*

"The alarm—" Matthias said.

"Her compatriots, no doubt."

"But—"

"Matthias, my men will take care of it. The Ice Court is secure." He glanced back at Nina's cell. "We could press the button right now."

"Won't she be a threat?"

"We've combined the *jurda parem* with a sedative that makes them more biddable. We're still working out the correct ratios, but we'll get there. Besides, by the second dose, the addiction does the work of controlling them."

"Not the first dose?"

"Depends on the Grisha."

"How many times have you done this?"

Brum laughed. "I haven't counted. But trust me, she'll be so desperate for more *jurda parem*, she won't dare act against us. It's a remarkable transformation. I think you'll enjoy it."

Matthias' stomach clenched. "You've kept the scientist alive then?"

"He's done his best to replicate the process of creating the drug, but it's a complicated thing. Some batches work; others are no better than dust. As long as he can be of service, he lives." Brum placed his hand on Matthias' shoulder, his harsh gaze softening. "I can scarcely believe you're really here, alive, standing before me. I thought you were dead."

"I believed the same of you."

"When I saw you in that ballroom, I barely recognised you, even in that uniform. You are so changed—"

"I had to let the witch tailor me."

Brum's revulsion was obvious. "You allowed her to—"

Somehow, seeing that response in someone else made Matthias ashamed of the way he'd reacted to Nina.

"It had to be done," he said. "I needed her to believe I was committed to her cause."

"That's all over now, Matthias. You are finally safe and among your own kind." Brum frowned. "Something is troubling you."

Matthias looked into the cell next to Nina's, then another, and another, moving down the hall as Brum followed. Some of the captive Grisha were agitated, pacing. Others had their faces pressed up against the glass. Others simply lay on the floor. "You can't have known about *parem* for more than a month. How long has this facility been here?"

"I had it built almost fifteen years ago with the blessing of the king and his council."

Matthias drew up short. "Fifteen years? Why?"

"We needed somewhere to put the Grisha after the trials."

"After? When Grisha are found guilty, they're sentenced to death."

Brum shrugged. "It is still a death sentence, just one a

little longer in the making. We discovered long ago that the Grisha could prove a useful resource."

A resource. "You told me they were to be eradicated. That they were a blight on the natural world."

"And they are – when they attempt to masquerade as men. They aren't capable of right thinking, of human morality. They are meant to be controlled."

"That's why you wanted *parem*?" Matthias asked incredulously.

"We have tried our own methods for years with limited success."

"But you've seen what *jurda parem* can do, what Grisha can do when in its grip—"

"A gun is not evil. Nor is a blade. *Jurda parem* ensures obedience. It makes Grisha what they were always meant to be."

"A Second Army?" Matthias asked, his voice thick with scorn.

"An army is made of soldiers. These creatures were born to be weapons. They were born to serve the soldiers of Djel." Brum squeezed his shoulder. "Ah, Matthias, how I've missed you. Your faith was always so pure. I'm glad you're reluctant to embrace this measure, but this is our chance to strike a deathblow. Do you know why Grisha are so hard to kill? Because they're not of this world. But they are very good at killing each other. They call it 'like calls to like'. Wait until you see all we've achieved, the weapons their Fabrikators have helped us develop."

Matthias looked back down the hall. "Nina Zenik spent a year in Kerch trying to bargain for my freedom. I'm not sure those are the actions of a monster."

"Can a viper lie still before it strikes? Can a wild dog lick your hand before it snaps at your neck? A Grisha may be capable of kindness, but that does not change her fundamental nature."

Matthias considered this. He thought of Nina standing terrified in that cell as the door slammed shut. He had longed to see her made captive, punished as he had been punished. And yet, after everything they'd been through, he was not surprised by the pain he felt at seeing it come to pass.

"What is the Shu scientist like?" he asked Brum.

"Stubborn. Still grieving his father."

Matthias knew nothing of Yul-Bayur's father, but there was a more important question to ask. "Is he secure?"

"The treasury is the safest place on the island."

"You keep him here with the Grisha?"

Brum nodded. "The main vault was converted to a laboratory for him."

"And you're sure it's safe?"

"I have the master key," said Brum, patting the disk hanging from his neck, "and he's guarded night and day. Only a select few even know he's here. It's late, and I need to make sure Black Protocol has been addressed, but if you like, I'll take you to see him tomorrow." Brum placed his arm around Matthias. "And tomorrow we'll deal with your return and reinstatement."

"I still stand accused of slave trading."

"We'll get the girl to sign a statement recanting the slaving charges easily enough. Believe me, once she's had her first taste of *jurda parem*, she'll do anything you ask and more. There will be a hearing, but I swear you will wear *drüskelle* colours again, Matthias."

Drüskelle colours. Matthias had worn them with such pride. And the things he'd felt for Nina had caused him so much shame. It was still with him, maybe it always would be. He'd spent too many years full of hate for it to vanish overnight. But now the shame was an echo, and all he felt was regret – for the time he'd wasted, for the pain he'd caused, and yes, even now, for what he was about to do.

He turned to Brum, this man who had become father and mentor to him. When he'd lost his family, it had been Brum who had recruited him for the *drüskelle*. Matthias had been young, angry, completely unskilled. But he'd given what was left of his broken heart to the cause. A false cause. A lie. When had he seen it? When he'd helped Nina bury her friend? When he'd fought beside her? Or had it been long before – when she'd slept in his arms that first night on the ice? When she'd saved him from the shipwreck?

Nina had wronged him, but she'd done it to protect her people. She'd hurt him, but she'd attempted everything in her power to make things right. She'd shown him in a thousand ways that she was honourable and strong and generous and very human, maybe more vividly human than anyone he'd ever known. And if she was, then Grisha weren't inherently evil. They were like anyone else – full of the potential to do great good, and also great harm. To ignore that would make Matthias the monster.

"You taught me so much," Matthias said. "You taught me to value honour and strength. You gave me the tools for vengeance when I needed them most."

"And with those tools we will build a great future, Matthias. Fjerda's time has finally come."

Matthias returned his mentor's embrace.

"I don't know if you're wrong about the Grisha," he said gently. "I just know you're wrong about her."

He held Brum tight, in a hold Matthias had learned in the echoing training rooms of the *drüskelle* stronghold, rooms he would never see again. He held Brum as he struggled briefly and as his body went slack.

When Matthias pulled away, Brum had slipped into unconsciousness, but Matthias did not think he imagined the rage that lingered on his mentor's features. He made himself memorise it. It was right that he should remember that look. He was a true traitor at last, and he should carry the burden of it.

When they'd entered the great ballroom, Matthias and Kaz had staked out a shadowy nook near the stairs. They'd watched Nina enter in that outrageous gown of shimmering scales – and then Matthias had spotted Brum. The shock of seeing his mentor alive had been followed by the terrible realisation that Brum was following Nina.

"Brum knows," he'd said to Kaz. "We have to help her."

"Be smart, Helvar. You can save her and get us Yul-Bayur, too."

Matthias had nodded and plunged into the crowd. "Decency," he'd heard Kaz mutter behind him. "Like cheap cologne."

He'd waylaid Brum by the stairs. "Sir—"

"Not now."

Matthias had been forced to step right in front of him. "*Sir.*"

Brum had halted then. His face had shown anger at being stopped, then confusion, and then wondering disbelief. "Matthias?" he'd whispered.

"Please, sir," Matthias had said hurriedly. "Just give me a moment to explain. There is a Grisha here tonight intent on assassinating one of your prisoners. If you'll bear with me, I can explain the plot and how it can be stopped."

Brum had signalled to another *drüskelle* to watch Nina, and shepherded Matthias into an alcove beneath the stairs. "Speak," he'd said, and Matthias had told him the truth – a bare sliver of it: his escape from the shipwreck, his near drowning, Nina's false charge of slavery, his captivity in Hellgate, and then the promise of the pardon. He'd blamed it all on Nina, and said nothing of Kaz or the others. When Brum had asked if Nina was alone in her mission, he'd simply said he didn't know.

"She believes I'm waiting to escort her over the secret

bridge. I broke away as soon as I could and came to find you."

A part of him was disgusted by how easily the lies came to his lips, but he would not leave Nina at Brum's mercy.

He looked at Brum now, mouth slightly open in sleep. One of the things he'd respected most in his mentor was his mercilessness, his willingness to do hard things for the sake of the cause. But Brum had taken pleasure in what he'd done to these Grisha, what he would have gladly done to Nina and Jesper. Maybe the hard things had never been difficult for Brum the way they'd been for Matthias. They had not been a sacred duty, performed reluctantly for the sake of Fjerda. They had been a joy.

Matthias slipped the master key from around Brum's neck and dragged him into an empty cell, propping him up against the wall in a seated position. Matthias hated to leave him there, chin flopped on his chest, legs sprawled in front of him, without dignity. He hated the thought of the shame that would come to him, a warrior betrayed by someone to whom he'd given his trust and affection. He knew that pain well.

Matthias pressed his forehead once, briefly, against Brum's. He knew his mentor could not hear him, but he spoke the words anyway. "The life you live, the hate you feel – it's poison. I can drink it no longer."

Matthias locked the cell door and hurried down the passage towards Nina, towards something more.

36

JESPER

ELEVEN BELLS

Jesper waited by the slit in the wall, a sniper's bolt, the perfect place for a boy like him. *What did we just do?* he wondered. But his blood was alive, his rifle was at his shoulder, the world made sense again.

So where were the guards? Jesper had expected them to rush into the courtyard as soon as he and Wylan triggered Black Protocol.

"I've got it!" Wylan called from behind him.

Jesper hated to give up the high ground before they knew what they were up against, but they were short on time, and they needed to get to the roof. "All right, let's go."

They raced down the stairs. As they were about to burst from the gatehouse archway, six guards came running into the courtyard. Jesper stopped short and held out his arm.

"Turn back," he said to Wylan.

But Wylan was pointing across the courtyard. "Look."

The guards weren't moving towards the gatehouse; all their attention was focused on a man in olive drab clothing standing by one of the stone slabs. *That uniform . . .*

A woman walked through the wall, a figure of shimmering mist that solidified beside the stranger. She wore the same olive drab.

"Tidemakers," Wylan said.

"The Shu."

The guards opened fire, and the Tidemakers vanished, then reappeared behind the soldiers and lifted their arms.

The guards screamed and dropped their weapons. A red haze formed around them. The haze grew denser as the guards shrieked, their flesh seeming to shrink against their bones.

"It's their blood," Jesper said, bile rising in his throat. "All Saints, the Tidemakers are draining their blood." They were being squeezed dry.

The blood formed floating pools in the vague shapes of men, slick shadows that hovered in the air, the wet red of garnets, then splashed to the ground at the same time as the guards collapsed, flaccid skin hanging from their desiccated bodies in grotesque folds.

"Back up the stairs," whispered Jesper. "We need to get out of here."

But it was too late. The female Tidemaker disappeared. In the next breath, she was on the stairs. She balanced her weight on the banisters with her hands and planted her boots against Wylan's chest, kicking him backwards into Jesper. They tumbled onto the black stone of the courtyard.

The rifle was jerked from Jesper's arms and tossed aside with a clatter. He tried to stand, and the Tidemaker cuffed him on the back of his head. Then he was lying next to Wylan as the Tidemakers towered above them. They lifted their hands, and Jesper saw the faintest red haze appear over him. He was going to be drained. He felt his strength start to ebb. He looked to the left but the rifle was too far away.

"Jesper," Wylan gasped. "Metal. Fabrikate." And then he started to scream.

In a flash, Jesper understood. This was a fight he couldn't win with a gun. There was no time to think, no time to doubt.

He ignored the pain tearing over his skin and focused all his attention on the bits of metal clinging to his clothes, the shavings and tiny particles from the severed link in the gate chain. He wasn't a good Fabrikator, but they didn't expect him to be a Fabrikator at all. He thrust his hands forwards, and the bits of metal flew from his uniform, a gleaming cloud that hung in the air for the briefest second then shot towards the Tidemakers.

The female Tidemaker screamed as the metal burrowed into her flesh, and she tried to turn to mist. The other Tidemaker did the same, features liquefying, but then solidifying once more, his face grey, speckled with bits of metal. Jesper didn't relent. He drove the metal home, into their organs, questing deeper. He could feel them attempting to manipulate the particles of metal. If the problem had been a bullet or a blade, they might have succeeded, but the flecks and shavings of steel were too many and too small. The woman clutched her stomach and fell to her knees. The man screamed, coughing up clotted black specks of metal and blood.

"Help me," the woman sobbed. Her edges blurred, her body vibrating as she struggled to fade to mist.

Jesper dropped his hands. He and Wylan scooted away from the writhing bodies of the Tidemakers.

Were they dying? Had he just killed two of his kind? Jesper had only wanted to survive. He thought again of the banner on the wall, all those strips of red, blue, and purple.

Wylan tugged at his arm. His face looked slightly transparent, the veins too close to the surface. "Jesper, we have to go."

Jesper nodded slowly.

"*Now.*"

Jesper made his feet move, made himself follow Wylan,

scale the rope to the roof. He felt woozy and lightheaded. The others were depending on him, he knew that. He had to keep going. But he felt as if he'd left some part of himself in the courtyard below, something he hadn't even known mattered, intangible as mist.

37
NINA

ELEVEN BELLS AND QUARTER CHIME

When Matthias opened the door to Nina's cell, she hesitated for the briefest moment. She couldn't help it. As long as she lived, she would never forget Matthias' face at that window, how cruel he'd seemed, or the doubt that had sprung up in her heart. She felt it again, looking at him standing in the doorway, but when he held his hand out to her, she knew they were done with fear.

She ran to him, and he swept her up in his arms.

He buried his face in her hair. She felt his lips move against her ear when he said, "I never want to see you like this again."

"Do you mean the dress or the cell?"

A laugh shook him. "Definitely the cell." Then he cupped her face in his hands. *"Jer molle pe oonet. Enel mörd je nej afva trohem verretn."*

Nina swallowed hard. She remembered those words and what they truly meant. *I have been made to protect you. Only in death will I be kept from this oath.* It was the vow of the *drüskelle* to Fjerda. And now it was Matthias' promise to her.

She knew she should say something profound, something beautiful in response. Instead, she spoke the truth. "If we make it out of here alive, I'm going to kiss you unconscious."

A grin split his beautiful face. She couldn't wait to see the real blue of his eyes again.

"Yul-Bayur is in the vault," he said. "Let's go."

As Nina raced down the hall after Matthias, the clanging bells of Black Protocol filled her ears. If Brum had known about her, then chances were the other *drüskelle* did, too. She doubted it would be long before they came looking for their commander.

"Please tell me Kaz hasn't gone missing again," she said as they hurtled down the corridor.

"I left him in the ballroom. We're to meet him by the ash."

"Last time I looked, it was surrounded by *drüskelle*."

"Maybe Black Protocol will take care of that."

"If we survive the *drüskelle*, we won't survive Kaz, not if we kill Yul-Bayur—"

Matthias put up a hand for them to stop before they turned the next corner. They approached slowly. When they rounded it, Nina made quick work of the guard at the vault door. Matthias took his rifle, then Brum's key was in the lock, and the circular entry to the vault was opening.

Nina raised her hands, prepared to attack. They waited, hearts pounding, as the door slid open.

The room was as white as all the others, but hardly bare. Its long tables were full of beakers set over low blue flames, heating and cooling apparatuses, glass vials full of powders in varying shades of orange. One wall was devoted to a massive slate board covered in chalk equations. The other was all glass cases with little metal doors. They contained blooming *jurda* plants, and Nina guessed the cases must be heated. A cot was pushed up against the other wall, its thin covers rumpled, papers and notebooks strewn around it. A

Shu boy was seated cross-legged on it. He stared at them, his dark hair flopping over his forehead, a notebook in his lap. He couldn't have been more than fifteen.

"We aren't here to harm you," Nina said in Shu. "Where is Bo Yul-Bayur?"

The boy brushed his hair back from his golden eyes. "He's dead."

Nina frowned. Had Van Eck's information been wrong? "Then what is all this?"

"Have you come to kill me?"

Nina wasn't quite sure of the answer to that. "*Sesh-uyeh?*" she ventured.

The boy's face crumpled in relief. "You're Kerch."

Nina nodded. "We came to rescue Bo Yul-Bayur."

The boy pulled his knees to his chest and wrapped his arms around them. "He's beyond your rescue. My father died when the Fjerdans tried to stop the Kerch from taking us out of Ahmrat Jen." His voice faltered. "He was killed in the crossfire."

My father. Nina translated for Matthias as she tried to take in what this meant.

"Dead?" Matthias asked, and his broad shoulders slumped slightly. Nina knew what he was thinking – all they'd endured, all they'd done, and Yul-Bayur had been dead the whole time.

But the Fjerdans had kept his son alive for a reason. "They're trying to make you recreate his formula," she said.

"I helped him in the lab, but I don't remember everything." He bit his lip. "And I've been stalling."

Whatever *parem* the Fjerdans had been using on the Grisha must have come from the original stock Bo Yul-Bayur had been bringing to the Kerch.

"Can you do it?" Nina asked. "Can you recreate the formula?"

The boy hesitated. "I think so."

Nina and Matthias exchanged a glance.

Nina swallowed. She'd killed before. She'd killed tonight, even, but this was different. This boy wasn't pointing a gun at her or trying to harm her. Murdering him – and it would be murder – would also mean betraying Inej, Kaz, Jesper, and Wylan. People who were risking their lives even now for a prize they'd never see. But then she thought of Nestor falling lifeless in the snow, of the cells full of Grisha lost in their own misery, all because of this drug.

She raised her arms. "I'm sorry," she said. "If you succeed, there will be no end to the suffering you unleash."

The boy's gaze was steady, his chin jutting up stubbornly, as if he'd known this moment might come. The right thing to do was obvious. Kill this boy quickly, painlessly. Destroy the lab and everything in it. Eradicate the secret of *jurda parem*. If you wanted to kill a vine, you didn't just keep cutting it back. You tore it from the ground by the roots. And yet her hands were shaking. Wasn't this the way *drüskelle* thought? Destroy the threat, wipe it out, no matter that the person in front of you was innocent.

"Nina," Matthias said softly, "he's just a kid. He's one of us."

One of us. A boy not much younger than she was, caught up in a war he hadn't chosen for himself. A survivor.

"What's your name?" she asked.

"Kuwei."

"Kuwei Yul-Bo," she began. Did she intend to pass sentence? To apologise? To beg forgiveness? She'd never know. When she found her voice, all she said was, "How fast can you destroy this lab?"

"Fast," he replied. He sliced a hand through the air, and the flames from beneath one of the beakers shot out in a blue arc.

Nina stared. "You're Grisha. You're an Inferni."

Kuwei nodded. "*Jurda parem* was a mistake. My father was trying to find a way to help me hide my powers. He was a Fabrikator. A Grisha, as I am."

Nina's mind was reeling – Bo Yul-Bayur, a Grisha hiding in plain sight behind the borders of the Shu Han. There was no time to let it sink in.

"We need to destroy as much of your work as we can," she said.

"There are combustibles," replied Kuwei, already gathering up papers and *jurda* samples. "I can rig an explosion."

"Only the vault. There are Grisha here." And guards. And Matthias' mentor. Nina would have gladly let Brum die, but though Matthias had betrayed his commander, she doubted he'd want to see the man who'd become a second father to him blown to bits. Her heart rebelled when she thought of the Grisha she'd be leaving behind, but there was no way to get them to the harbour.

"Leave the rest," she said to Matthias and Kuwei. "We need to move."

Kuwei arranged a series of vials full of liquid over the burners. "I'm ready."

They checked the corridor and hurried towards the treasury entrance. At every turn she expected to see *drüskelle* or guards storming their way, but they charged through the halls unimpeded. At the main door, they paused.

"There's a hedge maze to our left," Nina said.

Matthias nodded. "We'll use it for cover then make a run for the ash."

As soon as they opened the door, the clamour of the bells became almost unbearable. Nina could see the Elderclock on the highest silvery spire of the palace, its face glowing like a moon. Bright lights from the guard towers moved across the White Island, and Nina could hear the shouts of soldiers closing in around the palace.

She clung to the side of the building, following Matthias, trying to keep to the shadows.

"Hurry," Kuwei said with a nervous glance back at the lab.

"This way," Matthias said. "The maze—"

"Halt!" someone shouted.

Too late. Guards were racing towards them from the direction of the maze. There was nothing to do but run. They bolted past the entrance to the colonnade and into the circular courtyard. There were *drüskelle* everywhere – in front of them, behind them. Any moment they'd be gunned down.

That was when the explosion hit. Nina felt it before she heard it: A wave of heat lifted her off her feet and tossed her in the air, chased by a deafening boom. She came down hard on the white paving stones.

Everything was smoke and chaos. Nina struggled to her knees, ears ringing. One side of the treasury had been reduced to rubble, smoke and dust billowing into the night sky.

Matthias was already striding towards her with Kuwei. She pushed to her feet.

"*Sten!*" cried two guards breaking off from another group running in the direction of the treasury. "What's your business here?"

"We were just enjoying the party!" Nina exclaimed, letting all of her real exhaustion and terror fill her voice. "And then . . . then . . ." It was embarrassingly easy to let the tears flow.

He held up his gun. "Show me your papers."

"No papers, Lars."

The witchhunter's head snapped up as Matthias stepped forwards. "Do I know you?"

"You did once, though I looked a bit different. *Hje marden*, Lars?"

"Helvar?" he asked. "They . . . they said you were dead."

"I was."

Lars looked from Matthias to Nina. "This is the Heartrender Brum brought to the treasury." Then he took in Kuwei's presence, and understanding struck. "Traitor," he snarled at Matthias.

Nina raised her hand to drop Lars' pulse, but as she did, she caught movement in the shadows to her right. She cried out as something struck her. When she looked down, she saw loops of cable closing over her, binding her upper arms tight to her body. She couldn't raise her hands. She couldn't use her power. Matthias grunted, and Kuwei screamed as cables lashed from the darkness, snapping around their torsos, binding their arms.

"This is what we *do*, bloodletter," sneered Lars. "We hunt filth like you. We know all of your tricks." He kicked Matthias' legs from beneath him. Matthias went to his knees and sucked in a breath. "They told us you were dead. We mourned you, burned boughs of ash for you. But now I see they were protecting us from something worse. Matthias Helvar, a traitor, aiding our enemies, consorting with unnaturals." He spat in Matthias' face. "How could you betray your country and your god?"

"Djel is the god of life, not death."

"Are there others here for Yul-Bayur besides you and this creature?"

"No," lied Nina.

"I didn't ask you, witch," said Lars. "It doesn't matter. We'll get the information from you our own way." He turned to Kuwei. "And you. Don't think there won't be repercussions."

He made a signal in the air. From the shadows of the colonnade a row of men and boys emerged: *drüskelle*, hoods drawn up over long golden hair that glinted at their collars, dressed in black and silver, like creatures born from the dark crevasses that split the northern ice. They fanned out, surrounding Nina, Matthias, and Kuwei.

Nina thought of the white prison cells, the drains in the floors. Had all of the *parem* been destroyed with Kuwei's lab? How long would it take him to make another batch, and what would they subject her to before that? She cast a last desperate look into the darkness, praying for some sign of Kaz. Had someone got to him, too? Had he just abandoned them there? She was meant to be a warrior. She needed to steel herself against what was to come.

One of the *drüskelle* came forward with what looked like a long-handled whip attached to the cables that bound them, and handed it to Lars.

"Do you recognise this, Helvar?" Lars asked. "You should. You helped with its design. Retractable cables for controlling multiple captives. And the barbs, of course."

Lars flicked his finger over one of the cables, and Nina gasped as stinging little barbs jabbed into her arms and torso. The *drüskelle* laughed.

"Leave her be," Matthias growled in Fjerdan, the words bristling with rage. For the briefest second, she saw a flash of panic in his former compatriots. He was bigger than all of them, and he'd been one of their leaders, one of the best of these murderous boys. Then Lars gave another cable a hard flick. The barbs released, and Matthias let out a pained huff of breath, doubling at the waist, human once more.

The snickering that followed was furtive and cruel.

Lars gave the whip a sharp snap, and the cables contracted, forcing Nina, Matthias, and Kuwei to totter after him in an awkward parade.

"Do you still pray to our god, Helvar?" Lars asked as they passed the sacred tree. "Do you think Djel hears the mewling of men who give themselves over to the defilement of Grisha? Do you think—"

Then a sharp, animal yelp sounded. It took Nina and the

others a long moment to realise it had come from Lars. He opened his mouth and blood gushed over his chin and onto the bright silver buttons of his uniform. His hand released the whip, and the hooded *drüskelle* beside him lunged forwards to snatch it up.

A sharp *pop pop pop* came from the base of the sacred tree. Nina recognised that sound – she'd heard it on the northern road before they waylaid the prison wagon. When they'd brought the tree down. The ash creaked and moaned. Its ancient roots began to curl.

"*Nej!*" cried one of the *drüskelle*. They stood openmouthed, gaping at the stricken tree. "*Nej!*" another voice wailed.

The ash began to tilt. It was too large to be felled by salt concentrate alone, but as it tipped, a dull roar emerged from the gaping black hole beneath it.

This was where the *drüskelle* came to hear the voice of their god. And now he was speaking.

"This is going to sting a bit," said the *drüskelle* holding the whip. His voice was rasping, familiar. His hands were gloved. "But if we live, you'll thank me later." His hood slid off, and Kaz Brekker looked back at them. The stunned *drüskelle* lifted their rifles.

"Don't pop the *baleen* before you hit bottom," Kaz called. Then he grabbed Kuwei and launched them both into the black mouth beneath the roots of the tree.

Nina screamed as her body was yanked forwards by the cables. She scrabbled over the stones trying to find purchase. The last thing she glimpsed was Matthias toppling into the hole beside her. She heard gunfire – and then she was falling into the black, into the cold, into the throat of Djel, into nothing at all.

38

KAZ

ELEVEN BELLS AND THREE-QUARTERS CHIME

Kaz had considered trying to eavesdrop on Matthias and Brum in the ballroom, but he didn't want to lose sight of Nina when there were so many *drüskelle* around. He'd gambled on Matthias' feelings for Nina, but he'd always liked those odds. The real risk had been in whether or not someone as honest as Matthias could convincingly lie to his mentor's face. Apparently the Fjerdan had hidden skills.

Kaz had tracked Nina and Brum across the grounds to the treasury. Then he'd taken cover behind an ice sculpture and focused on the miserable task of regurgitating the packets of Wylan's root bombs he'd swallowed before they'd ambushed the prison wagon. He'd had to bring them up – along with a pouch of chloropellets and an extra set of lockpicks he'd forced down his gullet in case of emergency – every other hour to keep from digesting them. It hadn't been pleasant. He'd learned the trick from an East Stave magician with a firebreathing act that had run for years before the man had accidentally poisoned himself by ingesting kerosene.

Once Kaz was done, he'd let himself check the treasury perimeter, the roof, the entry, but eventually there was nothing for him to do but keep hidden, stay alert, and worry about all the things that might be going wrong. He remembered Inej standing on the embassy roof, aglow with some new fervour he didn't understand but could still recognise – *purpose*. It had suffused her with light. *I'm taking my share, and I'm leaving the Dregs.* When she'd talked about leaving Ketterdam before, he'd never quite believed her. This time was different.

He'd been hidden in the shadows of the western colonnade when the bells of Black Protocol had begun to ring, the chimes of the Elderclock booming over the island, shaking the air. Lights from the guard towers came on in a bright flood. The *drüskelle* around the ash left off their rituals and began shouting orders, and a wave of guards descended from the towers to spread out over the island. He'd waited, counting the minutes, but there was still no sign of Nina or Matthias. *They're in trouble*, Kaz had thought. *Or you were dead wrong about Matthias, and you're about to pay for all of those talking tree jokes.*

He had to get inside the treasury, but he'd need some kind of cover while he picked that inscrutable lock, and there were *drüskelle* everywhere. Then he saw Nina and Matthias and a person he assumed must be Bo Yul-Bayur running from the treasury. He'd been about to call out to them when the explosion hit, and everything went to hell.

They blew up the lab, he'd thought as debris rained down around him. *I definitely did not tell them to blow up the lab.*

The rest was pure improvisation, and it left little time for explanation. All Kaz had told Matthias was to meet him by the ash when Black Protocol began to ring. He'd thought he'd have time to tell them to deploy the *baleen* before they were all falling through the dark. Now he just had to hope that they wouldn't panic and that his luck was waiting somewhere below.

The fall seemed impossibly long. Kaz hoped the Shu boy he was holding on to was a surprisingly young Bo Yul-Bayur and not some hapless prisoner Nina and Matthias had decided to liberate. He'd shoved the disk into the boy's mouth as they went over, snapping it with his own fingers. He gave the whip a flick, releasing all of the cables, and heard the others scream as the strands retracted. At least they wouldn't go into the water bound. Kaz waited as long as he dared to bite into his own *baleen*. When he struck the icy water, he feared his heart might stop.

He wasn't sure what he'd expected, but the force of the river was terrifying, flowing fast and hard as an avalanche. The noise was deafening even beneath the water, but with fear also came a kind of giddy vindication. He'd been right.

The voice of god. There was always truth in legend. Kaz had spent enough time building his own myth to know. He'd wondered where the water that fed the Ice Court's moat and fountains came from, why the river gorge was so very deep and wide. As soon as Nina had described the *drüskelle* initiation ritual, he'd known: The Fjerdan stronghold hadn't been built around a great tree but around a spring. Djel, the wellspring, who fed the seas and rains, and the roots of the sacred ash.

Water had a voice. It was something every canal rat knew, anyone who had slept beneath a bridge or weathered a winter storm in an overturned boat – water could speak with the voice of a lover, a long-lost brother, even a god. That was the key, and once Kaz recognised it, it was as if someone had laid a perfect blueprint over the Ice Court and its workings. If Kaz was right, Djel would spit them out into the gorge. Assuming they didn't drown first.

And that was a very real possibility. The *baleen* only provided enough air for ten minutes, maybe twelve if they could keep calm, which he doubted they would. His own heart was hammering, and his lungs already felt tight. His body was numb and aching from the temperature of the water, and the darkness was impenetrable. There was nothing but the dull thunder of the water and a sickening sense of tumbling.

He hadn't been sure of the speed of the water, but he knew damn well the numbers were close. Numbers had always been his allies – odds, margins, the art of the wager. But now he had to rely on something more. *What god do you serve?* Inej had asked him. *Whichever will grant me good fortune.* Fortunate people didn't end up racing ass over teakettle beneath an ice moat in hostile territory.

What would be waiting when they fished up in the gorge? *Who* would be waiting? Jesper and Wylan had managed to engage Black Protocol. But had they managed to do the rest? Would he see Inej on the other side?

Survive. Survive. Survive. It was the way he'd lived his life, moment to moment, breath to breath, since that terrible morning when he'd woken to find that Jordie was still dead and he was still very much alive.

Kaz tumbled through the dark. He was colder than he'd ever been. He thought of Inej's hand on his cheek. His mind had gone jagged at the sensation, a riot of confusion. It had been terror and disgust and – in all of that clamour – desire, a wish that lingered still, the hope that she would touch him again.

When he was fourteen, Kaz had put together a crew to rob the bank that had helped Hertzoon prey on him and Jordie. His crew got away with fifty thousand *kruge*, but he'd broken his leg dropping down from the rooftop. The bone didn't set right, and he'd limped ever after. So he'd found himself a Fabrikator and had his cane made. It became a declaration. There was no part of him that was not broken, that had not healed wrong, and there was no part of him that was not stronger for having been broken. The cane became a part of the myth he built. No one knew who he was. No one knew where he came from. He'd become Kaz Brekker, cripple and confidence man, bastard of the Barrel.

The gloves were his one concession to weakness. Since that night among the bodies and the swim from the Reaper's Barge, he had not been able to bear the feeling of skin against skin. It was excruciating to him, revolting. It was the only piece of his past that he could not forge into something dangerous.

The *baleen* began to bead around his lips. Water was seeping in. How far had the river taken them? How far did they have left to go? He still had one hand gripped around Bo Yul-Bayur's collar. The Shu boy was smaller than Kaz; hopefully he had enough air.

Bright flashes of memory sparked through Kaz's mind. A cup of hot chocolate in his mittened hands, Jordie warning him to let it cool before he took a sip. Ink drying on the page as he'd signed the deed to the Crow Club. The first time he'd seen Inej at the Menagerie, in purple silk, her eyes lined with kohl. The bone-handled knife he'd given her. The sobs that had come from behind the door of her room at the Slat the night she'd made her first kill. The sobs he'd ignored. Kaz remembered her perched on the sill of his attic window, sometime during that first year after he'd brought her into the Dregs. She'd been feeding the crows that congregated on the roof.

"You shouldn't make friends with crows," he'd told her.

"Why not?" she asked.

He'd looked up from his desk to answer, but whatever he'd been about to say had vanished on his tongue.

The sun was out for once, and Inej had turned her face to it. Her eyes were shut, her oil-black lashes fanned over her cheeks. The harbour wind had lifted her dark hair, and for a moment Kaz was a boy again, sure that there was magic in this world.

"Why not?" she'd repeated, eyes still closed.

He said the first thing that popped into his head. "They don't have any manners."

"Neither do you, Kaz." She'd laughed, and if he could have bottled the sound and got drunk on it every night, he would have. It terrified him.

Kaz took a last breath as the *baleen* dissolved and water flooded in. He squinted against the rush of the water, hoping to see some hint of daylight. The river knocked him against the wall of the tunnel. The pressure in his chest grew. *I'm stronger than this*, he told himself. *My will is greater.* But he could hear Jordie laughing. *No, little brother. No one is stronger. You've cheated death too many times. Greed may do your bidding, but death serves no man.*

Kaz had almost drowned that night in the harbour, kicking hard in the dark, borne aloft by Jordie's corpse. There was no one and nothing to carry him now. He tried to think of his brother, of revenge, of Pekka Rollins tied to a chair in the house on Zelverstraat, trade orders stuffed down his throat as Kaz forced him to remember Jordie's name. But all he could think of was Inej. She had to live. She had to have made it out of the Ice Court. And if she hadn't, then he had to live to rescue her.

The ache in his lungs was unbearable. He needed to tell her . . . what? That she was lovely and brave and better than anything he deserved. That he was twisted, crooked, wrong, but not so broken that he couldn't pull himself together into some semblance of a man for her. That without meaning to, he'd begun to lean on her, to look for her, to need her near. He needed to thank her for his new hat.

The water pressed at his chest, demanding that he part his lips. *I won't*, he swore. But in the end, Kaz opened his mouth, and the water rushed in.

PART 6

PROPER THIEVES

39

INEJ

Inej's heart careened against her ribs. On the aerial swings, there was a moment when you let go of one and reached for the next, when you realised you'd made a mistake and you no longer felt weightless, when you simply started to fall.

The guards hauled her back through the prison gate. There were many more guards and many more guns pointed at her than the first time she'd come through this courtyard, when she'd stepped off the prison wagon with the rest of the crew. They passed through the mouth of the wolf and up the stairs, and dragged her down the walkway through the corridor with its giant glass enclosure. Nina had translated the banner for her: *Fjerdan might*. She'd smirked at that the first time she'd passed, gazing down at the tanks and weapons, one eye on Kaz and the others on the opposite walkway. She'd wondered what kind of men needed to display their strength to helpless captives in chains.

The guards were moving too fast. For the second time that night, Inej made herself stumble.

"Move," the soldier snapped in Kerch, dragging her forwards.

"You're going too quickly."

He gave her arm a hard shake. "Stop stalling."

"Don't you want to meet our inquisitors?" the other asked her. "They'll get you talking."

"But you won't look so pretty after they're through."

They laughed, and Inej's stomach turned. She knew they'd spoken in Kerch to make sure she understood.

She thought she might be able to take them, despite their guns and even without her knives. Her hands weren't bound, and they still thought they had a disgraced prostitute on their hands. Heleen had called her a criminal, but to them, she was only a little thief in scraps of purple silk.

Just as she was considering making her move, she heard other footsteps headed their way. She saw the silhouettes of two more men in uniform striding towards them. Could she manage four guards on her own? She wasn't sure, but she knew that if they left this corridor behind, it was all over.

She glanced again at the banner in the glass enclosure. It was now or never.

She hooked her leg around the ankle of the guard to her left. He pitched forwards, and she slammed her hand upwards, breaking his nose.

The other raised his gun. "You're going to pay for that."

"You won't shoot me. You need information."

"I can shoot you in the leg," he sneered, lowering his rifle.

Then he crumpled to the ground, a pair of beaten-up shears protruding from his back. The soldier standing behind him gave a cheery wave.

"Jesper," she gasped in relief. "Finally."

"I'm here, too, you know," said Wylan.

The guard with the broken nose moaned from the floor and tried to lift his gun. Inej gave him a good hard kick to the head. He didn't move again.

"Did you manage to get hold of a big enough diamond?" Jesper asked.

Inej nodded and slipped the massive jewelled choker from her sleeve. "Hurry," she said. "If Heleen hasn't noticed it's missing, she will soon." Though with Black Protocol in effect there wasn't much she could do about it.

Jesper snatched the choker from Inej's hand, mouth agape. "Kaz said we needed a diamond. He didn't tell you to steal Heleen Van Houden's diamonds!"

"Just get to work."

Kaz had given Inej two objectives: nab a big enough diamond for Jesper to work with and get herself into this corridor after eleven bells. There were plenty of other diamonds she could have stolen for their purposes and other trouble she could have made to attract the guards' attention. But it was Heleen she'd wanted to dupe. For all the secrets she'd gathered and documents she'd stolen and violence she'd done, it was Heleen Van Houden she'd needed to best.

And Heleen had made it easy. During the scuffle in the rotunda, Inej had made sure that she was too focused on being choked to worry about being robbed. After that, all of Heleen's attention had been devoted to gloating. Inej only regretted that she wouldn't be there to see Tante Heleen discover her prized necklace was missing.

Jesper lit a lantern and went to work beside Wylan. Only then did she see they were both covered in soot from their trip back down the prison incinerator shaft. They'd dragged two grubby coils of rope with them, too. While they worked, Inej barred the doors set into the arches on either side of the corridor. They had just a few minutes before another patrol came through and discovered a door that shouldn't be locked.

Wylan had produced a long metal screw and what looked like the handle of a massive winch, and was attempting to rig them together to form what Inej hoped would be an ugly but functional drill.

A thump came from one of the doors.

"Hurry," Inej said.

"Saying that doesn't actually make me work faster," Jesper complained as he concentrated on the stones. "If I just break them down, they'll lose their molecular structure. They have to be cut, carefully, the edges assembled into a single perfect drill bit. I don't have the training—"

"Whose fault is that?" put in Wylan, not looking up from his own work.

"Again, not helpful."

Now the guards were pounding on the door. Across the enclosure, Inej saw men storming onto the other walkway, pointing and shouting. But they couldn't very well shoot through two walls of bulletproof glass.

The glass was Grisha made. Nina had recognised it as soon as they'd passed through the display – Fjerdan might protected by Grisha skill – and the one thing harder than Fabrikator glass was diamond.

The doors on both sides of the walkway were rattling now. "They're coming!" Inej said.

Wylan secured the diamond bit to the makeshift drill. It made a scraping sound as they placed it up against the glass, and Jesper began turning the handle. The progress was painfully slow.

"Is it even working?" Inej cried.

"The glass is thick!"

Something smashed into the door on their right. "They have a battering ram," Wylan moaned.

"Keep going," urged Inej. She toed off her shoes.

Jesper turned the crank faster as the drill bit whirred. He began to move it in a curving line, sketching the beginnings of a circle, then a half moon. *Faster.*

The wood of the door at the end of the walkway started to splinter.

"Take the handle, Wylan!" Jesper shouted.

Wylan took his place, turning the drill as fast as he could.

Jesper grabbed the fallen guards' guns and pointed them at the door.

"They're coming!" he yelled.

On the glass, the two lines met. The moon was full. The circle popped free, tipping inwards. It hadn't even struck the floor before Inej was backing up.

"Out of the way!" she demanded.

Then she was running, her feet light, her silks like feathers. In this moment she didn't mind them. She'd duped Heleen Van Houden. She'd taken a little piece of her away, a silly symbol, but one she prized. It wasn't enough – it would never be enough – but it was a beginning. There would be other bawds to trick, slavers to fool. Her silks were feathers, and she was free.

Inej focused on that circle of glass – a moon, an absence of moon, a door to the future – and she leaped. The hole was barely big enough for her body, she heard the soft *swish* as the sharp glass rim sliced through the silks she trailed. She arced her body and reached. She would have only one opportunity to grab for the iron lantern that hung from the ceiling of the enclosure. It was an impossible leap, a mad leap, but she was once again her father's daughter, unbound by the rules of gravity. She hung in the air for a terrifying moment, and then her hands grasped the lantern's base.

Behind her, she heard the door in the walkway burst open, gunfire. *Hold them off, Jesper. Buy me time.*

She swung back and forth, building momentum. A bullet zinged past her. Accident? Or had someone made it past Wylan and Jesper to shoot at her through the hole?

When she had enough momentum, she let go. She hit the wall hard. There was no graceful way around it, but her hands clung to the lip of the stone ledge where the ancient axes were displayed. From there it was easy: ledge to beam to lower ledge, and down with a dull *clang* as her bare feet struck the roof of a massive tank. She slid into the metal dome at its centre.

She turned one knob then the next, trying to find the right controls. Finally one of the guns rolled upwards. She pulled on the trigger, and her whole body shook as bullets rattled against the enclosure glass like hail, pinging off in all directions. It was the best warning she could offer Jesper and Wylan.

Inej could only hope she could get the big gun working. She wriggled down in the cockpit of the tank. She rotated the only visible handle, and the nose of the long gun tilted into place. The lever was there, just as Jesper had said it would be. She gave it a hard pull. There was a surprisingly small *click*. Then, for a long horrible moment, nothing happened. *What if it isn't loaded?* she thought. *If Jesper's right about this gun, then the Fjerdans would be fools to keep this much firepower just lying around.*

A *thunk* sounded from somewhere in the tank. She heard something rolling towards her and had the terrifying thought that she'd done it wrong. The mortar was going to roll right down that long barrel and explode in her lap. Instead there was a hissing sound and a shriek like metal grinding against metal. The big gun vibrated. A skull-rattling *boom* split the air with a puff of dark grey smoke.

The mortar struck the glass, shattering it into thousands of glittering pieces. *Prettier than diamonds*, Inej marvelled, hoping that Wylan and Jesper had found time and space to take cover.

She waited for the dust to clear, her ears ringing badly. The glass wall was gone. All was still. Then two ropes attached to the walkway rail swung down, and Wylan and Jesper followed: Jesper like a limber insect, Wylan in stops and starts, wiggling like a caterpillar trying to make its way out of a cocoon.

"*Ajor!*" Inej shouted in Fjerdan. Nina would be proud.

She cranked the gun around. On the other side of the remaining glass wall, men were shouting from the walkway. As the barrel swivelled in their direction, they scattered.

Inej heard footsteps and clanging as Jesper and Wylan climbed onto the tank. Jesper's head appeared, hanging down from the dome. "You letting me drive?"

"If you insist."

She moved aside so he could climb behind the controls.

"Oh, hello, darling," he said happily. He pulled another lever, and the armoured wagon seemed to shudder to life around them, belching black smoke. *What kind of monster is this?* Inej wondered.

"That noise!" she cried.

"That engine!" cackled Jesper.

Then they were moving – and not a horse in sight.

Gunfire sounded from above. Apparently, Wylan had found the controls.

"For Saints' sake," Jesper said to Inej. "Help him aim!"

She squeezed in next to Wylan in the domed turret and aimed the second small gun, helping to lay down cover as guards burst into the enclosure.

Jesper was turning the tank, backing up as far as possible. He fired the big gun once. The mortar smashed the enclosure glass, sailed past the walkway, and struck the ringwall behind it. White dust and shards of stone scattered everywhere. He fired again. The second mortar hit hard, cracks splintering through the rock of the wall. Jesper had made a dent in the ringwall – a sizeable one – but not a hole.

"Ready?" he called.

"Ready," Inej and Wylan replied in unison. They ducked beneath the gun turret. Wylan had scratches from the glass all over his cheeks and neck. He was beaming. Inej grabbed his hands and squeezed. They'd come to the Ice Court scurrying like rats. Live or die, they were going out like an army.

Inej heard a loud *thunk*, the plunk and clang of gears turning. The tank roared; the sound was thunder trapped in a metal drum, clamouring to be let out. It rolled back on its treads, then surged forwards. They charged ahead, building momentum, faster and faster. The tank jounced – they must be out of the enclosure.

"Hold tight!" shouted Jesper and they slammed into the Ice Court's legendary, impenetrable wall with a jaw-shattering crash. Inej and Wylan flew back against the cockpit.

They were through. They rumbled over the road, the smatter and pop of rifle fire fading behind them.

Inej heard a chuffing noise. She righted herself and looked up. Wylan was laughing.

He'd pushed out of the niche of the dome and was looking back at the Ice Court. When she joined him, she saw the hole in the ringwall – a dark blot in all that white stone, men running through, firing futilely at the tank's dusty wake.

Wylan clutched his middle, still snorting laughter, and pointed downwards. Trailing behind them was a banner, caught in the tank's treads. Despite the smears of mud and gunpowder burns, Inej could still make out the words: STRYMAKTFJERDAN. *Fjerdan might.*

40

NINA

They emerged from the darkness, soaked, bruised, and gasping in the bright light of the moon. Nina's entire body felt as if it had been pummelled. The remnants of the *baleen* clustered in sticky gobs at the corners of her mouth. Her dress had frayed to nearly nothing, and if she hadn't been so desperately, giddily happy to be alive and breathing, she might have worried about the fact that she was standing barefoot and practically naked in the gorge of a northern river, still a mile and a half from the harbour and safety. In the distance, she could hear the bells of the Ice Court ringing.

Kuwei was coughing water, and Matthias was dragging a limp, unconscious Kaz out of the shallows.

"Saints, is he breathing?" asked Nina.

Matthias flipped him onto his back none too gently and started pressing down on his chest with more force than was strictly necessary.

"I. Should. Let. You. Die," Matthias muttered in time with his compressions.

Nina crawled over the rocks and kneeled beside them, "Let me help before you crack his sternum. Does he have a pulse?" She pressed her fingers to his throat. "It's there, but it's fading. Get his shirt open."

Matthias helped tear the *drüskelle* uniform away. Nina placed one hand on Kaz's pale chest, focusing on his heart and forcing it to contract. She used the other to pinch his nose shut and push his mouth open as she tried to breathe air into his lungs. More skilled Corporalki could extract the water themselves, but she didn't have time to fret over her lack of training.

"Will he live?" Kuwei asked.

I don't know. She pressed her lips to Kaz's again, timing her breaths with the beats she demanded of his heart. *Come on, you rotten Barrel thug. You've fought your way out of tougher scrapes.*

She felt the shift when Kaz's heart took over its own rhythm. Then he coughed, chest spasming, water spewing from his mouth.

He shoved her off of him, sucking in air.

"Get away from me," he gasped, wiping his gloved hand over his mouth. Kaz's eyes were unfocused. He seemed to be staring right through her. "Don't touch me."

"You're in shock, *demjin*," Matthias said. "You almost drowned. You should have drowned."

Kaz coughed again, and his entire body shuddered. "Drowned," he repeated.

Nina nodded slowly. "Ice Court, remember? Impossible heist? Near death? Three million *kruge* waiting for you in Ketterdam?"

Kaz blinked and his eyes cleared. "*Four* million."

"I thought that might bring you around."

He scrubbed his hands over his face, wet coughs still rattling his chest. "We made it," he said in wonder. "Djel performs miracles."

"You don't deserve miracles," said Matthias with a scowl. "You desecrated the sacred ash."

Kaz pushed to his feet, staggered slightly, drew in another shaky breath. "It's a symbol, Helvar. If your god is so delicate, maybe you should get a new one. Let's get out of here."

Nina threw up her hands. "You're welcome, you ungrateful wretch."

"I'll thank you when we're aboard the *Ferolind*. Move." He was already dragging himself up the boulders that lined the far side of the gorge. "You can explain why our illustrious Shu scientist looks like one of Wylan's school pals along the way."

Nina shook her head, caught between annoyance and admiration. Maybe that was what it took to survive in the Barrel. You could never stop.

"He's a friend?" asked Kuwei in skeptical Shu.

"On occasion."

Matthias helped her to her feet, and they all followed after Kaz, making slow progress up the rocky walls of the gorge that would lead them to the other end of the bridge above, and a bit closer to Djerholm. Nina had never been so exhausted, but she couldn't let herself rest. They had the prize. They'd got further than any crew. They'd blown up a building at the heart of the Ice Court. But they'd never make it to the harbour without Inej and the others.

She kept moving. The only other option was to sit down on a boulder and wait for the end. A rumbling began from somewhere in the direction of the Ice Court.

"Oh, Saints, please let that be Jesper," she pleaded as they pulled themselves over the lip of the gorge and looked back at the bridge festooned with ribbons and ash boughs for Hringkälla.

"Whatever is coming, it's big," said Matthias.

"What do we do, Kaz?"

"Wait," he said as the sound grew louder.

"How about 'take cover'?" Nina asked, bouncing

nervously from foot to foot. "'Have heart'? 'I stashed twenty rifles in this convenient shrubbery'? Give us *something*."

"How about a few million *kruge*?" said Kaz.

A tank rumbled over the hill, dust and gravel spewing from its treads. Someone was waving to them from its gun turret – no, two someones. Inej and Wylan were yelling and gesturing wildly from behind the dome.

Nina let out a victorious whoop as Matthias stared in disbelief. When Nina looked at Kaz, she couldn't quite believe her eyes. "Saints, Kaz, you actually look happy."

"Don't be ridiculous," he snapped. But there was no mistaking it. Kaz Brekker was grinning like an idiot.

"I'm assuming we know them?" asked Kuwei.

But Nina's elation dimmed as Fjerda's answer to the problem of the Dregs rolled over the horizon. A column of tanks had crested the hill and was crashing down the moonlit road, dust rising in plumes from their treads. Maybe Jesper hadn't got the *drüskelle* gate sealed. Or maybe they'd had tanks waiting on the grounds. Given the firepower contained behind the Ice Court's walls, she supposed they should count themselves lucky. But it sure didn't feel that way.

It wasn't until Inej and Wylan were thundering over the trestles of the bridge that Nina could make out what they were yelling: "Get out of the way!"

They leaped from the path as the tank roared past them, then came to a gear-grinding stop.

"We have a tank," marvelled Nina. "Kaz, you creepy little genius, the plan worked. You got us a tank."

"*They* got us a tank."

"We have *one*," Matthias said, then pointed at the horde of metal and smoke bearing down on them. "They have a lot more."

"Yeah, but you know what they don't have?" Kaz asked as Jesper rotated the tank's giant gun. "A bridge."

A metallic shriek went up from the armoured insides

of the tank. Then a violent, bone-shaking boom sounded. Nina heard a high whistling as something shot through the air past them and collided with the bridge. The first two trestles exploded into flame, sparks and timber plummeting into the gorge below. The big gun fired again. With a groan, the trestles collapsed completely.

If the Fjerdans wanted to cross the gorge, they were going to have to fly.

"We have a tank *and* a moat," said Nina.

"Climb on!" crowed Wylan.

They boosted themselves onto the sides of the tank, clutching at any groove or lip in the metal for dear life, and then they were rolling down the road towards the harbour at top speed.

As they roared past the streetlamps, people emerged from their houses to see what was happening. Nina tried to imagine what their wild crew must look like to these Fjerdans. What did they see as they poked their heads out of windows and doorways? A group of hooting kids clinging to a tank painted with the Fjerdan flag and charging along like some deranged float gone astray from its parade; a girl in purple silk and a boy with red-gold curls poking out from behind the guns; four soaked people holding tight to the sides for dear life – a Shu boy in prison clothes, two bedraggled *drüskelle*, and Nina, a half-naked girl in shreds of teal chiffon shouting, "We have a moat!"

When they entered the town, Matthias called, "Wylan, tell Jesper to keep to the western streets."

Wylan ducked down, and the tank veered west.

"It's the warehouse district," Matthias explained. "Deserted at night."

The tank clattered and clanked over the cobblestones, swinging right and left over kerbs and back again to avoid the few pedestrians, then sped into the harbour district, past taverns and shops and shipping offices.

Kuwei tilted his head back, his face bright with joy. "I can smell the sea," he said happily.

Nina could smell it, too. The lighthouse gleamed in the distance. Two more blocks and they'd be at the quay and freedom. Thirty million *kruge*. With her share and Matthias' they could go anywhere they wanted, live any life they chose.

"Almost there!" cried Wylan.

They rounded a corner, and Nina's stomach dropped.

"Stop!" she shouted. "Stop!"

She needn't have bothered. The tank jolted to a halt, nearly flinging Nina from her perch. The quay lay directly before them, and beyond it the harbour, the flags of a thousand ships snapping in the breeze. The hour was late. The quay should have been empty. Instead, it was crowded with troops, row after row of them in grey uniforms, two hundred soldiers at least – and every barrel of every gun was pointed directly at them.

Nina could still hear the bells of the Elderclock. She looked over her shoulder. The Ice Court loomed over the harbour, perched on the cliff like a sullen gull with feathers ruffled, its white stone walls lit from below, glowing against the night sky.

"What is this?" Wylan asked Matthias. "You never said—"

"They must have changed deployment procedure."

"Everything else was the same."

"I've never seen Black Protocol engaged," Matthias growled. "Maybe they always had troops stationed in the harbour. I don't know."

"Be quiet," Inej said. "Just stop."

Nina jumped as a voice echoed over the crowd. It spoke first in Fjerdan, then Ravkan, then Kerch, and finally Shu. "Release the prisoner Kuwei Yul-Bo. Put down your weapons and step away from the tank."

"They can't just open fire," said Matthias. "They won't risk hurting Kuwei."

"They don't have to," said Nina. "Look."

An emaciated prisoner was being led through the rows of soldiers. His hair was matted to his forehead. He wore a ragged red *kefta* and was clutching the sleeve of the guard closest to him, lips moving feverishly as if imparting some desperate wisdom. Nina knew he was begging for *parem*.

"A Heartrender," Matthias said grimly.

"But he's so far away," protested Wylan.

Nina shook her head. "It won't matter." Had they kept him down here with whatever troops were posted in lower Djerholm? Why not? He was a weapon better than any gun or tank.

"I can see the *Ferolind*," murmured Inej. She pointed down the docks, just a little way off. It took Nina a moment, but then she picked out the Kerch flag and the cheery Haanraadt Bay pennant flying beneath it. They were so close.

Jesper could shoot the Heartrender. They could try barrelling through the troops with the tank, but they would never make it to the ship. The Fjerdans would gladly risk Kuwei's life before they ever let him fall into anyone else's hands.

"Kaz?" called Jesper from inside the tank. "This would be a really good time to say you saw this coming."

Kaz looked out over the sea of soldiers. "I didn't see this coming." He shook his head. "You told me one day I'd run out of tricks, Helvar. Looks like you were right." The words were for Matthias, but his eyes were on Inej.

"I've had my fill of captivity," she said. "They won't take me alive."

"Me neither," said Wylan.

Jesper snorted from inside the tank. "We really need to get him more suitable friends."

"Better to go out with fists swinging than let some Fjerdan put me on a pike," said Kaz.

Matthias nodded. "Then we agree. We end this here."

"No," Nina whispered. They all turned to her.

The voice echoed out from the Fjerdan ranks once more. "You have a count of ten to comply. I repeat: Release the prisoner Kuwei Yul-Bo and surrender yourselves. Ten . . ."

Nina spoke to Kuwei rapidly in Shu.

"You don't understand," he replied. "A single dose—"

"I understand," she said. But the others didn't. Not until they saw Kuwei produce a little leather pouch from his pocket. Its rim was stained with rust-coloured powder.

"No!" Matthias shouted. He grabbed for the *parem*, but Nina was faster.

The Fjerdan voice droned on: "Seven . . ."

"Nina, don't be stupid," said Inej. "You've seen—"

"Some people don't get addicted after the first dose."

"It isn't worth the risk."

"Six . . ."

"Kaz is out of tricks." She plucked open the pouch. "But I'm not."

"Nina, please," Matthias begged. She'd seen the same anguish on his face that day in Elling when he thought she'd betrayed him. In a way, she was doing the same thing now, abandoning him once more.

"Five . . ."

The first dose was the strongest, wasn't that what they'd said? The high and the power could never be replicated. She'd be chasing it for the rest of her life. Or maybe she'd be stronger than the drug.

"Four . . ."

She touched Matthias'cheek briefly. "If it gets bad, find a way to end it, Helvar. I'm trusting you to do the right thing." She smiled. "Again."

"Three . . ."

Then she tossed her head back and poured the *parem* into her mouth, downing it in a single hard swallow. It had the sweet, burnt taste of the *jurda* blossoms she knew, but there was another flavour, too, one she couldn't quite identify.

She stopped thinking.

Her blood began to thrum, and her heart was suddenly pounding. The world broke up into tiny flashes of light. She could see the true colour of Matthias'eyes, pure blue beneath the flecks of grey and brown she'd put there, the moonlight gleaming off every hair on his head. She saw the sweat on Kaz's brow, the nearly invisible pinpricks of the tattoo on his forearm.

She looked out over the lines of Fjerdan soldiers. She could hear their hearts beating. She could see their neurons firing, feel their impulses forming. Everything made sense. Their bodies were a map of cells, a thousand equations, solved by the second, by the millisecond, and she knew only answers.

"Nina?"Matthias whispered.

"Move," Nina said, and she saw her voice in the air.

She sensed the Heartrender in the crowd, the movement of his throat as he swallowed his dose. He would be the first.

41

MATTHIAS

"Two . . . one . . ."

Matthias saw Nina's pupils dilate. Her lips parted, and she pushed past him, stepping down from the tank. The air around her seemed to crackle, her skin glowing as if lit from within by something miraculous. As if she'd tapped a vein of Djel directly, and now the god's power flowed through her.

She went for the Heartrender immediately. Nina flicked her wrist, and his eyes exploded in his head. He crumpled without a sound. "Be free," she said.

Nina glided towards the soldiers. Matthias moved to protect her as he saw rifles raised. She lifted her hands. "Stop," she said.

They froze.

"Lay down your arms." As one they obeyed her.

"Sleep," she commanded. Nina swept her hands in an arc, and the soldiers toppled without protest, row after row, stalks of wheat felled by an invisible scythe.

The air was eerily still. Slowly, Wylan and Inej climbed down from the tank. Jesper and the rest followed, and they stood in stunned silence, all language dissolved by what they'd witnessed, gazing out at the field of fallen bodies. It had happened so quickly.

There was no way to reach the harbour unless they walked over the soldiers. Without a word, they began to pick their way through, the hush broken only by the faraway bells of the Elderclock. Matthias laid his hand on Nina's arm, and she released a little sigh, letting him lead her.

Beyond the quay, the docks were deserted. As the others headed towards the *Ferolind*, Matthias and Nina trailed behind. Matthias could see Rotty clinging to the mast, jaw slack with fear. Specht was waiting to unmoor the ship, and the look on his face was equally terrified.

"Matthias!"

He turned. A group of *drüskelle* stood on the quay, their uniforms soaked, their black hoods raised. They wore masks of dully gleaming grey chainmail over their faces, their features obscured by the mesh. But Matthias recognised Jarl Brum's voice when he spoke.

"Traitor," Brum said from behind his mask. "Betrayer of your country and your god. You will not leave this harbour alive. None of you will." His men must have got him out of the treasury after the explosion. Had they followed Matthias and Nina to the river beneath the ash? Had there been horses or more tanks stationed in the upper town?

Nina raised her hands. "For Matthias, I will give you one chance to leave us be."

"You cannot control us, witch," said Brum. "Our hoods, our masks, every stitch of clothing we wear is reinforced with Grisha steel. Corecloth created to our specifications by Grisha Fabrikators under our control and designed for just this purpose. You cannot force us to your will. You cannot harm us. This game is at an end."

Nina lifted a hand. Nothing happened, and Matthias knew what Brum was saying was true.

"Go!" Matthias shouted at them. "Please! You—"

Brum lifted his gun and fired. The bullet struck Matthias directly in the chest. The pain was sudden and terrible – and then gone. Before his eyes, he saw the bullet emerge from his chest. It hit the ground with a *plink*. He pulled his shirt open. There was no wound.

Nina was walking past him. "No!" he cried.

The *drüskelle* opened fire on her. He saw her flinch as the bullets struck her body, saw red blooms of blood appear on her chest, her breasts, her bare thighs. But she did not fall. As fast as the bullets tore through her body, she healed herself, and the shells fell harmlessly to the dock.

The *drüskelle* gaped at Nina. She laughed. "You've grown too used to captive Grisha. We're quite tame in our cages."

"There are other means," said Brum, pulling a long whip like the one Lars had used from his belt. "Your power cannot touch us, witch, and our cause is true."

"I can't touch you," said Nina, raising her hands. "But I can reach them just fine."

Behind the *drüskelle*, the Fjerdan soldiers Nina had put to sleep rose, their faces blank. One tore the whip from Brum's hand, the others snatched the hoods and masks from the startled *drüskelle*'s faces, rendering them vulnerable.

Nina flexed her fingers, and the *drüskelle* dropped their rifles, hands going to their heads, screaming in pain.

"For my country," she said. "For my people. For every child you put to the pyre. Reap what you've sown, Jarl Brum."

Matthias watched the *drüskelle* twitch and convulse, blood trickling from their ears and eyes as the other Fjerdan soldiers looked on impassively. Their screams were a chorus. Claas, who had drunk too much with him in Avfalle. Giert, who'd trained his wolf to eat from his hand. They were monsters, he knew it, but boys as well, boys like him – taught to hate, to fear.

"Nina," he said, hand still pressed over the smooth

skin on his chest where a bullet wound should be. "Nina, please."

"You know they would not offer you mercy, Matthias."

"I know. I know. But let them live in shame instead."

She hesitated.

"Nina, you taught me to be something better. They could be taught, too."

Nina shifted her gaze to his. Her eyes were ferocious, the deep green of forests; the pupils, dark wells. The air around her seemed to shimmer with power, as if she was alight with some secret flame.

"They fear you as I once feared you," he said. "As you once feared me. We are all someone's monster, Nina."

For a long moment, she studied his face. At last, she dropped her arms, and the ranks of *drüskelle* crumpled to the ground, whimpering. Her hand shot out once more, and Brum shrieked. He clapped his hands to his head, blood trickling between his fingers.

"He'll live?" Matthias asked.

"Yes," she said as she stepped onto the schooner. "He'll just be very bald."

Specht shouted commands, and the *Ferolind* drifted into the harbour, picking up speed as the sails swelled with wind. No one ran to the docks to stop them. No ships or cannon fired. There was no one to give warning, no one to signal to the gunnery above. The Elderclock chimed on unheeded as the schooner vanished into the vast black shelter of the sea, leaving only suffering in her wake.

42

INEJ

They'd been blessed with a strong wind. Inej felt it ripple through her hair and couldn't help but think of the storm to come.

As soon as they were on deck, Matthias had turned to Kuwei. "How long does she have?"

Kuwei had some Kerch, but Nina had to translate in places. She did it distractedly, her glittering eyes roving over everyone and everything.

"The high will last one hour, maybe two. It depends how long it takes her body to process a dose of that size."

"Why can't you just purge it from your body like the bullets?" Matthias asked Nina desperately.

"It doesn't work," said Kuwei. "Even if she could overcome the craving for long enough to start purging it from her body, she'll lose the ability to pull the *parem* from her system before it's all gone. You'd need another Corporalnik using *parem* to accomplish it."

"What will it do to her?" asked Wylan.

"You've seen for yourself," Matthias replied bitterly. "We know what's going to happen."

Kaz crossed his arms, "How will it start?"

"Body aches, chills, no worse than a mild illness," Kuwei explained. "Then a kind of hypersensitivity, followed by tremors, and the craving."

"Do you have more of the *parem*?" Matthias asked.

"Yes."

"Enough to get her back to Ketterdam?"

"I won't take more," Nina protested.

"I have enough to keep you comfortable," Kuwei said. "But if you take a second dose, there is no hope at all." He looked to Matthias. "This is her one chance. It's possible her body will purge enough of it naturally that addiction won't set in."

"And if it does?"

Kuwei held out his hands, part shrug, part apology. "Without a ready supply of the drug, she'll go mad. With it, her body will simply wear itself out. Do you know the word *parem*? It's the name my father gave to the drug. It means 'without pity'."

When Nina finished translating, there was a long pause.

"I don't want to hear any more," she said. "None of it will change what's coming."

She drifted away towards the prow. Matthias watched her go.

"The water hears and understands," he murmured beneath his breath.

Inej sought out Rotty and got him to dig up the wool coats she and Nina had left behind in favour of their cold weather gear when they'd landed on the northern shore. She found Nina near the prow, gazing out at the sea.

"One hour, maybe two," Nina said without turning.

Inej halted in shock. "You heard me approach?" No one heard the Wraith, especially over the sound of the wind and sea.

"Don't worry. It wasn't those silent feet that gave you away. I can hear your pulse, your breathing."

"And you knew it was me?"

"Every heart sounds different. I never realised that before."

Inej joined her at the rail and handed over Nina's coat. The Grisha put it on, though the cold didn't seem to be bothering her. Above them, the stars shone bright between silver-seeded drifts of cloud. Inej was ready for dawn, ready for this long night to be over, and the journey, too. She was surprised to find she was eager to see Ketterdam again. She wanted an omelette, a mug of too-sweet coffee. She wanted to hear the rain on the rooftops and sit snug and warm in her tiny room at the Slat. There were adventures to come, but they could wait until she'd had a hot bath – maybe a few of them.

Nina buried her face in her coat's woollen collar and said, "I wish you could see what I do. I can hear every body on this ship, the blood rushing through their veins. I can hear the change in Kaz's breathing when he looks at you."

"You . . . you can?"

"It catches every time, like he's never seen you before."

"And what about Matthias?" Inej asked, eager to change the subject.

Nina raised a brow, unfooled. "Matthias is afraid for me, but his heart thumps a steady rhythm no matter what he's feeling. So Fjerdan, so orderly."

"I didn't think you'd let those men live, back at the harbour."

"I'm not sure it was the right thing to do. I'll become one more Grisha horror story for them to tell their children."

"Behave or Nina Zenik will get you?"

Nina considered. "Well, I *do* like the sound of that."

Inej leaned back on the railing and peered at Nina. "You look radiant."

"It won't last."

"It never does." Then Inej's smile faltered. "Are you afraid?"

"Terrified."

"We'll all be here with you."

Nina took a wobbly breath and nodded.

Inej had made countless alliances in Ketterdam, but few friends. She rested her head against Nina's shoulder. "If I were a Suli seer," she said, "I could look into the future and tell you it will be all right."

"Or that I'm going to die in agony." Nina pressed her cheek against the top of Inej's head. "Tell me something good anyway."

"It will be all right," Inej said. "You'll survive this. And then you're going to be very, very rich. You'll sing sea shanties and drinking songs nightly in an East Stave cabaret, and you'll bribe everyone to give you standing ovations after every song."

Nina laughed softly. "Let's buy the Menagerie."

Inej grinned, thinking of the future and her little ship. "Let's buy it and burn it down."

They watched the waves for a while. "Ready?" Nina said.

Inej was glad she hadn't had to ask. She pushed up her sleeve, baring the peacock feather and mottled skin beneath it.

It took the barest second, the softest brush of Nina's fingertips. The itch was acute but passed quickly. When the prickling faded, the skin of Inej's forearm was perfect—almost too smooth and flawless, like it was the one new part of her.

Inej touched the soft skin. Just like that it was done. If only every wound could be banished so easily.

Nina kissed Inej's cheek. "I'm going to find Matthias before things get bad."

But as she walked away, Inej saw Nina had another reason

to depart. Kaz was standing in the shadows near the mast. He had a heavy coat on and was leaning on his crow-head cane – he looked almost like himself again. Inej's knives would be waiting in the hold with her other belongings. She'd missed her claws.

Kaz murmured a few words to Nina, and the Grisha reared back in surprise. Inej couldn't make out the rest of what they said, but she could tell the exchange was tense before Nina made an exasperated sound and vanished belowdecks.

"What did you say to Nina?" Inej asked when he joined her at the rail.

"I have a job I need her to perform."

"She's about to go through a terrifying ordeal—"

"And work still needs to get done."

Pragmatic Kaz. Why let empathy get in the way? Maybe Nina would be glad for the distraction.

They stood together, gazing out at the waves, silence stretching between them.

"We're alive," he said at last.

"It seems you prayed to the right god."

"Or travelled with the right people."

Inej shrugged. "Who chooses our paths?" He said nothing, and she had to smile. "No sharp retort? No laughing at my Suli proverbs?"

He ran his gloved thumb over the rail. "No."

"How will we meet the Merchant Council?"

"When we're a few miles out, Rotty and I will row to harbour in the longboat. We'll find a runner to get word to Van Eck and make the exchange on Vellgeluk."

Inej shivered. The island was popular with slavers and smugglers. "The Council's choice or yours?"

"Van Eck suggested it."

Inej frowned. "Why does a mercher know about Vellgeluk?"

"Trade is trade. Maybe Van Eck isn't quite the upstanding merch he seems."

They were silent for a while. Finally, she said, "I'm going to learn to sail."

Kaz's brow furrowed, and he cast her a surprised glance. "Really? Why?"

"I want to use my money to hire a crew and outfit a ship." Saying the words wrapped her breath up in an anxious spool. Her dream still felt fragile. She didn't want to care what Kaz thought, but she did. "I'm going to hunt slavers."

"Purpose," he said thoughtfully. "You know you can't stop them all."

"If I don't try, I won't stop any."

"Then I almost pity the slavers," Kaz said. "They have no idea what's coming for them."

A pleased flush warmed her cheeks. But hadn't Kaz always believed she was dangerous?

Inej balanced her elbows on the railing and rested her chin in her palms. "I'll go home first, though."

"To Ravka?"

She nodded.

"To find your family."

"Yes." Only two days ago, she would have left it at that, respecting their unspoken agreement to tread lightly in each other's pasts. Now she said, "Was there no one but your brother, Kaz? Where are your mother and father?"

"Barrel boys don't have parents. We're born in the harbour and crawl out of the canals."

Inej shook her head. She watched the sea shift and sigh, each wave a breath. She could just make out the horizon, the barest difference between black sky and blacker sea. She thought of her parents. She'd been away from them for nearly three years. How would they have changed? Could she be their daughter again? Maybe not right away. But she wanted to sit with her father on the steps of the wagon eating fruit from the trees. She wanted to see her mother dust chalk from her hands before she prepared the evening meal. She wanted tall southern grasses and the vast sky above the Sikurzoi Mountains. Something she needed was waiting for her there. What did Kaz need?

"You're about to be rich, Kaz. What will you do when there's no more blood to shed or vengeance to take?"

"There's always more."

"More money, more mayhem, more scores to settle. Was there never another dream?"

He said nothing. What had carved all the hope from his heart? She might never know.

Inej turned to go. Kaz seized her hand, keeping it on the railing. He didn't look at her. "Stay," he said, his voice rough stone. "Stay in Ketterdam. Stay with me."

She looked down at his gloved hand clutching hers. Everything in her wanted to say yes, but she would not settle for so little, not after all she'd been through. "What would be the point?"

He took a breath. "I want you to stay. I want you to . . . I want you."

"You want me." She turned the words over. Gently, she squeezed his hand. "And how will you have me, Kaz?"

He looked at her then, eyes fierce, mouth set. It was the face he wore when he was fighting.

"How will you have me?" she repeated. "Fully clothed, gloves on, your head turned away so our lips can never touch?"

He released her hand, his shoulders bunching, his gaze angry and ashamed as he turned his face to the sea.

Maybe it was because his back was to her that she could finally speak the words. "I will have you without armour, Kaz Brekker. Or I will not have you at all."

Speak, she begged silently. *Give me a reason to stay.* For all his selfishness and cruelty, Kaz was still the boy who had saved her. She wanted to believe he was worth saving, too.

The sails creaked. The clouds parted for the moon then gathered back around her.

Inej left Kaz with the wind howling and dawn still a long while away.

43

NINA

The aches set in after dawn. An hour later, it felt as if her bones were trying to push through the places where her joints met. She lay on the same table where she'd healed Inej's knife wound. Her senses were still sharp enough that she could smell the coppery scent of the Suli girl's blood beneath the cleaner Rotty had used to remove it from the wood. It smelled like Inej.

Matthias sat beside her. He'd tried to take her hand, but the pain was too great. The chafe of his skin on hers made her flesh feel raw. Everything looked wrong. Everything felt wrong. All she could think of was the sweet, burnt taste of the *parem*. Her throat itched. Her skin felt like an enemy.

When the tremors began, she begged him to leave.

"I don't want you to see me like this," she said, trying to roll on her side.

He brushed the damp hair from her brow. "How bad is it?"

"Bad." But she knew it would get worse.

"Do you want to try the *jurda?*" Kuwei had suggested that small doses of regular *jurda* might help Nina get through the day.

She shook her head. "I want . . . I want – Saints, why is it so hot in here?" Then, despite the pain, she tried to sit up. "Don't give me another dose. Whatever I say, Matthias, no matter how much I beg. I don't want to be like Nestor, like those Grisha in the cells."

"Nina, Kuwei said the withdrawal could kill you. I won't let you die."

Kuwei. Back at the treasury Matthias had said, *He's one of us.* She liked that word. *Us.* A word without divisions or borders. It seemed full of hope.

She flopped back down, and her whole body rebelled. Her clothes were crushed glass. "I would have killed every one of the *drüskelle*."

"We all carry our sins, Nina. I need you to live so I can atone for mine."

"You can do that without me, you know."

He buried his head in his hands. "I don't want to."

"Matthias," she said, running her fingers through the close crop of his hair. It hurt. The world hurt. Touching him hurt, but she still did it. She might not ever get to again. "I am not sorry."

He took her hand and kissed her knuckles gently. She winced, but when he tried to pull away, she clutched him tighter.

"Stay," she panted. Tears leaked from her eyes. "Stay till the end."

"And after," he said. "And always."

"I want to feel safe again. I want to go home to Ravka."

"Then I'll take you there. We'll set fire to raisins or whatever you heathens do for fun."

"Zealot," she said weakly.

"Witch."

"Barbarian."

"Nina," he whispered, "little red bird. Don't go."

44

JESPER

As the schooner sped south, it was as if the whole crew was sitting vigil. Everyone spoke in hushed tones, treading quietly over the decks. Jesper was as worried about Nina as anyone – except Matthias, he supposed – but the respectful silence was hard to bear. He needed something to shoot at.

The *Ferolind* felt like a ghost ship. Matthias was sequestered with Nina, and he'd asked for Wylan's help in caring for her. Even if Wylan didn't love chemistry, he knew more about tinctures and compounds than anyone in the crew other than Kuwei, and Matthias couldn't understand half of what Kuwei said. Jesper hadn't seen Wylan since they'd fled the Djerholm harbour, and he had to admit he missed having the merchling around to annoy. Kuwei seemed friendly enough, but his Kerch was rough, and he didn't seem to like to talk much. Sometimes he'd just appear on deck at night and stand silently beside Jesper, staring out at the waves. It was a little unnerving. Only Inej wanted to chat with anyone, and that was because she seemed to have developed a consuming interest in all things nautical.

She spent most of her time with Specht and Rotty, learning knots and how to rig sails.

Jesper had always known there was a good chance they wouldn't make this journey home at all, that they'd end up in cells in the Ice Court or skewered on pikes. But he'd figured that if they managed the impossible task of rescuing Yul-Bayur and getting to the *Ferolind*, the trip back to Ketterdam would be a party. They'd drink whatever Specht might have squirreled away on the ship, eat the last of Nina's toffees, recount their close calls and every small victory. But he never could have foreseen the way they'd been cornered in the harbour, and he certainly couldn't have imagined what Nina had done to get them out of it.

Jesper worried about Nina, but thinking about her made him feel guilty. When they'd boarded the schooner and Kuwei explained *parem*, a tiny voice inside him said he should offer to take the drug as well. Even though he was a Fabrikator without training, maybe he could have helped to draw the *parem* out of Nina's system and set her free. But that was a hero's voice, and Jesper had long since stopped thinking he had the makings of a hero. Hell, a hero would have volunteered to take the *parem* when they were facing down the Fjerdans at the harbour.

When Kerch finally appeared on the horizon, Jesper felt a strange mixture of relief and trepidation. Their lives were about to change in ways that still didn't seem real.

They dropped anchor, and when nightfall came, Jesper asked Kaz if he could join him and Rotty in the longboat they were rowing to Fifth Harbour. They didn't need him along, but Jesper was desperate for distraction.

The chaos of Ketterdam was unchanged – ships unloading their cargo at the docks, tourists and soldiers on leave pouring out of boats, laughing and shouting to each other on their way to the Barrel.

"Looks the same as when we left it," Jesper said.

Kaz raised a brow. He was back in his sleek grey-and-black suit, immaculate tie. "What did you expect?"

"I don't know exactly," Jesper admitted.

But he felt different, even with the familiar weight of his pearl-handled revolvers at his hips and a rifle on his back. He kept thinking of the Tidemaker woman, screaming in the *drüskelle* courtyard, her face speckled black. He looked down at his hands. Did he want to be a Fabrikator? To live as one? He couldn't help what he was, but did he want to cultivate his power or keep hiding it?

Kaz left Rotty and Jesper at the dock while he went to find a runner to take a message to Van Eck. Jesper wanted to go with him, but Kaz told him to stay put. Annoyed, Jesper took the chance to stretch his legs, aware of Rotty observing him. He had the distinct sense that Kaz had told Rotty to keep him under watch. Did Kaz think he was going to bolt straight to the nearest gambling hall?

He looked up at the cloudy sky. Why not admit it? He was tempted. He was itching for a hand of cards. Maybe he really should get out of Ketterdam. Once he had his money and his debts were paid, he could go anywhere in the world. Even Ravka. Hopefully, Nina would recover, and when she was back to herself, Jesper could sit down with her and figure it out. No commitments right away, but he could at least visit, couldn't he?

A half hour later, Kaz returned with a message confirming that representatives from the Merchant Council would meet them on Vellgeluk at dawn the following day.

"Look at that," Kaz said, holding the paper out for Jesper to read. Beneath the details of the meet it said, *Congratulations. Your country thanks you.*

The words left a funny feeling in Jesper's chest, but he laughed and said, "As long as my country pays cash. Does the Council know the scientist is dead?"

"I put it all in my note to Van Eck," Kaz said. "I told

him Bo Yul-Bayur is dead, but that his son is alive and was working on *jurda parem* for the Fjerdans."

"Did he haggle?"

"Not in the note. He expressed his 'deep concern', but didn't mention anything about price. We did our job. We'll see if he tries to bargain us down when we get to Vellgeluk."

As they rowed back to the *Ferolind*, Jesper asked, "Will Wylan come with us to meet Van Eck?"

"No," Kaz said, fingers drumming on the crow's head of his cane. "Matthias will be with us, and someone has to stay with Nina. Besides, if we need to use Wylan to twist his father's arm, it's better that we not show our hand too early."

It made sense. And whatever discord existed between Wylan and his father, Jesper doubted Wylan wanted to hash it out in front of the Dregs and Matthias.

He spent a restless night tossing in his hammock and woke to a muggy grey dawn. There was no wind, and the sea looked flat and glassy as a millpond.

"A stubborn sky," murmured Inej, squinting out towards Vellgeluk. She was right. There were no clouds on the horizon, but the air felt dense with moisture, as if a storm was simply refusing to form.

Jesper scanned the empty deck. He'd assumed Wylan would come up to see them off, but Nina couldn't be left on her own.

"How is she?" he asked Matthias.

"Weak," said the Fjerdan. "She's been unable to sleep. But we got her to take some broth, and she seems to be keeping it down."

Jesper knew he was being selfish and stupid, but some petty part of him wondered if Wylan had deliberately kept away from him on the journey back. Maybe now that the job was complete and he was on his way to his share of the haul, Wylan was done slumming with criminals.

"Where's the other longboat?" Jesper asked as he, Kaz,

Matthias, Inej, and Kuwei rowed out from the *Ferolind* with Rotty.

"Repairs," said Kaz.

Vellgeluk was so flat it was barely visible once they were rowing through the water. The island was less than a mile wide, a barren patch of sand and rock distinguished only by the wrecked foundation of an old tower used by the Council of Tides. Smugglers called it Vellgeluk, 'good luck', because of the paintings still visible around the base of what would have been the obelisk tower: golden circles meant to represent coins, symbols of favour from Ghezen, the god of industry and commerce. Jesper and Kaz had come to the island before to meet with smugglers. It was far from Ketterdam's ports, well outside the patrol of the harbour watch, with no buildings or hidden coves from which to stage an ambush. An ideal meeting place for wary parties.

A brigantine was moored off the island's opposite shore, its sails hanging limp and useless. Jesper had watched it make slow progress from Ketterdam in the early dawn light, a tiny black dot that grew into a hulking blot on the horizon. He could hear the sailors calling to each other as they worked the oars. Now its crew lowered a longboat packed with men over the side.

When their own longboat made shore, Jesper and the others leaped out to pull it onto the sand. Jesper checked his revolvers and saw Inej touch her fingers briefly to each of her knives, lips moving. Matthias adjusted the rifle strapped to his back and rolled his enormous shoulders. Kuwei watched it all in silence.

"All right," Kaz said. "Let's go get rich."

"No mourners," Rotty said, settling down to wait with the longboat.

"No funerals," they replied.

They strode towards the centre of the island, Kuwei behind Kaz, bracketed by Jesper and Inej. As they drew closer,

Jesper saw someone in a black mercher's suit approaching, accompanied by a tall Shu man, dark hair bound at the nape of his neck, and followed by a contingent of the *stadwatch* in purple coats, all carrying batons and repeating rifles. Two men lugged a heavy trunk between them, staggering slightly with its weight.

"So that's what thirty million *kruge* looks like," said Kaz.

Jesper gave a low whistle. "Hopefully, the longboat won't sink."

"Just you, Van Eck?" Kaz asked the man in merch black. "The rest of the Council couldn't be bothered?"

So this was Jan Van Eck. He was leaner than Wylan, and his hairline was higher, but Jesper could definitely see the resemblance.

"The Council felt I was best suited to this task, as we've had dealings before."

"Nice pin," Kaz said with a glance at the ruby stuck to Van Eck's tie. "Not as nice as the other one, though."

Van Eck's lips pursed slightly. "The other was an heirloom. Well?" he said to the Shu man beside him.

The Shu said, "That's Kuwei Yul-Bo. It's a year since I've seen him. He's quite a bit taller now, but he's the spitting image of his father." He said something to Kuwei in Shu and gave a short bow.

Kuwei glanced at Kaz, then bowed in return. Jesper could see a sheen of sweat on his brow.

Van Eck smiled. "I will confess I am surprised, Mister Brekker. Surprised but delighted."

"You didn't think we'd succeed."

"Let's say I thought you were a longshot."

"Is that why you hedged your bets?"

"Ah, so you've spoken to Pekka Rollins."

"He's quite a talker when you get him in the right frame of mind," said Kaz, and Jesper remembered the blood on

Kaz's shirt at the prison. "He said you contracted him and the Dime Lions to go after Yul-Bayur for the Merchant Council as well."

With a niggle of unease, Jesper wondered what else Rollins might have told Kaz.

Van Eck shrugged. "It was best to be safe."

"And why should you care if a bunch of canal rats blow each other to bits in pursuit of a prize?"

"We knew the odds of either team succeeding were small. As a gambler, I hope you can understand."

But Jesper had never thought of Kaz as a gambler. Gamblers left something to chance.

"Thirty million *kruge* will soothe my hurt feelings," said Kaz.

Van Eck gestured to the guards behind him. They hefted the trunk and set it down in front of Kaz. He crouched beside it and opened the lid. Even from a distance, Jesper could see the stacks of bills in palest Kerch purple, emblazoned with the three flying fish, row after row of them, bound in paper bands sealed with wax.

Inej drew in a breath.

"Even your money is a peculiar colour," said Matthias.

Jesper wanted to run his hands over those glorious stacks. He wanted to take a bath in them. "I think my mouth just watered."

Kaz pulled out one of the stacks and let his gloved thumb skim over it, then dug down another layer to make sure Van Eck hadn't tried to bunk them.

"It's all here," he said.

He looked over his shoulder and waved Kuwei forward. The boy crossed the short distance, and Van Eck gestured him over to his side, giving him a pat on the back.

Kaz rose. "Well, Van Eck. I'd like to say it's been a pleasure, but I'm not that good a liar. We'll take our leave."

Van Eck stepped in front of Kuwei and said, "I'm afraid I can't allow that, Mister Brekker."

Kaz leaned on his cane, watching Van Eck keenly. "Is there a problem?"

"I count several right in front of me. And there's no way any of you are getting off this island."

Van Eck pulled a whistle from his pocket and blew a shrill note. In the same moment, his servants drew their weapons and a wind came out of nowhere – a howling, unnatural gale that whirled around the little island as the sea began to rise.

The sailors by the brigantine's longboat lifted their arms, waves gathering behind them.

"Tidemakers," growled Matthias, reaching for his rifle.

Then two more figures launched themselves from the deck of the brigantine.

"Squallers!" Jesper shouted. "They're using *parem*!"

The Squallers circled in the sky, wind whipping the air around them.

"You kept part of the stash Bo sent to the Council," said Kaz, dark eyes narrowed.

The Squallers lifted their arms, and the wind wailed a high, keening cry.

Jesper reached for his revolvers. Hadn't he wanted something to shoot at? *I guess this place is good luck*, he thought with a rush of anticipation. *Looks like I'm about to get my wish.*

45

KAZ

"The deal is the deal, Van Eck," Kaz said over the sounds of the growing storm. "If the Merchant Council fails to honour its end of this bargain, no one from the Barrel will ever traffic with any of you again. Your word will be meaningless."

"That *would* be a problem, Mister Brekker, if the Council knew anything about this deal."

Understanding came in a terrible flash. "They were never involved," Kaz said. Why had he believed Van Eck had the blessing of the Merchant Council? Because he was a rich, upstanding mercher? Because he'd dressed his own servants and soldiers in the purple uniforms of the *stadwatch*? Kaz had met with Van Eck in a quarantined mercher's house, not a government building, but he'd been taken in by a little set dressing. It was Hertzoon and his coffeehouse all over again, only now Kaz was old enough to know better.

"You wanted Yul-Bayur. You wanted the formula for *parem*."

Van Eck conceded the truth with an easy nod. "Neutrality is a luxury Kerch has too long enjoyed. The members of the

Council think that their wealth protects them, that they can sit back and count their money while the world squabbles."

"And you know better?"

"Indeed, I do. *Jurda parem* is not a secret that can be kept or quashed or stashed in a cabin on the Zemeni frontier."

"So all your talk of trade lines and markets collapsing—"

"Oh, it will all happen just as I predicted, Mister Brekker. I'm counting on it. As soon as the Council received Bo Yul-Bayur's message, I began buying up *jurda* fields in Novyi Zem. When *parem* is unleashed on the world, every country, every government will be clamouring for a ready supply of it to use on their Grisha."

"Chaos," said Matthias.

"Yes," said Van Eck. "Chaos will come, and I will be its master. Its very wealthy master."

"You will be ensuring slavery and death for Grisha everywhere," Inej said.

Van Eck raised a brow. "How old are you, girl? Sixteen? Seventeen? Nations rise and fall. Markets are made and unmade. When power shifts, someone always suffers."

"When profit shifts," Jesper shot back.

Van Eck's expression was bemused. "Aren't they one and the same?"

"When the Council finds out—" Inej began.

"The Council will never hear of this," Van Eck said. "Why do you think I chose scum from the Barrel as my champions? Oh, you are resourceful and far more clever than any mercenaries, I give you that. But more important, you will not be missed."

Van Eck lifted his hand. The Tidemakers spun their arms. Kaz heard a yell and turned to see a coil of water looming over Rotty. It slammed down on the longboat, smashing it to bits as he dove for cover.

"None of you will leave this island, Mister Brekker. All of you will vanish, and nobody will care." He raised his hand again, and the Tidemakers responded. A massive wave roared towards the *Ferolind*.

"No!" cried Jesper.

"Van Eck!" shouted Kaz. "Your son is on that ship."

Van Eck's gaze snapped to Kaz. He blew his whistle. The Tidemakers froze, awaiting instruction. Reluctantly, Van Eck dropped his hand. They let the wave fall harmlessly, the displaced sea sloshing against the side of the *Ferolind*.

"My son?" Van Eck said.

"Wylan Van Eck."

"Mister Brekker, surely you must know that I sent my son packing months ago."

"I know you've written to Wylan every week since he left your household, begging him to return. Those are not the actions of a man who doesn't care for his only son and heir."

Van Eck began to laugh – a warm, almost jovial chuckle, but its edges were jagged and bitter.

"Let me tell you about my *son*." He spat the word as if it were poison on his lips. "He was meant to be heir to one of the greatest fortunes in all of Kerch, an empire with shipping lines that reach all over the globe, one built by my father, and my father's father. But my *son*, the boy meant to rule this grand empire, cannot do what a child of seven years can. He can solve an equation. He can paint and play the flute most prettily. What my son cannot do, Mister Brekker, is read. He cannot write. I have hired the best tutors from every corner of the world. I've tried specialists, tonics, beatings, hypnotism. But he refused to be taught. I finally had to accept that Ghezen saw fit to curse me with a moron for a child. Wylan is a boy who will never grow to be a man. He is a disgrace to my house."

"The letters . . ." said Jesper, and Kaz could see the anger in his face. "You weren't pleading with him to come back. You were mocking him."

Jesper was right. *If you're reading this, then you know how much I wish to have you home.* Every letter had been a slap in the face to Wylan, a kind of cruel joke.

"He's your son," Jesper said.

"No, he is a mistake. One soon to be corrected. My lovely young wife is carrying a child, and be it boy or girl or creature with horns, that child will be my heir, not some soft-pated idiot who cannot read a hymnal, let alone a ledger, not some fool who would make the Van Eck name a laughingstock."

"You're the fool," Jesper snarled. "He's smarter than most of us put together, and he deserves a better father than you."

"Deserved," amended Van Eck. He blew the whistle twice.

The Tidemakers didn't hesitate. Before anyone could draw breath to protest, two huge walls of water rose and shot towards the *Ferolind*. They crushed the ship between them with a resonant boom, sending debris flying.

Jesper screamed in rage and raised his guns.

"Jesper!" Kaz commanded. "Stand down!"

"He killed them," Jesper said, face contorted. "He killed Wylan and Nina!"

Matthias laid a hand on his arm. "Jesper," he said calmly. "Be still."

Jesper looked back at the rocking waves, at the broken bits of mast and torn sail where a ship had been only seconds before. "I don't . . . I don't understand."

"I confess to being a bit shocked, too, Mister Brekker," said Van Eck. "No tears? No righteous protests for your lost crew? They raise you cold in the Barrel."

"Cold and cautious," said Kaz.

"Not cautious enough, it seems. At least you won't live to regret your mistakes."

"Tell me, Van Eck. Will you do penance? Ghezen frowns on broken contracts."

Van Eck's nostrils flared. "What have you given to the world, Mister Brekker? Have you created wealth?

Prosperity? No. You take from honest men and women and serve only yourself. Ghezen shows his favour to those who are deserving, to those who build cities, not the rats who eat away at their foundations. He has blessed me and my dealings. You will perish, and I will prosper. *That* is Ghezen's will."

"There's just one problem, Van Eck. You'll need Kuwei Yul-Bo to do it."

"And how will you take him from me? You are outgunned and surrounded."

"I don't need to take him from you. You never had him. That's not Kuwei Yul-Bo."

"A sorry bluff at best."

"I'm not big on bluffing, am I, Inej?"

"Not as a rule."

Van Eck's lip curled. "And why is that?"

"Because he'd rather cheat," said the boy who was not Kuwei Yul-Bo in perfect, unaccented Kerch.

Van Eck startled at the sound of his voice, and Jesper flinched.

The Shu boy held out a hand. "Pay up, Kaz."

Kaz sighed. "I do hate to lose a wager. You see, Van Eck, Wylan bet me that you would have no qualms about ending his life. Call me sentimental, but I didn't believe a father could be so callous."

Van Eck stared at Kuwei Yul-Bo – or the boy he'd believed to be Kuwei Yul-Bo. Kaz watched him wrestle with the reality of Wylan's voice coming from Kuwei's mouth. Jesper looked just as incredulous. He'd get his explanation after Kaz got his money.

"It's not possible," said Van Eck.

It shouldn't have been. Nina had been a passable Tailor at best – but under the influence of *jurda parem*, well, as Van Eck had once said, *Things become possible that simply shouldn't be*. A nearly perfect replica of Kuwei Yul-Bo stood before them, but he had Wylan's voice, his mannerisms, and – though Kaz could see the fear and hurt in his golden eyes – Wylan's surprising courage, too.

After the battle in the Djerholm harbour, the merchling had come to Kaz to warn him that he couldn't be used as leverage against his father. Wylan had been red-faced, barely able to speak the words of his supposed 'affliction'. Kaz had only shrugged. Some men were poets. Some were farmers. Some were rich merchers. Wylan could draw a perfect elevation. He'd made a drill that could cut through Grisha glass from parts of a gate and scavenged bits of jewellery. So what if he couldn't read?

Kaz had expected the boy to balk at the idea of being tailored to look like Kuwei. A transformation that extreme was beyond the power of any Grisha not using *parem*. "It may be permanent," Kaz had warned him.

Wylan hadn't cared. "I need to know. Once and for all, I need to know what my father really thinks of me."

And now he did.

Van Eck goggled at Wylan, searching for some sign of his son's features. "It can't be."

Wylan walked to Kaz's side. "Maybe you can pray to Ghezen for understanding, Father."

Wylan was a bit taller than Kuwei, his face a bit rounder. But Kaz had seen them side by side, and the likeness was extraordinary. Nina's work, performed on the ship before that first extraordinary high had begun to wane, was nearly flawless.

Fury lashed across Van Eck's features. "Worthless," he hissed at Wylan. "I knew you were a fool, but a traitor as well?"

"A fool would have been waiting to be smashed to bits on that ship. And as for 'traitor', you've called me worse in the last few minutes alone."

"Just think," Kaz said to Van Eck. "What if the real

Kuwei Yul-Bo had been on the ship you just turned into toothpicks?"

Van Eck's voice was calm, but an angry flush had crept up his neck. "*Where is Kuwei Yul-Bo?*"

"Let us safely off this island with our payment, and I'll gladly tell you."

"You have no way out of this, Brekker. Your little crew is no match for my Grisha."

Kaz shrugged. "Kill us, and you'll never find Kuwei."

Van Eck appeared to consider this. Then he stepped back. "Guards to me!" he shouted. "Kill everyone but Brekker!"

Kaz knew the instant he made his mistake. They'd all known it might come to this. He should have trusted his crew. His eyes should have stayed trained on Van Eck. Instead, in that moment of threat, when he should have thought only of the fight, he looked at Inej.

And Van Eck saw it. He blew on his whistle. "Leave the others! Get the money and the girl."

Hold your ground, Kaz's instincts said. Van Eck has the money. He is the key. Inej can fend for herself. She's a pawn, not the prize. But he was already turning, already sprinting to get to her as the Grisha attacked.

The Tidemakers reached her first, vanishing into mist, then reappearing at her side. But only a fool would to try to take Inej in close combat. The Tidemakers were fast – vanishing and reappearing, grabbing at her. But she was the Wraith, and her knives found heart, throat, spleen. Blood spilled over the sand as the Tidemakers collapsed in two very solid heaps.

Kaz caught movement from the corner of his eye – a Squaller hurtling toward Inej.

"Jesper!" he shouted.

Jesper fired, and the Squaller plummeted to the earth.

The next Squaller was smarter. He came in low, gliding over the ruins. Jesper and Matthias opened fire, but they had to face the sun to shoot and not even Jesper could aim blind. The Squaller barrelled into Inej and sped upwards with her into the sky.

Stay still, Kaz urged her silently, his pistol drawn. But she didn't. Her body spun, and she slashed out. The Squaller's scream was distant. He released her. Inej fell, plunging towards the sand. Kaz ran towards her without logic or plan.

A blur cut through his vision. A third Squaller swooped down, snatching her up seconds before impact and dealing her a vicious blow to the skull. Kaz saw Inej's body go limp.

"Bring him down!" roared Matthias.

"No!" shouted Kaz. "Shoot him and she falls, too!"

The Grisha dodged up and out of range, Inej clutched in his arms.

There was nothing they could do but stand there like fools and watch her shape get smaller in the sky – a distant moon, a fading star, then gone.

Van Eck's guards and Grisha closed in, sweeping the mercher and the trunk of *kruge* through the air, onto the waiting brigantine. Vengeance for Jordie, all Kaz had worked for, was slipping away. He didn't care.

"You have one week to bring me the real Kuwei," Van Eck shouted. "Or they'll hear that girl's screams all the way back in Fjerda. And if that still doesn't move you, I'll let it be known that you're harbouring the most valuable hostage in the world. Every gang, government, smuggler, and spy will be after you and the Dregs. You'll have nowhere to hide."

"Kaz, I can make the shot," said Jesper, rifle to his shoulder. "Van Eck is still in range."

And all would be lost – Inej, the money, everything.

"No," Kaz said. "Let them go."

The sea was flat; no breeze blew, but Van Eck's remaining Squallers filled the ship's sails with a driving wind.

Kaz watched the brigantine surge across the water towards Ketterdam, to safety, to a fortress built on Van Eck's impeccable mercher reputation. He felt as he had looking into the darkened windows of the house on Zelverstraat. Helpless once more. He'd prayed to the wrong god.

Slowly, Jesper lowered his rifle.

"Van Eck will send soldiers and Grisha to search for Kuwei," said Matthias.

"He won't find him. Or Nina." Not in the Slat or any other part of the Barrel. Nowhere in Ketterdam. The previous night, Kaz had ordered Specht to take Kuwei and Nina from the *Ferolind* in the second longboat – the one he'd told Jesper was being repaired. They were safely stashed in the abandoned cages below the old prison tower at Hellgate. Kaz had made a few inquiries when he'd visited the harbour to contact Van Eck. After the disaster at the Hellshow, the cages had been flooded to purge them of beasts and bodies; they'd been empty ever since. Matthias had hated the idea of letting Nina go anywhere without him, especially in her state, but Kaz had convinced him that keeping her and Kuwei aboard the *Ferolind* would leave them exposed.

Kaz marvelled at his own stupidity. Dumber than a pigeon fresh off the boat and looking to make a fortune on East Stave. His greatest vulnerability had been right beside him. And now she was gone.

Jesper was staring at Wylan, his eyes roving over the black hair, the golden eyes. "Why?" he said at last. "Why would you do this?"

Wylan shrugged. "We needed leverage."

"That's Kaz's voice talking."

"I couldn't let you all walk into a hostage exchange thinking I was some kind of insurance."

"Nina tailored you?"

"The night we left Djerholm."

"That's why you disappeared during the journey," said Jesper. "You weren't helping Matthias care for Nina. You were hiding."

"I didn't hide."

"You . . . how many times was it you standing beside me on the deck at night when I thought it was Kuwei?"

"Every time."

"Nina might not be able to put you back, you know. Not without another dose of *parem*. You could be stuck like this."

"Why does it matter?"

"I don't know!" Jesper said angrily. "Maybe I liked your stupid face." He turned to Matthias. "You knew. Wylan knew. Inej knew. Everyone but me."

"Ask me why, Jesper," Kaz said, his patience at an end.

Jesper shifted uneasily on his feet. "Why?"

"*You* were the one who sold us out to Pekka Rollins." He thrust an accusatory finger at Jesper. "You're the reason we were ambushed when we tried to leave Ketterdam. You almost got us all killed."

"I didn't tell Pekka Rollins anything. I never—"

"You told one of the Dime Lions you were leaving Kerch, but that you'd be coming into big money, didn't you?"

Jesper swallowed. "I had to. They were leaning on me hard. My father's farm—"

"I told you not to tell anyone you were leaving the country. I warned you to keep your mouth shut."

"I didn't have a choice! You had me locked up in the Crow Club before we left. If you'd let me—"

Kaz turned on him. "Let you *what*? Play a few hands of Three Man Bramble? Dig yourself deeper in with every boss in the Barrel stupid enough to extend you credit? You told a member of Pekka's gang you were about to be flush."

"I didn't know he'd go to Pekka. Or that Pekka knew about *parem*. I was just trying to buy myself some time."

"Saints, Jesper, you really haven't learned anything in the Dregs, have you? You're still the same dumb farm boy who stepped off the boat."

Jesper lunged for him, and Kaz felt a surge of giddy violence. Finally, a fight he could win. But Matthias stepped between them, holding them each back with a massive hand. "Stop. Stop this."

Kaz didn't want to stop. He wanted to beat them all bloody and then brawl his way through the Barrel.

"Matthias is right," said Wylan. "We need to think about what's next."

"There is no *next*," Kaz snarled. Van Eck would see to that. They couldn't go back to the Slat or get help from Per Haskell and the other Dregs. Van Eck would be watching, waiting to pounce. He'd turn the Barrel, Kaz's home, his little kingdom, into hostile territory.

"Jesper made a mistake," said Wylan. "A *stupid* mistake, but he didn't set out to betray anyone."

Kaz stalked away, trying to clear his head. He knew Jesper hadn't realised what he was setting in motion, but he also knew he could never really trust Jesper again. And maybe he'd kept him in the dark about Wylan because he wanted to punish him a little.

In a few hours, when they'd failed to make contact, Specht would row out for them in the longboat. For now, there was nothing but the flat grey of the sky and the dead rock of this miserable excuse for an island. And Inej's absence. Kaz wanted to hit someone. He wanted someone to hit him.

He surveyed what remained of his crew. Rotty still hovered by the wreckage of the longboat. Jesper sat with elbows on knees, head in hands, Wylan beside him wearing the face of a near-stranger; Matthias stood gazing across the water in the direction of Hellgate like a stone sentinel. If Kaz was their leader, then Inej had been their lodestone, pulling them together when they seemed most likely to drift apart.

Nina had disguised Kaz's crow-and-cup tattoo before

they'd entered the Ice Court, but he hadn't let her near the *R* on his bicep. Now he touched his gloved fingers to where the sleeve of his coat covered that mark. Without meaning to, he'd let Kaz Rietveld return. He didn't know if it had begun with Inej's injury or that hideous ride in the prison wagon, but somehow he'd let it happen and it had cost him dearly.

That didn't mean he was going to let himself be bested by some thieving merch.

Kaz looked south towards Ketterdam's harbours. The beginnings of an idea scratched at the back of his skull, an itch, the barest inkling. It wasn't a plan, but it might be the start of one. He could see the shape it would take – impossible, absurd, and requiring a serious chunk of cash.

"Scheming face," murmured Jesper.

"Definitely," agreed Wylan.

Matthias folded his arms. "Digging in your bag of tricks, *demjin*?"

Kaz flexed his fingers in his gloves. How did you survive the Barrel? When they took everything from you, you found a way to make something from nothing.

"I'm going to invent a new trick," Kaz said. "One Van Eck will never forget." He turned to the others. If he could have gone after Inej alone, he would have, but not even he could pull that off. "I'll need the right crew."

Wylan got to his feet. "For the Wraith."

Jesper followed, still not meeting Kaz's eyes. "For Inej," he said quietly.

Matthias gave a single sharp nod.

Inej had wanted Kaz to become someone else, a better person, a gentler thief. But that boy had no place here. That boy ended up starving in an alley. He ended up dead. That boy couldn't get her back.

I'm going to get my money, Kaz vowed. *And I'm going to get my girl.* Inej could never be his, not really, but he would find a way to give her the freedom he'd promised her so long ago.

Dirtyhands had come to see the rough work done.

46

PEKKA

Pekka Rollins tucked a wad of *jurda* into his cheek and leaned back in his chair to survey the raggedy crew Doughty had brought to his office. Rollins lived above the Emerald Palace in a grand suite of rooms, every inch of them covered in gilt and green velvet. He loved flash – in his clothes, his friends, and his women.

The kids standing before him were the opposite of anything properly stylish. They wore the costumes of the Komedie Brute, but no one got access to his office without showing his face, so the masks had come off. He recognised some of them. He'd hoped to recruit the Heartrender Nina Zenik at some point, but now she looked as if she might not last out the month – all jutting bones, dark hollows, and trembling hands. Seemed he'd dodged a bad investment there. She leaned against a giant Fjerdan with a shaved head and grim blue eyes. He was huge, probably former military. Good muscle to have around. Where did Kaz Brekker find these people?

The boy next to them was Shu, but he looked far too young to be the scientist they'd all been so desperate to get their hands on. Besides, Brekker would never bring such a prize to the Emerald Palace. And then, of course, Rollins knew Jesper Fahey. The sharpshooter had run up an astonishing amount of debt at nearly every gambling den on East Stave. His loose talk had put Rollins wise to the knowledge that Brekker was sending a team to Fjerda. A little digging and a lot of bribes had yielded the where and when of their departure – intelligence that had proved faulty. Brekker had been one step ahead of the him and the Dime Lions. The little canal rat had managed to make it to the Ice Court after all.

It was a good thing, too. If not for Kaz Brekker, Rollins would still be sitting in a cell in that damned Fjerdan prison waiting for another round of torture – or maybe looking down from a pike atop the ringwall.

When Brekker had picked the lock on his prison cell door, Rollins hadn't known if he was about to be rescued or assassinated. He'd heard plenty about Kaz Brekker since he'd risen to prominence in the Dregs – that sorry outfit Per Haskell called a gang – and he'd seen him around the Barrel a few times. The boy had come from nowhere and been a slew of trouble since. But he was still just a lieutenant, not a general, a terrier nipping at Rollins' ankles.

"Hello, Brekker," Rollins had said. "Come to gloat?"

"Not exactly. You know me?"

Rollins had shrugged. "Sure, you're the little skiv who keeps stealing my customers."

The look that passed over the boy's face then had taken Rollins aback. It was hatred – pure, black, long simmering. *What have I ever done to this little pissant?* But in seconds the look was gone, and Rollins wondered if he'd imagined it altogether.

"What do you want, Brekker?"

The boy had stood there, something bleak and mad in his gaze. "I want to do you a favour."

Rollins noted Brekker's bare feet and prison clothes, the hands shorn of his legendary black gloves – a ridiculous affectation. "You don't look like you're in a position to do anyone favours, kid."

"I'm going to leave this door unlocked. You're not stupid enough to go after Bo Yul-Bayur without a crew to back you. Wait for your moment and get out."

"Why the hell would you help me?"

"You weren't meant to die here."

Somehow it sounded like a curse.

"I owe you, Brekker," Rollins had said as the boy exited his cell, hardly believing his luck.

Brekker had glanced back at him, his dark eyes like caverns. "Don't worry, Rollins. You'll pay."

And apparently the boy had come to collect. He stood in the middle of Rollins' opulent office looking like a dark blot of ink, his face grim, his hands resting on a crow-handled walking stick. Rollins wasn't surprised to see him, exactly. Word had it that the exchange between Brekker and Van Eck had gone sour and that Van Eck had eyes on the Slat and the rest of Kaz Brekker's haunts. But Van Eck wasn't watching the Emerald Palace. He had no reason to. Rollins wasn't even sure the merch knew he had made it back from Fjerda alive.

When Brekker finished explaining the bare bones of the situation, Rollins shrugged and said, "You got double-crossed. You want my advice, give Kuwei to Van Eck and be done with it."

"I'm not here for advice."

"The merchers like the taxes we pay. They let the occasional bank heist or housebreak slide, but they expect us to stay here in the Barrel and leave them to their business. You go to war with Van Eck, and all that changes."

"Van Eck's gone rogue. If the Merchant Council knew—"

"And who's going to tell them? A canal rat from the worst

slum in the Barrel? Don't kid yourself, Brekker. Cut your losses and live to fight another day."

"I fight every day. You're telling me you'd just walk away?"

"Look, you want to shoot yourself in the foot – the good foot – I'm happy to watch you do it. But I'm not going to ally with you. Not against a merch. No one will. You're not courting a little gang war, Brekker. You'll have the *stadwatch*, the Kerch army and its navy arrayed against you. They'll burn the Slat to the ground with the old man in it, and they'll take Fifth Harbour back, too."

"I don't expect you to fight beside me, Rollins."

"Then what do you want? It's yours. Within reason."

"I need to get a message to the Ravkan capital. Fast."

Rollins shrugged. "Easy enough."

"And I need money."

"Shocking. How much?"

"Two hundred thousand *kruge*."

Rollins nearly choked on his laughter. "Anything else, Brekker? The Lantsov Emerald? A dragon who craps rainbows?"

"You have the money to spare, Rollins. And I saved your life."

"Then you should have negotiated back in that cell. I'm not a bank, Brekker. And even if I were, given your current situation, I'd say you're a pretty poor credit risk."

"I don't want a loan."

"You want me to *give* you two hundred thousand *kruge*? And what do I get for this generous gesture?"

Brekker's jaw set. "My shares in the Crow Club and Fifth Harbour."

Rollins sat up straighter. "You'd sell your stake?"

"Yes. And for another hundred thousand I'll throw in an original DeKappel."

Rollins leaned back and pressed his fingers together. "It's

not enough, you know. Not to go to war with the Merchant Council."

"It is for this crew."

"This crew?" Rollins said with a snort. "I can't believe you sorry lot were the ones to successfully raid the Ice Court."

"Believe it."

"Van Eck is going to put you in the ground."

"Others have tried. Somehow I keep coming back from the dead."

"I respect your drive, kid. And I understand. You want your money; you want the Wraith back; you want a bit of Van Eck's hide—"

"No," said Brekker, his voice part rasp, part growl. "When I come for Van Eck, I won't just take what's mine. I'll carve his life hollow. I'll burn his name from the ledger. There will be nothing left."

Pekka Rollins couldn't count the threats he'd heard, the men he'd killed, or the men he'd seen die, but the look in Brekker's eye still sent a chill slithering up his spine. Some wrathful thing in this boy was begging to get loose, and Rollins didn't want to be around when it slipped its leash.

"Open the safe, Doughty."

Rollins doled out the cash to Brekker, then had him write out a transfer order for his shares in the Crow Club and the goldmine that was Fifth Harbour. When he held out his hand to shake on the deal, Brekker's grip was knuckle-crushing.

"You don't remember me at all, do you?" the boy asked.

"Should I?"

"Not just yet." That black thing flickered behind Brekker's eyes.

"The deal is the deal," said Rollins, eager to be done with this strange lot.

"The deal is the deal."

When they'd gone, Rollins peered through the big glass window that overlooked the gambling floor of the Emerald Palace.

"An unexpectedly profitable end to the day, Doughty."

Doughty grunted agreement, surveying the action taking place at the tables below – dice, cards, Makker's Wheel, fortunes won and lost, and a delicious slice of all of it came to Rollins.

"What's with those gloves he wears?" the bruiser asked.

"A bit of theatre, I suspect. Who knows? Who cares?"

Rollins watched Brekker and his crew moving through the crowded gambling hall. They opened the doors to the street, and for a brief moment, they were silhouetted against the lamplight in their masks and capes – a cripple trailed by a bunch of kids in costumes. Some gang. Brekker was a wily thief and tough enough, Pekka supposed, inventive, too. But unlike those poor stooges at the Ice Court, Van Eck would be ready for Brekker. The boy was going into a real battle. He didn't stand a chance.

Rollins reached for his watch. It had to be about time for the dealers to change shifts, and he liked to supervise them himself.

"Son of a bitch," he exclaimed a second later.

"What is it, boss?"

Rollins held up his watch chain. A turnip was hanging from the fob where his diamond-studded timepiece should have been. "That little bastard—" Then a thought came to him. He reached for his wallet. It was gone. So was his tie pin, the Kaelish coin pendant he wore for luck, and the gold buckles on his shoes. Rollins wondered if he should check the fillings in his teeth.

"He picked your pocket?" Doughty asked incredulously.

No one got one over on Pekka Rollins. No one dared. But Brekker had, and Rollins wondered if that was just the beginning.

"Doughty," he said, "I think we'd best say a prayer for Jan Van Eck."

"You think Brekker can best him?"

"It's a long shot, but if he's not careful, I think that merch might walk himself right onto the gallows and let Brekker tighten the noose." Rollins sighed. "We better hope Van Eck kills that boy."

"Why?"

"Because otherwise I'll have to."

Rollins straightened the knot of his pinless tie and headed down to the casino floor. The problem of Kaz Brekker could wait to be solved another day. Right now there was money to be made.

Acknowledgements

I have a degenerative condition called osteonecrosis. This basically translates to 'bone death', which sounds kind of gothy and romantic, but actually means that every step I take is painful and that I sometimes need to walk with a cane. It's no coincidence I chose to create a protagonist struggling with similar symptoms, and I often felt that Kaz and I were limping along this road together. We wouldn't have made it to 'The End' without a lot of wonderful people.

All the love to my crew of outcasts and troublemakers: Michi, Rachael, Sarah, Robyn, Josh, and especially Morgan, who gave this book its name and helped me finish it. Many thanks also to Jimmy, who dragged me off to Santa Barbara and smashed my writer's block just by being wonderful.

Bless Noa Wheeler for helping me solve this particular puzzle and for staying patient when I get prickly and bring out the whiteboard. I am deeply grateful to Jean Feiwel, Laura Godwin, Jon Yaged, Molly Brouillette, Elizabeth Fithian, Rich Deas, April Ward, and the countless people at Henry Holt and Macmillan Children's who have helped bring the Grisha world to life and who let me continue to explore it with readers. Joanna Volpe at New Leaf: 'Stalwart and true' should definitely be on your résumé. I can face just about any challenge knowing you have my back. Thanks also to Pouya 'he was a young' Shahbazian, Kathleen Ortiz, Danielle Barthel, Jaida Temperly, and Jess Dallow. And a big thank you to Team Grisha in the UK: Fiona Kennedy, and the wonderful crew at Orion – most especially Nina Douglas, who is an extraordinary publicist, an excellent travelling companion, and a born Ravenclaw. Thank you to the readers, librarians, booksellers, BookTubers, and bloggers who celebrate stories all over the world.

Any good heist requires talented specialists, and I've been aided by the best:

Steven Klein offered invaluable expertise on how beginners learn magic and pointed me to the work of Eric Mead and Apollo Robbins, gentleman thief. Angela DePace did her best to help me find a real way to knock out a room full of prisoners, but the chloro pellet ended up being a work of pure fabrikation. (Don't try it at home.) Richard Wheeler advised me on how government buildings and high-security facilities actually keep out ne'er-do-wells. Emily Stein walked me through knife wounds and introduced me to the beautiful phrase 'apex of the heart'. Conlang king David Peterson tried to nudge me in the right direction and let me be very stubborn about straats. And Hedwig Aerts, my dear friend and Soberumi, thank you for helping me mangle Dutch more thoughtfully.

Marie Lu, Amie Kaufman, Robin LaFevers, Jessica Brody, and Gretchen McNeil keep me laughing and put up with so much whining. Thanks also to Robin Wasserman, Holly Black, Sarah Rees Brennan, Kelly Link, and Cassandra Clare for plot advice, margaritas, and foisting *Teen Wolf* upon me. I will never be the same. Anna Carey can be blamed for the Fjerdan guard's nosebleed. Send her your complaints.

Christine, Sam, Emily, and Ryan, I am so lucky to call you family. And dearest Lulu, *you have failed your city*. Thank you for weathering my moods and caring about my little band of thugs.

Many books helped Ketterdam, the Barrel, and my team of crows take shape, but the most essential titles were Sarah Wise's *The Blackest Streets: The Life and Death of a Victorian*

Slum; *The Coffee Trader* by David Liss; *Amsterdam: A History of the World's Most Liberal City* by Russell Shorto; *Criminal Slang: The Vernacular of the Underworld Lingo* by Vincent J. Monteleone; David Maurer's *The Big Con: The Story of the Confidence Man*; and *Stealing Rembrandts: The Untold Stories of Notorious Art Heists* by Anthony M. Amore and Tom Mashberg.

One more thing: This book wanted to be revised to the sounds of the Black Keys, the Clash, and the Pixies, but it was born in a drafty old schoolhouse with *In a Time Lapse* playing on a continuous loop, and a bat flapping around the eaves. Many thanks to composer Ludovico Einaudi. And the bat.

To read more about the magical world of
the Grisha, look out for

Shadow and Bone
Siege and Storm
Ruin and Rising